THE
GANJA
COAST

The Ganja Coast

PAUL MANN

FAWCETT COLUMBINE

NEW YORK

A Fawcett Columbine Book
Published by Ballantine Books

Copyright © 1995 by Paul Mann

All rights reserved under International and Pan-American
Copyright Conventions. Published in the United States by Ballantine Books,
a division of Random House, Inc., New York, and simultaneously
in Canada by Random House of Canada Limited, Toronto.

Mann, Paul.
  The Ganja Coast / Paul Mann.
    p.   cm.
  ISBN 0–449–90769–4
  1. Drug traffic—India—Goa (State)—Fiction.
2. Americans—India—Goa (State)—Fiction.
3. Goa (India : State)—Fiction.
I. Title.
PS3563.A53623G36   1994
813'.54—dc20   93–46505
                                                       CIP

Text design by Ann Gold

Manufactured in the United States of America
First Edition: February 1995
10   9   8   7   6   5   4   3   2   1

FOR SARAH, THE INDOMITABLE

The white moth to the closing bine,
The bee to the opened clover,
And the gipsy blood to the gipsy blood
Ever the wide world over.

Rudyard Kipling, "The Gipsy Trail"

ACKNOWLEDGMENTS

India is a country where anything can happen and often does, which is what makes it so fascinating to write about. It can also be overwhelming, which is why good local contacts are essential to the well-being and frequently the survival of the inquisitive outsider. Even though this book is a work of fiction, much of the material that has gone into it is factual and could not have been acquired without the generous assistance of many Indian friends. In particular, I would like to express my thanks to Dr. Pritam Phatnani, Deputy Coroner of Bombay; Manohar Krishna Patwardhan, senior counsel to the High Court of Bombay; Ms. Sumedha Rao, advocate to the High Court of Bombay; Allwyn Fernandes, special correspondent to the *Times of India*; Kiran Wagle, sales manager for the Taj Group of Hotels; Dr. Silvano Dias Sapeco, medico-legal officer at Margao Hospital in Goa; and Anthony Fernandes, news editor of the *Herald* in Panjim. I would also like to give special thanks to my editor at Fawcett, Daniel Zitin, who coaxed, guided, and bullied me through several key passages and thus saved me from making a fool of both of us.

THE
GANJA
COAST

CHAPTER 1

Sometimes it seemed the whole world wanted a piece of him. Men wanted his friendship. Children wanted his approval. Women wanted him for his looks. And the freaks wanted him for his plentiful supply of good dope. That was how it seemed to Cora and that was how it had always been. Piece by piece they tried to win her husband away from her. And piece by piece she won him back. An endless tug-of-war between them and her. A contest that never ended.

Cora understood why as she watched him from the jostling anonymity of the beach. She understood perfectly. He was beautiful, which had always been a problem. He was clever, which made people want to please him. And he projected an effortless self-possession, which set him apart from other men. Which was why he sat alone now at the edge of the cliff, a slender, darkening profile on a blunt shelf of rock lit from behind by the neon glare of the sun. He had been there for hours, in the lotus position, his lightly bearded face tilted to the sky, his nickel-colored hair stirred by the inshore breeze. Separate and aloof. Calculated and compelling. Like a Hindu idol, a focal point between heaven and earth. For once, everybody on the beach seemed willing to remain at a distance, in an act of collective homage to the perfection of the moment that Drew had created for himself.

Anyone who had dared to climb the cliff and approach him would have seen that he was naked, his only clothing a thin cotton *lungi*, folded carefully and set to one side with a stone on top of it so that it would not blow away. He had arranged a handful of incense sticks in a half circle in front of him, so that coils of smoke flitted briefly around him like wraiths before they were snatched away by the wind. His eyes were closed and his only expression was a smile that suggested he could see things that no one else could see. He had composed himself with his forearms balanced on his knees so that his hands dangled loosely in the air, the third finger of each hand lightly touching the tip of each thumb. The only sound he made was a soft, murmuring drone, so faint it was lost in the grumble of the surf. It was a sound that echoed the sacred harmonic of the universe. The Shabda Brahman, the music of the cosmos that flowed from Brahma the Creator and resonated through all things. The words were the words of his mantra:

> *"Brahman Satyam, Jagan Mitya.*
> *Jeevo Brahmaiva Naparah."*

> Brahman alone is Truth, the world is unreal.
> The individual soul is the only Brahman.

Cora repeated the words softly to herself as she watched from the beach below. "Brahman alone is Truth, Brahman alone . . ."

"Ba-Ba-Ba-Ba-Barbara-Ann . . ." Somebody chanted the first few bars of the old Beach Boys song in her ear.

She turned, startled, and saw that her friend Cass had come up on her unnoticed in the crowd.

"So . . ." Cass said. "He been to the bathroom yet or is he going for a new personal best in bladder control?"

Cora smiled grudgingly. "It's not a stunt," she said.

"Did I say it was?" Cass answered, and handed Cora one of two red plastic cups she was holding. "Here," she said. "A girl's second best friend—except this stays stiff all night."

Cora took the cup and looked at the scummy gray liquid inside. Feni and coconut water. Feni was the local liquor, a sweet, colorless syrup distilled from cashew nuts. It had a kick like tequila and came in quart bottles that cost a dollar each, which made it the drink of choice in Goa. She sipped it respectfully. It tasted sweet and warm and carried a sinister afterburn. She would have to be careful. She didn't want to get drunk. Not this early in the evening.

"Have you seen the kids?" she asked.

"Sara's in the water with Tina," Cass said, and waved vaguely down the beach. Some of her drink spilled down the front of her dress and she looked at it as if she didn't know how it got there. Cass's real name was Karen Henke and she had come to Goa from Ann Arbor three years earlier with her husband, Rick, and their daughter, Tina. Long before that, when she was still in high school, her friends had called her Cass because nobody could look at her without seeing Cass Elliot of the Mamas and the Papas.

"I'm pretty sure I saw Paul with Otto when I came down," she said, dabbing halfheartedly at the stain on her massive chest.

Cora nodded. Like most twelve-year-olds, her son was fascinated by gadgets. Otto was the balding Dutch hippie who managed the sound-and-light show at all the full-moon parties, and Paul had wormed himself into the role of Otto's assistant.

Cora got up on her toes and strained to see over the bobbing heads of the crowd. The music that boomed out over the beach came from a battery of amplifiers on a small, ramshackle stage tucked into a stand of coconut palms whose trunks had been painted phosphorescent shades of pink and blue and green. She glimpsed her son briefly, hurrying across the stage to fix some blown fuse or frayed piece of wire. Even if he hadn't been her son, her eye would have been drawn to him. He wore indecently frayed cutoffs, had sun-bleached, shoulder-length hair that flowed behind him like a banner, and the wild, feral look of a child who had never seen the inside of a schoolroom.

Paul was Cora's elder child, his name a westernized version of Parvati, the consort of Shiva. Usually a female name, it was also meant to symbolize the perfect union between man and woman, which was how Cora and Drew had felt about their first-born. Their daughter, Sara, was nine years old and her name was short for Saraswati, the goddess of learning and wisdom.

Cora dropped back down onto the soles of her feet and gave Cass a quick, nervous smile. She worried more about her kids than Cass worried about Tina and she was sure Cass thought her borderline neurotic. She opened her mouth to say something, but somebody in the crowd bumped her and it was her turn to spill her drink. The plum-colored T-shirt she wore molded instantly to her breasts.

"Shit," she swore, and pulled the sticky fabric away from her skin. She looked apologetically at Cass, then turned and started threading her way through the crowd toward the water. Cass sighed and lumbered after her, her feet leaving a trail of small craters in the sand. The crowd thinned out considerably along the waterline, though there was a steady flow of naked and semi-naked bodies in and out of the surf. Most people preferred to laze in the shallows drinking Kingfisher beer from quart bottles, sipping feni with lime juice or coconut water, and passing fat soggy joints back and forth. A few people threw Frisbees while others tried to catch the sluggish swells, and some floated far beyond the surf line, blissfully stoned and drifting unimpeded toward Africa.

Cora gave Cass what was left of her drink and waded through the shallows till the water tugged at the hem of her *lungi*. Then she stopped, pulled her T-shirt over her head, and bent down to rinse it in the water. Cora wore only a bikini thong beneath her *lungi* and was proud of the fact that she carried very little fat anywhere. Her belly was a small rounded cup, her hips slender, and her legs slim and shapely. Her skin was a pretty biscuit color with no sign of stretch marks, and there were no tan lines. At forty-two, Cora was five years older than Cass but could have been five years younger. Her reddish-brown hair was shiny and thick and untouched by any hint of gray. She was aware of Cass watching her enviously from the shore as she rinsed the feni and coconut water out of her T-shirt.

A shrill scream pierced the monotonous thump of the music and Cora jolted upright and looked down the beach.

"Yours, I think," Cass said. "But it sounded like fun to me."

Cora nodded. She was familiar with the full repertoire of her daughter's screams. Still, it was getting late and she wanted both her children where she could see them before night fell and the hard-core craziness started. Traditionally, the full-moon parties at Anjuna were about cutting loose and having a good time. But there were dangers, too—temptations and jealousies, under-currents of excess waiting to pull the unwary down. People overdosed. People fought. People died. Things happened after dark that a nine-year-old girl and a twelve-year-old boy ought not see.

Cora wrung out her T-shirt and pulled it back over her head. It was wet and clingy, but the heat would dry it in minutes. She stepped out of the water and scanned the beach until she saw two small bodies playing in the surf about fifty yards away.

"I see them," she said, and set off again along the sand.

Cass grumbled to herself, held on to the drinks, and shuffled after her.

"Hey, you two," Cora called as she came within earshot of the two girls. "You stay in there much longer, you're going to need gills."

Tina heard her first, and she grabbed Sara by the arm to get her attention. Sara was poised to dive through an oncoming wave and shrugged her friend away, giggling, thinking it was part of the game. Tina grabbed her again, a little harder this time, and turned her around so she could see her mother calling to her from the shore.

Cora felt a clutch at her heart when she looked at the two of them together, their eyes bright with mischief, their elfin faces flushed with the excitement of play. Friends for almost three years—an eternity in a child's lifetime—and so similar in appearance they could have been sisters. They were like water sprites, she thought. A portrait of naked innocence. And that was what bothered her the most. In the early days the full-moon parties had been like block parties for friends and neighbors. Two or three hundred people sharing food, drink, dope, and sometimes each other. Since then, they had lost their innocence. Now they attracted thousands. Creeps, flashers, freeloaders, tourists, and other voyeurs lured by the promise of mass nudity, cheap dope, and anonymous sex.

"It's getting dark," Cora said.

"Oh Mom . . ." Sara's voice turned to a whine and her face to an expression of deep tragedy.

"How you doin', hon?" Cass wheezed to her own daughter as she caught up. "Everythin' okay?"

Cora felt a pang of annoyance. It was the kind of question that demanded an affirmative answer, and it made her feel even more guilty.

"Sure," Tina said. "We're only playing."

They all looked accusingly at Cora.

"Come up here, honey," Cora said to her daughter. "I want to talk to you a minute."

"Mom . . ." Sara protested.

"Now," Cora insisted. "Okay?"

The tone in her mother's voice told Sara there was nothing to be gained by arguing and she trudged sullenly out of the water.

"Where's your towel and your things?"

"I don't know," Sara said. "Over there, someplace . . ."

Cora looked around and saw what looked like a bundle of rags trampled into the sand. She picked them up and shook them clean. There was a towel, a T-shirt, and a small pair of bikini pants. She turned back to her daughter and knelt down while she wrapped the towel around her. As she did so she leaned forward and spoke softly in Sara's ear.

"Honey, you haven't done anything wrong," she said. "I just don't like you going naked when the beach is busy like this. It's okay when there's only me and your father and a few friends, but you're getting to be a big girl and from now on . . ."

Her words died in her throat when she realized they were being watched by a man in the crowd a scant few feet away.

"Shit," she breathed.

She saw him distinctly amid the swirl of people that surrounded her—a smallish, thin-faced man with a neat mustache, light brown pants, a pair of cheap leather sandals, and a pale, blue-checked shirt worn outside his pants. He stood with his hands in his pockets, his head tilted slightly to one side, one clear image in a blur of faces. His name was Tony Dias and he was the chief of the drug squad in Panjim. If he was at the party, it meant only one thing. There was going to be a raid. The rest of his men would be spread out among the crowd, making friends with the unwary, picking out their busts before they called in the trucks and the armed reinforcements. She could see that Dias knew he'd been recognized, but he didn't look away or try to hide. Instead, he continued to stare at her, his flat brown eyes empty of all expression.

"Just do what I tell you," Cora said, and she dressed her daughter quickly under the towel. "There are a few creeps hanging around. We're going to get Paul and we're going back to the garden right now, where it's safe, okay?"

Sara saw the concern on her mother's face and heard a note of fear in her voice that hadn't been there a moment ago, and she did what she was told without further protest. When Cora got to her feet, she saw that Cass had found Tina's clothes and was helping her to get dressed, too, though she moved slowly and grudgingly, as if she had been coerced into it. Cora moved over and took her friend by the elbow.

"I knew there were bad vibes here tonight," she said.

Cass looked questioningly at her.

"I just saw Tony Dias," Cora said.

The skepticism on Cass's face shifted abruptly to a look of dismay. She followed Cora's gaze to where Dias had been a moment earlier, but he was gone, lost in the crowd.

"You sure?"

"Yeah, I'm sure," Cora said. "He was right there and he was looking at me like he knew something was going down tonight."

"Ah . . . shit."

Cass's husband, Rick, had been arrested for selling hash at the Anjuna flea market three months earlier. It had cost them thirteen hundred dollars, all the spare cash they had, to get Dias to tear up the paperwork. The alternative was a long stay in jail followed by a trial that would bring certain conviction and then, if Rick was lucky, deportation. If he was unlucky he would get more jail time. And no foreigner, man or woman, emerged from an Indian jail unscathed. Everybody in Goa had heard the story about the young Austrian woman who had been flown home sedated and belted to a stretcher after eighteen months in Panjim jail. The word was that she was clean when she was busted, but Dias had planted dope on her so he could keep her in jail to entertain him and his friends. If Rick was busted again, there was no way Cass could come up with money to buy him out of jail this time.

"You'll watch Tina for me?" she asked.

"No problem," Cora said. "You know where he is?"

"I'll find him," Cass said. She bent down and spoke briefly to her daughter before heading off into the crowd in search of her husband. As soon as both girls were dressed, Cora took them by the hand and led them in the direction of the soundstage to get Paul. Once there, it was several minutes before Otto was able to persuade her son to come out of hiding. He had seen his mother coming and knew that his evening of fun was about to end before it had started. Paul liked the beach parties. He liked to sneak around after dark and watch the orgies in the dunes. And there was always the chance that he'd find some accommodating female willing to help him lose his virginity again.

As soon as she had all three children safely together, Cora began shepherding them back along the beach toward the sanctuary of the garden. It was getting late. The sun was foundering on the horizon and the encroaching darkness only made her more anxious. She could feel the change of mood in the crowd. Hours of drink and dope were taking their toll. People were getting loose and stupid.

It was a big party, she realized. The biggest of the year. At least two thousand people, maybe more. Most of them half-naked in thongs, baggies, polychromatic surfer shorts, or the *lungi*, the wraparound native skirt worn indecently low on the hips by men and women. Some of the women wore body paint and little else, their breasts daubed with spirals, flowers, and Sanskrit symbols. Some of the men wore dreadlocks as thick as rope and streaked yellow by the sun. Others, of both sexes, had shaved their heads completely or etched bizarre patterns into the stubble. Everyone wore jewelry—chains, bracelets, anklets, amulets, studs, medallions, earrings, nose rings, and nipple rings—cheap, fantastic jewelry made from copper, silver, or coarse-grained Indian gold. Some wore beaded vests and mirrored pillbox caps bought from the Banjaras—tribal women who hawked a living along the beach. A few of the white women had copied the Rajasthani fashion of chains, laden with charms or medallions, that reached from nose to ear.

By the time Cora's little procession had reached the garden, they were hot, sweaty, and bad-tempered. She paused to catch her breath at the top of the path while the children trooped past her looking for something to drink and a place to lie down. The garden was not a garden at all but a sandy hollow in the dunes with a box-seat view of the beach. It was the preferred haunt of Anjuna's hippie elders and a place where the uninvited could be made to feel most unwelcome. A dozen people had settled in for

the night, including Drew, who had ended his clifftop meditation. A small campfire had been lit and coir mats scattered
around on the sand. Cora knew everyone who was there, most of
them friends and neighbors from the colony of cheap rental cot-
tages around the village of Anjuna, where eight hundred dollars
could rent a three-bedroom bungalow for a year. Some had
brought food as well as drink and dope to see them through the
night. There were wicker baskets and palm-thatch shoulder bags
filled with oranges, mangoes, sugar bananas, and papaya. Aggie
was there, too, a leathery Danish woman who ran a health-food
stall at the flea market. She had a couple of bags stocked with banana cake, molasses cookies, coconut slices, and brownies made
with hashish. There were also several bottles of feni and a couple
of coolers filled with beer, wine, and fruit juice. Incense sticks
had been lit and at least two joints were in circulation, so that the
air was thick with the intermingled aromas of incense and ganja.

As usual the focus of attention was Drew. The garden was a
kind of ashram for him when he wasn't taking classes at Vagator,
the next town up the coast. Wearing only his *lungi*, he sat, lotus
fashion, on a strip of coir matting. Everyone else was arranged
around the hollow in a crude ellipse, some of them in the lotus,
others sprawled in the sand, comfortably stoned. The fire was in
the middle of the ellipse, and in the light of the flames, Drew
could easily have been taken for a Hindu mystic. Only the voice
was out of place. After thirteen years in India he still spoke with
a lazy Southern Californian drawl.

Cora listened to him for a moment. He was talking about the
Tamils, who were said to be the only true Hindus left in India. He
had spent a couple of months with Tamil priests at a temple in
Madurai and observed some of their oldest rituals. The Tamils
were the only Hindus not to have been corrupted by the Moghuls
or the British, he said. Only they were the true interpreters of the
Srutis, the Vedas, and the Upanishads, the Hindu articles of faith
handed down by the Creator at the beginning of time. His audi-

ence listened with what was either rapt fascination or rapt insensibility. Cora couldn't be sure which.

"I'm hungry," Paul said, and stalked irritably across the clearing to where Aggie sat. He squatted down beside her and began picking through her bags looking for something to eat. He found the brownies and went to put one in his mouth. Cora started to protest and Aggie caught his hand in midair. She pried the brownie from his fingers and put it back in the bag.

"Not that one, darling," she said in her heavy Danish accent. "Here, have one of—"

"It's okay," Drew interrupted. "He can have one of those."

"Drew . . . ?" Cora looked at her husband, annoyed.

"Half won't hurt him," Drew said.

Aggie looked at Cora. "These are pretty mellow," she said.

Cora sighed. She knew what Drew wanted. If their son ate a hash brownie, he would be asleep in minutes and unable to make a nuisance of himself.

"Okay," she said, too tired to argue. "But you can carry him home."

Aggie broke the brownie in two and handed half to Paul. He took it, chewed it briefly, then spat it into the sand.

"Tastes like dog shit," he said, and reached for an open bottle of Kingfisher.

"Like you'd know," Sara taunted her brother.

"Ugh." Tina shuddered and tried not to smirk. "You guys are disgusting."

Cora looked apologetically at Aggie and leaned down to take the beer from her son's hand. She gave him a bottle of fruit juice instead. He turned his back on her and sipped it sullenly. In a few minutes, when she wasn't looking, he would spike it with feni. Cora found some food and drink for the girls, then looked for a place where she could settle. She found a seat near Aggie, retrieved a bottle of mineral water from a cooler, and took a long, calming drink. She felt better now that the children were safe where she could keep an eye on them, though she was still worried about Cass and Rick.

The sun was almost below the horizon. A few minutes more and the dense tropical night would close in. She stared pointedly at her husband, willing him to finish his monologue about the Tamils so she could speak to him, but he seemed not to notice. She looked back along the shore, knowing that Dias and his men were still out there. The coconut palms unfolded their raw-knuckled shadows down the beach and reminded her of claws, the claws of a silent and malevolent beast stealing over the heads of the unsuspecting crowd, seeking out fresh victims, choosing those who would be in jail by morning—and those who would be dead. Her T-shirt was bone dry now and the air cloyingly warm, but still she shivered.

"Are you all right?" Aggie asked.

"Just tired," Cora said.

Aggie's eyes were glazed. "You've lost weight," she said. "Are you eating properly? Are you worried about something?"

Cora smiled. It would be an admission of personal failure to admit to anxiety in paradise. "Why would I be worried?"

Aggie shrugged. She offered Cora the joint she was holding. Cora took it, inhaled briefly, and passed it on. Then she leaned back on her elbows, closed her eyes, and listened to the music for a while as it pulsed down the beach. Earlier it had been Pink Floyd and *The Dark Side of the Moon*. Now it was Trilithon and *Children of the Future*. Acid rock. Loud, repetitive, and numbing. Acid had made a big comeback in the past few years. It was too intense for Cora, but Drew still liked to do it from time to time. He was the living embodiment of the old hippie adage that reality was for people who couldn't handle drugs.

"Something happening?"

Cora opened her eyes, surprised to see that her husband had joined her. She hadn't heard him sit down, hadn't realized he was right there beside her until he spoke. She pushed herself up so she could talk to him.

"I saw Dias down there," she said. "There's going to be trouble. I can tell by the way he looked at me."

"Maybe," Drew said.

Cora frowned. It wasn't the answer she wanted to hear.

"He's just making a nuisance of himself," Drew added. "Letting us know he's around. We'll be okay here. He knows not to come up here."

"You sure?"

Drew shrugged. "I'm not sure about anything," he said. "What happens happens. We deal with it—when it happens."

Cora fell silent. It was frustrating, but she knew he was right. People made their own karma, including Cass and Rick. She only wished she could be as relaxed about it as Drew. Nothing seemed to surprise him. Nothing seemed to bother him. He was the all-seeing eye at the center of every storm. Which was why he was the guru and she was the dutiful wife. Something stirred in the corner of her eye and she noticed that the girls were getting restless, especially Tina. She looked drowsy, but she was fidgeting and having trouble getting comfortable. Cora thought she must be fretting about her parents.

"Come over here, honey," she said. "Your mom and dad will be fine. They'll be here real soon, you'll see."

Tina hesitated only momentarily, then got up, walked woodenly across to Cora, and lay down beside her with her head in her lap. In a couple of minutes she was asleep. Cora brushed a few grains of sand from Tina's face. There were a few crumbs stuck to her long blond eyelashes, but Cora left them there. Lightly, she stroked Tina's cheek, feeling the smoothness of her skin, admiring the perfection of her face. It was the kind of moment she rarely shared with her own children anymore. Paul rejected just about every display of affection from his mother and Sara seemed to be going through a stage in which she preferred to be with her father. When Sara saw Tina with her mother, she moved over to her father's side and pulled his arm around her. In a little while her face, too, acquired the familiar vacancy that preceded sleep.

Cora realized that Drew was watching her, smiling. She smiled back, knowing he was thinking the same thing. The simplest moments were the best.

One by one the children fell asleep. Then the adults, too, began to drift off into their stoned slumber. Cora watched the fire for a while, struggling to find the calmness that eluded her, her mind returning constantly to Cass and Rick. Something must have happened. It had been too long. Something had gone wrong. Then, through the darkness, she saw a couple of shapes struggling up the path toward them. Drew saw them, too. He eased Sara gently down onto the sand and went to help.

When they came into view Cora realized what had taken so long. Rick was barely conscious and Cass had been forced to carry him for half the length of the beach. Two of the men around the fire stirred themselves to give Drew a hand. Between them they were able to carry Rick up into the hollow and lay him down on the sand. For a joke, one of the guys put Rick's feet together and folded his hands across his chest as though he were a corpse. A few people sniggered. Rick was oblivious to it all. He lay quite still, his long black hair fanned out around his head, his stubbled jaw slack beneath his thick mustache. Then he began to snore.

"Ripshit," Cass wheezed. "I found him passed out with his head against an amp."

She struggled the last few steps to a cooler, lowered herself awkwardly to the sand, and took out a jug of fruit juice.

"Going to be deaf in that ear," she muttered between drinks. "Totally deaf . . . got to be."

The novelty of Rick's arrival passed and everyone slipped back into a private haze. Aggie lit a joint and gave it to Cass to mellow her out. Cora somehow returned Tina to her mother without waking her.

Down on the beach bonfires had been lit, some of them quite big. People screamed and called lewdly to one another. Naked bodies could be seen moving in the firelight, dancing, playing, coupling. Up above, in a sky lit by the cold brilliance of the stars, the ravaged face of the moon leered down approvingly on the whole pagan spectacle.

Drew got up again and padded across the clearing. Cora watched him, disappointed, wondering where he was going. When he came back she saw the familiar Red Man tobacco tin and she relaxed. It was his stash tin, so old that the picture on the lid had been worn to a shine. He pried it open, took out a neatly rolled joint, and lit it with a twig from the fire. He inhaled twice, deeply, then handed it to her. She hesitated and looked around one last time. Paul and Sara were both asleep. Cass was exhausted and seemed to have fallen into a doze, her head bowed to her chest. Aggie was snoring softly. It looked as if Cora and Drew were the only ones awake.

"Just . . . do it," Drew said.

Cora smiled. Everybody seemed to think she was so uptight. She put the joint to her lips, took a couple of pulls to prime it, then inhaled deeply. She held the smoke inside for a long time before letting it go.

"And suddenly . . ." Drew deadpanned, "the whole world became a better place."

Cora tried not to laugh. She took another toke, then another. It was only when her lungs started to burn that she passed the joint back to him. He took a last leisurely pull then flicked what was left into the fire. Nobody bothered with roach clips in a place where dope was cheaper than bottled water.

Cora made herself comfortable and waited for the rush. When it came it was more powerful than she had anticipated. She felt as though she had been tied to the nose of a rocket ship and propelled into space. There was a sensation of rapid acceleration accompanied by breathlessness and a flutter of panic as the ground seemed to fall away beneath her. The stars spiraled in the sky and the leering face of the moon rushed at her, making her feel giddy. Her throat tightened and her mouth felt gluey. She swallowed, telling herself it was only a rush. For a moment the nausea was so bad she thought she would be sick. Then, as suddenly as it had started, it was over. The rush peaked, slowed, and glided into something gentle and serene. The giddiness was replaced by a sensation of absolute calm. She was free again. Free of gravity, free of care, free of all worldly concern, floating in a waking dream. Instantly, everything slipped into perspective. Everything was the way it was supposed to be. Nothing bad could touch her now. Drew was right. Dope was beautiful. The world was beautiful. For the first time that day she felt happy.

She had no idea how long she lay like that, riding that first irresistible rush. All she knew was that she didn't want it to end. Then, gradually, it started to ebb, leaving her with a warm and sensual afterglow.

"Whooo . . ." she exhaled softly. "What . . . is . . . that . . . ?" Her voice sounded loud and funny and she giggled.

Drew smiled. "I picked it up yesterday," he said. "Serious shit, isn't it?"

"Serious . . . shit . . . serious?" The words tripped over each other and she giggled again. This time it was a while before she could stop. She sat up feeling spacey and weak and dabbed at her eyes with the heel of her hand.

"Oh God . . ." she mumbled. "Laughing weed . . . you might have warned me."

"Shouldn't have too much trouble moving it," he said.

Drew had learned a long time ago that the guru business offered very little money, unless you wanted to be a corporate guru like the Maharishi, which brought with it other problems. So he had fallen back on the industry that provided many hippies with cash flow in India. He had become a dealer. Two hundred kids worked for him now, pushing dope from Arambor in the north to Betul in the south. They had a home-delivery service that arrived in less than half an hour. Better than Domino's Pizza. But he never sold drugs personally. He was always careful, never greedy.

Cora thought it a tribute to his cleverness that he had never spent a day in jail.

She heard a noise from the other side of the garden, a rhythmic, panting sound. She peered dazedly through the darkness, trying to see what was going on. She saw a man and a woman, both naked, but couldn't tell who they were. The woman was on top, riding the man slowly, deliciously. Cora watched for a minute then looked away.

"We should go home," she said. For a long time Drew didn't respond. She thought he hadn't heard, so she opened her mouth to speak again, but then he turned toward her, put a finger to her lips, and followed it with a kiss—a familiar, hungry kiss. He had been watching them, too, and it had turned him on. She hesitated, uncertain. Then she kissed him back. He leaned closer, put his arms around her, and lowered her gently to the sand. He slid his hand beneath her T-shirt and caressed her breasts until he felt her nipples harden. She moaned softly, the sensation of his touch heightened by the ganja. He moved his hand slowly downward, his fingertips tracing the soft curve of her belly, following the natural descent to her crotch. He worked her *lungi* loose and spread it around her like wrapping paper. She saw the way he looked at her and she savored the feel of his eyes on her body. He paused to take off his own *lungi*, then lay down beside her and kissed her again, tenderly. Cora pulled him against her and kissed him hard, shocked by the immediacy of her own need. She reached between his legs, took hold of him, and guided him into her, eager to feel him inside her, to keep him and hold him there . . . so that no one else could have him.

Afterward she lay in his arms while he slept, listening to the sound of his breathing, knowing that he belonged to her for at least another night. Then she felt herself sliding toward sleep, too, and she went reluctantly, wishing the night would never end.

In the blur of waking she thought she had only been asleep for a little while. But when she opened her eyes, she found herself looking at the gray half-light of dawn. For a moment she thought she had imagined the scream, that it was part of an unremembered dream. Then she heard it again, a woman's scream, harsh and terrible. She tried to move but found she was still wrapped in Drew's arms. He stirred but didn't wake. Other people had heard the screams, too, and they began to stir. Grudgingly, Cora disentangled herself from her husband's protective grasp, put on her clothes, and started down the path to the beach.

At the water's edge she stopped. More people arrived and began crowding around her.

"Oh, man . . ." somebody murmured.

"Shit," somebody else said.

Cora realized they were looking at something in the water, something long and pale, like a broken surfboard or a sheet of plastic, floating just beneath the surface. A few people waded out to it. Cora took a few tentative steps after them. She was concerned, too, but she wasn't sure she wanted to get too close.

There was a man nearby and he looked at her. "It's a kid," he said.

A stab of pain pierced her through the chest.

It? Like it wasn't human anymore.

"A kid . . . ?" she repeated. She thought of Paul and Sara. She hadn't checked either of them before she had left the garden. She waded into the shallows, trying to hurry, cursing as the water clutched at her legs, slowing her down.

Then she saw the body.

The man was right. It was a child, floating faceup, eyes open, a halo of blond hair spread around the head like a sea fan. Cora stopped, unable to go farther. She put a hand to her throat as if to push back the sickness she felt rising there.

"Sara . . . ?" she said, her voice weak and distant.

The sun broke through the cloud and illuminated the dead child's face. Her skin seemed to have been leeched of all color so that it was as white as cuttlefish bone. Her eyes and mouth were open, locked in an expression of disbelief, the haunting awareness of her own death frozen on her perfect face.

But it wasn't Sara.

It was Cass's daughter, Tina.

CHAPTER 2

Annie Ginnaro glanced at the clock on the newsroom wall and swore under her breath. It was five to eight. There was no way she would make her dinner date on time. She finished the sentence she was working on, hit the save keys, and watched the trembling green letters vanish from the screen. She swept her notes and her cassette recorder into a drawer and got to her feet. Half a cigarette was burning in the ashtray and she went to stub it out, then changed her mind and put it in her mouth. It wasn't too polite to walk around with a cigarette in her mouth—it made her look hard—but it wasn't easy to find Kents in Bombay, and when she did find them, they weren't cheap. Besides, this was India. There were worse sights on the street. She gathered the rest of her things into a bulky leather bag, slung it over her shoulder, and made a quick detour by the night editor's desk on her way to the door.

"My piece on the dowry burnings will be ready tomorrow, Sylvester," she said as she hurried past.

Sylvester Naryan, somber-faced night editor for the *Times of India*, looked over the top of his glasses at her.

"You are going to lose the front page of the insight section," he said. "I have done all I can for you, Annie. If you don't get it to me by tomorrow, I will have to bump it inside."

"It'll be in your directory when you get in tomorrow," she called back to him. "Promise."

Naryan sniffed and went back to his word processor. Annie was already gone, the newsroom door swinging behind her. The elevator was slow and unreliable, so she took the stairs and ran down three flights. When she emerged onto the street, the usual flotilla of black-and-yellow taxicabs was waiting at the curb. She made her way through a besieging mob of drivers and climbed into the first empty cab.

"The Café Naaz," she said. "Malabar Hill."

The driver stared at her vacantly.

"Where, memsahib?"

Annie sighed. Malabar Hill was a major landmark and its name was the same in any language. She switched to Hindi and told the driver to take the Gandhi Marg overpass to Marine Drive, past Chowpatty Beach, and up Walkesar Road to the hanging gardens on the old Nepean Sea Road.

"*Acha, memsahib.*" The driver nodded vigorously and started the engine, his manner transformed now that he knew his passenger was not entirely helpless.

Annie smiled faintly. Despite her red hair, white skin, and American accent, the *salwar khameez* she wore was intended to give her the look of someone who belonged. Most of the younger working women in Bombay preferred the loose-fitting smock and pant suit to the traditional but restrictive sari, and as well as the extra comfort it offered, she hoped it would spare her at least some of the aggravation inflicted on tourists. But Bombay taxi drivers spared no one. Everybody in the newsroom had heard the story of the taxi driver who persuaded an Arab businessman that the correct fare from the airport was twelve hundred American dollars.

Annie's driver raked through the gears of the aging Premier

taxicab and lunged into the passing traffic without waiting for an opening. Cars braked, buses swerved, tires screeched, horns blared, drivers yelled, and Annie ignored it all. She sat back in her seat and calmly finished her cigarette. She had recognized long ago that the fastest way to appreciate the concept of karma was to use any form of public transportation in India. If you survived, your karma was good. If you did not, your karma was bad. It was that simple. This daily demonstration of karmic logic had convinced her that Hinduism was far in advance of anything the West had yet devised. American scientists had only just discovered the theory of chaos as the prevailing logic of the universe. Hindus had been living it for five thousand years.

The cab charged up Dadabhai Naoroji Road to Lohar Chowk, a traffic circle where six major roads met to create a drag race from hell. The chaos was exacerbated today because of a cow that had wandered into a center lane to graze on a fallen cardboard box. Annie watched, fascinated, as a crowded double-decker bus threatened to broadside the stupid beast. With only a few yards to go, the driver saw the sacred animal and instantly abandoned all concern for the safety of his passengers. He spun the steering wheel and the bus heeled over like a frigate in a gale. A dozen men clinging to the back of the bus screamed in unison as they were tossed back and forth like pieces of loose rigging. One of them scraped the pavement with his feet and took a series of giant running strides to avoid the wheels of the pursuing traffic.

The bus missed the cow and almost hit a truck carrying a load of loose gas cylinders. The truck veered away from the bus and threatened to crush a family of four Sikhs on a scooter. The scooter driver swore and shook his fist at the truck driver. The truck swayed, the gas cylinders jostled and clanged, but miraculously, none spilled out onto the road. At last Annie's cab hurled itself free of the traffic circle's deadly orbit. She turned and looked through the rear window as the cow receded behind her, contentedly chewing its ersatz cud, unperturbed by the mayhem it had caused.

Minutes later the cabdriver tried to stand the taxi on its nose when he stomped on the brakes outside the Café Naaz. Annie was ready with one arm braced against the seat back in front of her, so she wasn't thrown through the windshield. She handed the driver a fifty-rupee note and opened the door to get out. Her foot barely touched the sidewalk when the driver reached after her, grabbed her by the arm, and fixed her with what she had come to call "the Look."

His mouth was a writhing grimace, his face an anguished mask of betrayal, his eyes the eyes of a whipped dog. He waved the fifty-rupee note back at her as if she had given him her dirty underwear.

"Please, memsahib," he whined. "Is so little money . . . so many childrens at home . . . so many sick childrens . . . please, memsahib . . ."

Annie jerked her arm away.

"Vedya zala aheska," she snapped back at him. *"Halkat melya."*

He flinched and his face rearranged itself into a scowl. He stuffed the money into his shirt pocket, muttered something about her ancestry, and restarted the engine. Annie slammed the cab door and hurried up the path to the restaurant. She had given him a twenty-rupee tip on a thirty-rupee fare and still he'd tried the guilt routine on her. She had called him a madman and a scoundrel and told him to drop dead. It wasn't the worst Hindi she knew, but it was enough to tell him that she wouldn't be pushed around. She also knew enough to make a quick departure once the words were out of her mouth. Indian men would tolerate some abuse from a woman if she was from a higher caste or if she was white. But not always. Bombay might think itself the most enlightened city in India, but it was still a city where women were beaten to death for the crime of talking back to men.

The Café Naaz was a three-story cement box with standard

food and the aesthetic charm of an artillery bunker. But for the price of a meal, it offered the best view on the peninsula. Annie nodded to Mr. Ahbay at the cashier's desk and took a circular stone staircase up to the third floor. She emerged, panting, onto the rooftop to find a dozen empty tables and only one customer. For a moment he didn't realize she was there and she thought how forlorn he seemed and it made her feel guilty again. Then he heard the slap of her sandals on the flagstones and turned to look at her. As he got to his feet his face was transformed by an expression of such genuine pleasure it thrilled her just to see it. Annie Ginnaro could think of few things more exciting in life than to see how much she was wanted by the man she loved.

George Sansi was in his early forties and had the manner of a man who was at ease with the world and his place in it. He wore a tan suit cut from quality linen, though he had removed the jacket and draped it across the back of a chair. He wore a pale blue shirt with the tie loosened at the collar and the cuffs rolled midway up his forearms in a way she found terribly sexy. A man of average height and build, he looked anything but average. He wore his hair longish, and swept straight back from his forehead. He had a straight nose and a mouth that seemed always to be on the verge of a smile. His skin was a light coffee color, the color of the half-caste. But as pleasing as his features were, he might have been only routinely handsome were it not for one remarkable feature.

His eyes were blue.

Like the color of his skin they were the genetic legacy of an English father and an Indian mother.

"Just when I was certain you'd abandoned me," Sansi said. His English was impeccable, the accent refined by three years at Magdalen College, Oxford. He leaned forward to kiss Annie on the cheek, but she guided his face toward her so she could kiss him on the lips. She kissed him long enough and warmly enough to let him know just how bad she felt for keeping him waiting.

"I'm sorry I'm late," she said.

"If this is how you make up for a few minutes"—he smiled—
"I would have been willing to wait all night."

"Let's not leave it quite that long," she said, leaving no doubt
how she intended to make it up to him.

Sansi pulled out a chair for her. When she sat down it rocked
precariously and she had to shuffle it a few times till she was
comfortable. There wasn't a chair in the place that sat evenly, but
it hardly mattered. The floor wasn't even either.

"Would you like a drink?" Sansi asked.

"Badly," she said.

What she wanted was a whiskey, straight up. But the Café
Naaz had no liquor permit, so she would have to make do with
something tamer.

"Lime soda will be fine," she said.

Sansi ordered the drinks from the only waiter, a stooped old
man in dirty shorts and T-shirt who sat at the top of the stairs,
smoking a *bidi*. When he had gone the two of them relaxed and
enjoyed the view of the city through the branches of the encroaching mango trees. From the rooftop of the Café Naaz, they
could look out over the jumble of roofs that crowded the south-
eastern flank of Malabar Hill, past the gaudy lights of the *bani
puri* stalls on Chowpatty Beach and the oily waters of Back Bay
to the elegant arc of streetlights along Marine Drive that was still
known as Queen Victoria's Necklace. It was a view reserved pri-
marily for Bombay's wealthiest residents: the business moguls,
property tycoons, and powerful government *babus* who lived in
the high-priced apartment buildings that clotted the hillside. But
it wasn't only the view that made it the priciest real estate in the
city. The soothing breezes of the Arabian Sea kept the tempera-
ture and the mosquitoes under control. The governor of Maharashtra also lived in a heavily guarded estate at Malabar Point,
which provided him ready access to escape by fast boat at times
of civil unrest.

From where they sat they could also see Sansi's home in one
of the oldest and smallest apartment buildings on the hill. A pink

and white wedding cake of a building, it had once been occupied
by the families of senior British army officers and high government officials of the Raj. The apartment had been bought by
Sansi's father, General George Spooner, who gave it to his mis-
tress, Pramila, when he left India with the remnants of the
British army in 1947. Sansi had grown up on Malabar Hill. It was
his backyard. Every weekday morning for twelve years he had
run down Walkesar Road to Chowpatty Beach, where he had
chased seagulls while waiting for the bus that took him to Cam-
pion School in Colaba. His mother had taken him to the Café
Naaz for ice cream when he was a little boy, usually on Sundays
after he had tired of the rides in Kamala Nehru Park. Now he was
gathering new memories there with the mettlesome but unpunc-
tual Annie Ginnaro, who had swapped the good life in California
for an impossible life in India. Tonight, it seemed, she had been
reminded of the awfulness of what she had taken on.

"Difficult day?" he asked softly.

"Shit of a day," she said, and expelled a long thin column of
smoke.

Sansi waited to see if she wanted to talk about it.

"They're fighting me every step of the way on the dowry-
burnings piece," she went on. "I had to fight to get it into the paper and I've had to fight to keep it there. Now they're threatening
to bury it inside somewhere. The problem is I've given them the
excuse they need because now I'm late with it. I keep finding new
material and it's all worse than the stuff I got before."

"The problem, I suppose, is that it has been around so long,"
Sansi suggested cautiously. "There's nothing new in it."

"That's exactly the problem," Annie answered. "But maybe
you can tell me how any society can let itself get complacent
about thousands of women who are burned to death each year
just because their family can't ante up enough cash for a decent
dowry. It's barbaric . . . it's the kind of thing that should have
gone out with the Middle Ages."

Sansi was well acquainted with the saga of dowry burnings. He had been a police inspector for twenty years. His mother was a lecturer in feminist studies at the University of Bombay and had spent most of her life opposing a whole raft of institutionalized injustices against women in Maharashtra, of which dowry burnings were only a part.

"I went to the burns ward at the hospital yesterday," Annie continued. "I spoke to a woman, a girl really—she was nineteen. She's been there for eight months getting grafts and she'll be there for a while yet. When they brought her in she had burns over eighty percent of her body and wasn't expected to live. She did . . . but I think she wishes she hadn't. She showed me a photograph of her on her wedding day. She was beautiful, absolutely beautiful. Anyway, her father promised a whole bunch of things for her dowry—cash, jewelry, a TV set—all the usual stuff. But because he wasn't rich he asked for time to deliver the TV set. The groom's family gave him six months. But the father didn't come up with it by the deadline, and so they started on her. First the mother-in-law, calling her names, slapping her around, beating her with a broom handle. Pretty soon the whole family was involved, including her husband. They beat her just about every night for a month because her father couldn't come up with a goddamn TV set on time. And when they decided they'd waited long enough, they held her down in the kitchen, poured kerosene over her, and set her on fire. They waited two hours before calling an ambulance. Can you imagine what she went through in that time? The only reason they called the ambulance was because she wouldn't die . . . and they couldn't kill her any other way. They had to be able to say it was an accident. So she went to the hospital and somehow she survived. But she's scarred from head to toe. She'll never grow hair, she'll never be able to sit in the sun again."

"Will her family take her back?" Sansi asked.

"Her father says he'll live with the shame," Annie said. "Most

of them won't. That's why we have to get some money for shel-
ters—for the women who have nowhere to go when they get out
of the hospital."

Sansi knew how Annie felt. He experienced the same feelings
of frustration and helplessness whenever he ran into the brick
wall of Indian inertia. But he was part Indian. He had learned to
do things the Indian way. He had learned when to push and when
to yield. He had learned the Indian arts of patience and compromise. Annie was an American. When she saw something wrong
she wanted to change it overnight, regardless of the fact that it
had been practiced in India since before Christopher Columbus
was a boy.

"My mother tried—" Sansi began.

"I know," Annie interrupted. "She's been pushing for the
same thing for years. All I hope is that this piece will move things
along a little further. But I guess that depends on whether the
people who run this state are capable of human emotions like
guilt and shame."

"In my experience," Sansi said, "the only way to shame the
government into action is through the successful prosecution of
a known offender. That way they have no alternative but to acknowledge the seriousness of the problem. Otherwise . . ."

He ended the sentence with a shrug.

"And that's how I have to angle my story," Annie said. "The
police won't prosecute because the victims won't make formal
complaints. But even if you can get a victim to overcome a lifetime of conditioning and testify against her husband and her in-
laws, all that happens is that the family pays the cop off and he
never files the charges. So here we are, stuck with this mysterious
epidemic of kitchen fires that kill and maim thousands of women
every year but nobody wants to talk about."

"All the time I was in the police service," Sansi said, "I never
saw one dowry burning come to court."

Annie looked bleakly at him.

"There were one hundred and thirty-seven burnings last

month," she said. "In Bombay alone. We don't know how many
there are in the towns and villages because nobody keeps figures.
Sometimes I wonder if this country really wants to be part of the
modern world."

Sansi folded his arms on the table and leaned forward. "This
girl you were talking about. Would she be willing to go to court?"

Annie thought about it. "She might. If we could find a cop
willing to bring charges. Then we'd have to find a prosecutor
who'd take the case . . . and a judge who couldn't be bribed by her
in-laws."

Sansi smiled faintly. "I talked to the secretary of the bar council today," he said. "He does not anticipate any difficulty in getting the council to recognize my degree from Magdalen. I have
also found two attorneys to sponsor me. Both are quite influen-
tial in the council. All I am waiting for now is a vote at next
month's meeting. If there are no objections . . ."

"You'll be allowed to practice law in Bombay." She finished
the sentence for him.

"Before any court in the land if I want to," he said.

Annie slumped in her chair for a moment as if the news were
too good to be true. "I don't believe it," she breathed.

"I wouldn't be the first policeman to practice law in Maharashtra," Sansi said. "But I must say, I'm finding it easier to break
in today than I did twenty years ago. I suppose this is what comes
of living long enough to become respectable."

Annie smiled. Sansi was well equipped to be a lawyer. The
only reason he had pursued a career in the police service at all
was because he had returned from England as a young man to
discover that in the perverse world of Indian politics, the excel-
lence of his qualifications only made him more of an outcast.
Back then the country had been in the grip of Indianization and
any law firm that sought the government's favor found it expedi-
ent to employ full-caste Indians with degrees from third-rate Indian universities rather than an Anglo-Indian bastard with an
honors degree from Oxford. Sansi joined the police force because

it was the only job open to him where he thought he might do something useful. An instinct for politics and his sheer doggedness as an investigator had carried him to the rank of inspector in crime branch, the only department in the police service of Maharashtra untainted by the stench of corruption. Then, to the consternation of all those who had marked him as a future chief of crime branch, he had resigned to pursue the legal career he had always wanted.

"Perhaps what made the difference is that this time I know most of the lawyers in council," he said with a small smile. "I know what scoundrels they all are. They must have decided I would make a better friend than an enemy."

"It's wonderful," Annie said. "When will you be able to start?"

"I could start tomorrow," Sansi said. "I won't be ready to appear in court for another few months, of course. I'll need time to find chambers, to hire a clerk, a secretary, to find the odd client or two."

"And you'd take cases like this?"

"The greatest need is still for good defense lawyers," he said. "And that is where I will concentrate most of my energies. But as far as your dowry-burning victim is concerned, I might be able to find a police officer to lay charges. And there are a couple of honest prosecutors in the system—at least they are honest some of the time—who might be willing to take the case. There is nothing we can do to stop the in-laws from trying to bribe the judge, but it ought to be possible for you to publicize a case like this in such a way that it would make the judge wary about calling attention to himself. If that doesn't work we can still consider a civil court action against the in-laws to get her some compensation. If you are right about the time it took the family to call the ambulance, it shouldn't be too hard to prove negligence. That way, if we are unsuccessful in the criminal court but successful in the civil court, it could be even more embarrassing to the government. One way or another, we might get them to take the issue of dowry burnings a little more seriously."

Annie put her hand behind his neck and pulled him toward her so she could kiss him again on the lips. "You think you'll take more cases like this?" she asked.

Sansi laughed.

"Considering the type of women with whom I seem to surround myself, I think it would be hard for me to do otherwise," he said.

Annie smiled and leaned back in her chair. "I was feeling so defeated before I came here," she said. "Now I feel there's a reason to be hopeful. Does Pramila know?"

"I only found out myself this afternoon."

"We should celebrate," Annie decided. "We should go to the Taj so we can get champagne."

"Actually . . . I think I'd rather eat first," Sansi said.

"Actually . . . ?" she teased. From the day they had met she had been amused by the meticulousness of his English and the particularly English way in which he drawled certain words. They seemed quaint and idiosyncratic coming from an Indian man but, along with the blue eyes, they reminded her constantly of the extraordinary Englishman whose genetic imprint lingered indelibly within the extraordinary Indian.

Sansi's news helped restore both Annie's spirits and her appetite. When the waiter returned with their drinks, the two of them were ready to eat. Annie ordered a light chicken *dhansak* and Sansi the pomfret with green chutney baked in banana leaves. He also ordered side dishes of saffron rice and *masala dahl*, a black lentil stew spiked with red chilis. When the food came they ate in the Indian fashion, with their fingers. Afterward, Sansi watched her, a curious look in his eye.

"What?" she asked, and dabbed self-consciously at her chin.

"So, you're in the mood for something special?" he asked.

"I think that would be nice."

"Something different?"

She eyed him warily. "How different?"

But Sansi only smiled mysteriously and got up to go. He held

her hand as they left the restaurant and took the long wooden
staircase down the hill to Walkesar Road. They walked past the
beach at Chowpatty, where *kulis* squatted beneath the palm trees
smoking *bidis* and playing cards while children in rags played
cricket under naked lightbulbs strung from bamboo poles. From
there it was a short stroll up Pandita Ramabai Road to the point
where it joined three other roads. Sansi led her into a gloomy
side street where she could see only palm-thatch shanties, cook-
ing fires, and the dark shapes of people sleeping on the pavement.
There were other shapes in there, too, the small, animated shapes
of rats foraging for food. Annie would have gone with him, without hesitation, but he stopped and nodded at a small group of
men clustered in front of a brightly lit alcove on the opposite side
of the street.

The alcove was set into the side of one of the stately Victorian
town houses that had once been occupied by senior British civil
servants when Bombay was the most desired posting in the em-
pire. Now the house was rotten with neglect, the stonework
chipped and pitted and glazed with mildew. Like all the other
houses on the street, the ground floor had been turned into a
storefront and the floors above into noisy, overcrowded apartments. The city had been designed to accommodate a million
people but was now home to ten million. The strains were evident everywhere in the swarming, clamorous streets, the plague-
ridden slums, the festering apartment buildings, and the solemn
faces that crowded every door and window.

"Let me introduce you to Pandit," Sansi said. "The Chowpatty
paan wallah."

Sansi guided her through the crowd of customers to the *paan*
wallah's stall. Annie was intrigued. She had never been this close
to a *paan* wallah before. *Paan* was a predominantly male ritual
and she hadn't seen the attraction of hanging out with a bunch of
the guys at the end of the day while they chewed thick wads of betel leaf, spat spectacular jets of brown saliva into the gutter, and

passed comment on every woman who walked by. But she was well aware of the importance of the ritual in the lives of Indian men, from the lowliest *kuli* to the mightiest *babu*. It was a vice as old as India, as common to Indian men as chewing tobacco was to baseball players in the United States. Its popularity was evident in the maroon splashes that decorated every building and pavement in the city.

The *paan* wallah sat cross-legged on a green plastic cushion that was cracked with age. Over his head a couple of bare electric bulbs dangled from an extension cord to give him the light he needed for his work. Laid out neatly beside him on a length of coconut matting were the tools of his trade and an impressive array of powders and potions. Directly in front of him was a shiny piece of plywood that he used as his workbench. On it were two tin mugs that held the same kind of spoons and spatulas a pharmacist might use. On one side he kept a stack of fresh green betel leaves arranged in an attractive swirl, each one shaped like a human heart and about the same size as the palm of a man's hand. On his other side was a bigger stack of *paan* leaves, which his assistant, a serious-faced boy of about twelve, continually dipped in a pail of water to keep them fresh and supple. The rest of the alcove was filled with jars, shakers, and cans of all shapes and sizes, many of them labeled in elegant Sanskrit script. The jars and shakers held a variety of spices; the cans were filled with dark pastes that looked as appetizing as shoe polish.

"Pandit has been here for more than twenty years," Sansi told Annie quietly. "His father had this place before him and his father before him. That's his eldest son, Manoj, helping him. In another twenty years or so Manoj will inherit this stall from his father."

Annie was impressed. The *paan* wallah's stall might be nothing more than a hole in the wall, but in the teeming streets of Bombay where space was never wasted, it was worth money. Some, she knew, would be siphoned off by the local gang lord in the form of *hafta*, a weekly bribe to ensure that the humble alcove stayed exclusively in Pandit's family.

Annie gazed at the cans of paste. "What is that stuff?" she whispered, ignoring the curious looks of the men who pressed in around her.

"It is called *kimam*," Sansi answered. "It's tobacco paste. You have different types of betel leaf and you have different types of tobacco. There is refined tobacco and unrefined tobacco. The un-refined tobacco is called *bhala* and it is numbered according to its quality from 1-20 to 1-60 to 300 and 600. It is quite harsh and re-ally only for the *kulis*. The more refined tobacco starts with Chalu, which is the cheapest and still a little harsh and then it goes up through Kashmiri, Rajratan, and Navratan till you get to six hundred again—and that is the best."

"You expect me to put that stuff in my mouth?" she said.

"East and West can always teach each other new things."

"This isn't exactly what I had in mind."

"Taking tobacco this way is no worse than smoking it," Sansi reminded her.

Annie sighed. She was well aware what he thought of her smoking habit. "How do I know what to have?" she asked. "I don't know what betel leaf tastes like."

"I'll order for you," he said. "The cheapest leaf is Banarasi. Then there's Calcutta and Poona and then Magai. If you haven't had it before, the cheaper leaf can seem very coarse, very chewy. Magai is a small, brown leaf. When women take *paan* that's the one they choose most often because it is very sweet, like candy, it practically melts in the mouth."

She wanted to know more, but they were at the front of the line and it was their turn to order.

"*Kya khabar, Pandit?*" Sansi said to the *paan* wallah. It was Hindi for "What's up?"

Pandit looked up from his workbench and grinned when he saw who it was. The *paan* wallah had reason to be grateful to

Sansi. It was Sansi who had told the uniformed cops to stop bleeding the *paan* wallahs dry by getting their *paan* for free. He hadn't put an end to the practice—that would have been too much to expect—but he had cut it back enough to stop the drain on Pandit's meager profit.

Sansi introduced Annie. Then he and the *paan* wallah spoke for a minute in Hindi that was too rapid for her to follow. Pandit expressed genuine regret that Sansi was no longer a policeman but nodded knowingly when Sansi told him he was going into business as a lawyer.

"The cops are only small-time bandits," the *paan* wallah observed. "It is the lawyers who make the real money."

Sansi translated the last part for Annie and she nodded her agreement.

"It's the same where I come from," she said.

Sansi gave the *paan* wallah their order and coaxed Annie in closer so she could see how it was done. Pandit made hers first. He opened a jar and picked out a delicate golden leaf that was only half the size of the green *paan* leaves. He laid it out gently on the board in front of him and sprinkled it lightly with water. Then he took a clean wooden spatula, dipped it into one of the cans, and spooned out a morsel of paste the size of her little fingernail.

"That's *katechu*," Sansi explained. "It's an astringent made from crushed betel nuts."

"What does it do?" she asked.

"If you take too much of it," he said, "it makes your head go numb."

Pandit smeared the paste lightly over the leaf, then picked up a fat shaker and added a dash of fine white powder.

"*Mawa*," Sansi explained before she could ask. "Lime powder. Too much of that and you burn the top right off your tongue."

"I can hardly wait," Annie breathed. "Tell him to get his measures right, will you?"

"Pandit is one of the best *paan* wallahs in Bombay," Sansi re-assured her. "Something of a celebrity in his own right. The big names in the movie business all come down from Film City to get their *paan* here."

He hesitated, then shrugged. "Most of them want the *palang-tod* for their girlfriends."

"*Palang-tod?*" Annie repeated, a little too loudly. Sansi tried to quiet her, but it was too late. Some of the *kulis* had overheard and laughed to each other as they studied the red-haired American memsahib more closely.

"What is it?" Annie whispered.

"It has cocaine in it," Sansi whispered. "It's supposed to be an aphrodisiac. Translated literally, *palang-tod* means 'break out the cot.' "

Annie nodded thoughtfully.

"I don't think I need it," she said.

She turned her attention back to the street theater in front of her and watched, fascinated, as Pandit's hands fluttered from jar to jar, taking a smear of this, a dash of that, a dab of something else, mixing and blending, working to some ancient recipe, adding again and again to the mysterious cocktail on the tiny golden leaf. His hands moved with such speed and grace she was reminded of the hands of a concert pianist. Suddenly he was finished. He folded the leaf into a wad about the size of a matchbook and offered it to her with a smile. It had taken less than a minute.

"I told him to use six hundred tobacco and to add a little coconut," Sansi told her. "That way you get the taste of the betel and everything else that is good, but the coconut and the Magai leaf will take away the bite . . . or most of it."

Annie held the *paan* between finger and thumb and studied it closely.

"Hurry, or it will start to dissolve in your hand," Sansi urged. "Push it inside your cheek and hold it there."

"Yeah?" Annie paused. "Then what?"

"Then you wait for the different tastes to come through," he said, as though explaining himself to an idiot. "The first taste is the strongest and the best, then you chew it for a while to get all of it."

Annie hesitated a moment longer, then did as she was told. She felt as if she'd just shoved a wet tea bag into her mouth. Almost immediately the leaf began to dissolve and there was a surge of competing flavors, all of them merging together into a bizarre rush of sensation. First there was the leaf, as sweet as sugar, just as Sansi had promised. Then there was the scorching hit of the lime, followed by the sour jolt of tobacco, then something sweet again that must have been the coconut. Then there was something else that tasted like wood shavings and may have been sliced betel nut.

Her saliva glands reacted by trying to put out the fire and her mouth flooded. She tried to swallow, but there was too much fluid and the trickle she managed to get down burned her throat. She started to gag. She got scared and pushed her way through the crowd. Her stomach spasmed, a ripple of nausea radiated through her entire body, her head tilted back and then forward. The crowd parted before her, knowing what was coming. A great gout of scarlet liquid spurted from her mouth and landed twenty feet away in the roadway. The *kulis* nearby roared their approval. Annie barely noticed. She took a series of quick, short steps to the curb and gasped for air, afraid that she was going to throw up. Her mouth burned and her tongue thrummed like a guitar string. An awful image came back to her. When she was a kid she had gone to the state fair in Sacramento, where she had seen a sideshow geek eat a lightbulb. Now she knew how it felt.

More liquid poured into her mouth. She spat, coughed, hawked, and spat some more, heedless of the spectacle she knew she was making of herself. Gradually the burning subsided. Her saliva glands retreated from red alert and she knew she was going to live. She took out her handkerchief and dabbed daintily at her face. Sansi strolled up beside her, his cheek distended with a wad of *paan*.

"Well," she gasped, lowering the handkerchief from her mouth. "Parts of it were okay. . . ."

Sansi chewed the *paan* down to a manageable size. "I'll say one thing for you," he said at last. "You know how to spit like an Indian."

CHAPTER 3

Annie sipped a large vodka and tonic to purge the memory of the *paan* from her palate and watched Sansi get undressed. It was a fastidious process and was attended by such self-consciousness on his part that it constituted a kind of amused foreplay to her. He stood with his shirttails bunched around his bare thighs and his trouser cuffs tucked under his chin, smoothing the pant legs into their proper creases all the way down to the waistband. When he was satisfied he gripped the pants tightly at the knee between the thumb and forefinger of each hand and let the cuffs fall out from under his chin so that they dropped into a neat fold. Then he hung them carefully over the back of a chair. Next he unbuttoned his shirt, shook out the wrinkles, and arranged it tidily on the chair over the top of his trousers. The only time he departed from his punctilious striptease was when it came time to take off his undershorts. Then he turned slightly away from her, took them off quickly, and slipped into bed sideways so she barely got a glimpse of him.

Annie smiled. She was already naked, her body barely covered by a single top sheet, her own clothes in a heap at the foot of the bed. She was very comfortable with her own nudity and she found Sansi's modesty affecting, though she knew from past experience how quickly it would evaporate once she got her hands and mouth to work on him.

"You've got the best little butt," she said. "Like a couple of footballs pumped up nice and tight."

Sansi looked solemnly at her. "That is a very sexist remark," he said. "Under certain circumstances a gentleman such as myself might be offended."

Annie put down her drink and snuggled close to him. "Come here," she said. "I'll show you the meaning of the words *sex object.*"

Afterward they lay together in an exhausted tangle and slipped into a sleep so deep that neither of them was ready for the morning. They both slept through the alarm, and if Sansi had not been awakened by the sun in his eyes, Annie might have missed her story deadline. They dressed in a rush and left her apartment together. They held hands in the back of the cab all the way from Nariman Point into the city, but by the time they reached the *Times of India* building Annie's mind was already focused on the job ahead. She kissed Sansi good-bye, took a breath, and launched herself out of the cab and into the task of finishing the piece on the dowry burnings—before her bosses could find another excuse for bumping it. Sansi took the cab on to Malabar Hill, wishing there was more he could do to help her, wondering if he could get her away from work for a while, away from the unrelenting pressures of Bombay.

When he got to his apartment building, he paid off the driver and tipped him ten rupees. The man looked as if Sansi had spit in his hand, but Sansi was already through the main door and on his way to the elevator. He rode up to the fifth floor and let himself into the apartment he shared with his mother. He stopped briefly to look out on the terrace, where Pramila was drinking coffee and working her way through the morning newspapers.

His mother took in his puffy eyes and unshaven face and

said, "Don't you think you're getting a little old for this sort of thing?"

"I didn't expect to spend the night," Sansi lied. "I fell asleep."

"Of course you did, darling," his mother said. "Men your age always fall asleep after they've made love. You should know that by now."

Sansi grunted irritably in a way that reminded her of his father and disappeared in the direction of the bathroom. His mother smiled and turned her attention back to the papers. There were at least a dozen daily newspapers in Bombay and they came in three languages, English, Hindi, and Marathi. Pramila was fluent in all three. Sansi was fluent in five: English, the language of the bureaucracy; Hindi, the language of northern India; Marathi, the language of Maharashtra; Urdu, the language of Muslim India; and Tamil, the language of the south. Only a handful of scholars were known to have mastered all thirteen of India's official languages.

Sansi felt better after a shave and shower. He had no particular plans for the day and so he put on his *kurta* pajamas, the collarless tunic and trousers that many Indian men wore to relax at home. He walked out onto the terrace in his bare feet to join his mother for coffee. He knew she would be leaving soon for her morning tutorial at the university and thought he could be polite for at least a few minutes. He sat down in a thickly cushioned cane chair, picked through the pile of newspapers, and selected that day's copy of the *Hindustan Times*. A moment later the *bai*, Mrs. Khanna, appeared from the kitchen with a pot of fresh coffee. Sansi watched while she filled a fresh cup and lightened it with a splash of hot milk. He drank it while it was still scalding.

"I don't know how you can do that without burning your mouth," his mother remarked without looking up from her paper. Sansi wondered if he should have stayed inside.

"What would you like for breakfast, sahib?" Mrs. Khanna asked.

"The coffee will do fine," he said.

"I could make *masala dosa*," she offered.

Sansi shook his head. "The coffee will be fine, Mrs. Khanna," he insisted, thinking that one mother was more than enough.

Mrs. Khanna frowned and headed back to the kitchen. Sansi knew the cause of her displeasure. He had lost weight since he had gotten involved with the American woman. Obviously, it was her influence that was to blame. Western women had no idea what was attractive in a man. Like most of her generation, Mrs. Khanna admired plumpness. In a country where thinness was a sign of poverty, plumpness was an indication of status. Mrs. Khanna took pride in the fact that her husband was of generous proportions—and so was she.

Sansi watched her go with a smile of amusement. "I'll try to make up for it at lunch," he called after her.

He drank his coffee and scanned the front page of the paper. There was little that was new. Another bribery scandal in New Delhi, another Indian Airlines crash, thirty-seven poisoned by bad liquor in Chittorgarh, twenty-three killed in riots in Kashmir, eleven passengers on the Faizabad Express murdered by *dacoits*. Corruption, mayhem, and murder. Another twenty-four hours in the life of India.

A gust of wind darted across the terrace and tried to snatch the newspaper from his grasp. He snatched it back and scrambled to keep the other papers from becoming airborne. The potted palms in Pramila's rooftop jungle rasped and chafed at each other. Sansi looked on as the same prankish wind that tried to steal his newspaper now painted the murky waters of Back Bay with restless patterns of spindrift. The sky had been swept clean of all clouds, and on the far side of Back Bay, the city trembled in the heat of the sun. Sansi knew he should be out looking at offices to rent, but when he thought of the heat and the choking dust clouds the wind would create in the filthy city streets, he decided he could wait for another day.

"I suppose I'd better get going." Pramila sighed, reluctant to leave her rooftop oasis.

Sansi tried to look sympathetic. Pramila smiled, knowing how much he liked to have the apartment to himself. She was unusually pretty for a woman in her midsixties and there was a warmth in her face that echoed the loveliness of her youth. Only her eyes seemed old. They were the eyes of a woman who had seen all the lunatic extremes of human behavior and survived them all. Her hair was gray, though she wore it short and pert, and when she moved she moved with the grace of a much younger woman. She had attracted many suitors over the years and rebuffed them all. Sansi often wondered if they had any idea how lucky they were. He loved his mother and admired her unreservedly, though she could annoy him in ways that no other human being had ever been able to do. Except perhaps Annie. Pramila thought it the best joke of all that he had fallen for a woman who so resembled her in temperament.

"You and Annie can sleep together here, you know," Pramila said abruptly. "It has to be more comfortable than that poky little flat of hers."

It was a discussion they'd had before and Sansi was not inclined to go through it again. "Yes, Mother," he said. "I'll mention it."

Pramila hesitated then leaned forward and kissed him on the top of his head. "She's my friend, too, you know," she added. "And we have many more interesting things to talk about than you."

Sansi looked self-conscious again. It was a recurring fear of his that he would get up one morning and find Annie at the breakfast table discussing the most intimate details of their sex life with his mother.

"Yes, Mother," he repeated.

She heard the tone in his voice and recognized that it was her cue to leave. Minutes later Sansi heard the front door close. He felt a momentary pang of guilt, shrugged it away, and poured himself a fresh cup of coffee. Then he retrieved the *Hindustan Times* from the mess on the table and moved to a lounge chair in a sheltered corner of the terrace where he could stretch his legs and read in peace, unmolested by the wind or anything else.

He read for half an hour, but he was tired and his attention kept wandering. He put the paper down on his lap and closed his eyes for a moment. The next thing he knew he was being shaken gently but persistently by the shoulder. He opened his eyes with some difficulty and looked around. His mouth tasted stale and the newspaper had slipped to the floor beside his chair.

"I fell asleep," he said, surprised. He looked at Mrs. Khanna. "How long have I been asleep?"

"For some time," Mrs. Khanna answered helpfully. "I would not disturb you, sahib, but there is a man on the telephone and he says he has important business with you. He says he won't wait and he will not call back. He is a very rude man. I think it is Commissioner Jamal, but he will not tell me his name."

Sansi looked at his watch. It was almost midday. *"Are Bapre."* It was the Hindi expression for "my God." He had been asleep for two hours. He got to his feet, walked stiffly to the kitchen, and picked up the phone. "This is Sansi."

"Congratulations," the deep male voice on the other end said. "I understand you've been admitted to the bar."

Mrs. Khanna was right. It was Narendra Jamal, the joint commissioner of crime branch and Sansi's former boss. Crime branch was an elite investigative unit within the Maharashtran Police Service, a force within a force with a mandate to pursue anyone anywhere. It was a role that made Jamal the most powerful policeman in the state and caused him to be hated every bit as much as he was feared.

"Thank you, Commissioner," Sansi answered politely. "I'm afraid you're a little early. My admission hasn't been confirmed yet."

"It will be," Jamal said.

Sansi smiled faintly. "I am encouraged by your optimism, Commissioner," he said.

It was typical of Jamal to let Sansi know what was going to happen to him before it happened. But it was worrisome only because Sansi knew it was not the real reason Jamal had called. Sansi had no illusions about his place in the hierarchy of Bombay. He was a nobody. His mother, the firebrand feminist, carried more weight than he. Jamal was one of the city's leading power brokers. He would never have called Sansi about something so trifling unless he wanted something more. Sansi waited, curious and apprehensive at the same time.

"There is a matter of some importance I must discuss with you, Sansi," Jamal added abruptly.

Sansi hoped that once he had left crime branch he would no longer be subject to Jamal's machinations. Clearly, it had been hope in vain. Jamal needed his pawns and he intended Sansi to be one of them. Nor was it a simple matter for Sansi to deny Jamal now that he was out of uniform. The commissioner was one step below cabinet rank. He expected to be chief minister one day. Sansi fully expected him to make it. In the meantime, if Sansi wanted to practice law unhindered, he could not afford to make an enemy of Jamal.

"Commissioner." Sansi tried to sound apologetic. "I haven't had much time—"

"I know I can count on you, Sansi," Jamal interrupted. "But this is not a matter that can be discussed over the telephone. I must meet with you in person. All I can tell you is that it is a matter of considerable importance to the state."

Sansi sighed. Considerable importance to the state meant considerable importance to Jamal and perhaps no one else.

"I do have certain commitments in the next few days," Sansi tried again.

"Affairs of state take precedence over personal matters," Jamal insisted. "I'll see you at three-o-clock."

An awkward silence stretched out between the two of them.

Sansi had thought he might be able to stall Jamal for a day or two in the hope that the moment of crisis, whatever it was, would pass him by. But Jamal would not be denied.

"Very well, Commissioner," Sansi said at last. "I will be waiting for you."

"Your mother must not see me there," Jamal added. "And you have a *bai*, do you not?"

"My mother will be at the university all day," Sansi said. "I will see that Mrs. Khanna goes home early."

"Acha," Jamal said. "Three-o-clock. I will see you then."

"Commissioner . . . " Sansi tried one last time.

But the line was dead. Sansi hung up the phone and wandered back out onto the terrace. A mocking gust of wind lunged at him, ruffled his hair, pulled at his clothes, and flung the discarded sheets of newspaper at his feet.

CHAPTER 4

When Sansi opened the door of his apartment, he was shocked by the commissioner's appearance. Jamal was a vain man who wore pristine white shirts, designer ties, and expensive suits. He went everywhere in an air-conditioned Contessa chauffeured by a police driver so that he always arrived cool and composed and in control. It was all part of the image of a man who was comfortable with power and who expected deference wherever he went. This Jamal had the breathless and disheveled look of a fugitive. His neatly barbered hair was slick with sweat, his tie was loose at the collar, and his shirt clung to his body in big wet patches. In one hand he carried an attaché case and in the other his suit jacket, bunched up like a rag.

"I left my driver at Walkesar Temple," he said, seeing the look in Sansi's eyes. "I told him to wait for me there."

Sansi nodded as if he understood. "Welcome to my home, Commissioner," he said politely. "Please, come in and make yourself comfortable. You look as if you could do with a drink."

Jamal followed Sansi into the living room, threw his jacket

49

carelessly on the arm of a sofa, and put down his attaché case. Sansi continued across the living room to the open kitchen.

"Something cold, Commissioner?" he offered. "I have beer. . . ." It occurred to him that something stronger was called for. He knew Jamal liked good scotch.

"I have a rather nice single malt."

Jamal shook his head. "Can you make a salt lime?"

"Of course," Sansi said, and took two glasses down from a shelf.

"I have to appear before state cabinet tonight," Jamal explained. "I'm going to need a cool head."

Sansi thought it might already be too late. On the telephone it had sounded like the same old Jamal—abrupt, demanding, impatient. This Jamal was someone else. This Jamal had a look of desperation, the look of a drowning man. Sansi felt a pang of sympathy. He tried to suppress it. Drowning men weren't too particular about whom they pulled down with them.

He filled the glasses from a pitcher of lime juice in the refrigerator, added a pinch of salt, and gave each a brisk stir. Then he slid one across the counter to Jamal and watched while he drained it.

"Rather an unpleasant day out there," Sansi observed idly.

"Rather," Jamal agreed. He put down the empty glass and dabbed at a trickle of lime juice on his chin before it dripped onto his shirt.

"Another?" Sansi offered.

"You are very kind," Jamal said, and pushed his glass back across the counter. Like Sansi, the commissioner had come to the police service twenty years earlier with a law degree. Unlike Sansi, he had the right connections and had gone straight to headquarters with a lieutenant's pips on his shoulders while Sansi had been made a constable and sent to a hellhole called Tamori five hundred miles from Bombay. Jamal was tough in his way, but he had no idea what it was like to hunt *dacoits* in the desert or walk the streets of Bombay. Sansi made another salt lime and invited the commissioner to follow him out to the terrace.

"I would prefer that we stayed inside," Jamal said.

"It is quite private," Sansi reassured him.

"No," Jamal insisted. "Nobody knows I am here, Sansi. Nobody knows we have kept in touch since you turned in your resignation. As far as everyone at crime branch is concerned, you have lost favor with me—and I would prefer it if they continued to think that way."

It was the first time Jamal had acknowledged openly that Sansi might have embarrassed him with his resignation over the Cardus affair, an investigation the department had quietly tried to bury. Sansi nodded but said nothing. He turned back to the living room and took one of two fat armchairs opposite a rattan coffee table that had once belonged to his father. Jamal sat down on the sofa on the other side of the table, within easy reach of his attaché case. The two of them sat quietly for a moment and savored the cooling draft of the ceiling fan as it swished rhythmically over their heads.

Sansi was struck by how much older Jamal looked since they had last seen each other. The commissioner was a big man, well over six feet, and inclined to the kind of fleshiness that afflicted most big men in middle age. But he had lost weight since Sansi had seen him last and looked worse for it. His skin hung loose on his big-boned frame, like a suit that was a size too big. Where there had once been a comfortable double chin, there was now a slack fold of skin that suggested a much older man. Jamal seemed to have lost much of his energy, too, and with it, much of his physical authority. There was also a hint of pallor beneath the skin and dark, mottled pouches beneath the eyes. Clearly, something big had happened, something catastrophic, perhaps, to have had such an effect on him.

"I can turn on the air-conditioning," Sansi said, noticing that Jamal was still sweating. He wondered if the commissioner had come down with a touch of fever in his weakened state.

"Please." Jamal lifted his hand. "It isn't necessary."

Sansi waited. It was an odd moment for both of them. In all the years they had known each other, they had never socialized, never been to each other's homes, never met each other's families. All Sansi had seen of Jamal's private life were the photographs on his desk at work. An appropriately plump wife and two grown-up children. A daughter who was in public relations with the Oberoi hotel group in New Delhi and a son in his final year of law at Cambridge.

It was the first time Jamal had been to Sansi's home, but he did not seem surprised by the comfortable surroundings, which were well beyond the means of a police inspector's salary. There was little about Sansi's life that Jamal did not already know. Sansi harbored no illusions about his former boss. There would be a thick dossier on George Louis Sansi in Jamal's secret files. A dossier that listed all his flaws as well as his strengths. Undoubtedly there was a file on Pramila, too, bigger than Sansi's, and possibly a newer file on Annie Ginnaro. Sansi knew all of this and accepted it as something he could not change, as karma. He had not been a conventional policeman. Nor would he make a conventional lawyer. Jamal knew this also.

"Sansi," the commissioner began at last. "I come to you today in need of a great service."

Sansi nodded, his face blank.

"But it is not only for myself that I ask," Jamal continued in a portentous tone. "I am sure you will see this as an opportunity to perform a great service for the people of Maharashtra."

Considering how Jamal thought the fate of Maharashtra was closely allied with his own fate, the commissioner was hardly an unbiased judge, Sansi thought. He nodded politely and waited.

"You are aware of the national debate concerning the free port?" Jamal asked, taking the conversation in an unexpected direction.

"*Acha*," Sansi said. "But only what I've seen in the newspapers."

For years the government in New Delhi had studied the feasibility of turning a piece of Indian territory into a free port, a duty-free haven for international trade, banking, and manufacturing that would duplicate the success of Singapore and transfuse the Indian economy. Only recently had the government moved into high gear by setting up a committee to investigate potential sites.

"I know they've narrowed the field down to, what, half a dozen places?" Sansi said. "Tuticorin, Goa, Pondicherry . . ."

"The free port will be built at Goa," Jamal said. He said it with such certainty that Sansi could not doubt that it was true.

"Delhi has already made up its mind," Jamal went on. "The only reason the announcement has been delayed is so the thieves in government can buy up as much land as possible before the boom starts—when they make a formal announcement to the rest of the world. A mini-boom has already started in Goa. Property is changing hands at crazy prices . . . and it's going to get a lot crazier. The greed in cabinet is so thick you could choke on it."

Until this moment Sansi had thought there was little that could shock him about the scale and extent of corruption in India. Indians cheated each other all the time. It was a national vocation. Cheating foreigners was a national responsibility. But cheating the rest of the world? Sansi was impressed. A free port would suck in investments worth billions of dollars. First by the federal government, then by the big banks and corporations in India, and then by the big banks and corporations in the rest of the world. Mammoth construction projects would be involved; new port facilities, roads, railways, airports, factories, service industries, telecommunications. New hotels would be built to accommodate the millions of tourists lured to Goa by the promise of vast beaches and shopping malls packed with duty-free goods. The potential rake-off for those who got in early was fantastic. In the short term there would be so much money flying about that nobody would know where it was going. The long term was for somebody else to worry about.

"I don't suppose it would come as a surprise to you to know that Banerjee is leading the investment charge into Goa," Jamal added.

"*Are Bapre,*" Sansi breathed.

Rajiv Banerjee was the newly appointed minister for economic development, a racketeer who controlled the northern industrial suburb of Bhandup and had used his money and influence to buy himself a seat in the state assembly. The outcry that followed his appointment to the post of minister was enough to shame the devil—but not the state cabinet. A despairing editorial writer at the *Times of India* compared it to putting a fox in charge of the henhouse. But the plaintive voice of the media had been silenced by a flurry of writs from Banerjee's lawyers, who claimed their client was a successful businessman, a generous donor to charity, a worthy and honorable man who had been singled out unfairly by a vindictive and inaccurate press.

"As you know, we've been building a case against Banerjee for years," Jamal continued. "Now he thinks he's too big for us. He thinks we can't touch him." The commissioner shrank further into the sofa. "And he may be right," he added wearily.

Sansi shifted uncomfortably in his seat. It wasn't pleasant watching a man wither in front of him. Even a manipulative and self-serving bastard like Jamal, whose ego had once seemed unassailable. Most people learned early in life to endure compromise and defeat. Jamal had little experience of either—and he handled both with a singular lack of grace.

"You don't really believe that," Sansi said, wishing he sounded more convincing.

"Banerjee has the protection of the cabinet because he can make them all rich," Jamal added. "He will put money into Goa on their behalf and they will go along with him, for a year or so, until they've made their fortunes. The moment they have their money secreted safely in Dubai, they'll find an excuse to get rid of him. He is too much of an embarrassment to keep around indefinitely. There will be a few threats and recriminations from both

sides, but none of it will stick. Banerjee will go back to his rackets knowing how it feels to be used by a worse bunch of
scoundrels than him—but nobody will complain too loudly because everybody will have made their profit."

Sansi remained silent. The scenario Jamal had outlined was
all too plausible. For a while the only sound in the room was the
rhythmic swish of the ceiling fan.

"Of course, Banerjee thinks he has cabinet in his pocket," Jamal added. "His mistake is to think it will always be that way. He
thinks that all he has to do is get some dirt on them and he can
blackmail them into doing what he wants—perhaps even making
him chief minister."

Sansi looked at the floor to hide any hint of amusement there
might be in his eyes. Clearly Jamal did not appreciate the irony of
his predicament. His secret files were the armament of a master
blackmailer. Perhaps what bothered him most was that Banerjee
would use the same weapon to beat him to the chief minister's
chair.

"I am the only man who can stop him, Sansi," the commissioner was saying. "And the only way I can stop him is to destroy
him."

Abrubtly Sansi realized the real purpose of Jamal's visit—and
the fleeting glow of amusement curdled inside him.

"You can't close the case?" he said. It was more a statement
than a question.

Jamal leaned forward on the sofa and fidgeted with the rings
on his hand. "I have a warehouse full of evidence," he said. "But
I must have something more. I need something conclusive, something damning so there isn't a politician in the country who
would stand by him."

Sansi sipped at his salt lime, hardly tasting it.

"Goa is a federal project," Jamal went on. He spoke quickly,
drawing on nervous energy. "New Delhi won't like it if Banerjee
does anything to sabotage the free port before it can be presented
to international finance markets. They can't afford to have the

stink of corruption around it. A little land speculation at the local level is acceptable, inevitable perhaps, but more than that won't be tolerated. And that is where Banerjee has made his biggest mistake. Greed has made him reckless. He is trying to buy up everything on the coast—him and his new cronies in cabinet."

"Something like this . . ." Sansi looked levelly at Jamal. "If it gets out, it could bring down the government."

"I don't want to bring down the government," Jamal answered sharply. "I am trying to save the government by bringing down Banerjee. I am trying to stop these fools from destroying themselves—and if they weren't so insane with greed, they might understand that."

Sansi paused. What Jamal was doing was trying to shore up his own political aspirations. The way to do that, in his mind at least, was to keep the present government in office—but amenable to his wishes, not Banerjee's.

Sansi feigned ignorance. "If the joint commissioner of crime branch can't prevail upon cabinet—"

"It's too late for that," Jamal cut him short. "With the chief minister on his side, Banerjee holds the balance of power in cabinet. To correct that balance, I must discredit him completely. I must destroy him—and soon."

"Commissioner, you have all the sources of crime branch at your command," Sansi said. "With the best will in the world, I do not see what help I can be to you in this situation."

"If Banerjee gets his way, I won't have the resources of crime branch at my command much longer," Jamal answered dully.

Sansi looked puzzled.

"Banerjee has found a way to get rid of me before I have a chance to move against him," Jamal said.

Sansi waited. For a moment Jamal paused, clearly loath to explain how he had been outmaneuvered by such a lowly adversary as Rajiv Banerjee.

"Until recently I believed there were only two ways Banerjee could get rid of me," Jamal finally said. "He could bribe me—or he could kill me. He has already tried to bribe me by inviting me to share in his scheme—through no less an intermediary than the home minister, I might add. I turned him down. That left him with the other option. But that would involve an unacceptable level of risk to him. The murder of a joint commissioner of crime branch falls into the same category as political assassination—and it would attract exactly the kind of attention from Delhi that he wants to avoid."

"To have you dismissed or demoted requires a full vote of cabinet," Sansi responded. "You think that's what he intends to do?"

"No." Jamal shook his head. "That would attract almost as much attention as my death. I know what they have in mind for me, Sansi. They're going to send me to a place where I can't make trouble for them. They're going to put me in quarantine."

"Quarantine?"

"They have decided to make me district commissioner of Tamori, effective next month. I believe it is a place you know rather well."

Sansi gave a soft grunt of recognition. It was perfect. No wonder Jamal looked beaten. It wasn't necessary to have him fired, demoted, or killed. He would simply be shunted sideways—with minimum fuss and maximum humiliation—to a place called Tamori in the deserts of northeastern Maharashtra, a wretched outpost in a wretched landscape infested by scorpions, *dacoits*, and Naxalites, where the only industry was famine relief and the main activity of the police was the rescue of kidnapped foreign-aid workers. Tamori was a legend in the police service. For decades it had been a dumping ground for drunks, fools, psychopaths, and other misfits who had become an embarrassment to the department. Sansi had spent his first year there because he would not join the bidding game at the police academy that decided what recruits got the choicest postings. He still bore a scar on his side, from his own exile in Tamori, where a Naxalite insurgent had stabbed him with a knife.

Over the years Joint Commissioner Jamal had banished
many men to Tamori. Now it was his turn. Like those who went
before him, he had a simple choice—take it or resign. If he were
to resign he would spare cabinet the bother of getting rid of him.
Sansi could not help but be impressed.

"You can laugh at me if you want," Jamal said. "Everybody
else is laughing behind my back."

Sansi shook his head. There was much about Jamal that
could be despised. In his mind the advancement of justice was in-
extricably bound up with the advancement of his own career. Yet
despite his vanity, he had his own code of honor, a peculiar,
frayed, Indian kind of honor. In a world where there were no absolute truths, he clung to the notion of dharma, his duty. And he
discharged that duty the only way he knew how. He broke many
of the laws he was sworn to uphold. He was unscrupulous in his
use of power. He manipulated the course of justice to suit himself. But he feared no one. Some of the most powerful criminals
in the state of Maharashtra had been brought down by him. In
India, his was the fairest face that justice had to offer.

But more sobering to Sansi was the knowledge that Jamal
was the last remaining restraint on a cabinet grown reckless with
greed. If he was removed, to be replaced by someone more
amenable to the dictates of a cabinet influenced by Rajiv Banerjee, crime branch would be ruined. The eighty million people of
Maharashtra would lose their last bulwark against corruption.

Sansi felt Jamal's gaze on him like a pressing weight. To
Sansi it was no longer a question of whether he should ally himself with Jamal in the looming power struggle but whether Jamal
could be saved—and whether Sansi would be sticking his neck
out needlessly. It was not a decision he cared to make in haste.
But Jamal had wanted it this way so that Sansi had no alternative
but to declare himself now, friend or enemy. There could be no
in-between. The commissioner was desperate, but he was not a
fool. He wanted to see how Sansi reacted, to watch the doubt and

deliberation on his face, to study the emotional circuitry just beneath the surface, to gauge for himself precisely how much he
could trust Sansi.

"Commissioner," Sansi said slowly and deliberately. "How is
it that I may assist you in your time of trouble?"

For a moment Jamal stayed quite still. Then the tension
seemed to coil out of him like a departing evil spirit. He leaned
back in the sofa, looked frankly at Sansi, and nodded.

"Thank you, Sansi," he said. "I owe you a great debt . . . the
state owes you a great debt."

Sansi nodded slightly and waited. It wasn't over yet. There
was still much to be resolved. Jamal had made it hard for Sansi
to refuse him. If Sansi let him get away with it, it meant nothing
had changed between them. He was still in Jamal's power. Still
his pawn. Sansi couldn't let it stay that way. There had to be a
change in the balance of power between them. There had to be
a price for his assistance.

"As you would be aware, Sansi," the commissioner continued, "the common characteristic of all land booms is that they require large amounts of money. Hard currency. Not notes and
promises. Which means large amounts of cash are locked up until a profit can be turned. And Rajiv Banerjee is not the only spec-
ulator in Goa. Every land shark in India with a connection to the
government has people in Goa looking for property, many of
them waving a bundle of notes in one hand and a piece of lead
pipe in the other. The shooting war will start when all the best
land has gone and they have to start taking it from each other.
Right now there's still plenty available and it's an old-fashioned
land rush. Whoever buys the most the fastest wins the biggest."

"So Banerjee needs cash?"

"He can't get his hands on it fast enough. And we both know
the best business in the world for generating a lot of cash in a
hurry."

"Drugs," Sansi said quietly.

"Banerjee has been in the drug business a long time," Jamal added. "Mostly domestic distribution, though he started moving small amounts of heroin to the Gulf States a few years ago because it was easy. Until recently, Goa was a nice little franchise operation. His people down there made a bit of money selling to the tourists and the hippies. That reached saturation level years ago—you can't make everybody a junkie, no matter how hard you try. So his people had to look for other ways to make money. That wasn't too hard because there were always a few small-time traffickers looking for a kilo of heroin to take home with them. It gave Banerjee's people the idea for a nice little racket of their own. They would sell a couple of kilos to some foreign buyer then tip off their pals in the police department. The police would raid the buyer's hotel, make the arrest, and seize the drugs. Banerjee's people would split the drug money with the police and get the drugs back to sell again. Most of them anyway. The police had to keep some around as evidence in case the buyers weren't able to bribe their way out of jail. It was a nice little racket. Everybody made money and nobody got burned except a few stupid foreigners—and they had to keep their mouths shut if they wanted to get a deportation deal instead of twenty years in Panjim jail."

Sansi nodded.

"The only problem was that it was an unreliable source of income," Jamal went on. "Many buyers knew enough to stay away from Banerjee's people. They bought the heroin elsewhere and got out before anybody knew. It was only a matter of time before Banerjee decided if it was that easy to get drugs into Europe, he might as well do it himself. He started a couple of years ago. Small quantities at first. Two or three kilos, mules only, the condom-in-the-stomach routine. One of his mules died at the airport in Athens after a condom burst. Another went into a seizure during a flight to Rome. But Banerjee is so desperate he's moving the heroin out in bigger quantities all the time. Mules, containers, boat drops, light planes, any way he can. It has grown so big he

can't keep track of it all. He has to rely more and more on subor-
dinates and they're not always reliable. He had to send one of his
people down there a few months ago to take over the Goan end of
the operation. A man called Prem Gupta. I think you've heard
of him."

Sansi recognized the name. Gupta was a career thug with a
long list of killings to his name for someone not yet turned thirty.

"A man by the name of Sharma had been in charge of the Goa
operations," Jamal added. "Banerjee decided Sharma was cheating him, so he sent Gupta down to clean things up. Everything is
run from Banerjee's house in Panjim. Gupta stayed there for a
week, acting friendly, as if nothing was wrong. One day Gupta
dragged him into the garage and hacked him to pieces with a
sword while somebody taped it with a video camera."

Sansi was not surprised. This sort of thing was horrific but
nothing new in gangland. Videotapes of executions were a pecu-
liarity of the Bombay underworld—a useful tool for keeping dis-
cipline in the ranks.

"He's getting careless," Jamal said. "Careless and stupid. And
we are that close to nailing him. . . ." He held up his thumb and
forefinger so they were almost touching.

"It seems to me you have everything you need to move
against him now," Sansi said.

"No," Jamal said. "I can connect him to the rackets in
Bhandup. I can prove he has moved large sums of money
through front companies in Bombay to front companies in Goa.
I can prove there is money from at least five cabinet ministers
mixed in with the dirty money Banerjee is sending to Goa—and
none of them knows whether the money goes to buy land or to
support Banerjee's drug operation. I have information from Interpol to show that the mules they picked up all worked for
Banerjee's front companies. I can get a lot of the people around
him, Sansi. I can show he is involved in fraud, racketeering, and
money laundering and I can implicate him in a hundred other

crimes including murder. But it's not enough. Not now. I have to
go outside the state. I have to show a level of criminality in Goa
that will offend the government in New Delhi and every foreign
investor who is thinking of putting a single paise into the free
port. And I have to do it soon."

Sansi tried to suppress the queasiness that stirred inside him.

"I want you to go to Goa on my behalf," Jamal said. "I need
evidence that will connect Banerjee directly to the international
trafficking of drugs. I need a detailed, evidentiary picture of the
situation down there, Sansi—the scale of the operation, the size
and frequency of shipments, destinations, the extent of police involvement. I have to show New Delhi how dirty Goa is and I have
to be able to prove that Banerjee is up to his neck in it."

Reflexively, Sansi found himself shaking his head. Under
ideal circumstances an investigation of such size and complexity
would require a support team of twelve men and take up to a
year, perhaps longer. Sansi would be working alone, with no protection, and he had less than one month. It wasn't possible.

"Commissioner," he began. "With the best of intentions . . ."

Jamal raised his hand in that annoying, imperious way that
he had. "I know you are not a miracle worker," he said. "But I
have paid you the highest compliment I can pay any man, Sansi.
I have put my faith in you. And I do not do that lightly. You are
one of the best investigators I have ever known. You are percep-
tive. You are resourceful. You are tenacious. And"—he paused
artfully—"you do your best work when you are free to follow
your intuition, when there is no one in authority standing over
you."

Sansi smiled thinly.

"You are the only man I can trust to do this thing for me,
Sansi," Jamal said.

The armchair creaked as Sansi got to his feet and walked
slowly to the window overlooking the terrace. He watched the
wind torment the shrubs and plants for a while, but then his gaze

retracted and he found himself looking at his own face in the glass. What he saw was a reflection of his own dismay.

"Most of the work will be straightforward surveillance," Jamal continued behind him. "It is your eye and your experience that will make the difference. I will give you unrestricted access to all my files. You will know how to proceed from there. And you won't be alone, Sansi. I have friends in Goa. People who want to help. People like you, who care about what is right."

The reflection in the glass showed a warped smile. "Not inside the police department," Sansi said.

"No," Jamal confirmed. "You will not be able to rely on the local police for anything. They are rotten with Banerjee's spies. It would be prudent if the Goan police did not know you were there at all."

Sansi remained silent for a long time, gazing at the jumbled, empty dimensions in the window. Prudent, he thought, and turned the word over in his head. This was India, the most corrupt society on earth. Prudent men went mad here.

"Of course," Jamal added, "I will pay you for your services."

Sansi heard two metallic clicks and turned around as Jamal sprang his attaché case open on the coffee table. The joint commissioner looked up to make sure that Sansi was watching, then turned it around so that he could see inside it. It was filled with money, brightly colored new rupee notes in large denominations.

"There are two and a half lakhs there," Jamal said. "Generous payment for a month's work—even for a Bombay attorney."

Sansi looked at the neatly stacked bundles of money. Two hundred and fifty thousand rupees. About ten thousand American dollars. Five years' pay if he was still an inspector. Some things, then, had changed.

"Goa is not an unpleasant place to work," Jamal went on. "I think you should take your lady friend with you. Miss Ginnaro, isn't it? It would be better that way. It would look normal. Two lovebirds on holiday?"

Sansi's gaze shifted from the money to Jamal and then back to the money again. It wasn't exactly a bribe. But it was too much money for a month's work, even a hazardous month's work. Sansi knew what it was. It was an attempt to keep the relationship between them unequal, an attempt by Jamal to show that Sansi's private wealth did not matter. It was meant to show that Jamal was still the boss, just as he'd always been. At that moment Sansi knew how to get what he wanted from Jamal.

"It is not enough," he said quietly.

For a moment Jamal seemed stunned, then suspicion replaced the astonishment in his eyes.

"There is something you must understand . . . Narendra Jamal." Sansi used the commissioner's full name with deliberate emphasis, a gesture of unprecedented familiarity in their long and turbulent relationship. "I will not do this thing for money. I will do this for you as I would do a favor . . . for a friend."

Jamal's expression wavered for a moment between frustration and uncertainty. Then it was replaced by a slow smile of resignation. Sansi knew what Jamal would do once he had rid himself of Banerjee. Taking into consideration what was really at stake here, the contents of the attaché case were meaningless. Sansi wanted more, much more. He knew where Jamal was headed and he wanted a piece of him when he got there.

"If it is at all in my power," Jamal acknowledged.

"It will be," Sansi said, an echo of Jamal's smug prediction about Sansi's acceptance to the bar.

The commissioner closed his briefcase with a snap and set it down on the floor. Sansi returned to the armchair opposite and the two men contemplated each other silently for a moment, adjusting to the implications of their new partnership.

"You could still come back to crime branch, you know," Jamal said. "I need someone there I can trust. You could be joint commissioner one day."

"I don't think so," Sansi said. "Too much politics."

Jamal laughed softly. Sansi thought it his first display of genuine emotion since he had set foot in the apartment.

"Assuming I get you the evidence you need," Sansi asked, "will you use it against Banerjee?"

"Oh yes," Jamal answered. "Nothing will save Banerjee . . . nothing."

Sansi heard the undercurrent of loathing in Jamal's voice and nodded. "You know you shouldn't stop there," he said. "You should put the whole damn cabinet in jail. It's where they belong."

Jamal shrugged. "It would serve no useful purpose," he said. "And it would shake public confidence in the system."

Sansi thought just the opposite—that throwing a few cabinet ministers in jail was exactly what was needed to restore public confidence in the system.

"Once I have the evidence to make my move against Banerjee, all I have to do is present it to the cabinet," Jamal added. "I doubt there will be any need to involve New Delhi. The threat alone will be enough. The chief minister can't allow any public disclosure of Banerjee's cash transfers from Bombay to Goa. Every man in cabinet will know his money is mixed in with Banerjee's drug money. Banerjee doesn't know the meaning of the word *betrayal* until he sees how fast cabinet will turn on him."

He paused and added with a small smile, "I want to see their faces when they realize they will never see any of their money again. That will be punishment enough."

Not quite, Sansi thought. With Banerjee gone, Jamal would be free to launch his own coup against cabinet—armed with dossiers full of incriminating new evidence, much of it provided by Sansi. All of it would be used as leverage to pave the way for Narendra Jamal to become the next chief minister of Maharashtra.

Sansi had not anticipated a role as kingmaker for himself. It wasn't a role he particularly wanted. But if he had to play the game, he would play it as if his life depended on it. Because it

did. Somehow he would learn to live with the stain on his conscience. As the philosopher Chanakya, adviser to the Mauryan
kings, had declared two thousand years before Machiavelli, the
exercise of morality and the exercise of statecraft were separate
arts.

CHAPTER 5

Annie walked quickly through the wrought-iron gates in front of the strawberries-and-cream confection that had once been the town hall and was now the Bombay Sessions Court. She moved quickly through the crowd, scanning the glum faces waiting their turn inside, but there was no sign of Sansi. She checked her watch. He had asked her to meet him at noon. It was now twenty to one. He must have gone back inside to look for her there, she decided.

Reluctantly she attached herself to a slow-moving column of people shuffling toward the only entrance on this side of the building, a single doorway inside a narrow stone portico. The closer she got to the door, the worse the crush became. It was at its worst inside the portico, where those struggling to get in confronted those struggling to get out in an awkward L-shaped space the size of an elevator car. Annie steeled herself for the press of sweating bodies and the grind of bony elbows. Incredibly, in a corner of the portico, a group of men was loitering, heedless of the awful crush. Annie gave them a dirty look. One of them

smiled at her with teeth turned to rust by betel juice. She muttered under her breath and concentrated her energies on surviv-
ing the bottleneck.

Outside, in the harsh glare of the sun, it had been hot. Inside
the portico it was a taste of hell. People cursed and pushed each
other, the air was rank with the smell of sweat, cigarette smoke,
and cologne. Then Annie felt a hand on her right hip. For a
moment she thought it was a mistake. Just another accidental
familiarity in the crowd. Then the hand slid down around
her right thigh and tried to force its way between her legs. She
tensed and looked around. All she saw was a mélange of anonymous, sweating faces, most of them looking as desperate as she
felt.

She struggled to free her right hand and wormed it down the
side of her body. Her fingers closed on the intruder's wrist. There
was no reaction. No attempt to pull away. Nothing. She scrabbled for a finger, found one, and twisted it back hard enough to
break it at the knuckle. A straggly-haired man in his twenties
screeched in pain and snatched his hand away.

"*Melya,*" she swore at him. "*Tula aya bahini nahit ka?*" And
then, for good measure, she added: "*Ba zarvat gelas.*"

The man stared at her, astonished, his eyes moist with pain.
Everyone around her fell silent. Annie saw her chance. She
pushed between the people in front of her and broke free of the
logjam. The momentary lull was drowned by a renewed chorus of
angry voices as the crowd surged into the gap she had left. But
nobody directed their anger at her. Nobody dared challenge the
memsahib who could claw like a tigress and curse like a *kuli.*

The words she used had not come from Sansi. They had come
from a young woman she knew at the office.

Melya was hindi for "rascal." *Tula aya bahini nahit ka?* was a
standard rebuke for men who pestered women. It meant: "Don't
you have a mother and sisters?"

Ba zarvat gelas was in a different category altogether and
rarely used by women. It was Hindi for "Go fuck your father."

In the ocean of indignities that washed over Indian women every day, maybe it didn't count for much. But it made her feel better to think there was one creep who might hesitate before he groped a woman in a crowd again.

Annie straightened her clothes and looked around. She was at the end of a long, high-ceilinged corridor filled with the surge and babble of people. Its only light came from a few narrow windows set high in the walls and a handful of fluorescent ceiling lamps. Some of the lamps were broken, and beneath them were dense pools of darkness that heightened the impression of being in a tunnel. A number of ancient electric fans wobbled uncertainly from the ceiling and threatened to spin loose and decapitate those passing underneath. The walls of the corridor were peeling and latticed with the arcs and slashes of expectorated betel juice. The crevices between the flagstones were black with it and the floor felt gummy underfoot. Annie shuddered. She felt as if she had stepped into a giant cuspidor.

She got up on tiptoe and tried to see over the seething mass of heads but saw no sign of Sansi. The right side of the corridor was punctuated by a number of open doorways. People drifted through them constantly—policemen, lawyers, white-jacketed ushers, plaintiffs, and petitioners. Sansi could have been anywhere.

Annie's spirits sank. Usually she could manage the crowds. Today her tolerance was running low, especially after the business with the creep at the door. But she wouldn't go back. She had to go forward. Resignedly she started to work her way through the slow-moving streams of people. At the first door she found a stifling, windowless office where women in saris worked at ancient black typewriters on desks piled shoulder-high with legal files. She kept going.

The next door had a sign outside that said ADVOCATES' CANTEEN. Inside, it was the size of a high-school classroom and filled with rows of white plastic tables where lawyers ate greasy food cooked at a fire pit set into a wall. The next door opened onto a change room where lawyers put on their uniforms—formal black jackets and white legal collars—before stepping back out to the corridor to consult their clients on last-minute changes of strategy.

Sansi wasn't among them.

Halfway down the corridor she came to a major junction where a baroque staircase led to the courtrooms on the next two floors. She took the stairs, staying well clear of the inside corners, which looked as if they had been used as toilets. On the second floor was another long corridor, though this one was airier and better lit than its twin on the ground floor because of a series of high arched windows that were open to the outside. The open windows offered an irresistible invitation to the pigeons that fluttered in and out to add their own distinctive signatures to the betel stains. Here, too, were the crowds, shuffling back and forth, in and out of the courtrooms, their faces showing the same cold calculation as shoppers in a bazaar looking for a bargain. Which was precisely what they were doing, she realized. These people were shopping for judges the way they would shop for carpets or gemstones.

Sansi had warned her what to expect. The Bombay Sessions Court was not a law court in any sense that she might understand. While it had been established by the British and retained some of the characteristics of British jurisprudence, the system had been corrupted over the years to the point where it was now little more than a state-run collection agency. Businessmen, property developers, landlords, shopowners, gem traders, and silk merchants used the court to get enforcement orders that enabled them to have their debtors thrown in jail if they did not pay up. The speed and ease with which a case would be heard depended on how much the clerk of the court had been paid to get it on the court list. Judgments usually depended on which of the rival parties got to the judge first. Sansi had told Annie that the only way to guarantee a fair trial in the sessions court was to make sure that both parties bribed the judge.

He had also told her that petty lawbreakers often spent years in jail while the business community ate up the court's time with their money-grubbing feuds. The *Times* had run a story about a *kuli* arrested for riding on a city train without a ticket who spent twenty years in jail waiting for his case to come to trial. The attorney general dismissed it as "one of those unfortunate cases where someone falls through a hole in the system."

The *kuli*, at least, had survived his incarceration. Some defendants, also accused of the most trifling offenses, died in jail without ever seeing the inside of a courtroom. Even on the outside, waiting times of ten to fifteen years were not uncommon for plaintiffs who naively believed they could go through the courts to get justice. The frustration that resulted had helped create a booming new industry for the city's gangs. Instead of going through the legal system, honest and unscrupulous citizens alike found it cheaper and quicker to go to a *thod-johd*, a kangaroo court run by the underworld to settle scores, collect debts, and mete out whatever form of justice was required.

"Hello," a familiar voice said behind her. "Looking for a good lawyer?"

Annie turned and saw Sansi at last.

"You think I'll find one here?" she asked.

Surprised by the edge in her voice, he said "There are one or two who care about what they are doing."

She seemed not to hear the injury in his voice.

"I've never been in a whorehouse before," she said. "But this place has that feel about it, don't you think? The only difference is that it isn't sex that's for sale in here, it's power. You choose your pimp"—she waved dismissively at a passing lawyer—"you hand over the money, the judge turns the trick, and you get to show everybody what a big man you are."

Sansi looked at her. Her face was flushed and a few strands of hair clung damply to her forehead. There was a harassed look about her and a puffiness around her eyes that hadn't been there a few days earlier.

"Come on," he said, and took her gently by the elbow. "I think we should get out of here."

"What's the hurry?" she said. "Afraid I might get struck by lightning for telling the truth?"

"Keep talking like this and you'll have me disbarred before I'm accepted," he muttered.

"Maybe I'd be doing you a favor," she said. But she had seen the look in his eyes and she allowed him to steer her toward a door marked PRIVATE. The sessions court was next door to the sprawling fortress of police headquarters and the two were connected by a web of corridors, stairways, and secret tunnels. After twenty years in the police service Sansi knew them all. He opened the door and took Annie down a steep flight of stairs to the first floor, where another door opened onto an empty, oak-paneled vestibule. Their footsteps echoed on the shiny marble floor as they passed the offices of the Sheriff of Bombay and exited through a pillared colonnade into the eastern precincts of police headquarters. The guards at the precinct gate recognized Sansi and saluted as he passed.

"It isn't far," Sansi said as they turned north up Mahatma Gandhi Road.

"Good," Annie said.

"Do you have to be back by any particular time?"

"No."

"You finished the piece on the dowry burnings?"

"Yes."

"Happy with it?"

She shrugged.

"Are they happy with it?"

"They've bumped it inside. Sylvester says it's too long. He's going to cut it."

Sansi nodded and fell silent. They walked on for a while, the silence lengthening awkwardly between them. Then each turned to the other and spoke at the same time.

"Look—" Annie began.

"I didn't mean—" Sansi said.

They stopped and smiled self-consciously at each other. Currents of blank faces swirled and eddied around them on the sidewalk.

"You've done nothing to apologize for," Annie added quickly. "It's me who was making a scene."

"I shouldn't have suggested you meet me there," Sansi said. "But you wanted to see it—and today seemed as good a day as any."

"I did want to see it," Annie said. "It's me. I seem to be operating on a pretty short fuse lately. It's been a hell of a week . . . a hell of a month actually."

"Actually?" Sansi echoed.

She smiled.

"I'm not usually so squeamish," she added. "Today, I don't know, it was more than I could bear. I found the whole thing . . . sickening. I wanted to scream at those people in there. I wanted to do something. . . ."

"You aren't the only person who wants to tear everything down and start all over again," he said. "I know how awful it is. It grinds people down . . . everybody."

"Everybody but you?"

"I've had longer to get used to it," Sansi said. "But I have no illusions about the place where I will be working."

"And you really think you can accomplish something in there?"

"I have to work with the system that exists," Sansi said. "Sometimes I will win. Sometimes it will be enough just to make it hard for them. You know the English expression there is more than one way to skin a cat? There are ways and means, even in there."

"And what . . . you wind up just as dirty as the rest of them?"

Sansi paused. He reached for her hand and gave it a squeeze.

"This is India," he said. "Revolution is not the answer. We tried that and it didn't work. Millions die and it changes nothing. We have to take a different approach. We have to be patient."

"Oh," she said. "So I'm just another dumb foreigner who thinks she understands more than she does but has no idea what's really going on—is that it?"

"You've been here for one year," Sansi answered. "Our country is five thousand years old. Quite a bit happened before you got here, Annie. I'm still learning about it myself."

She looked down and tapped her foot restlessly on the sidewalk. Then she looked up at him, a small, crooked smile on her face.

"Okay," she said. "You're right. It is your country. And maybe you do know how to work the system. Maybe it is the smart way to go. And maybe I am getting a little bit ahead of myself here, given that I am just another impetuous Yank and the whole world knows of our desperate need for instant solutions to everything. But there's still something I want to tell you."

Sansi waited.

"Five thousand years is a mighty long time to get your fucking act together."

Sansi chuckled. "I will see what I can do to speed things up."

She looked skeptically at him, then added, "There's something else."

Sansi paused.

"Don't hand me that this-is-India-we-do-things-differently-here bullshit anymore. You're not so different from other people. Dirt is dirt. Greed is greed. You've just been at it longer than everybody else, that's all."

She turned and started walking again, relieved to have unburdened herself of some anger. "So," she asked, "where are we going?"

"I'm not sure it's such a good idea anymore," Sansi said, hurrying to catch up. "I don't know if I have the courage. . . ."

"Oh, please . . ." She gave him her most pained look.

"We're almost there," Sansi responded.

They were perhaps twenty yards from the junction of Mahatma Gandhi Road and Nariman Road when Sansi pointed out a number of young men hanging around the corner wearing black jackets and white legal collars and carrying clipboards. Some were working the crowd at a bus stop while others accosted passersby. All of them were younger, fresh-faced versions of the lawyers Annie had seen inside the sessions court. She knew that this was the city's legal district. The civil and criminal courts, as well as the high court, were all within a few blocks of each other, and lawyers were a common sight on these streets. The young men must have been here on other days, she realized, though she hadn't paid them much attention before.

"They're law-school graduates," Sansi said. "They can't find any law firms to employ them, so they look for business on the street."

Annie looked doubtful. "What kind of things can they sell on the street?"

"Simple legal services—depositions, sworn statements, small claims. There are many small business transactions that must be accompanied by a sworn statement. Anything that requires the stamp of the court."

"So they just walk up to people and ask if they need a court order to go?"

"Yes," Sansi answered. "It's a bargain really . . . and very quick. If you want any kind of document notarized by the court, you can have it done while you wait. One of those young men will go inside and do it for you and come back in about half an hour with an official stamp. Or you can swear out a claim against a debtor right here and now and have it registered with the court. Sometimes it's enough to do the trick."

"What does it cost?"

"It is negotiable," Sansi said. "The starting price might be around one hundred rupees, but if business is slow you can get them down to sixty or seventy pretty quickly."

Annie stared as the eager young lawyers in their choirboy collars worked the crowd, hawking their legal services in competition with barbers, shoeshine boys, fortune-tellers, snake charmers, and all the other hucksters who scrabbled for a living on the streets of Bombay.

"My God," she breathed. "Do they ever get anywhere doing this?"

"Oh yes," Sansi said. "Some of them are very good and make quite a lot of money. And once they can show they know how to make money, they usually find some law firm to take them on. I doubt if there's a harder apprenticeship anywhere else in the world."

"It's disgusting," Annie said.

"Far more disgusting than ambulance-chasing lawyers in America," Sansi remarked blandly.

Annie made a face but, for once, remained silent. This time, she knew, Sansi was right. As she had observed only moments earlier, the face of corruption was the same the world over. The only difference was its makeup.

They had stopped to wait for the traffic lights, and the moment the lights changed they found themselves swept across Mahatma Gandhi Road by the momentum of the crowd. Fortunately, it was the direction Sansi wanted. They continued northward on the other side of the road for half a block then turned into a busy side street. It was called Dalal Street, and after about fifty yards it led to a narrow, noisy intersection commanded on the northeastern corner by a dowdy, four-story office building. Time and dirt had stained the building the color of tea and there was nothing much to distinguish it from all the other dowdy office buildings in the area except for the grace of its curved front corner. A sign over the corner door said LENTIN CHAMBERS. A list of tenants beside the doorway indicated that the building was occupied mostly by legal firms.

"My new chambers," Sansi said. "I've had my eye on this building for a while. It's close to court, air-conditioned, and secure; there are washrooms on every floor and it's not too expensive. I wanted to get the landlord down a bit more, but I couldn't afford to wait any longer, so we signed the lease two days ago. I got him to come down a little. I said I would have the suite repainted."

"It looks okay, I guess," Annie said guardedly.

Sansi knew that to American eyes most buildings in Bombay looked like slums.

"Why the rush?" she asked. "You said you had a couple of months before you could start. Have you heard something?"

Sansi nodded.

"What?" she asked impatiently.

"Let me show you the offices first," he answered, and started across the narrow street. The inside of the building was musty and gloomy. Corridors branched off in both directions. At the entrance to the right-hand corridor was a flight of stairs and an antique elevator with a greasy concertina-wire gate. Two uniformed security guards slouched on metal stools just inside the doorway.

Sansi told them that he was going to the fourth floor and one of them pried himself reluctantly from his stool and opened the gate to the elevator. The elevator car was little more than a steel-mesh cage and it bounced when they stepped inside. Sansi pushed the worn brass button and there was a frighteningly loud clang followed by a chorus of pneumatic grunts and groans as the ancient pulleys hauled the elevator upward. Annie noticed every cobweb, every rusting cog and rivet as the cage cranked slowly past each floor. It was not a pleasant ride and Annie thought she could have reached the top floor faster if she'd climbed the stairs on her hands and knees.

The cage jolted to a halt and swayed unsettlingly on its creaky cables. Annie shuddered as a gust of stale air moaned up the shaft and tugged with ghostly fingers at the hem of her *salwar khameez*. Sansi pushed back the gate and they both stepped out onto the top floor.

Sansi's chambers were at the end of the corridor. The door was open and the sinuous sound of sitars accompanied by the thump of tablas could be heard coming from a radio. As the two of them drew closer they heard a tuneless male voice attempting to follow the music, a popular tune by the Bengali folk singer Ajoy Chakraborti.

Sansi rapped loudly on the door and stepped inside, followed by Annie.

"Mr. Mukherjee?" he called, trying to project his voice over the music. No one answered.

Annie looked around. The first room was a reception area. The walls were an ugly, mottled brown and the floor was covered with disintegrating linoleum in a pattern that had long since been scuffed to a scaly blur. What furniture there was had been pushed into the middle of the floor—an L-shaped desk, a couple of chairs, and a chipped wooden bench that could have come from a railway station. The room was lit by fluorescent ceiling lights and there were two uncurtained windows, one of which held a rattly air conditioner. To the rear of the room were glass-paneled doors that opened into two more offices. Annie could see that each was furnished similarly, with a plain wooden desk, a couple of chairs, and a number of dented metal filing cabinets. The only differences were that the office on the right was bigger and accommodated a massive plywood-and-veneer bookcase. The furniture in these two offices had also been pushed into the middle of the floor.

"You have to keep the furniture?" Annie asked.

The tone of her voice told Sansi what she thought of it.

"It comes with the lease."

"What about the previous tenant?" she added. "Won't he want it?"

"Highly doubtful," Sansi said. "The former occupant of these chambers was stabbed to death by a dissatisfied client. The bloodstain is still on the floor, close to where you're standing, I believe."

Annie couldn't tell whether he was joking or not. She looked down at the linoleum and saw a massive Rorschach blot that could have been blood. She stepped around it with a slight grimace and joined Sansi at the door to the larger of the two offices, where the sitar music and the singing were loudest. From there she could see that there was a connecting door between the inner offices and each had its own small window with a view of the same brick wall. There was also a young man standing on a chair with his back to them. He was wearing dirty blue jeans and an undershirt that might once have been white but was now gray. The music came from a portable stereo on the desk in the middle of the floor. On a chair next to the young man was a bucket of soapy water and a bottle of detergent. His feet were bare, his arms were slick with water, and he was spotted with flecks of gray foam. In his hands was a nylon-bristled brush that he used to scrub the wall in short, rapid strokes. The results of his labors were striking. The section of wall he had scrubbed so far was no longer brown but a blotchy, milky color. The rest of the room remained hidden beneath years of accumulated grime. At this rate, Annie thought, it would take him a month just to clean the walls. Then there were the ceilings, the paintwork, and the scabrous linoleum floor that had to be stripped and polished. The young man scrubbed diligently and sang along with the music on the radio, oblivious to their presence.

"Mr. Mukherjee?" Sansi called out, louder this time.

The young man's head snapped around and he almost lost his footing. He teetered precariously on one leg for a second, regained his balance, and jumped down. He dropped the scrubbing brush into the bucket, switched off the radio, and pressed his soapy palms together.

"*Namaste, Sansi sahib,*" he said, and bobbed his head respectfully. Then he turned to Annie and bobbed a second time. "*Namaste, memsahib.*"

Sansi only nodded, but Annie was so impressed she put the palms of her hands together and returned the greeting formally.

"Namaste, Mister . . . Mukherjee?" she said hesitantly.

"Mr. Jeet Mukherjee," Sansi confirmed. "Distinguished alumnus, University of Bombay, class of ninety-three. Even more distinguished alumnus, University of Nariman Road, class of ninety-four. I have engaged Mr. Mukherjee to be my clerk, researcher, and legal assistant. He is currently preparing for these important positions by cleaning and painting my chambers."

Now Annie understood why Sansi had pointed out the white-collared hustlers on the corner of Nariman Road. A few days earlier Mukherjee had been one of them.

"Mr. Mukherjee," Sansi continued with the same mock formality. "I would like to introduce my good friend Ms. Annie Ginnaro. Ms. Ginnaro is a reporter with the highly esteemed newspaper the *Times of India.*"

"Acha," the young law graduate responded. Then, in heavily accented English, he said, "I am very charming to be making your acquaintance, memsahib."

"You don't have to keep calling me memsahib," she said. "My name is Annie."

Mukherjee smiled and waggled his head from side to side in the Hindu gesture of approval. He was a good-looking boy with an innocent round face and long, fashionably cut hair. His perfect, white-toothed smile belonged on the cover of one of Bombay's many fan magazines that peddled movie heartthrobs to adoring teenage girls. Annie suspected he wasn't quite as innocent as he looked. Doubtless he had been as successful with the female students at Bombay University as he had been with his legal studies. And if he was good enough to hustle a living from the law on the streets of Bombay, he knew exactly how much an honest face was worth. When her eyes met his, he looked away and she realized that he had been appraising her as carefully as she had been appraising him. It only confirmed her opinion. Behind the easy, boyish charm was the calculating mind of an ambitious young man who knew exactly what he had going for him and would use all of it to get where he wanted.

"I wanted to show Ms. Ginnaro our new chambers," Sansi said. "And to make sure you have everything you need."

"Oh yes, sahib." Mukherjee waggled his head again. "Everything is going along most splendidly. I will be finished this work very soon." Then he added, almost as an afterthought, "I know a place where I can buy the paint for a very good price, sahib."

Sansi smiled faintly. "This place would not be owned by a close relative of yours by any chance?"

"My uncle Bakul is a very honest man, sahib," Mukherjee said eagerly. "He will give me very best quality at very best price. Family does not cheat family, sahib."

Sansi gave it some thought. He knew that the price would be substantially lower than he had budgeted and Jeet and his uncle would pocket the difference between them. At least his new assistant had not attempted to lie about it, and that was promising.

"Just make sure you do a good job," Sansi said. "Or I will make you do it over again—and the price of the new paint will come out of your pocket."

"You will see, sahib," Jeet promised solemnly. "When you come back everything will be beautiful like a nawab's palace."

Sansi winced and glanced furtively at Annie.

The wheels in Annie's mind were already turning. Come back from where? She could see for herself how much time was involved in cleaning and painting these offices. It would take several weeks at least. Where was Sansi going for that length of time?

"I don't want a palace," Sansi was saying. "I want it to look like a law firm. I want the walls to be a plain ivory color. And the woodwork is to be brown—rich, mahogany brown. No crazy colors, you understand?"

"No crazy colors," Jeet agreed emphatically. "Ivory and mahogany. Very nice, sahib. I am understanding to perfection."

Sansi pressed his hand lightly against Annie's back to signal that it was time to leave. "We shall see, Mr. Mukherjee," he said cautiously. "We shall see."

"Please do not be concerning yourself," Mukherjee added, his voice brimming with reassurance. "And good-bye to you, Annie. And please be having a most relaxing time, Sansi sahib."

Annie waited until they were out in the corridor before she said anything. When she spoke her voice betrayed a fragile calm.

"You've been busy."

"It's been frantic."

"Oh . . . frantic?"

"Unbelievably so."

"You must be tired."

Sansi smiled feebly.

"I'm grateful you could squeeze me in."

Somehow the absence of any irony in her voice made it worse.

"I am afraid Mr. Mukherjee's limited experience has left him rather lacking in certain matters of discretion," Sansi said.

"Yes." Annie nodded graciously. "I can see where you'll have to watch him. But, as you're inclined to remind me, often, you do know what you're doing . . . don't you?"

Her last sentence was honed to such an edge it gleamed as it cut through the air toward him.

"This is not exactly what I intended," Sansi said.

Annie folded her arms and slowly started to pace.

"Look," he said, struggling. "I had wanted to do this over a nice lunch. I've even booked the table."

Annie rotated slowly on one heel and looked at him. "Do what, exactly?"

"Oh, bugger." Sansi threw up his arms in a gesture of surrender. "All right—how do you feel about coming to Goa with me?"

Annie's face remained set. She stood for a long time, silhouetted against a dusty shaft of light from a window at the end of the corridor, arms tightly folded, rocking slightly on the ball of one foot.

"Goa?" she said at last, her voice flat and noncommittal. "The Goa with all the beaches . . . that Goa?"

"Yes," Sansi added. "That Goa . . . for about a month. I'm not sure exactly how long it will be because it depends on some work I have to do down there. But I think we'd both benefit from some time away together, don't you? God knows you're ready for a break. You've worked your heart out for more than a year; they must owe you some holiday time. . . ."

His voice trailed off into a wretched sigh. The only sound left in the corridor was the music from Mukherjee's radio and his tuneless singing in the background. Annie nodded thoughtfully, considering Sansi's proposition. Then she walked slowly back to him, rose up on her toes, and touched his lips lightly with her own.

"Good recovery," she said. Then she turned and walked back toward the elevator. "Now you can buy me lunch."

CHAPTER 6

The Indian Airlines 727 descended through a scrappy layer of cloud, and Annie leaned toward the plastic lens of her porthole window to get her first look at Goa. For a while there was only the usual patchwork of parched browns and pallid greens, the scrubby hills and plains of rural India, sparsely veined with rivers, creeks, and stagnant irrigation ditches. Then the plane banked to the west and the landscape changed and softened as it scrolled slowly past her window. Creeks converged and rivers broadened. The stark patchwork of the interior melded into the dark tropical greens of a rich coastal plain. Lush jungle appeared, then farms, coconut groves, the pewter sheen of a wide estuary. Her eye was drawn to the plane's shadow as it skimmed the surface of the estuary. The plane banked once more, the shadow leaped into extinction, and the land yielded abruptly to a shimmering expanse of ocean. Separating the two was a chain of golden crescents that started far to the south and stretched northward into infinity—the fabled beaches of Goa.

The plane came around and the airport slid into view, a white cross on a majestic, palm-studded headland. The plane dipped its nose, the wing flaps clawed at the slipstream, and the undercarriage grunted into position. There was no announcement from the cabin crew, but Sansi and Annie were veterans of many Indian Airlines flights and already had their seat belts fastened. They were within seconds of touchdown when they heard a commotion behind them. A passenger, a middle-aged Sikh wearing a green suit with a metallic shine and an outsized turban, was on his feet emptying the baggage locker behind theirs. A flight attendant shouted at him to sit down, but he shouted back and tugged determinedly at his luggage. Annie and Sansi put their hands over their heads. The plane hit the runway with a smack, bounced, and braked hard. The Sikh cartwheeled down the center aisle with a shrill scream. The contents of the open locker cascaded after him. A stunned silence settled throughout the cabin. Sansi leaned out and saw the man lying in a dazed heap against the cockpit door, his luggage piled around him.

Sansi leaned over to Annie and whispered, "We call them the Yorkshiremen of India."

Once inside the tiny airport terminal, they had to collect their bags and fight their way through the usual waves of shock troops—bus drivers, taxi drivers, rickshaw drivers, hotel hustlers, pickpockets, black-market money changers, and all the other pests who waited to ambush arriving passengers. At last Sansi saw a young man in a smart white uniform holding a piece of cardboard with Sansi's name scrawled on it. Sansi identified himself and the young man shouted his welcome to friendly, relaxed Goa. He took their bags and led them outside to a cream-colored, humpbacked Ambassador. Moments later they pulled through the airport gate and onto the road that would take them across the Zuari River to Panjim, the capital of Goa.

The road was a two-lane switchback with dense vegetation on both sides and coconut palms that leaned sixty feet into the air. Because the Ambassador had no air-conditioning, the windows were rolled down and the wind filled the car with all the sounds and smells of the tropics. The deafening screech of parrots, the

background drone of cicadas, and the sweet fragrances of frangi-
pani and bougainvillea mixed with the rank stench of rotting
vegetation. The closer they got to Panjim, the more the jungle receded and the country flattened out. They passed dried-up rice
paddies where tiny children with sticks rode massive, docile water buffalo. They passed elegant Portuguese villas painted yellow,
burgundy, and blue, with pretty white window shutters and elaborate balustrades. They passed farms that were no more than
mud-brick hovels, where mongrel dogs and ferocious hogs fought
each other for scraps.

They came to a small village where the car was forced to a
crawl because of a traffic jam. Annie heard loud Western rock
music and she followed the sound to a single-story whitewashed
building on the main road. Its red tile roof was carpeted with
grapevines, and there was a terrace down the side that was
packed with long-haired foreigners. It looked as though it should
have been in Lisbon rather than India. Its name, painted on a
banner over the front door, was Casa Manic.

By the time they reached Panjim, it was almost dark and the
streets were clogged with people and traffic. The Ambassador
joined a long line of cars, trucks, and motor scooters waiting on
Dayanand Bandodkar Road to take the ferry across the Mandovi
River. The hotel driver told them it would be a while before it was
their turn to board, so Sansi and Annie got out to stretch their
legs.

It had been a long day. Their plane had been scheduled to
leave Bombay at the ghastly time of 5:45 that morning and they
had arrived at the airport an hour before the sun came up. But
because Indian Airlines regarded passengers as a nuisance and
had its own idea of what a flight schedule should be, there had
been no aircraft, no ground staff, and no explanation. When an
aircraft was finally produced, it had not been ready for takeoff
until three in the afternoon, and so, what should have been a
ninety-minute commute had evolved into a daylong odyssey. Be-

cause of that, perhaps, Annie felt as if she had left India and arrived in another country.

As she and Sansi joined the other strollers on the riverside and walked down toward the ferry ramp, she noticed that there were still plenty of Indian faces on the street, but somehow it no longer seemed like the India she knew. The architecture was different. The buildings were Mediterranean in style rather than British colonial or Hindu. There were no temples and few symbols of Hinduism but many churches and symbols of Catholicism. Annie remembered what Sansi had told her. Goa had been a Portuguese colony for four hundred years, until annexed by India in 1961, which made it the most recent and least Indian of the states. Two thirds of the population were Catholic, only one third Hindu, and the remainder Muslim.

The mood was different, too. There were more Westerners on the street than she had seen anywhere else in India, except perhaps for Agra, the home of the Taj Mahal. And their behavior was different. In the bigger cities they looked wary and confused, travel weary veterans in a large and volatile country seeking exotic new experiences despite the ceaseless assaults of its inhabitants, who seemed interested only in parting them from their money. On the streets of Panjim these same visitors looked happy and relaxed, confident to the point of boisterousness—as if they owned the place. Their accents came from everywhere—England, France, Germany, Scandinavia, Japan, Australia, Italy, Holland, the United States.

A ragged burst of cheers and whoops erupted from the other side of the street. Annie looked up to the second-floor balcony of the Hotel Mandovi, where a group of half-naked young people were having a beer fight. That was when she knew exactly what it was—the same kind of raucous carnival atmosphere she had found in places like Cabo and Tijuana, where she and her friends from USC had gone during spring break to get drunk and wild. Like those places, Goa was part of the third world but a part that had lost its independence already, this time to a new, more subversive invader. Instead of soldiers with muskets looking for gold and everlasting glory, it was hedonists with credit cards looking for ganja and the everlasting party. Goa had survived centuries of colonization by one foreign power only to be conquered by another. This time the colonists wore surfer shorts and beads, and their idea of culture was a beer fight on the main street.

The ferry ride across the Mandovi River took five minutes and the drive to the Fort Aguada Hotel another half hour. The scenery changed dramatically during the last half mile, from rice paddies and farms to walled-in estates, gem shops, clothing boutiques, expensive restaurants, and the clean, manicured lines of well-tended resorts. At last they drove through the gates of the Fort Aguada resort and rode in silence up an avenue of palm trees lit pink, blue, and green. The hotel looked new. With its sleek white lines, liveried porters, and middle-aged guests, who could be seen drifting across the spacious, marbled lobby, it could have been another glitzy hotel in Acapulco.

Annie waited in the car with her head back and her eyes closed while Sansi took care of the registrations. He returned after a few minutes with a porter. The driver pulled away from the main portico, drove into another gated enclosure, and continued up a long, curving driveway to a cluster of hillside villas that proclaimed their exclusivity from the rest of the hotel. This compound within a compound bore the lofty title of the Hermitage.

They stopped in front of a smart white bungalow with a red tiled roof and mahogany shutters. The porter opened the door and showed them inside while the driver followed with their bags. Annie endured the guided tour without listening to anything the porter said, but she admired the dark mahogany furniture, rattan armchairs, plush sofas, and bowls of fresh flowers. The few touches of modernity included climate control as well as teak-bladed ceiling fans and TV sets in the living room and bedroom. The only Indian touches were a few framed prints of Lakshmi, Ganesh, and Hanuman on the walls. It was an evocative blending of East and West that suggested a wealthy tea planter's bungalow in the hills of Assam.

The porter opened a pair of French windows to show off a pretty, white-pillared verandah with a table, chairs, and a couple of Bombay fornicators: wooden lounge chairs with extendable arm slats that could be pulled out to support the occupant's legs. Every time Annie saw one she was reminded of past visits to the gynecologist.

The verandah overlooked a lawn enclosed by hedges of chest-high kuri bush, which provided privacy and protection from the onshore winds while allowing the guests to look out over everything. Spread out below them, like an electric map, was the rest of the hotel and its sister resort next door, the family oriented Taj Holiday Village. Beyond the lights was a vast expanse of beach that glowed milky in the moonlight, and beyond that, the dark, sinister reaches of the ocean.

Annie unpacked her bags in the master bedroom and hung up her clothes while Sansi paid off the driver and the porter. When they had gone she went back into the living room and examined the contents of the liquor cabinet. She found what she was looking for in the bar fridge—a half bottle of French champagne.

"I have a little ritual," she explained to Sansi as she opened the bottle. "My vacation hasn't started until I'm up to my neck in bubble bath and I have a glass of champagne in my hand."

"I can't bear the thought of you having so much fun without me," Sansi said as he slid a couple of champagne flutes toward her.

She managed to open the bottle without spilling its contents and filled both their glasses. Then she picked up her glass, touched it to his, and offered a toast.

"The fun starts now," she said.

"You're on vacation," Sansi reminded her. "I have to go to work tomorrow."

She leaned forward and kissed him provocatively on the lips. "I've seen the bath," she said softly. "It's big enough for two."

They were only in the bath for a few minutes before the inevitable happened. Events moved rapidly back to the bedroom and finished in a tangle of damp bedsheets. Afterward they showered, put on clean white bathrobes, and curled up together on the bed with the last of the champagne and the French windows open so they could smell the ocean and see the night sky.

"I guess I could get to like Goa," Annie said after a while.

"I am already enjoying it more this time than I did last time," Sansi said.

Annie moved closer to him. "I didn't know you were here before," she said.

"With my mother in 1963," he said. "Two years after annexation. We spent most of our time looking at churches. Pramila said it was important to understand everything about India. The only time I went to the beach I cut my foot on a shell and I had to stay out of the water the rest of the trip."

He lifted his right foot for her, and there, on the instep, was a small scar in the shape of a new moon, milky white against his tea-colored skin. She leaned down and kissed it, then nestled back into his chest, her damp red hair spread across his shoulder, so he could smell its perfume.

"No scars this time," she said. "Only happy memories."

Sansi did not answer, but she sensed rather than felt a certain tightening inside him.

"You're worried about something," she said.

"Of course," he admitted.

"This job," she said. "How dangerous is it?"

Sansi hesitated before answering. He had told her as little as possible about the real reason for his visit to Goa. He had told her about the free port, and he had told her he was to conduct an informal investigation into the land speculation that surrounded it. He had made her swear she would not breathe a word to anyone at the newspaper and she had promised him willingly. She trusted him completely. Without knowing it, she had put her life in his hands. Her readily given trust made him feel worse. Guilt gnawed at him constantly. But he couldn't tell her about Banerjee and he couldn't tell her about Jamal, not only because the leadership of the state was at stake, but because Annie despised Jamal and knew that Sansi despised him too. She would be horrified at the idea that Sansi had made a deal with him. She had made it abundantly clear what she thought of Sansi's dabbling in corruption at even a modest level. How dirty was too dirty? Was he sure that he really knew anymore? Sansi considered himself an intelligent man, but he could miscalculate. India was a country in perpetual chaos. Events had a way of spinning out of control quickly. What if she was right? What if he had miscalculated? How could he protect her then?

"There are some very dangerous people in Goa," Sansi said. "And the kind of money that is involved in the free port makes them even more dangerous. I will have to be careful. If I decide the situation is getting out of control, we will leave. I won't put our lives at risk."

"Tell me something," she said quietly. "Am I here because you want me here . . . or because you need me here?"

Sansi had to think about it for a minute. "Both," he decided.

Annie remained silent for a long time. Then she leaned over and kissed him. "Good," she said. "Because I don't mind you using me. Just as long as you don't lie to me."

CHAPTER 7

Sansi stepped out of the shower and toweled himself dry. He dressed quickly and stood before the bathroom mirror. According to his daily routine, he had shaved before showering. Now he could depart from routine.

Instead of brushing his hair straight back from his forehead and letting it dry as it liked, he took a comb from his travel bag, started at the scalp line near the outside corner of his left eyebrow, and traced a neat part in his hair. At first his hair refused to do as he wanted. The hair on the left side of the part tried to fan out and the hair on the right tried to flop back into its old position and hide the part altogether. He persevered. He added more water and a dab of gel. Finally, the hair below the part stuck to the side of his head as if it had been glued there, while the hair on the right lay to the side in a thick, resentful clump. It was close to the effect he wanted. He looked like a dork.

Next, he took a small black plastic case and a bottle out of his bag and put them on the countertop. He opened the case first and examined the two curved pieces of colored silicone resting on their tiny foam-rubber pillows. He picked up a piece of silicone and squeezed two tiny drops of solution onto it from the bottle. The liquid trembled momentarily then covered the lens with a fine glossy coat. He put the contact lens up to his left eye and carefully slid it over the pupil. His eye watered and he blinked rapidly to clear it. A small tear ran down his cheek. Then he looked in the mirror. So far, so good. One blue eye, one brown eye. He repeated the process with the second contact lens and slid it over his right eye.

When he had finished, the eyes that looked back at him were plain, nondescript dark brown, like the eyes of most Indian men.

Now he was ready for work. He dried his hands, patted his hair in place one last time, and stepped out of the bathroom.

Annie was already on the verandah eating breakfast. She had ordered papaya, yogurt, and a couple of honey *dosas* with coffee from room service. She was delicately dicing a piece of papaya when she glanced up at him and did a double take. The man who had gone into the bathroom half an hour earlier was her handsome, exotic, blue-eyed lover. The man who stood in front of her now, with a cheap haircut, a pair of cheaper brown pants, and a long-sleeved white shirt, was a stranger. The difference was stunning. Even his skin looked darker.

"Sansi," she said, a forkful of fruit suspended in the air, "are you in there somewhere?"

Sansi was pleased with himself. It was exactly the reaction he wanted. After twenty years of detective work he had found that the only disguise he really needed was a pair of brown contact lenses and a set of street clothes. His blue eyes were his most distinctive—and therefore his most memorable—physical feature. Everyone who met him remarked on them. Everyone remembered him as "the blue-eyed Indian."

The addition of a pair of brown contact lenses changed everything. A change of hairstyle completed the transformation. The original Sansi had vanished. He had become another brown face in the anonymous teeming masses of India.

"A very good morning to you, memsahib." Sansi slipped into

his most outlandish Indian accent. "My name is Ram. I am understanding you are in most urgent need of a handyman."

Annie smiled. Ram was a nickname given by the bored wives
of Bombay businessmen to handsome young male servants who
performed more than the usual array of domestic services. She
got up and walked coyly over to him and stopped with her face
only inches away from his.

"You know, you're kind of cute," she breathed. "If we hurry
we can have a little fun before my boyfriend gets back . . . take
your shirt off."

Slowly, she started to unfasten his shirt buttons. Sansi smiled
and took hold of her wrist.

"Very sorry, memsahib," he said. "None of the hanky-panky
this morning. Ram is having enough of the hanky-panky last
night to be lasting the rest of the year."

"Gee." Annie pouted and turned to go back outside. "And I
thought I was going to get a little fun on the side without having
to feel guilty about it."

Sansi followed her and sat down at the breakfast table across
from her. She was wearing a plain red T-shirt and khaki shorts
that showed off her legs. Her hair shone like copper and her face
had the glow of contentment. It was as if she had slept ten hours
and he had slept three. He thought it unfair that making love to
a beautiful woman only seemed to add to her beauty while the
man wound up looking tired and spent.

Sansi ate lightly and then, as they had arranged, he kissed Annie good-bye and left her to begin her vacation while he went off
to work. For once in her life Annie was not sorry to watch her
man go off to slay the dragon while she stayed behind. She
needed this vacation and she intended to make the most of every
day—in case things went bad and they had to leave town in a
hurry. She hadn't forgotten everything Sansi had said last night.

Sansi's first stop was the hotel service desk, where he made
arrangements for a rental car. It took more than an hour and he
was told that a car would not be available until the next day. In

the meantime he would have to rely on taxis. He caught a cab at the front of the hotel and took it to the Mandovi ferry, where he paid off the driver and continued the rest of the way on foot. Once he had disembarked on the Panjim side of the river, he walked the short distance from the waterfront to Ormuz Road and the forbidding walled enclosure of the nineteenth-century army fort that now accommodated Goa's police headquarters. In one sense it was the last place he should go, in case someone from Bombay was in town who might know him despite the disguise. But the investigation could not begin without Sansi making contact with the men whose names Jamal had given him. Of the two, the man at police headquarters promised to be the more useful.

He walked through the archway that guarded the main entrance and asked a constable armed with a bolt-action Lee Enfield where he could find the police surgeon's office. The constable barely glanced at him before directing him to a row of offices in the shade of a wide colonnade that encircled the dusty parade ground. The office doors were all open and a number of people—clerks, typists, policemen in and out of uniform—lounged outside on old benches and rickety chairs, smoking *bidis* and passing the time of day. Sansi drew a few curious glances, but none lingered. He looked like a nobody.

The third door along he saw a sign that said POLICE SURGEON and stepped inside. He found himself in a poorly lit room that had been divided into two offices. The outer office held an assortment of scarred wooden desks, chairs, and battered filing cabinets. The door to the inner office was closed, but Sansi could see through the dimpled glass windows in the partition walls that no one was inside. A couple of ceiling fans clicked over his head, stirring papers left carelessly out on the desks. A couple of sheets had blown onto the floor. Sansi resisted the temptation to pick them up and look at them.

"You are looking for somebody?"

Sansi turned. A short, sinewy man with wavy hair and a

neat mustache had left his perch outside to see what the visitor wanted.

"Dr. Sapeco?" Sansi inquired. He knew before the man answered that he was not the police surgeon, but Sansi did not want to seem too clever.

"Who is asking for him?" the man asked.

"My name is Kumar," Sansi said.

"You have an appointment?"

"No," Sansi said. "I did not know it was necessary."

"Why do you want to see Dr. Sapeco?"

"I have some business with him," Sansi answered with just enough irritation to show that he was not intimidated.

"What kind of business?" the man persisted.

"Are Bapre," Sansi muttered.

"You are from Bombay?" the man asked.

Sansi cursed himself silently. He had used an expression common to Bombay Hindus. Native Goans spoke Konkani and their expressions were different.

"Acha," Sansi said. "I am here on holiday. I was at university with Dr. Sapeco, and when I heard he was police surgeon in Panjim, I thought I would look him up . . . for old times' sake."

Even to Sansi it sounded lame. It was impossible to know from the look on the man's face whether he believed it or not.

"You are a doctor?" the man asked.

Sansi decided it was time for a little display of temper. He couldn't allow some little police *babu* to push him around too easily.

"Who are you?" he asked in a voice that suggested he was a man of authority.

The man stiffened, then answered, "I am Pawar, clerk in chief to the police surgeon."

"My business is with your superior, not you," Sansi said officiously. "When is Dr. Sapeco expected back?"

The approach seemed to be working. The chief clerk seemed less sure of his ground.

"Dr. Sapeco will not be back," he answered sullenly.

"What do you mean?" Sansi said. "Today . . . tomorrow?"

The man hesitated, then said, "Dr. Sapeco is no longer with the department."

Sansi didn't have to pretend he was confused. He looked around the empty office while his mind ran quickly through the possibilities. Sapeco must have left suddenly—within the past few days—or Jamal would have known. A twinge of unease stirred in him.

"When did this happen?" Sansi asked sharply.

The clerk did not answer. Instead he found his nerve again and gestured to the door. "You must go now," he said. "You cannot stay here. You have no official business."

Sansi knew he had no alternative but to go quietly. The last thing he wanted was to make a scene and be remembered. But there was something he could try, something that was not at all out of the ordinary. He reached into his pocket and took out a bundle of rupee notes. He watched the clerk's eyes as he peeled off a hundred and dangled it loosely by his side.

"Where can I find Dr. Sapeco now?" he asked.

The clerk looked at the money then at Sansi. He hesitated only a moment. "You might find him at the hospicio in Margao."

Sansi passed Pawar the hundred rupees, then stepped around him and walked outside. From the corner of his eye he saw the clerk examine the note to make sure it was clean and whole, that there were no tears or pieces missing. It was against a man's pride to accept a note that was torn or dirty.

Sansi strolled back along the colonnade, imagining he was being watched every step of the way. Once outside, he felt safer, though he was worried that Jamal's intelligence was already out-of-date. Sapeco's departure might be coincidental; it might have nothing at all to do with this investigation; but Sansi had learned never to believe in coincidence where human behavior was concerned.

Sansi's next step was to call on his other contact, Mr. Ramesh

Rao, whom Jamal had identified as one of his oldest friends. A Brahmin and an eminent lawyer in Panjim, Rao was a man Sansi ought to be able to visit without arousing suspicion.

Mr. Rao's offices were only a couple of blocks away, on Swamy Vivekanand Road, in a row of two-story houses that had been converted into shops on the first floor and offices on the second. The entrance was next to a shop that sold used electrical appliances. Beside the door was a brass plate that proclaimed RAO & RAO, SOLICITORS AND ADVOCATES. Sansi assumed that Mr. Rao was part of a legal dynasty and the other Rao was a father or son.

He climbed a flight of worn stone steps and found himself in a narrow corridor with flaking blue paint and one door on each side. He went to the door that bore Mr. Rao's name and turned the handle. It wouldn't open. Sansi thought it might be stuck and gave it a push. It was locked. Anxiety stirred in him anew.

He turned to the door on the other side of the corridor—the sign said it was the office of a trademark agent—and tried the handle there. It opened easily. A middle-aged woman in a green sari looked up from her desk as Sansi appeared. Behind her was a large empty office.

"Good afternoon," the woman said formally. "How may I help you, please?"

"I have come to see Mr. Ramesh Rao," Sansi said. "I wondered—"

"Their offices are on the other side of the hall."

"Yes. I am afraid they seem to be closed. I don't understand because I have an appointment with Mr. Rao."

"How silly," the woman said. "How very silly."

Sansi wondered if she meant him or Mr. Rao.

"They didn't open yesterday and now they're not open today," she went on, her voice reflecting her indignation. "It is most unprofessional. Nisha only told me on Friday that Mr. Rao was going away. She didn't say the office would be closed."

"Please . . ." Sansi asked politely. "Who is Nisha?"

"Mr. Rao's secretary. She isn't there either?"

"The offices seem to be locked," Sansi said.

"Oh dear," the woman said disapprovingly. "No manners at all. They could have asked me and I would have been happy to take messages for them."

She stopped and held up a dozen sheets of yellow memo paper. "See," she said, "I'm doing it anyway. But they could have asked."

"Do you happen to know where Mr. Rao was going?" Sansi persisted. "Is he still in Panjim or has he gone away?"

Even as he asked, Sansi knew the answer. Rao had skipped town. The lawyer had been unable to tell Jamal directly, but obviously he wanted no part of the commissioner's problems and would not be dragged into any investigation. Typical Brahmin duplicity, Sansi thought. He had always found the lower castes more reliable than the upper castes.

"To visit his father in Bangalore, I expect," the woman answered. "That's where he usually goes. Nisha came in yesterday afternoon for a few minutes. She might be in later today to pick up the messages. I could ask her, if you wish. Would you care to leave a message?"

Sansi hardly heard her. "No, thank you." He smiled. "I don't think that will be necessary. I think I know what has happened."

Sansi left her muttering about the general decline in standards of courtesy and headed back toward the river. His investigation was barely an hour old and already it looked like it was going no farther. Both Jamal's leads had turned out to be dead ends. One had lost his job and the other had fled town. At this rate, Sansi realized, he could shut down the investigation today. He and Annie could fly back to Bombay tonight, and tomorrow he would face the thankless task of telling Jamal that none of his supposed friends could be relied upon to help him.

Sansi came to the corner of Swamy Vivekanand Road and paused, wondering where to go next. He looked at his watch. It was a few minutes before eleven. Most of the day stretched emptily ahead of him. He had to do something. He leaned out into the traffic and waved down a black-and-yellow Premier taxicab.

"Yes, sahib?"

"Margao," Sansi said. "The hospicio."

■ ■

Once Sansi had gone and room service had picked up the breakfast things, Annie determined to make the most of her time alone. She took off everything but her bikini bottom, basted herself with suntan lotion, and lay on a towel in the garden with a copy of *Padmavati the Harlot*, a collection of short stories by Kamala Das, which she'd bought six months earlier and still not started. She read for about an hour until she decided she'd had enough sunbathing for the first day. Then she showered, dressed, picked up her purse, and went off on a solo exploration of the hotel and its surrounds.

First she cruised the lobby shops and decided that the gold bracelets, ivory carvings, and silk blouses were priced for New York rather than India. She bought only one item she considered essential, a stylish straw hat with a wide brim. It suited her, but it cost ten times more than it should have, and she decided she wouldn't buy anything more until she'd seen what prices were like outside the hotel.

She arranged the hat to her liking and wandered out onto a broad, sunlit terrace with a smallish swimming pool and a circular bar that overlooked the beach. There was no one in the pool, though the chairs and tables that surrounded it were occupied by a number of darkly tanned Europeans, most of them Germans, she gathered, from their shouted conversations with each other. She continued across the terrace and took a short flight of steps down to a footpath that branched out in opposite directions. One branch led down to the beach and a wooden walkway that linked the hotel to the pink stucco Taj Holiday Village next door. The other followed the contour of the coast to a small, diamond-shaped headland a hundred yards away. The headland was crowned by a brown-stoned embattlement that nudged uncertainly into the sea, as if it would rather not be noticed than pick an unnecessary quarrel with a passing pirate ship. A remnant of the original Fort Aguada, she assumed, and the only sign that the hotel was built on an historic site. Everything that had been built around it was white, modern, and bland, like a shiny new cap on the stump of an old tooth. A nice cosmetic touch, perhaps, but lacking in character.

She took the pathway out to the fort and found it smaller and cruder than she expected. Anything of interest had long since been scavenged or removed to a museum, and the only other signs of human visitation were discarded candy wrappers and soda bottles. The footpath went no farther, and so, still restless, she followed it back to the hotel and continued down to the beach.

To Annie the beach was startlingly empty. Then she realized it only looked that way because the people on it were lost in a Saharan vastness that stretched up the coast for miles. Intimidated by its immensity, most people had set themselves up within easy walking distance of the two resorts, as if they were afraid to stray too far from room service. To Annie, the emptiness beyond was like an invitation.

She set off across the sand until she reached the water's edge, then took off her sandals and continued through the shallows, enjoying the soothing splash of the water against her legs. She wanted to go for a swim. But not here, she decided; farther up the beach, where she could enjoy that rarest of all luxuries in India—solitude.

As she got farther and farther away from the resort end of the beach, she saw how the beach culture changed, subtly at first, then dramatically. For a little while there was nothing—no resorts, no houses, no buildings of any kind. Just palm trees and scrub, a kind of buffer zone between Aguada and the rest of the beach. Then she saw a few houses among the palm trees, once

Portuguese villas, formerly the beachfront homes of Goa's colonial masters, now salt-stained slums converted into overcrowded guest houses or rentals for the hippies. Then there were the first of the hippie beach bars, each little more than a platform on the sand with a thatched roof and a few scraps of furniture. Each had a row of armchairs facing the sea so the customers could sit and drink and smoke and watch their lives slide over the horizon with the sun each night.

Then she came across a palm-thatch shelter where a group of Banjaras women—tribals from Rajasthan in bright-colored robes and glittering jewelry—rested from their treks up and down the beach hawking trinkets, fruit, and brightly dyed cottons to the hippies. Annie detoured toward them, and when they saw her coming, they greeted her with open delight. It wasn't often that a customer came to them. She spent an enjoyable half hour with them, picking through their cottons, choosing, comparing, bargaining, bluffing, laughing at each other's lies. Eventually she decided on a richly patterned green-and-blue *lungi* and a cream silk scarf. Together they came to seventy-five rupees—less than three dollars. The cheapest *lungi* at the hotel had been priced at twelve hundred rupees.

A woman with blue-black skin and a chain from nose to ear laden with silver medallions showed Annie how to drape the *lungi* across her hips and to fasten it so that it felt comfortable and secure. Then Annie tied the scarf around the crown of her straw hat and left the ends trailing down the back to give it the careless touch of elegance it had been lacking. When she got up to go, she did a mock pose and the women murmured their approval. One of the women held up a mango and a couple of sugar bananas, but Annie shook her head and turned to leave. The woman got up after her and pressed the fruit into her hands, making it plain it was a gift. Then Annie felt guilty and wanted to pay, but the woman waved her away, smiling, and went back to her friends under the shelter. Annie waved good-bye and left with the feeling that she'd just done business with a group of women who knew more about public relations than all the boutique owners in the ritziest hotel on the beach.

She walked back down to the water and continued her exploration of the beach, feeling more optimistic than she had in weeks. She glanced briefly behind her and saw that the Fort Aguada Hotel was little more than a molten white puddle on the southern horizon. Up ahead, she knew, were the other hippie beaches of Candolim, Calangute, Baga, Anjuna, and Vagator, with their reputations for drugs, nudity, and full-moon parties that were little more than orgies. There was a bungalow in the trees ahead and she watched as a man with long blond hair emerged from it and walked down to the water's edge a little ahead of her. When he got to the waterline he undressed leisurely, slipping off his sandals, his T-shirt, and his *lungi* until he was naked except for a black G-string. From a distance she had thought he was young, but as she drew closer she saw that his skin was leathery and loose on his bones and his hair was not blond but gray, though he wore it in a seventies rock-star cut, bristly on top and long at the sides. He turned to look at her as she came up on him and she smiled and was about to say something friendly, but he looked through her and scuttled into the water like a crab, as if he wanted to get away from her.

She walked on, unwilling to let a spaced-out old hippie spoil her mood. He had to be at least sixty, she thought. He'd probably fried his brain on acid years ago.

A little farther on she found someone new—a young girl on her knees at the water's edge poking around in the sand as if looking for something she'd lost. Her hair was a tangle of glossy black curls and she wore only a bikini bottom, so that her breasts jiggled as she moved back and forth. When Annie got closer she saw that the girl hadn't lost anything at all but was making something, a sand castle or a sculpture. After the encounter with the grouch Annie found it charming.

"What are you making?" she asked.

The girl sat back and Annie was startled to see that she

wasn't a girl at all but a middle-aged woman with wrinkles around her eyes and mouth. The gloss in her hair was shiny strands of gray and her breasts, which had looked so young and pretty at a distance, hung slackly on her chest. Beneath the woman's tan Annie saw the pearly trail of stretch marks across her belly. This was somebody's mother, and ten, maybe twenty years older than Annie.

"Not makink," the woman answered in a sharp-edged accent that could have been German or Dutch. "Drawink."

Her tone reflected the same indifference as her eyes, as if she could hardly be bothered to explain herself to . . . to what? Annie wondered. To an outsider? To somebody who wouldn't understand?

Without another word the woman lowered her head and went back to her art. Annie hesitated a moment, looking at the picture in the sand, an abstract arrangement of symbols, squares, and spirals. What she had thought charming a moment ago now seemed silly and indulgent. What was it with these people? she wondered. Were they hostile to all outsiders? Or was it something about her, the way she looked, or the way she was dressed?

She smiled at this last stab of insecurity and walked on for a little longer. It was a big beach. The shacks faded from view and she came to a long stretch of beach where she could see no one. It was a good time to stop and go for a swim. She took off her clothes and laid them in a pile on the sand. She hesitated when she came to her bikini pants, then pushed them down and flicked them to one side with her toe. She walked down the slope to where the beach dropped away sharply into the ocean. She took only a few steps and the water rose quickly to her waist. She dived beneath the first big swell, surfaced, and went into a practiced and purposeful crawl to carry her out beyond the breakers. She swam until she was about a hundred yards from shore, then rolled onto her back and fanned the water gently with her hands while she caught her breath. All she could see was the sky, all she could hear was the soothing mutter of the ocean, and all she could feel was the warm passage of the water across her skin.

Suddenly Annie understood what had happened to her these past few weeks. It was cultural dyspepsia, circuit overload. She had begun to buckle beneath the weight of the fantastic, that was all. It had happened to others before her. Sometimes India was too much and the coddled Western mind recoiled. Naively, she had assumed she was immune. A few more days like this, she knew, and she would feel better. Her energy would return, her spirits would be replenished, and she would be ready once more for whatever India cared to throw at her—however fantastic.

CHAPTER 8

Margao, located some twenty miles south of Panjim, was a small commercial and administrative center with wide, leafy streets, grand colonial villas, and a lively market. Once Sansi's taxi had passed through the center of town the streets became narrower and more crowded, and he glimpsed the dusky insides of warehouses where sweating *kulis* built pyramids of coconut, mango, papaya, cashews, and sackloads of spices that peppered the air with an aromatic mist. Some of the *kulis*, exhausted by their labors, slept on top of their barrows, oblivious to the tumult, while others loitered in the shade and chewed strips of dried chili while they waited for the next truck to arrive.

The hospicio was on a busy main road on the south side of town. A cantonment with a high wall, a half-dozen older buildings, and two newer cement towers with balconies from which the lame and the incurable could watch the world outside as it passed them by. Sansi paid off the cabdriver at the main gate and went in search of the administration building. He passed a number of patients whose arms and legs ended in bandaged stumps or whose faces had been eaten away by lesions. He knew enough not to look away in disgust. Leprosy was still common in India and its victims so numerous they were treated as outpatients at many hospitals.

The reception area at the Margao hospicio looked old and worn, but it was kept clean and smelled of antiseptic. There was an atmosphere of calm that was absent in most Bombay hospitals. The nurses wore white saris with smart green trim and silver crosses pinned to their shoulders. Sansi asked one of them where he might find Dr. Sapeco and she directed him to the sixth floor. The elevators were at the back of the building but, like the elevators in Bombay hospitals, out of order.

By the time he had climbed the stairs to the top floor, Sansi was reminded of how unfit he was; he had to wait a moment while his breathing settled. He found himself in an empty corridor whose only light came from the open doorways of offices on both sides. The muted sounds of people at work could be heard from inside most of the offices. He started along the corridor, checking the sign above each door for the name and specialization of the occupant. Occasionally somebody in a white coat glanced up at him as he passed, but nobody was curious enough to ask who he was or what he wanted. A third of the way along he found a sign that said DR. F. SAPECO. PATHOLOGY. Inside, a small, dark-haired man with glasses was sorting through some papers on his desk. Sansi went to knock on the open door, but the man sensed he was there and turned abruptly to look at him. He said nothing but looked over the top of his glasses at Sansi with an expression that indicated wariness.

"Dr. Sapeco?" Sansi said.

"Yes."

"My name is George Sansi. I think you might be expecting me. I was referred to you by Narendra Jamal."

For a moment Sapeco didn't react at all. Then, when he took off his glasses, slid off his chair, and stepped toward the door, Sansi had to hide his surprise. Dr. Sapeco was only slightly taller standing up than he was sitting down. He had the size and build of a racehorse jockey, but there was a peculiar doll-like prettiness about him. His features were delicate to the point of daintiness. His eyelashes were long and thick and his lips such a pale pink against his dark skin that they looked painted on, the way they would be painted on the face of a doll. His clothes and his hair were meticulously neat and he smelled good, as if he used a lot of cologne.

The look on Sapeco's face told Sansi something he would rather not have known. The doctor was not pleased to see him. Sapeco put his hand on the door as if he was thinking of closing it on Sansi.

"I had trouble finding you," Sansi said.

The doctor did not respond and this time Sansi let the silence stretch out till it became clear that he was not going to just turn around and walk away. Sapeco began to look nervous. He tapped his fingers lightly against the door. At last he stood aside.

"You had better come in, Mr. Sansi," he said.

The voice fit the man—tinny and tremulous, the miniaturized voice of a doll.

Sansi stepped through the open door and looked around. Apparently, Sapeco's fussiness about his personal appearance did not extend to his taste in office decor. The metal tube-frame furniture had a charmless, institutional look—chipped, scuffed, its bile-green paint worn to a shine at the corners, its only merit its indestructibility. There was a row of metal filing cabinets against one wall and two metal shelves bowed beneath the weight of files, medical books, and corkscrewed stacks of paper held together with string. What the shelves and filing cabinets couldn't hold was stacked on the floor in cardboard boxes, evidence of the recent move from the police surgeon's office in Panjim. The only other chair in the room was stacked with boxes, too.

Sapeco went back to his desk, leaving Sansi standing just inside the open doorway.

"I am sorry, Mr. Sansi," he said. "I don't mean to be rude . . . but there is very little point in your coming here."

Sansi looked at him. "I thought you were expecting me?"

Sapeco shrugged. "Jamal told me he was sending someone. I told him there was no point."

Sansi hesitated. "He never told me."

"No," Sapeco said. "He wouldn't."

"He said you would help him."

"Perhaps some time ago," Sapeco added. "Not now. It's too late. As usual Jamal took too long to make up his mind. I cannot help him now. I am not in a position to help anybody . . . except perhaps the patients here at the hospicio."

"He said you were a friend."

Sapeco smiled faintly. "I have known Jamal for some time," he said. "That is not the same thing as friendship."

Sansi allowed himself a small smile of recognition. Whatever else he might be, Sapeco was not a fool.

"Doctor, I did not make the decision to come here lightly," Sansi said. "I know there are risks involved, considerable risks—for both of us."

Sapeco looked at Sansi as if he was hearing something he had heard many times before.

"Do you know how much difficulty Jamal is in?" Sansi asked.

"All that surprises me is that it didn't happen sooner," the doctor answered. "I am sorry your journey has been wasted, Mr. Sansi. Now, please, if you don't mind, I still have a lot of unpacking to do."

The doctor looked directly at Sansi, willing him to leave, but Sansi stayed where he was. Without somebody to point him in the right direction, his investigation was over before it had begun. He turned and put his hand on the door handle as if to leave. Then he closed the door quietly and turned back to Sapeco. The doctor seemed frightened.

"I won't hurt you, Doctor," Sansi said. "And I won't threaten you or blackmail you. If you want me to, I will go and you will not hear from me again. But you must understand, you won't be left alone. If Rajiv Banerjee is not stopped now, there won't be any peace, for you or for anybody. You think you are afraid today; it is nothing compared to the fear you will know when Banerjee and his goons take over."

Sapeco smiled feebly. "You haven't been listening, Mr. Sansi. It is already too late. Banerjee is more powerful than you realize. I warned Jamal months . . . a year ago. He chose to ignore my warnings because it didn't suit him to do anything at the time. Now it is too late. Banerjee sent a new man to take care of things here, Prem Gupta. He is cleverer than Sharma ever was and much more dangerous. It is Gupta who tells the government what to do now. You can see them every day, the ministers and the *babus*, going up to Gupta's house in their official government cars to get their orders. They don't even bother to pretend anymore."

"We can bring them down," Sansi said. "We can bring Banerjee down and Gupta and all the rotten politicians."

Sapeco shook his head. "If you stay here, Mr. Sansi, you'll get us killed. You'll get us both killed. There is no law here."

"I am not here to work within the law," Sansi said.

Sapeco blinked, his exquisite doll's eyelashes trembling.

"This isn't about the law," Sansi said. "It is about power. The balance of power has shifted to suit our enemies. We have to shift it back."

"And you think you can do that?"

"If I can prove that Banerjee's activities present a threat to the interests of the federal government, I can force New Delhi to act."

"You think New Delhi would step in?"

"The viability of the free port depends on the goodwill of foreign lenders," Sansi said. "If the prime minister has to choose between billions of dollars in foreign investment and a few state politicians from opposition parties who happen to have the wrong connections, I think I know which way he will go."

An awkward silence descended between the two of them. Sunlight poured warmly through the windows and bathed the office in a sepia glow. The doctor remained immobile in his chair. Sansi's eye was drawn to a galaxy of dust particles that spiraled slowly in the sunlight. The doctor stirred.

"Would you like some chai, Mr. Sansi?" he asked.

Sansi smiled a brief tight smile, then nodded.

Sapeco pointed him to the only other chair and picked up the phone. Sansi moved the cardboard boxes from the chair to the floor, sat down, and listened. Sapeco spoke rapid Konkanese. It was similar enough to Marathi that Sansi could follow it if he paid attention. He felt better when he heard Sapeco send for two cups of tea and not two security guards.

The doctor hung up and leaned back in his chair. "You are a stubborn man, Mr. Sansi," he said, switching back to English.

Sansi inclined his head a fraction, a tiny gesture of acknowledgment. "Perhaps it is more that I am the victim of a compulsion," he said. "Like straightening a crooked picture."

Sapeco smiled wanly. "You look at a crooked picture long enough and it starts to seem normal," he said. "You have known Jamal a long time?"

"Almost twenty years. And you?"

"Since university in Bombay," the doctor said. "He recruited me to the student council on behalf of the Congress Party. He was good at getting people to do what he wanted. I was surprised when he went into the police service. I was certain he would go into politics."

"He did," Sansi said. "He just took a slightly different route."

Sapeco nodded. "I was fascinated by forensic medicine," he continued. "The investigative side of the job intrigued me. The battle of wits with the criminal mind. People who thought they could get away with murder. After I graduated, I worked in pathology at Glaxo for a while. Then Jamal arranged for me to be taken on at crime branch. I worked there for four years before I came back to Panjim."

"When did you come back?"

"Nineteen seventy-three."

Sansi nodded. It was the year he had joined the police service. The year he spent in Tamori tracking Naxalites and trying not to get himself killed.

"Did Jamal get you the police surgeon's job in Panjim?"

"Yes."

Sansi wasn't surprised. Jamal maintained a vast and elaborate network of contacts that extended throughout India from the highest circles of power to the lowest circles of the criminal underworld. He guarded it jealously and spent hours on the phone each day servicing it with a combination of threats and promises, rewards and favors. It was his secret power base and it had saved his neck more than once. Now Sansi was part of that secret network, too, and it was his turn to save Jamal's neck.

"So," Sansi said. "You were police surgeon in Panjim for a long time."

"Oh yes, but it's not the same job now, Mr. Sansi. Everything has changed. Just walk around the streets. Look at the people's faces. You will see what we're up against."

"Fear?"

"No, Mr. Sansi. Greed. Corruption is our biggest employer now. It is the only part of the economy that works, and it is bringing more money to Goa than ever before. Now everyone has a chance to get rich. The only thing they have to fear is staying poor."

"But that will change," Sansi said.

"It hasn't changed yet. There is plenty of competition for land and plenty of money to pay for it. People look no further than the bottom of their pockets. If they can make a profit and get out before things turn nasty, they don't care what happens to their neighbors. So far most of the violence has been between the gangs fighting each other. Bodies turn up in the rice paddies every week, mostly goons from outside. As long as it's not local people getting hurt, nobody complains too loudly."

"And if they did?"

"It wouldn't matter. Certainly, no one would be so foolish as to take their complaints to the police. They have their own rackets to run and they don't like troublemakers."

"What about the newspapers?"

"From time to time they make a fuss," Sapeco conceded. "It doesn't change anything. You are right about that much, Mr. Sansi. You can't shame politicians into doing anything; you have to threaten them directly."

The doctor was opening up. Sansi was encouraged.

"It also explains why the government was so quick to crack down on the activists," Sapeco went on. "Obviously they don't want New Delhi to get the idea that they can't handle any opposition to the free port."

"Opposition?"

"Yes," the doctor said. "From environmental groups."

Sansi looked blankly at him.

"You don't know about the railway?"

Sansi shook his head.

Sapeco sighed.

"It started about two years ago. A consortium made up of the government and a few private investors was buying up property in a corridor that cuts north to south across some of the best land in the state. It made no sense that they wouldn't come in from another direction, where they could build the railway on land that was no good. At that time nobody was thinking about a free port. So people protested. An environmental movement was formed. The government strung them along, promised independent inquiries, public hearings, ecological surveys, but nothing happened. Now everybody knows . . . the consortium was betting all along that Goa would get the free port and they wanted to be in a position to control all the freight moving up and down the coast. Construction started a few months ago and that's when everybody realized the government never had any intention of rerouting the railway. So the protestors took to more dramatic measures."

"How dramatic?"

"Vandalism . . . sabotage. Work sites have been attacked, machinery destroyed. They're getting bolder. Two weeks ago they blew up a crane. Nobody has been hurt yet, but the government is nervous and the police have been cracking down on anybody who has had anything to do with the protest movement. Especially the hippies. It seems that some of the hippies have been showing the protesters how to make bombs."

"Are Bapre," Sansi whispered. Behind the curtain of graceful palms, beautiful beaches, and its image of dope-smoking indolence, Goa was a war zone. "What about Banerjee," he asked, "is he part of this consortium?"

"Nobody has said so," Sapeco answered. "But it is impossible to believe that he has not had a hand in it somewhere."

Sansi paused a moment, then said, "If we can show that Banerjee is behind the drug trade and at the same time connect one of his companies to this railway consortium, it will prove that the government has been in bed with a major drug exporter for a long time. I don't see how New Delhi could allow such a government to continue in office and expect to keep the confidence of the international finance community, do you?"

Sapeco shook his head. "It's not enough," he said, growing agitated. "The police are the biggest armed gang in Goa. They are a law unto themselves. To do the job properly, New Delhi would have to send in the army and rebuild the police force from the top down. That could only be done through the declaration of a state of emergency. I can't see them going that far."

Sansi knew Sapeco was right. A new cabinet would create an impression of stability; a state of emergency would do exactly the opposite.

"Is that who you're afraid of?" Sansi addressed Sapeco sharply.

The doctor looked at him.

"The police?" Sansi added.

Sapeco lapsed into silence once more.

"Why did you leave the police service after nineteen years?" Sansi pushed him. "Were you threatened by somebody inside the police force?"

Sapeco remained silent, his childish face set in an expression of nervous obstinacy.

"Doctor, you have to—"

He was stopped by a knock at the door.

Both men stiffened.

Sapeco opened his mouth to speak, but before he could say anything, the door opened and an old man in a white *kurta dhoti* appeared carrying a tray with two cups of tea. Sapeco told him to leave the tea on the desk. They both waited until the old man had gone, then Sapeco got up and locked the door after him. He returned to his desk, curled one hand protectively around his cup, and stared at it fixedly, though he did not seem interested in drinking it. Sansi lifted his cup to his lips and took a careful sip. The tea was sweet and scalding, made with condensed milk and heavily sugared. The cup slipped when he went to put it back in the saucer and it made a clacking sound that seemed unnaturally loud. Sapeco flinched.

Sansi waited, feeling the doctor's torment, then said quietly, "You have to tell me, Doctor. It's already gone too far. You have to tell me . . . what you know."

For a long time Sapeco did not move at all. Then he nodded, and when he began to speak it was as if all the life had gone out of him. His voice had the same defeated quality it had when he first spoke to Sansi.

"I liked my work, Mr. Sansi," he said. "I suppose that sounds ridiculous, considering what it is I do. It wasn't only because it was fascinating. It was because I knew I was doing something right. But that all changed some time ago."

Sansi waited patiently. Sapeco continued to stare at the teacup cradled in his hand.

"Much of the police surgeon's work in Goa is taken up with drug overdoses," he went on. "One or two a month is about normal. Things get busier whenever there is some dirty heroin around. Dirty or pure, it doesn't matter, the result is the same. Last February I had five. One of them was an English girl, eighteen years old. Unlucky the first time. Most drug overdoses involve foreigners and most are straightforward. They are the least interesting aspect of my work. I establish the cause of death, issue the death certificate, and turn the body over to the police for release to the family. About a year ago things got more complicated."

He looked up at the window, in the direction of the road Sansi's cab had come in on. The noise of the traffic was a steady drone punctuated by the occasional howl of a passing motorbike.

"We see them riding around on their rented motorcycles, rushing from one party to another, one high after another. Sometimes we even envy them. We envy their youth, at least. Nobody could envy their stupidity. But they all have families, and when they die we tell the consul and someone comes to take them home. A father, brother—someone. If the family can't afford to send someone, the consulate makes the arrangements. In a few cases, when there is no family and no instructions from the consul, the bodies are cremated here."

"And the ashes?"

Sapeco shrugged. "The wind takes care of the ashes."

"And the families know this?"

"That is why most of them prefer to take the body home," Sapeco said. "They'll borrow the money if they have to. And the police know this." His voice caught and he stopped for a moment.

"It's one of the ways they make their money," he went on. "The family has to pay a fee before the body is released to their care. If they won't pay, the police come up with some excuse to hang on to the body while the family runs up bigger and bigger hotel bills. Eventually the father or brother comes to understand there is no other way. It is cheaper to pay the bribe."

"What about the consuls?" Sansi asked.

"They go along with it because the government of Goa goes along with it," Sapeco answered. "When the family leaves it to the consul, they probably never find out. It is hidden in the bill, they pay it back, and they don't know any different. I suppose the consuls think they are sparing the feelings of the families."

Sansi wasn't unduly surprised. In India there was no stage of the human life cycle that was not touched by the hand of commerce. Whether it was the high cost of sandalwood for a fragrant pyre, an admission fee to the burning ghats of Varanasi, or a bribe to speed the passage of a dead foreigner through the bureaucracy, death was just another industry. In a country where death was only another step in the endless cycle of rebirth, a little *hafta* to smooth the transition was no more immoral than a toll fee.

"And some of this money went to you?" Sansi asked.

"No," Sapeco answered firmly. "I am a Christian. The idea of a trade in human souls is sickening to me. I never touched any of that money."

"But you're ashamed," Sansi said softly. "You're ashamed of something."

Sapeco lifted his gaze and looked at Sansi again, his eyes glistening. "I haven't told anyone," he said. "Even the priests would not forgive me."

Sansi waited, scarcely breathing. The room was still and felt suffocatingly hot.

"When I resigned there were nine bodies in the morgue awaiting postmortem examination," Sapeco said, his voice little more than a whisper. "All of them foreigners . . . all of them murdered."

A bead of sweat itched its way down Sansi's spine, then another and another. He dabbed absently at the damp patch in the small of his back as Sapeco continued.

"You wonder how I know they were murdered, without benefit of a postmortem?"

There was an edge to his voice and Sansi was afraid the doctor was beginning to crack. He was careful to keep his own voice level and calm.

"The same cause of death . . . for all of them?"

"Most of them," Sapeco said. "Most of them were drug overdoses. Not all, but most of them."

Sansi nodded. He had guessed as much. But there was nothing that could have prepared him for what the doctor said next.

"You want to know what is so unusual about them, Mr. Sansi? You want to know what kind of evil you are up against here?"

Sansi shifted slightly to ease the discomfort in his legs and realized how tensely he had been holding himself.

"They were—harvested, I think is the word," Sapeco said.

Sansi looked uncertainly at the doctor. "Harvested?"

"Yes," Sapeco said. "The way you would harvest a field of rice, by walking through the field and picking out the best shoots. Only this is not the work of farmers. This is the work of the police. They go through the countryside picking out the choicest victims from each new crop of tourists. They are looking for tourists who come from families with money, families who would pay a great deal to get the bodies of their children back."

For a moment Sansi was stunned. When he spoke his voice was strained. "They kill people with drug overdoses . . . then sell the bodies back to the families?"

Sapeco nodded, apparently gratified by the effect his revelation had had on Sansi and relieved that at last he could vent some of the poison that had been trapped inside him.

"How can they get away with it . . . on such a scale?" Sansi asked.

"Because nobody cares when some stupid tourist dies from a drug overdose," Sapeco answered. "That's why most of them come here—for the drugs. The cause of death is listed as accidental overdose and the condition of the body supports the diagnosis. God knows what would happen if one of the families were to demand a real postmortem once they got the body home. I kept waiting for it to happen. I thought somebody would get suspicious sometime, but no one did. Because the families expected it to end this way, Mr. Sansi. They are not surprised. There is nothing to be suspicious about. Goa is a haven for outcasts. When someone dies here they fulfill all our expectations. All that is left is the paperwork."

"What . . . kind of money do they get?"

"Five hundred American dollars is usual. But it can go as high as two, three thousand if the family has money."

Sansi cleared his throat and tasted something bitter in his mouth. He picked up his cup and washed it away with the tea.

"Two thousand dollars is a lot of money in Goa," Sapeco added. "You can buy a house and land for ten thousand dollars. The police want to share in the boom like everybody else."

"And they needed you to take care of the paperwork?"

"It was my fault. I was drawn into it without realizing it was happening."

Sansi looked at him.

"I was not as thorough as I should have been," Sapeco continued. "It is just as I told you, Mr. Sansi, overdoses are common. The symptoms are nearly always the same. It is the perfect disguise for murder. I have no idea how many victims I certified as accidental death because I wasn't suspicious."

"But if you had not become suspicious, you would still be there," Sansi added.

Sapeco nodded. "The police became arrogant and careless," he said. "They brought in a couple of victims who did not fit the pattern. One of them was a young man, twenty-six years old, with a very good physique. There was no indication of previous drug use, no tracks, no bruises, nothing to indicate he was part of the drug culture. On the contrary, he was a man who took care of himself, who exercised and took pride in his appearance. But there was enough heroin in his blood to kill a mule. He also had abrasions to his head and shoulders, injuries which could only have occurred shortly before death. It was clear to me what had happened. Someone had held him while he was injected, and he had put up a fight. . . ."

Sapeco stopped, unable to go on.

Sansi waited, giving the doctor a moment to compose himself. "You said there were two?" he asked gently.

"The other one was a child."

"A child?"

"A little girl, nine years old. From the hippie colony up at Anjuna. Obviously they could not represent her as a drug overdose, so they tried to tell me it was an accidental drowning."

"And it wasn't?"

"There were bruises around her neck. She was strangled or somebody held her under the water until she drowned."

"What did you do?"

"I started to do my job. I started to ask questions."

"What happened?"

"I was told to mind my own business and put down accidental death like always."

"And did you?"

Sapeco sighed. "Not at first. I thought I could go over their heads. I tried to meet with the commissioner, for all the good it would have done. Before I could see him, some men came to my office at police headquarters."

"Other police officers?"

"Yes."

"Who were they?"

"They are all in the drug squad. One of them was Inspector Dias; he's the chief of the drug squad. The others do what he wants. There are two in particular, Costa and Perez. Everybody in Goa knows who they are."

"Did they threaten you?"

"First they offered me money," Sapeco said. "When I told them I didn't want money, they made it plain what would happen to my family—to my children."

"So you agreed to play along?"

"May God forgive me," he said, and crossed himself. "I put my name to false death certificates. To my eternal shame I signed three death certificates before I left."

"I don't think you should worry too much about eternity," Sansi observed.

Sapeco looked puzzled.

"You think this man Dias will leave you in peace, considering all you know?"

The doctor shifted uncomfortably. "Dias knows I cannot expose him without exposing my part in it, too. He knows I am no threat to him."

"This Dias doesn't sound to me like a man I would be willing to entrust with my life," Sansi said.

Sapeco looked miserably at him.

"What else can you tell me about Dias?" Sansi asked. "What does he look like?"

The doctor thought for a moment then leaned down beside his desk and searched through a boxful of papers. After a moment he produced a back copy of Panjim's English-language daily newspaper, *O Heraldo*, and spread it on his desk. He turned to an inside page and pointed to a black-and-white photograph. Sansi leaned forward. It was a picture of several rows of uniformed policemen on the parade ground at police headquarters. In the foreground was an officer with an inspector's insignia on his shoulders and an impressive array of ribbons on his chest. He was saluting as he accepted something from the governor of Goa.

"That is Dias," Sapeco said. "It was taken a few weeks ago when he received a citation for his efforts in keeping Goa drug free. He draws up the figures himself and the government sends them to New Delhi to make them look good."

Sansi looked at the man in the picture, a slender man of medium height with a mustache, bad skin, and an insincere smile. There was nothing remarkable about him, nothing distinctive or memorable. He would be an easy man to underestimate.

"Does he work for Banerjee . . . or Gupta?"

"He takes money from everybody," Sapeco said. "He likes to play the gangs against each other. Whoever emerges the victor will be his friend."

Sansi leaned back in his chair, his eyes fixed on the picture of Dias.

"There is nothing to be gained by changing the government if Dias keeps his job," Sapeco said. "It only drives the problem underground for a while."

Sansi switched his gaze back to the doctor. "You want me to get rid of Dias, too?" he said quietly.

"I help you get rid of Banerjee," Sapeco said. "You help me get rid of Dias."

Sansi reflected a moment. "It would be difficult to imagine a situation where a new government could in all conscience allow a corrupt officer to remain in charge of the drug squad," he said carefully. "It should be possible to speak to someone."

It was enough. Sapeco nodded with satisfaction.

"I don't care about Jamal," he admitted. "I care about my job. I want it back, Mr. Sansi. That is the only way I will be able to atone for the wrongs I have done."

But Sansi hardly heard him. A man's need for atonement was an abstract virtue at best. Sansi's attention had shifted back to the smiling face of the man in the newspaper and the threat he posed to all those well-heeled foreign visitors who thought they knew what they were doing by slumming it in the third world. And what about Annie? What perverse logic had permitted him to bring her to this nightmarish place?

CHAPTER 9

"**I** think you should go back to Bombay."

"I'm sorry?"

For a moment Annie thought she hadn't heard him properly. The two of them were seated on the verandah of their bungalow at the Hermitage, Sansi in a hotel bathrobe, Annie in a billowy white T-shirt and khaki shorts with the cuffs turned up. Her hair was still damp from the shower and she wore it combed straight back from her face. To Sansi's eyes, she looked younger and more vulnerable than usual. She sat with her chair turned away from the breakfast table and her feet propped up on a footstool. Her legs were pink from too much sun and the sensitive bridges of her feet almost scarlet. She had mentioned her nude swim the day before and he had been strangely quiet about it through breakfast. She had taken this as a sign of disapproval. For a man who spent much of his life exploring the seamier side of human nature, there were times when Sansi could be maddeningly prim. Even so, she had expected nothing quite like this.

"It was a mistake to bring you here," he said, sipping his coffee. "I think you should go back—today."

123

"I just got here."

"I know. I agree, it's a bother."

"A bother?" she echoed. "Sunburn is a bother. What you're suggesting is ridiculous."

"I can't let you stay. I can't work properly when I'm worrying about you all the time."

"Just because I went for a little skinny-dip? I told you, nobody was there."

"It's not about that. It's about Goa. The kind of place it is. It may not look like it on the surface, but it is dangerous here, much more dangerous than I expected."

"Why?" Annie demanded. "Why is it suddenly so dangerous?"

"I talked to someone yesterday," Sansi said. "A man who knows Goa very well. He told me some of the things that are happening here—gang wars, political unrest, murder for profit. The embassies don't warn you about these things, but tourists especially are at risk. I can't keep you safe here, Annie. I want you to go back to Bombay."

Annie turned so she could face him properly, wincing as she scuffed her burned feet. "Why don't you tell me what's going on here," she said. "Maybe I can help."

"It would be easier for both of us if you'd just do what you're told."

"I know it must be very irritating for you," she said. "It's called free will."

Sansi fell silent. He played idly with the sugar spoon, drawing patterns in the tablecloth.

"All right," he said. "But you must keep it between us. This is not a news story. It's off-the-record."

"Nothing is *on* the record when I'm on vacation," Annie answered.

Sansi seemed unconvinced. Reluctantly, he went ahead. "There are many problems here," he said. "The gangs, the police, the free port, the drug trade, they're all major problems, but they're all interconnected, like gears in a big, dirty machine. And somebody like you, somebody who doesn't know what's going on, you could slip between those gears and get yourself killed—very easily."

"Killed?" she repeated skeptically.

"Yes, killed," Sansi said, and he repeated what Sapeco had told him about the police involvement in murder and the traffic in human corpses.

"My God," Annie breathed, when he had finished. "And nobody asks questions? Don't the consuls get suspicious?"

"The victims come from different countries," Sansi said. "I don't suppose anyone is keeping track. Drug overdoses in Goa are as common as snake charmers at the Taj Mahal. People get cynical."

"Meaning?"

"Meaning that some consular people may have an idea what is going on, but they don't do anything about it. Because it's too much trouble. Because nothing will change. Because—"

"Because some of them might be on the take?" she interrupted.

Sansi shrugged.

She sat quietly for a while, drawing on her cigarette. "And you're afraid something like that could happen to me?"

"You think it couldn't?"

Annie glanced around at their safe, comfortable surroundings, the lush gardens, the shining opalescent sea. She listened to the sounds of people having fun on the beach, children laughing.

"Every place has its sleazy side," she said. "I'm sure it's possible to vacation in Goa without getting into too much trouble. Other people seem to do it okay."

"You're going to be spending a lot of time on your own," he added. "You're American, you have money, you're open to new experiences—"

"I can also look like a whole lot of trouble."

Sansi sighed. "I warned you that if things got dangerous you would have to go home," he said.

"No," she reminded him. "You said if things got dangerous we'd both go. You didn't say anything about sending me home on my own because you decided I couldn't take care of myself."

Sansi shook his head. "The situation here is far more complicated than I realized," he said. "It may look peaceful on the surface, but it is very unstable, very volatile. This investigation will be difficult enough without me worrying about you all the time, where you are, who you're with."

"Look," Annie said. "I *will* be careful. I always am, whether you believe it or not. But I need this vacation. And now that I'm here, I'm not about to pick up and go home just because you think I can't tell the bad guys from the good guys. You've got to have a little more faith in me than that."

She leaned closer to him. "Besides," she added, "I'm not that bad a judge of character. . . ."

Instead of reassuring him, her words seemed only to make him more uncomfortable. She was puzzled. When he looked back at her, there was a pain and a regret in his eyes that was quite unexpected. Then she realized what was wrong.

"You haven't told me everything, have you?" she asked.

Sansi hesitated and in his hesitation she saw her answer.

"This business about the free port—it's not the real reason you're here?"

"It's part of it," he said, hedging. "The free port has instilled a kind of madness in people. There is so much money involved. . . ."

She leaned away from him. "I think you should tell me everything," she said coolly. "I've gone about as far as I'm going to go on blind trust."

Sansi stopped, annoyed with himself. He had wanted to protect her but had succeeded only in alienating her. Now he had to tell her everything and hope he didn't look like too much of a fool.

"It's politics," he began, embarrassed at how lame it sounded.

"Bombay politics?"

Sansi shrugged. "You're aware of this business with Rajiv Banerjee," he said. "You know how bad things have been since he got into cabinet. We've talked about it."

"This is about Rajiv Banerjee?"

"He has interests here," Sansi said. "Interests that have acquired a certain sensitivity with the approval of the free port."

Annie exhaled, a short, shallow breath.

"There is a good chance we can get to him through Goa," Sansi added. "He is very vulnerable here."

"We . . . ?"

"Jamal has been building a case against him for some time—he asked me to help."

Annie stared disbelievingly at him. "You're working for Jamal again?"

Sansi grimaced at her choice of words.

"You couldn't wait to get away from him," she said.

"This situation is not of my choosing," he said.

Annie sagged back in her chair, wincing as she forgot about her sunburn. It was a moment or two before she recovered her composure.

"What's it going to be?" she said. "Charges or a deal?"

"No deal," Sansi said. "Jamal wants to put him away. He'll give cabinet just enough warning to allow them to cut Banerjee loose, if they're smart enough."

She looked impressed. "You think he can do that?"

"If anybody can . . ."

"From what I understand, he's none too secure himself."

"He can do it if he acts soon. New Delhi will have to back him up."

"He could blow it and take you down with him."

"Yes."

"And that's a chance you're willing to take?"

"I've thought about it," he said. "I daresay there are one or two legal firms in England that would not look askance at a chap with a law degree from Oxford. The experience would be useful."

"You'd give up the chance to practice law in Bombay?" she asked. "After all you've been through?"

"If I try to help Jamal and fail and Banerjee retains control of cabinet?" he said. "I couldn't stay in Bombay . . . even if I wanted to."

Annie watched him for a moment. "And that's the real reason you're here—to dig up some dirt on Banerjee so you can help Jamal put him away?"

"It wasn't something I went looking for," he said. "I was offered a choice. I had to take sides."

"Oh boy," Annie breathed.

"I didn't tell you because I didn't think you'd understand," he added.

She remembered the way she had ranted at him about corruption at the law courts in Bombay, as if he were in a position to do something about it overnight.

"I think I understand," she said. "I'm just disappointed, that's all."

Sansi smiled faintly. "I disappoint myself continually," he said. "I thought if I were clever enough, you wouldn't notice."

"He'd never stick his neck out like this for you, you know. He'd drop you in a second if it suited him."

"That's why you have to go back," Sansi said. "I can't allow him to put us both at risk."

"He knew I was coming?"

Sansi paused. "He thought it was a good idea. He thought you'd be good cover for me."

"And now you're scared because the situation here is worse than he led you to believe?"

"I don't think he knows how bad it is. He thought he had friends here, people he could count on. I went to find them yesterday and they didn't want to know me. One of them closed his business and left town rather than face me. They know how dangerous it is here, Annie. You can't stay. You have to go back."

"Well," she said, "I'm not going—especially not now. I'll go when you go."

"Are Bapre . . ."

Annie shrugged. "If you leave India because of this, I'll be going with you," she said. "Which means that the course of my life will pretty much be decided by a bunch of strangers. In which case, this could well be the last vacation I'll have in this country. So, if you don't mind, I'd goddamn well like to decide for myself how I spend it." She lifted herself delicately out of her chair. "Now I think I'll go inside and put a little more suntan lotion on my legs."

Sansi stayed where he was, stunned and silent. As she passed behind him she leaned down and kissed the top of his head.

"You know, for somebody who's supposed to be so much smarter than the rest of us," she said, "you have an absolute gift for painting yourself into a corner."

CHAPTER 10

The rental car was waiting in front of the hotel, a new Maruti Suzuki hatchback in fire-engine red that could be seen twenty miles away. Sansi was not pleased. He had asked for white or green or brown, any color except red. They had assured him there would be no problem. And they had given him red. The rental agent said it was a brownish red. Sansi signed the papers and took delivery. To insist on another car would only cost him another day and invite the kind of speculation he didn't want.

He followed the highway from Aguada back to the Mandovi River and endured the half-hour wait to make the ferry crossing. Once on the Panjim side, he turned left along the riverfront and circled the Hotel Mandovi slowly, looking for Sapeco. They had arranged to meet in town this time so the doctor could show Sansi one of Goa's more dubious landmarks. For a few minutes Sansi couldn't find Sapeco. The front of the hotel was obscured by a clutter of parked scooters, people loitering, talking, and riders constantly weaving in and out. Then he recognized the diminutive figure of the doctor leaning against a scooter, cradling a chipped blue helmet in his arms. Sansi stopped and sounded his horn. The doctor hurried over to the red Maruti, climbed into the front passenger seat, and tried to make himself look even smaller than he was.

"Take the river road west," he said.

Sansi obediently turned onto Dayanand Bandodkar Road and drove westward out of the city. Minutes later they were on the busy two-lane blacktop that followed the southern shoreline of the Mandovi River for a couple of miles until it broadened into an estuary whose grubby southern shore was known as Miramar Beach. Because Miramar was the closest beach to Panjim, it was the busiest beach in Goa. The road that ran alongside it was clogged with cars, taxis, scooters, motorbikes, and buses. There was a long line of trashy food stalls, mobs of peddlers and beggars, and the beach was jammed with day-trippers.

Sapeco peered over the dashboard and told Sansi to pull over at the end of the road. There was a small turning space where the road elbowed sharply away from the beach and climbed into the hills that overlooked the mouth of the Mandovi River. Sansi double-parked beside an empty tourist bus and Sapeco squirmed around in his seat so he could get a better view of the hillside.

"You see those houses up there?" he said, gesturing toward the grand Mediterranean-style homes that dotted the hillside. "There's a big pink house on the right, almost at the top of the hill."

Sansi squinted through his open window. The hills reared back from the coast like a steeply ascending stairway, most of them carpeted thickly with jungle, except for those closest to the beach, which had been cleared to make room for the mansions of the rich. The houses were big and uniformly vulgar, with grandiose flourishes such as pillared balconies, lookout towers, and bulbous white cupolas. Most had broad, terraced gardens with lawns, shrubs, ornamental palms, and neatly tended flower beds that knitted together to form a lush tropical quilt. The seams of the quilt were visible as walls and fences that strictly determined the lines of demarcation between each property. The walls were painted the same pastel shades as the houses—greens and blues and yellows—and were topped with jagged, white-washed stones, as pretty as icing sugar from a distance. The glittering chain-link fences had been draped with purple flowering bougainvillea to soften the glare of the razor wire. It was an attempt at camouflage that only served to emphasize rather than diminish the underlying message: this was a protected place, a place for the rich and privileged. Outsiders were not welcome.

At last Sansi found the house, about a half mile distant. It was an imposing, three-story villa with arched wings on either side, salmon-pink walls, red tile roof, and pretty white brickwork around the windows and balconies.

"I see it," he said.

"That is Rajiv Banerjee's house," Sapeco added. "That is where Prem Gupta is now."

"Can we get closer?" Sansi asked.

Sapeco looked nervous. "We'll have to be careful," he said. "They don't like strangers and you can't stop at the gate without making them suspicious. You will have to drive past slowly, as if you are looking for a different address."

Sansi put the car in gear, turned back onto the main road, and started the long, slow climb up the first hill. A third of the way up they got stuck behind a truck carrying what looked like a load of slurry with a half-dozen dirt-caked *kulis* sitting on top—men, women, and children. The *kulis* watched blankly as the mud drizzled out the back of the truck and spattered over everyone and everything that came too close. Sansi's first instinct was to hang back, but then he changed his mind and edged closer to the truck. The more mud that splashed over the car, streaking the paintwork and dulling its shine, the more Sansi liked it. When Sapeco told him to take a sharp left turn a hundred yards before the brow of the hill, the car was a mottled, grayish color with occasional patches of red, and Sansi felt much better.

They bumped off the blacktop and onto a groomed gravel

track with walls of jungle on either side. They followed it for fifty yards until they came to a fork where one track sloped to the left and the other climbed to the right. Sapeco told him to take the track to the right. A moment later the jungle ended abruptly and was replaced by a high, chain-link fence behind which they could see a broad expanse of lawn and an elegant, dun-colored bungalow. Sansi drove on at a steady twenty miles per hour, past a pair of low, wooden gates and then more chain-link fence until the jungle swooped in on each side again. Sansi assumed they were getting close when Sapeco shrank lower and lower in his seat until the top of his head could no longer be seen through the open window. After about a minute the jungle yielded to a clay brick wall about seven feet high and crusted with broken glass.

"This is it," Sapeco hissed. "Whatever happens, don't stop, keep going."

The wall continued for another sixty or seventy yards and then ended abruptly to be replaced by a pair of gates that appeared to be made entirely of stainless steel. There was nothing pretty or ornamental about them. They were the kind of gates Sansi saw in prison yards—brutish, functional, and solid enough to stop a truck. Both gates were closed, though there was a gatehouse just inside, the same salmon pink as the house. Sansi glimpsed a couple of uniformed security guards through a gatehouse window and then the wall leaped back into view.

He muttered under his breath and kept going. It wasn't enough. But Sapeco was right. There was nowhere to stop where he could get a better look at the house without attracting suspicion. He followed the track past two more houses until it took a downward loop that would take them back to the main road via the houses on the lower side of the slope. He stopped the car, did an awkward reverse turn, and headed back toward the pink house. This time he slowed to around ten miles an hour as he drove past the gates. Sapeco moaned softly and lowered his head even farther. It was just long enough for Sansi to get a glimpse of the house. A stately Portuguese villa set well back from the main gate amid wide lawns sparsely studded with ashoka trees and yellow budded gulmohur trees. The driveway was big enough for a single car and curved past the front of the house in a kind of question mark shape to finish under a high-roofed portico at the side. There was no movement anywhere, no wandering guards or guard dogs. But one of the men in the gatehouse noticed the car and started to get up. Sansi accelerated away gently and a moment later he pulled out onto the main road and continued up the hill. Beside him, the doctor slowly began to unfold.

They followed the undulating blacktop for several minutes, climbing one hill after another until they crested the final ridge and were confronted by the coastal panorama of Cabo Raj Bhavan and the beach at Doña Paula. This was the beach preferred by students from the University of Goa's medical school, whose mustard-colored buildings could be seen clustered around the hilltop a few miles away at Bambolim. Sansi pulled over to the side of the road and switched off the engine.

"I'm going to walk back and see if I can get closer on foot," he said.

"It will make no difference," Sapeco said. "If they see you hanging around, they will want to know what you are doing there. They may take you inside and use force on you until they are satisfied you are telling the truth. Remember, there is no law here. They have nothing to fear from anyone."

"It looks to me as if there is nothing but jungle at the rear of the house," Sansi answered. "Perhaps I can find a way in there. The elevation would work in my favor. I don't have to get too close. Only close enough to see."

"Oh Mary, Mother of God," Sapeco moaned. "It is very dangerous, Mr. Sansi. The jungle is very hard. If something goes wrong, you will not be able to get out quickly."

"No," Sansi agreed. "But I can hide. I have to start my surveillance somewhere, Doctor. I will have to make sure they don't see me."

Sapeco watched silently while Sansi rummaged around on

the backseat and retrieved his sun hat and a small camera bag. Then the doctor picked up his crash helmet and put it on his knee.

"I will help you as best as I can," he said.

"It is quite all right, Doctor," Sansi tried to reassure him. "You've done enough for today. If you drop me at the side of the road, that will be fine. You can come back and pick me up later."

"No, Mr. Sansi." The doctor shook his head. "I am afraid I can't."

"Doctor, you will be in no danger . . .

"I can't drive a car," Sapeco interrupted. "Without special controls I find it very uncomfortable. That is why I go everywhere on my scooter. I am afraid we're stuck with each other for today, Mr. Sansi. We may as well make the best of it."

Sansi looked at the doctor, saw how his head barely cleared the dashboard, how his feet left room to spare on the floor. The Maruti was a small car, but Sansi doubted Sapeco's feet would even reach the pedals.

"*Acha,*" Sansi said. "I will be pleased to have you along."

"Only promise me one thing . . ." Sapeco put his small hand on Sansi's arm. "You will not attempt anything heroic with me in the vicinity. If you are intending to do something heroic, please let me know in advance so that I may leave quickly."

"Don't worry, Doctor," Sansi said. "I regard heroism much the same way I regard the beach at Chowpatty."

Sapeco stared in puzzlement.

"I think it is best admired from a distance," Sansi explained.

He restarted the engine and did a U-turn that took them back the way they had come. They were about a mile from the turnoff that led to the pink house when Sansi slowed down to search for a place to park. It wasn't easy. The road was narrow and the shoulders spongy and treacherous and obscured by overhanging jungle. At last Sapeco spotted a break in the scrub and Sansi pulled in and parked as far off the pavement as possible.

Sansi nosed the Maruti delicately into the opening and

turned off the engine. When he and Sapeco got out of the car, Sansi arranged a few branches and palm fronds to cover the car, then took the added precaution of attaching a note to a windshield wiper that explained that it had broken down. Then he put on his hat, shouldered his camera bag, and started down the slope into the eerie green twilight of the jungle.

When he got to the bottom, he paused to wait for Sapeco. He smiled when he saw the doctor easing his way gingerly down the slope. Sapeco had put on his crash helmet. The doctor saw Sansi's face and shrugged.

"Bullets," he said.

"Of course," Sansi said.

Still smiling, he turned and started picking his way through the thickly tangled scrub. Progress was every bit as hard as Sapeco had predicted. The greatest hazard for Sansi was the false floor of the jungle, a slick and treacherous carpet of decaying vegetation, fallen branches, and thickly matted vines two or three feet above ground level. Sansi broke through the false floor, continually risking a broken leg, a twisted ankle, or the venomous bite of whatever malevolent creatures scuttled and slid underneath. Sapeco, who weighed so much less, found the going easier. But the mosquitoes tormented both men equally. So did the pretty palm shrubs whose spiny leaves cut and slashed like straight razors. They had to be careful where they put their hands, too. The slimy tree trunks were home to poisonous centipedes and swarms of carnivorous ants. The most surprising thing was the noise. Sansi had expected it to be quiet beneath the jungle canopy, but instead it was a bedlam of whining, harping insects, screeching parrots, and chattering tree monkeys.

They plodded doggedly onward for almost an hour. At last, Sansi heard something above the clamor of the jungle that told him they were getting close. He signaled Sapeco to be quiet and they covered the last few yards in silence. Then Sapeco heard it, too. The screams and laughter of children playing. A moment later they noticed the jungle was thinning. Broad patches of sky appeared and the green twilight dissolved into bright sunlight. Then, just ahead, they saw a high chain-link fence and behind it a neatly tended lawn that sloped down to the dun-colored bungalow. Behind the bungalow, but hidden from the front gate, was an L-shaped swimming pool where three children played, watched over by a woman in a plastic lawn chair.

Sansi kept to the cover of the tree line and followed the chain-link fence. The fence was replaced by the mud-brick wall that encircled Banerjee's house. On the other side of the wall was a stretch of open lawn that sloped gently down to the house, about eighty or ninety yards away.

A fallen tree trunk a few yards back from the tree line offered a tolerable seat and an acceptable view of the house. Sapeco settled for the leaning trunk of a palm tree, made himself as comfortable as possible, and gazed apprehensively in the direction of the house.

"So," he whispered, "this is surveillance?"

"Yes," Sansi whispered back.

"And now what do we do?"

"We wait."

"For what?"

"I don't know," Sansi said. "Perhaps I will know when I see it."

He opened his camera bag, took out a pair of binoculars, and pressed them to his eyes. He roamed slowly and carefully over the magnified image of the house, pausing at each window to see if any faces were visible on the inside. There were none. The house and grounds were so quiet there might have been nobody home. Sansi felt a pang of uncertainty.

He put the binoculars back in the bag and took out a camera and a telephoto lens. He attached the lens, put the camera to his eye, and trained it on the house so he could set the focus. Surveillance was not for everyone. It was an art that suited some personalities better than others. It was the art of endurance, of waiting and watching for hours that dragged into days that dragged into weeks that often dragged into months. It required the patient expectation that one day the object of surveillance would make a slip that would suggest a way to get at him—a clue, a fragment of information, a sliver of an opening just big enough for the tip of a chisel that would eventually turn into a battering ram. It was an uncertain art at best.

The first hour passed slowly and miserably. The second was worse. The sun burned down on the filmy jungle canopy and turned everything underneath into a fetid, steaming broth. Clouds of mosquitoes swarmed through the haze and followed the scent of carbon dioxide to the warm-blooded creatures who were its source. Both men buttoned their collars and sleeves and tucked their pants into their socks, but the mosquitoes lanced impudently through the thin fabric and attacked every millimeter of exposed flesh. After a while each man's fingers were stained the color of beetroot with blood squeezed from the carcasses of bloated mosquitoes. Blood flecked their clothing and fat itchy welts erupted all over their bodies. They both began to suffer for lack of water.

"I am not sure how much more of this I can take, Mr. Sansi," Sapeco said. "If I continue to lose fluid at this rate, I will be too weak to make the journey back . . . and I don't think you want to carry me on your shoulders."

Sansi felt wretched, too, but he hated to leave with nothing. He trained the binoculars at the house below and surveyed it one more time.

"There has to be somebody there," he muttered to himself.

"One half hour," Sapeco added. "Then I will have to go back, Mr. Sansi. With you or without you."

"*Acha,*" Sansi said. He resigned himself to returning the next day, better prepared and without Sapeco.

There was a flash of reflected sunlight from the direction of the main gate and Sansi quickly raised the camera. The gate was opening to admit a battered brown-and-white Mahindra Jeep with a half-laden roof rack. It was smeared with dust and looked as if it had been driven a long way. Sansi lifted his camera, aimed at the license plate, and reeled off three shots in quick succession as the Jeep drove toward the house. He wasn't optimistic. The focus wasn't set for the driveway and the license plate was caked with dirt.

The Jeep pulled under the portico at the side of the house and stopped with only its snout in view. Sansi took a close-up of the license plate. Even though the numbers were obscured, he might be able to enhance them later. The sound of car doors slamming drifted up the hill. Sansi counted three. Two men came into view, then a third. The first two were short and stocky, and they wore street clothes, one of them with a round pillbox cap. The third had a heavy mustache and wore a turban with a puggaree and white *kurta* pajamas with a long black vest over the top. They were talking to each other but were too far away to be overheard. The body language between them suggested the man in the turban was the boss. Sansi passed the binoculars to Sapeco.

"Do you know them?" he whispered.

Sapeco stepped forward warily and peered through the binoculars while Sansi closed in through the camera viewfinder.

"No," the doctor said. "I haven't seen them before. I don't think they're from Goa."

"It looks like they've driven a long way to get here," Sansi said. "I'd like to run a check on that license plate."

"From the look of them I would say they're from the north," Sapeco added.

"They could be from Bombay."

"No, further north."

Sansi gave him a sideways glance.

"Look at their features, their build, their clothes. They're not from the south, they're not tribal, they're not from the desert."

"They're not Punjabi," Sansi said.

"No," Sapeco agreed. "But they're from the north, one of the Himalayan states, I think. Except for the man in the turban. I think he's Afghani."

"Afghani?" Sansi repeated.

"I have a good eye for physiognomy," Sapeco said. "You get a knack for it in my line of work."

Amused that professional curiosity was helping the doctor to overcome his fear, Sansi looked back at the man in the turban. He had assumed that Gupta's heroin would come by road from Banerjee's warehouses in Bombay. Before that, it would have come into India from Pakistan through the usual supply route, across the Thar Desert of southern Pakistan by camel train, through the thinly patrolled border with India, and into the Great Indian Desert of northwestern Rajasthan, where Banerjee's trucks would be waiting. But that didn't explain the presence of the Afghani at Gupta's house, assuming the doctor was correct. Afghani smugglers rarely strayed far from their home territory, preferring to keep to the lawless northwest frontier and the labyrinthine trails of the Hindu Kush, where they made good money smuggling drugs, guns, and gold in a three-way trade between Pakistan, Afghanistan, and the Muslim secessionists in Jammu and Kashmir.

"They could be Muslims," Sansi mused out loud. The pillbox hat was a style favored by Muslims. The Afghani would certainly be Muslim. And the Muslim community had close ties to the Indian underworld. It was Muslims who had used the underworld to orchestrate a series of devastating explosions in the heart of Bombay a few years earlier in retaliation for Hindu attacks on the city's Muslim community.

"We know Gupta is clever," Sansi said. "Cleverer than the man he replaced."

"Sharma was a clown," Sapeco answered. "Nobody is laughing at Gupta."

"I wonder if he's clever enough to do what Sharma couldn't do?"

Sapeco lowered the binoculars to his chest and looked at Sansi.

"Banerjee has a lot to occupy his mind at the moment," Sansi added. "You said Gupta pretty well runs Goa on Banerjee's behalf. There's no way Banerjee could know exactly how much heroin Gupta is shipping out of Goa."

"You think Gupta would be cheating Banerjee?"

"It looks to me like Gupta is bypassing Bombay and getting at least some of his drugs from other sources," Sansi said. "Banerjee may or may not be aware of that."

He turned his attention back to the men below. If they were longtime smugglers, or if they had connections to the secessionist movement in Jammu and Kashmir, there was a good chance that one or more of them would be known to the security forces. In which case, crime branch in Bombay ought to be able to come up with an identification. And if Gupta was doing business with Muslim smugglers and secessionists, with or without Banerjee's knowledge, it would give Jamal everything he needed to drive a wedge between Banerjee and cabinet. There wasn't a government in India that could stand by a minister with ties to those elements.

Sansi felt a pinprick on his arm. He swatted a mosquito and left another bloody smear on his shirtsleeve. It didn't seem to matter quite so much now. He had a lead.

"Somebody's coming out of the house," Sapeco said.

Sansi aimed the camera at the door just visible under the portico. It was open and two men had appeared. Both looked like goons. They spoke briefly to the three visitors and patted them down. When they were finished one of them went to the car and started poking around inside. Then another man appeared at the door, slim with longish black hair.

"That's Gupta," Sapeco said.

Sansi recognized Gupta from past photographs. He was young, good-looking, and deceptively boyish for a man who had spent a lifetime in the gangs. Sansi thumbed the shutter button rapidly, shooting frame after frame until the roll was gone. It was all evidence now, evidence that placed Gupta and the heroin smugglers—if that was what they turned out to be—at Banerjee's house.

The man in the turban was the first to approach Gupta. They clasped hands like old business acquaintances and spoke familiarly to each other. Then Gupta turned and disappeared back into the house followed by his visitors and his goons. The door closed; Sansi lowered his camera and wiped the sweat from his face.

"We can go now, Doctor," he said. "Gupta is at home . . . and open for business."

CHAPTER 11

Annie stirred and put down her book. She was sitting with her feet up on the sitting-room sofa and the book was *Padmavati the Harlot*. She had been depressed enough by the title story of a woman who sold herself into whoredom to provide for her family, only to be spurned by them in the end, but it was the story of a twelve-year-old girl betrayed into a life of prostitution by her own parents that had finished her off. Annie swung her feet off the sofa, wandered over to the open French window, and looked past the garden at the ocean. Maybe that would be her first job when she got back to Bombay—an investigative piece on child prostitution. Then again, she thought, maybe this wasn't the kind of reading she ought to be doing when she was on vacation.

It was only an hour since Sansi had left and already she was restless. She was mindful of his warning not to stray too far from the hotel, but she was starting to feel confined. She had never been someone who could spend long periods in her room. Inevitably, her mind kept drifting back to her work and all the social ills of India that she couldn't put right no matter how hard she tried.

She picked up the TV remote and clicked rapidly through CNN, the BBC's world service news, Doordashan, the government channel from Bombay, and finally MTV courtesy of Star TV from Hong Kong. After a few seconds of Salt 'n' Pepa she switched off. She looked at the video listings. Three-hour Hindi musicals, soft-core porn from England, and American movies that were so bad they had never seen airtime in the United States.

She went to the bedroom and picked through the other books in her bag. There was the first English translation of *Raag Darbari*, a supposed comedy about village life in Uttar Pradesh; *A Goddess in the Stones*, an anthology of all that was bizarre in modern India, which she doubted could compete with her own experience; and there was *The Namaste Book of Indian Short Stories* by a selection of India's best-known writers. She picked it up and took it back to the sitting room. Then she picked up her hat, her purse, and her room keys and went out in search of somewhere more agreeable to read. There had to be a restaurant or a café somewhere where she could sit in the shade, drink tea, read a little, and observe the passing parade for a while.

She found what she was looking for next door at the hotel's sister resort, the Taj Holiday Village—a big, comfortable, thatched-roof restaurant right on the boardwalk overlooking the beach. It was two-thirds empty and those who were there were mostly breakfast stragglers and late risers who looked like they needed more than coffee to help them embrace the new day.

Annie chose a table in a well-shaded corner that offered privacy and an unimpeded view of the beach. She had noticed that there were already a few swimmers, sunbathers, and Frisbee throwers out there as well as her friends the Banjaras, stoically hawking their trinkets and cottons. She took a seat and arranged her things in a way that said she was staying awhile. A waiter sauntered over and she ordered a pot of coffee. Then she took out her book and lit a cigarette while she skimmed the pages looking for something cheerful and uplifting that would compensate for all the squalor and degradation she had wallowed in since breakfast.

After a few minutes the coffee arrived and the waiter poured it in the traditional Indian manner—by the yard. He held the pot at arm's length and, the moment he began to pour, raised the pot and lowered the cup until they were at least three feet apart. He gauged it finely until the cup was almost full and then yanked the pot away with a flourish. The severed ribbon of coffee twirled down into the cup and settled without a splash. It was all a show for the tourists, but it was, nevertheless, rooted in custom. It was the way servants had poured coffee in the palaces of the nabobs and the viceroys. The theory was that the coffee cooled as it passed through the air so that patrician lips would not be scalded. Annie smiled her appreciation. The waiter left the pot on the table, bobbed politely, and disappeared.

It was good strong Javanese coffee and Annie savored it while she tried to work her way into a story by the Urdu author Ram Lall. But it was no good. She was tired of reading, and after a few minutes her attention started to wander. Slyly, she scrutinized her neighbors. There were a couple of families, one Indian, the other Italian, both with equally awful children. There were three blond English girls who complained a little too enthusiastically about their hangovers to a handsome young waiter who appeared willing to solve all their existing problems by giving them others to worry about. There were a couple of sinister, middle-aged German men whom Annie suspected were gay, though she couldn't tell whether they were there for each other or the plentiful supply of young boys. Probably both, she decided. And there was an earnest young Scandinavian couple who seemed to be worried about money and kept going over and over the same set of figures with a notebook, pencil, and calculator.

Then her eyes settled on a couple who didn't fit, a man and a woman with the same feral look as the hippies she had seen on the northern beaches the previous day, though they had made an effort to clean themselves up. The woman had done better than the man. Like Annie she wore khaki shorts, though they were badly creased and looked as if they hadn't seen an iron since the day they were bought. Her top was a sleeveless orange shirt that looked like silk and was so loose at the armholes it exposed a lot of breast when she leaned forward. She had come wearing leather clogs, though she had kicked them under the table so she could prop her foot up on the edge of her chair. It was a pose that implied the supple arrogance of youth, though she was not a young woman. She was pretty, with small, elfin features and perfect white teeth that looked even whiter against her dark tanned skin, but when she smiled there were creases around her eyes. Annie put her in her mid-to-late thirties. Her hair, however, was spectacular. A glossy auburn cape that cascaded over her shoulders in waves and reached as far as her waist. Annie suspected the waves were not natural but the result of meticulous braiding that had been taken out just that morning. Dozens of fine bracelets jangled from both arms, she wore a gold and silver chain around her left ankle, and her toenails had been newly painted red. What Annie thought most impressive was the delicate, pale blue orchid the woman wore behind her left ear. Annie thought it was neither affectation nor enticement. It was the gesture of a woman who wanted to make herself feel special.

The man she was with could have beamed in directly from Woodstock. He wore a black T-shirt with the Grateful Dead logo on the front, green drawstring pants, and nothing on his feet. He was bald except for a horseshoe fringe of gray hair that reached his shoulders and a graying walrus mustache. The skin on top of his head was the color of polished rosewood and reminded Annie of a large antique puppet. She couldn't see his left ear, but his right ear was crenelated with a number of silver rings. He wore a chain and a couple of beaded necklaces around his neck. He had metal bracelets on both arms and his right forearm was covered by something that looked like an ornate silver gauntlet.

Both of them smoked hand-rolled cigarettes and drank coffee with the studied nonchalance of gate-crashers who hoped nobody would notice that they didn't belong. From the fragments of conversation she overheard, Annie knew the woman was American, though the man spoke English with a heavy accent that could have been Dutch.

The woman seemed to realize that she was being watched. She looked around and her eyes locked with Annie's. Annie smiled, embarrassed, and returned to her book. The woman smiled back, a friendly smile, and returned to her conversation. Gradually, Annie found herself sliding into a funny story about an arranged marriage gone wrong. But she had only read a few pages before she was distracted again, this time by the sound of voices raised in anger. She looked up and saw that the hippie couple appeared to be having a problem with a waiter. Annie assumed it was because they hadn't bargained for the resort prices and couldn't pay their bill. She was wrong.

"We want some more coffee, okay?" the woman spoke in a plaintive, escalating whisper. "Here . . ." She pulled a small beaded wallet from her purse and brandished a thick wad of rupee notes at the waiter.

"No, I am sorry." The waiter shook his head. "This place is only for guests of the hotel. No one else can come here."

"What is wrong?" the woman demanded, her voice rising from a whisper. "Has somebody complained?"

Her male friend smoked his cigarette and gazed stolidly out to sea as if the argument had nothing at all to do with him.

"I am sorry, madam," the waiter persisted. "But you and the gentleman must go now."

"I don't see the problem here." The woman held her ground. "This is a public place. We've got money . . . we're not hurting anybody."

"Madam, this is not a public place," the waiter retorted. "This is private property and it is for the use of hotel guests only. You must go now, please."

Then he stepped behind her chair and took hold of it as though he intended to push her out of it.

"Hey . . ." Her companion got to his feet, his passivity dispelled in a sudden burst of outrage. He might have been a balding caricature of a hippie, but he was tall and well muscled and capable of causing some damage if the situation got much worse. The waiter hesitated, his hands still on the chair. The restaurant filled with a tense silence.

"I don't believe this," the woman said. She threw a couple of bills onto the table and got up to go.

"I don't think this is necessary," Annie said.

The attention of everyone in the room shifted to her. It made her feel acutely uncomfortable because she had no idea what she should say or do next. Her remark was quite spontaneous and without any thought for its effect. The last thing she wanted was to inject herself into someone else's quarrel. All she knew was that she was offended by what was happening and wanted to do something to stop it. She looked around as if in search of support and her eyes fell on her room keys. Impulsively, she picked them up, got out of her chair, and walked across to the other table.

"They're my guests," she said, and threw the keys down on the table. "I'm staying at the hotel . . . and they're here at my invitation."

The couple stared at her. The waiter stared down at the keys and then at her. Annie stared at the waiter. It pleased her to see the consternation in his eyes as he struggled to make up his mind. He had made such an issue out of the hippie couple's presence it would be humiliating for him to back down now. But he recognized the keys from the exclusive Fort Aguada bungalows. If he didn't back down, he risked a far costlier confrontation with a guest from the big-money end of the resort. The instinct for self-preservation prevailed. Intransigence melted from his face to be replaced by a smile of professional insincerity.

"As you wish, memsahib," he said politely. He stepped away from the chair and gestured to the hippie couple to resume their seats. "You would like more coffee?" he inquired.

The couple hesitated. For a moment neither of them seemed sure what they wanted to do. Annie waited, letting them decide.

"What do you want to do?" the woman asked her companion.

"I don't care."

The woman looked at Annie and smiled wryly. "I really want some more coffee," she said.

Annie looked at the waiter.

"I guess we're having more coffee," the woman said.

The waiter bobbed his head and disappeared in the direction of the kitchen. The bald hippie slumped down in his chair and turned his attention back to the beach. Then the woman, too, sat down. The tension in the room eased and the murmur of conversation returned gradually.

"Will you join us?" the woman asked.

Annie hesitated. "No, it's okay," she said, and turned to go back to her table. "I don't think they'll throw you out now."

"Come and sit down." The invitation was more emphatic this time. "We're tired of talking to each other."

Annie smiled. "Okay," she said.

She went back to her table, took a minute to collect her things, then returned to the hippie couple's table and sat down.

"My name is Cora," the woman said. "Cora Betts. And this is Otto."

"Hi Otto," Annie said.

He grunted something in reply but wouldn't look at her.

"He's a musician," Cora said.

"Ah," Annie responded.

"My name is Annie Ginnaro. It's, ah . . . I'm very pleased to meet you."

They both smiled at their stilted observance of Western formalities, then Annie did what she always did when she was unsure of herself. She reached for a cigarette. She took the Kents out of her bag and offered one to Cora, who looked pleased at the prospect of an American cigarette.

"Does he . . . ?" Annie nodded in Otto's direction.

"Otto," Cora said, "do you want a real cigarette?"

Otto turned to see what was being offered. Seemingly, he approved. He extended a silver-plated arm, took a cigarette, stuck it under his walrus mustache, and waited for a light. Annie thumbed her lighter, lit Cora's cigarette, then Otto's, and then her own. Otto grunted and went back to his reverie.

"That business with the waiter," Annie asked, "does it happen a lot?"

"It didn't used to happen at all," Cora answered. "Now it happens more and more all the time. They used to be glad to take our money. Suddenly it's like we're bad for business . . . like we might scare the real big spenders away, you know?"

Annie smiled faintly. "It's called greed," she said. "If you figure out a cure, let me know."

Cora grimaced in a way that could have meant anything and drew on her cigarette. "When we first came here, there was nobody," she said. "It was real laid-back, you know? You camped on the beach. Somebody would rent you a room in their house for a buck-fifty a week. The cops were cool. Nobody hassled you. Then they realized they could make money off of us. The rents went up. They started running bus tours up the coast so the tourists could look at the freak show. We got used to it. They did that around the Haight, too. And it isn't like we discovered this place or anything. So I guess we should have seen it coming. Now they're going to build condos and tennis courts, make some real money. We've outlived our usefulness, I guess. They'd rather we stayed up at Anjuna with all the other hippie trash till they decide to kick us out of there, too."

She leaned forward and deposited a neat cylinder of ash in the ashtray. "And it won't be long," she said with a resigned sigh. "It won't be long at all."

"You've lived at Anjuna awhile?"

"You could say that," Cora answered.

Otto looked over his shoulder and Annie caught a glimpse of a smirk.

"Am I missing something?" she asked.

"It's home." Cora shrugged. "We've been there a long time."

"How long?"

Cora had to think about it. "About twelve years," she said.

Annie caught her breath. Twelve years was a long time. And now the developer's bulldozer had caught up with them. Annie could understand the hostility of the hippies she had met during her stroll the previous day. To them it must seem like there was nowhere they could be left alone anymore.

"Under the circumstances," she said, "I'd say you're handling it pretty well."

"Yeah, right." Cora chuckled.

"So," Annie said. "You're down here checking out where to put the bombs?"

Cora smiled. Even Otto turned and gave her what looked like half a smile.

"I wish," Cora said. "But it isn't that glamorous."

Annie waited.

"It's the coffee," Cora explained. "They serve really good coffee here. You didn't used to be able to get a good cup of coffee in Goa. And that's funny, you know, because it was the only thing I really missed from the States. Now they're building these places all over and they have to have coffee for the tourists. So I guess I just bow to the inevitable and I come down about every two weeks now and get my caffeine fix. So you see, that's my price. The price of a good cup of coffee."

She had tried to be glib about it, but Annie heard the rancor underneath and she knew that Cora wasn't handling it quite as well as she pretended.

"It's funny," she responded. "The only thing I miss about the States is Oreos. I pay eight bucks a bag to get them here."

"Hey," Cora said, "we all need something to get us by." She smiled. "So . . ." she added. "You traveling?"

"No, not really," Annie said.

"You don't live here?"

"No—I live in Bombay."

"What, you work there?"

"Yes, for a newspaper."

"Yeah?" Cora brightened.

"The *Times of India*—you know it?"

"Sure," Cora answered. "I love the papers here, they're a riot."

Annie knew exactly what Cora meant. English-language newspapers in India were compendiums of the eccentric and the bizarre written in a form of English that existed nowhere else on earth.

"You a reporter?" Cora asked.

"Yes."

"You down here on a story?"

It sounded innocent enough, but Annie knew that Cora was fishing. She got the feeling that Otto was listening to their conversation more keenly now. This was a place where people had reason to be wary of journalists.

"No," she said. "I'm on vacation."

"I thought, maybe, you might be doing something about the railroad," Cora said.

"The railroad?"

"Yeah, the big environmental thing . . . the bombings?"

"I don't know anything about it," Annie said.

"Shit," Cora said. "I thought that was what you were talking about before, you know . . . ?"

"No," Annie said. "Why, is somebody trying to blow up the railroad?"

Cora pulled on her cigarette and looked at Annie more closely, as if to discern whether she was lying or not. "It's the big story down here," she added. "Been all over the papers for months now."

"Well," Annie said with a shrug, "it's had very little ink in Bombay."

At that moment the waiter returned with their coffee. This time he poured it by the yard for the three of them, then put down the pot, bobbed courteously, and left. Cora shot a hostile look at his departing back.

"He didn't do that for us before."

Annie smiled faintly and took a sip of coffee. Cora and Otto did the same. Annie thought Otto would be a slurper and he was. He drank like a horse at a trough, and when he put down his cup, great glistening globules of brown fluid clung to his mustache. This time she turned away from him.

"You're really not interested in the railroad?" Cora asked, apparently unable to accept that there was such a thing as an off-duty reporter.

"It's not that I'm not interested," Annie said, trying to justify her indolence. "It's just that I'm not interested . . . now."

"It's a horror story," Cora said.

"India is full of horror stories. I can't do them all."

Cora paused and Annie assumed she was disappointed because she had been denied an opportunity to press the environmental issue with someone who might be able to help with the propaganda war.

"Look," Annie added. "I'm only two days into my vacation. Maybe if I wasn't suffering from such a bad case of burnout . . ."

"It's not a problem," Cora said. "I just thought, you know, professional curiosity . . . ?"

"I'll pick up a few clippings before I go," Annie promised. "When I get back to Bombay I'll mention it to somebody. I'm sure we have a correspondent down here who knows the situation better than I do."

"That's cool," Cora said. "I didn't mean to make a big deal out of it. I guess it's like meeting a doctor on vacation. Somehow you just wind up talking about your stiff neck or something."

"You want to talk about medical problems?" Annie said jokingly.

Cora smiled and drank her coffee.

"What about you?" Annie said, glad to take the conversation in a new direction. "Where are you from?"

"L.A."

"You're kidding me," Annie said. "I'm from L.A."

"No shit," Cora said. "Which part?"

"Canoga Park is where I grew up. When I left home I lived down near USC for a while. Then, after I was married, I was back out at Brentwood for two years."

"Are you here with your husband?"

"No." Annie shook her head. "We split up a while back, before I decided to come out here. He wouldn't have liked India. When he heard I was coming out here to work, it just confirmed all his worst suspicions about me."

Cora smiled broadly and Annie saw from her reaction that she understood exactly what Annie was talking about.

"What about you?" Annie asked. "Which part of L.A. are you from?"

"Chatsworth," Cora said.

"That's twenty minutes from where I grew up," Annie said.

"I know."

"Where did you go to high school?"

"Northridge."

"Jesus," Annie breathed. "I know Northridge. I used to play basketball against Northridge. You didn't play basketball, did you?"

Cora laughed. "No."

"Wow." Annie leaned back in her chair. "I know that school. I played there eight, nine times a year. There were some tough girls played for Northridge."

"I wouldn't have been one of them," Cora said. "Jocks, cheerleaders, that whole sports thing never appealed to me. I wasn't the classic Southern California girl." She stopped and pulled a strand of thick auburn hair between her fingers. "Wrong kind of hair."

Annie smiled.

"Anyway," Cora added, "I would have been before your time."

"What year did you graduate?"

"Sixty-eight . . . I went on to teachers' college."

Annie paused. She had guessed wrong. Cora couldn't be in her mid-to-late thirties. She had to be over forty, at least ten years older than Annie.

"When I was seventeen," Cora said. "If that makes it any easier . . . ?"

"I was out by a mile," Annie conceded.

"You probably knew my mother," Cora said. "Joy Gilman?"

Annie recognized the name immediately. "The Joy Gilman who was mayor of Glenvale?"

"Gilman was my family name," Cora said.

"It's 'Time for Joy'?" Annie exclaimed.

"That was one of them," Cora acknowledged. "Another big one was 'Vote Family, Vote Joy.' "

"I liked 'You're on Top with Joy.' "

"She never saw the humor in it," Cora said. "I thought it was a gas."

"She looked like Florence Henderson."

"Dye and a nose job," Cora said. "Her real hair was the same as mine. Nothing about that woman was real. Especially the joy part."

"Oh." Annie paused. She had heard the chill undercurrent in Cora's voice again. "I didn't mean to stir up unpleasant memories."

"It's okay," Cora said. "It's my life, too. But we don't keep in touch."

Annie could see Joy Gilman clearly in her mind's eye—tough, capable, and feisty, the kind of successful businesswoman-turned-politician whom traditional feminists despised, a carica-ture of a California Republican and a tireless campaigner on the family values platform, a legend in local politics who served a record five consecutive terms as mayor of Glenvale before retiring in the early 1980s. There wasn't a journalist in Los Angeles who hadn't heard of her. Annie recalled a husband who played a docile supporting role and a son, but she couldn't remember anything about a daughter.

"There's always one black sheep," Cora said, reading Annie's mind.

"I'm sorry," Annie said.

"Don't be," Cora added. "Some things in life get broken and can't be mended."

Annie nodded. If Cora was telling the truth, it was obvious why she and her mother had never gotten along. There was absolutely nothing about this beautiful gypsy woman to suggest she could have been related in any way to a woman like Joy Gilman. Or the public persona of Joy Gilman, at least.

"God," Annie said. "I don't believe it. Halfway around the world to meet another Valley girl."

"A Valley girl?" Cora said. "Is that good or bad?"

"It's a joke," Annie said. "I guess you wouldn't know it, but the whole San Fernando Valley is one big fashion mall now and there's this thing about Valley girls. It's another name for all the spoiled little rich girls."

"Sounds just like me," Cora said.

Annie smiled faintly. She had been enjoying herself. Now, it seemed, the conversation had foundered on an unpleasant memory. It was a pity, she thought. They had been getting along fine.

"What time is it?" Cora asked.

Annie noticed that neither Cora nor Otto wore watches. "A quarter to twelve," she said.

"Yeah," Cora said. "I think we better get going."

Otto heard her and stirred. He pushed his empty coffee cup away, stubbed out his cigarette, and got up to go. Cora took a couple of hundred-rupee notes out of her purse and tucked them under the ashtray.

"That should take care of the coffee."

"Oh no," Annie protested. "I'll take care of it."

"No, really," Cora insisted. "I'd feel better."

She stood up, slipped her feet into her clogs, and shouldered her purse. Otto stepped around behind Annie and slouched off toward the door without a word to either of them.

"Nice meeting you," Annie called after him.

Otto grunted over his shoulder.

Cora grinned.

"Do you mind if I ask you something personal?" Annie said.

"Okay," Cora said.

"Are you two, ah, close?"

"You mean together close?"

Annie nodded.

"No," Cora said. "He gave me a ride down here . . . on his bike. He's the only person who'll come here with me. Everybody else I know thinks this place sucks."

Annie was relieved. She wasn't sure why except that Cora and Otto as a couple made no sense.

"He's a very sweet guy," Cora added. "It's just that he's . . ." She searched vainly for an explanation.

"Marching to a different drummer?"

"That's it."

"Well," Annie said, "I enjoyed meeting you."

"Me, too. See you next time."

"Sure."

Cora turned to go, then stopped as if she, too, was reluctant to break the contact. She turned and looked back at Annie.

"You should come up for a visit," she said.

"Where . . . Anjuna?" Annie asked.

"It's not far from here. You should come up on Wednesday. That's market day. It gets pretty crowded, but there's a lot to see—you might enjoy it."

"Sure," Annie said. "Maybe I will."

Cora nodded. "Okay, maybe we'll see you up there." Then she turned and disappeared after Otto.

Annie poured herself another cup of coffee and tried to get back into her book. After a while she gave up. She lit a fresh cigarette and wondered what Sansi would say if she told him she wanted to visit Anjuna. He would probably try to discourage her. Maybe it would be better if she didn't tell him. After all, he had been known to keep the occasional secret from her when it suited him. And what possible harm could come to her from a bunch of aging hippies?

CHAPTER 12

In the darkroom of the hospicio at Margao, Sansi watched the figure of a man materialize through a pool of developing fluid.

First there was the outline of the white *kurta* pajamas and then the stark black contrast of the vest. Then the turban appeared, and finally the dour, mustached face of the Afghani.

Sansi took the print carefully between finger and thumb and lifted it, slick and dripping, out of the tray. He shook it lightly and clipped it to an overhead line with a plastic clothespin. Then he studied it closely in the amber glow of the darkroom light. After a moment a small smile appeared on his face. He turned and looked at Sapeco.

"This is the best," he said. "It will make an excellent enlargement."

Sapeco stepped out of the gloom and together they surveyed the row of black-and-white photographs drying on the line. The first pictures were of the Mahindra coming up the drive at the pink house and were blurred and useless. According to Sansi, there were only two photographs of the Jeep that would be any good. They were the shots he had taken of the license plate after the Jeep had stopped with its nose peeking out from under the portico. Like the rest of the car, the plate was smeared with dust, but fragments of numbers were visible and Sansi believed that crime branch in Bombay could use computer enhancement to bring up the definition of the hidden numbers and give an accurate reading of the plate.

The other pictures were of the Afghani and his two accomplices shown at various stages under the portico and then Gupta greeting them. Sansi was confident the prints were good enough to enable Jamal to come up with an identification. But it was still only a beginning. What Sansi had to do next was to establish the location of Gupta's drug cache. To find out where it was and how and when it would be moved out. And then, somehow, he had to tie it all to Banerjee. And he had no idea how he was going to do that.

When they had finished, Sansi and Sapeco cleaned up after themselves so there was nothing for the darkroom staff to find when they came in the next day. Then the two of them took the prints and the negatives upstairs to Sapeco's office. Sansi had made two sets of prints and planned to send both to Bombay. One set would go to Jamal. The other would go to Mukherjee at Sansi's chambers, as an added precaution. In the meantime Sansi wanted Sapeco to hang on to the negatives for safekeeping. He slid them into an envelope and offered them to the doctor.

"Can you keep them somewhere for me until I leave Goa?" he asked.

Sapeco didn't look too happy about it, but he didn't offer any protest. He looked around for a moment then went to one of his overloaded bookshelves, pulled out a big green textbook, and tucked the envelope between the pages.

"I can't help you tomorrow," the doctor said. "I have a lot to do here at the hospicio, otherwise people will start to get suspicious."

"I would appreciate the use of your darkroom again," Sansi said.

"What time?"

"Late . . . I can't tell you exactly when."

Sapeco sighed. "You're going back to do more surveillance?"

"I have to," Sansi said. "I have to catalog everything that goes on at Banerjee's house. If I am lucky Gupta will have a shipment going out soon. But I have to know who and where and when. I have to get some hard evidence."

"There is always something dirty going on at that house," Sapeco said.

"I am counting on it, Doctor," Sansi said. Then he added, "We all are."

Sapeco nodded. "I will wait for you here," he said.

Sansi felt sorry for Sapeco. He didn't want to bully the doctor. Sapeco looked so small and fragile, so ill equipped to deal with the brutish forces that had been unleashed all around him.

Sansi wanted to say or do something that would reassure him, but he knew he could promise nothing. He almost reached out and patted him on the shoulder, but he stopped himself. There was still a long way to go. There was still a lot that could go wrong if the doctor lost his nerve. Sansi contented himself by wishing Sapeco a good night's rest. Then he picked up the envelopes containing the spare sets of prints and let himself out, glad to get away from Sapeco's fear.

The top-floor corridor was dark and deserted except for the odd puddle of light that spilled through an open door. Voices echoed back and forth between the wards, but Sansi passed no one as he walked down the corridor and took the elevator to the ground floor. There were a couple of nurses on duty at reception and a few patients drifting aimlessly in and out, but none of them gave Sansi a second glance.

Outside, it was oppressively warm. Frogs and cicadas chafed at the night, competing with the noise of the traffic outside the walls. The grounds of the hospicio were badly lit and the spaces between buildings filled with dense shadows. Shapes brushed past him in the darkness, lepers shuffling like zombies through their own endless shadowland. Occasionally someone cried out in pain, and the echo of suffering rang throughout the cantonment.

Sansi found the Maruti where he had left it, in the street behind the hospicio, unremarkable beneath its crust of dried mud. He drove slowly and carefully from Margao back to Panjim, careful not to do anything that might attract the attention of the police. Still, on the drive from the ferry to Aguada, he almost had an accident. He dozed off at the wheel and was jolted awake by the sound of tree branches snapping and clawing at the side of the car. He snatched at the wheel, took his foot off the gas, and let the car coast to a halt while he caught his breath. One little accident was all it would take. The moment the police were aware of his existence, the moment they started checking into his background, the investigation was dead. He got out and looked around. He was lucky. Apart from a few stray dogs, the road was empty. When he looked at the car, it seemed undamaged except for a few more scratches that added nicely to its camouflage.

It was after twelve when he finally let himself into the bungalow. Annie had waited up, and when he saw the expression on her face, he remembered how awful he must look. His clothes were ripped, spotted with blood, and stained with the foul ooze of the jungle. He smelled of sweat and other indeterminate odors and his body was latticed with welts. Annie switched off the television and walked over to him.

"I take it there's not another woman involved," she said.

Tired as he was, Sansi smiled.

She led him into the bathroom and made him strip off all his clothes. While he showered she stuffed them into a plastic laundry bag and dumped it into the garbage. After the shower he dried off gently. Then he sat on the edge of the bed with a towel around his waist while she dabbed calamine lotion on his mosquito bites. When she had finished he was covered from head to toe with pale pink smudges.

"You look really, really sexy," she said.

He put on a bathrobe while she called room service and ordered him a club sandwich and a Kingfisher. When it arrived he ate it in bed with the tray on his lap while she lay beside him and watched CNN. When he had finished she took the tray away for him, shut off the TV, and lay back down beside him, hoping he might feel like talking.

"Hard day at the office, hon?" she asked.

Sansi lay with his hands folded across his stomach and his eyes closed. His only response was the slightest hint of a smile, though his eyes stayed shut. He would tell her—in due course. But not now. Not tonight.

When she realized he wasn't about to volunteer anything, she decided to tell him her own little bit of news. "I'm thinking of going up to Anjuna," she said. "To see the market."

It wasn't everything, but it was enough. She waited while he appeared to give it some thought. A moment later he started to snore.

Annie sighed. Then she reached past him and turned off the light.

■   ■

Six hours later, without the prompting of an alarm, Sansi opened his eyes, prodded into wakefulness by a subconscious awareness that he had slept enough and there was still much that had to be done. By the time Annie had stirred he was showered, dressed, had put in his contacts, and eaten breakfast. He leaned over the bed to kiss her good-bye.

"Is today going to be like yesterday?" she asked.

"Probably."

"You won't be back till late?"

"Probably not."

"In the same condition? Because if you come back in that shape every night, you're going to go through your wardrobe pretty darn quick."

"I intend to do something about that."

"Did you spend the day in a swamp?"

"I am watching some people," he said. "If they knew I was watching them, they would not be happy."

"Banerjee's people?"

He didn't answer, but his eyes spoke for him.

"Can I ask you one more thing?"

He waited.

"Are you getting anywhere?"

"Surveillance takes time. I don't have a lot of time. So I need luck. Without luck . . ." He left the sentence hanging.

Annie nodded. She considered asking him about Anjuna again, but she could see that he was anxious to leave. "Well, next time you're passing through . . ." she said.

Sansi bent down and kissed her again. "I love you," he said.

"Be careful," she said.

When he got to Panjim his first stop was the post office, where he sent two envelopes air express to Bombay. One envelope held a set of prints for Jamal at crime branch. The other held the duplicates and was addressed to himself at Lentin Chambers. He planned to call both Jamal and Mukherjee sometime in the next twenty-four hours. He needed to go over a few things with Jamal and he had to tell Mukherjee where to put the duplicate prints for safekeeping.

His next stop was a store that sold surplus clothing and equipment from the armed forces. He picked up a pair of jungle-green trousers and matching shirt, a hat with mosquito net attached, and a water bottle. Next, he stopped at a pharmacy and picked up insect repellent and a bottle of salt tablets. He filled the water bottle in the washroom of the Hotel Mandovi then got into his car and drove back out toward Miramar. He hid the Maruti in the same place as before. He took off his street clothes, doused himself from head to toe with bug repellent, then put on his jungle greens and hat. When he was ready he picked up his camera bag and set off once more through the scrub in the direction of the pink house. A little after ten he was back in place at the fallen tree on the edge of the jungle. He made himself as comfortable as he could and settled in for a long wait.

Unlike the previous day he didn't have to wait long before there was some activity—though not the kind of activity he had hoped for. Half an hour after he took up his position, a smoke-blue Contessa pulled out of the garage, drove slowly around the house, and stopped under the portico. Sansi lowered the binoculars, picked up his camera, and peered through the viewfinder, his finger poised over the shutter button. The side door to the house opened and Gupta appeared with the same two goons. All three climbed into the Contessa, and a moment later the car turned down the drive and disappeared through the open gates.

"*Bhagwan,*" Sansi groaned. His prime suspect had just gone and there was no way of knowing for how long. It could be for a few hours or it could be for a few days. He could even be on his way to Bombay to see Banerjee. Sansi had no choice but to stay put and hope Gupta would be back soon. If he had been a religious man, perhaps he would have prayed a little.

For the next three hours the house remained still and quiet. All that happened was that the sun climbed higher and higher in the sky, the jungle became foul and vaporous, and swarms of mosquitoes attacked him anew, probing his defenses, daring the noxious fumes of the repellent, many of them paying the ultimate price in their thirst for blood. The Indian in Sansi knew what it was like to wait. He bore it stoically; watching, listening, observing the microcosmic dramas of the insect world in his little jungle perch, rationing the water in his canteen to a few warm sips every hour. A little after 1:30 the gate opened again. It was the Contessa coming back.

Sansi put the binoculars to his eyes and watched as the car eased to a halt beneath the portico. The goons appeared first, then Gupta and the three of them went into the house. Once they

had gone, the driver drove around the back of the house and returned the Contessa to the garage. Sansi sighed with relief. It
looked like Gupta was back for the day. There was still a chance.

Half an hour later another car arrived, another Contessa. Except this one was white and seemed to have some kind of official
insignia on the license plate and the driver was wearing a uniform. Sansi took a couple of quick shots with his camera and
willed the car to stop in the same place as the Jeep the day before,
with its nose sticking out, so he could get a clear shot of the license plate. It didn't. It stopped right under the portico, hidden
from view.

The sound of car doors slamming floated up the hill. A man
came briefly into view—tall, straight-backed, distinctive white
hair, and snow-white *kurta* pajamas. He was accompanied by
his driver, who hurried in front of him to open the door to the
house. Sansi pumped the shutter button. He thought he got off
six good shots before the white-haired man disappeared, leaving
his driver outside. A few minutes later a servant appeared with a
cold drink for the driver. The two of them chatted amiably for a
few minutes, as if they knew each other, then the servant went
back into the house.

Whoever the white-haired man was, he did not stay long.
Forty minutes after he had arrived he came out of the house and
climbed stiffly back into the Contessa. Sansi ran off another series of shots as the car rolled down the drive, trying to get the license plate. About half an hour had passed and then another,
almost identical car arrived—a white, official-looking Contessa.
Sansi felt a slight tremor of excitement. They were government
cars. They had to be. Sapeco had told him that ministers came up
regularly to consult with Gupta, but Sansi had still not expected
it to be quite so blatant.

This time the car stopped with its nose clear of the portico
and Sansi got a clear shot of the plate. Again the man at the wheel
wore a uniform, though the occupant was nowhere near as dis-

tinguished as the first visitor. This man was bald and bulky and wore a lime-green safari suit with short sleeves that revealed a pair of brutish forearms. He stayed for about the same length of time. Sansi finished his first roll of film as the car pulled out through the gates, and had to scramble to reload.

He had barely gotten the camera shut when somebody else arrived, not a Contessa this time but a gray Ambassador, old and careworn. The driver did not wear a uniform and his passenger got out without waiting for the door to be opened for him—a nondescript man in his late forties with untidy hair and untidy clothes and a slow, unhurried way of moving. Sansi was able to get several clear shots, both as the man arrived and as he left, about an hour later.

When the man had gone Sansi checked the position of the sun and guessed he had an hour, perhaps ninety minutes before darkness fell. Despite his discomfort, his thirst, and his empty belly, Sansi felt elated. He was eager to get back to Margao to process the film and have Sapeco identify some of the scoundrels who had been to the pink house today. Despite the unpromising start it had turned out to be a busy afternoon.

It was a little after six when the sun began to settle on the horizon and the first long shadows started up the hillside. Sansi climbed down from his perch and tried to massage some of the stiffness out of his joints. He was putting the camera back in its case when he heard something—the sound of a motorbike on the road in front of the house.

It heightened, faded, then died away completely. Sansi assumed it was somebody bound for one of the other homes farther along the lane. Then the gate opened a sliver and the harsh bark of a 250cc engine reverberated up the hillside. Sansi looked through the binoculars as a red-and-white Yamaha approached the house. The driver was a man, a hippie, naked to the waist. Sansi would have put him in his mid-to-late thirties were it not for his ashen beard and his long matching hair. His passenger was a woman in her twenties with gypsy hair, a pink T-shirt, and a *lungi* tucked up high around her thighs so that everyone could see how fine her legs were.

The hippie cut the engine and let his machine roll to a halt well within Sansi's view. Sansi put down the binoculars and took the camera back out of its case. He watched the two of them as they talked idly for a few moments. No one emerged from the house, either to welcome them or discourage them. Sansi took a few shots then waited, reluctant to waste film. It was hard to see how a couple of hippies could be important to a man like Gupta. Sansi speculated that they were probably no more than cogs in Gupta's distribution network—but that didn't explain what they were doing at his house. What was apparent was that no one was in any particular hurry to greet them.

The man got off the Yamaha, settled it on its stand, and walked to the door. He wore ragged denim cutoffs, sandals, and had a shirt tied carelessly around his waist. He looked as if he didn't have two *paise* to rub together let alone the money for a motorbike. A low-level pusher rather than a distributor, Sansi decided. He took another couple of shots.

There was a delay of several moments before the door opened and the hippie disappeared inside the house. The woman watched him go, then hitched herself up on the motorbike seat, crossed her legs, and draped her arms loosely across her knees with the finger and thumb of each hand touching. Sansi watched her through the binoculars and smiled. She was meditating.

Sansi had discovered long ago that many Westerners had an extraordinary faith in the powers of meditation. It was no surprise to him that so many self-styled gurus had made a fortune in the West by exploiting the gullible with a hodgepodge of Eastern mysticism and transcendental quackery. When he was younger and at Oxford and the Beatles had extolled the virtues of meditation, he had felt obliged to try it himself. He had found it nowhere near as enjoyable as a nap on a secluded bank of the Cherwell.

The woman's meditation was interrupted after only a few

minutes when the door opened and her silver-haired companion reappeared, accompanied by one of Gupta's goons. Sansi picked up his camera and aimed it at them. The gestures between the men indicated a degree of hostility and their voices were raised high enough for Sansi to hear a few shouted fragments, but that was all. It seemed clear that the couple was being turned away and the hippie wasn't happy about it. It was equally clear to Sansi that the man must be very foolish or uninformed to provoke a confrontation with a man like Prem Gupta or any of his goons. The exchange came to an abrupt end with the hippie gesturing angrily and returning to the woman and the motorbike. The goon contributed a parting comment of his own and closed the door with a crash. Seconds later the two hippies rode out through the open gate and the sound of the motorbike faded down the hillside.

Sansi put down the camera wondering what, if anything, to make of this last visit. He had several shots of the hippie and his girlfriend. He would ask Sapeco. The doctor would know whether they were important or not, though Sansi doubted that they were.

The sun was setting quickly and darkness was rushing through the hills and hollows like a tide of spilled ink. Sansi put the camera back in its case, slung it across his shoulder with the empty water bottle, and started back through the undergrowth. By the time he got back to the car, it was quite dark. He changed into his street clothes, stowed his camera safely in the trunk, then climbed behind the wheel and drove directly to Margao. It was almost eight when he parked in his usual spot behind the hospicio. As promised, Sapeco had waited for him.

The doctor let Sansi into the darkroom then went to the canteen to get him something to eat. By the time he returned with a greasy *masala dosa* and two cups of chai, Sansi was hanging up the first pictures. Sansi turned his attention to the food while Sapeco sipped his tea and examined the sticky, curling prints.

The first roll of film included the white-haired man in the

kurta pajamas and the bald man in the green safari suit. Sapeco knew them both.

"The first man is Santosh Pawar," the doctor said, a note of distaste in his voice. "He is minister of industry. Until a few months ago he was minister of environment. He spoke out loudly against the free port, and the environmentalists thought he was their only friend in government. They know better now. His appointment to industry was supposed to give the project the stamp of legitimacy."

"He came in a government car," Sansi said. "So did the other one. There was nothing discreet about it."

"They don't have to be discreet," Sapeco said. "They have no reason to be afraid."

"Good," Sansi said. "As long as they keep thinking that way, they will continue to make mistakes and that will make our job so much easier. What about the other one?"

Sapeco turned to the man in the safari suit. "That is Jaffer Dev. No surprises about him. He is a member of the opposition, a bagman and a fixer. He has been on Banerjee's payroll a long time. It is his job to see that the opposition doesn't ask too many embarrassing questions in the assembly."

Sansi nodded. He put down the *masala dosa* with only a couple of bites missing and went back to the darkroom. Hungry as he was, the *dosa* was inedible and he would wait until he got back to the hotel. It took him a short while to make prints from the second roll. Sapeco looked at the untidy man in the gray Ambassador.

"I know him—but I'm not sure of his name. He has something to do with the unions, I think."

"Transportation . . . airlines . . . shipping?" Sansi said.

Sapeco thought for a moment. "The docks, I think. Yes, it is the docks. His name is Azad and he is an important man in the docking unions."

The doctor turned and looked at Sansi. "How did you know?"

"I didn't," Sansi said. "I was guessing."

Sansi slid a fresh print into the developing tray. "A case like this looks as if it should be easy," he said. "We know Banerjee is guilty, we know what he is doing, and we know where—but we don't know how. It is like putting together a jigsaw puzzle. We know what the final picture is supposed to look like, but even when we have it in front of us, we don't know how to put it together."

He paused while the image of two people on a motorbike coalesced on the print in the developing tray. When it was ready he lifted it out, wiped off the excess fluid, and pinned it to the line beside the others. They looked at the picture together while Sansi continued.

"We pick up the wrong pieces, we put them in the wrong places, we throw the right pieces away and forget where we put them. We get frustrated and make stupid mistakes. But we get there eventually through the process of elimination. Only it is time-consuming—and time is something we do not have. So it would help us greatly to know which pieces of the puzzle we need next and where we might find them."

"To know where Gupta is getting his drugs," Sapeco said. "And if he is cheating Banerjee."

"That would be useful," Sansi admitted. "But only as leverage we might want to use later. First we need to know what Gupta plans to do with his heroin. If we assume our Afghani friend is a smuggler and Gupta has just taken delivery of a fresh consignment, he will have to move it soon. We have to find out how and when and where."

Sapeco looked dubiously at Sansi. "Who is going to tell us that?"

"These people." Sansi gestured at the rogues' gallery dripping on the line. "They have already told us a great deal."

The doctor looked from Sansi to the prints then back at Sansi.

"Gupta can't move a large consignment of heroin out of the country unless he feels safe," Sansi explained. "He has to talk to

people. He has to know what the government is doing, if there
have been any directives from New Delhi, if there are new security measures at the airport and the docks, if there are any labor
troubles on the way, if there is a new boss for the customs service
. . . all these things."

The doctor thought about it for a moment. "And you think
he's moving the drugs by sea?"

"The whole point of using Goa is that it is easier to move large
quantities of drugs from here than it is from Bombay," Sansi answered. "The airport is too small, there are too many federal
agencies, and it is too easy for something to go wrong. But the
docks are enormous, the labor force is under Gupta's control,
and hundreds of ships come and go all the time."

"So that's why he was talking to Azad?"

"I am guessing that is why he was talking to Azad," Sansi
said.

Sapeco shook his head. "There are so many ships, Mr. Sansi.
How are we supposed to find out which of them is carrying
Gupta's heroin?"

"If Gupta is as clever as I think he is, he wouldn't risk a whole
consignment on one ship," Sansi said. "He probably has several
ships leaving for several ports on several different dates."

The doctor looked gloomily at Sansi.

"Actually, it works in our favor," Sansi said. "We only have to
find one. If we can give Jamal the name of one ship, he can
arrange an intercept through Interpol and we can roll up the
pipeline all the way back to Banerjee through Gupta here in
Goa."

"It's not possible," Sapeco said. "The docks are too big, there
are too many ships . . . and Gupta has spies there."

"We don't have to search the docks," Sansi said. "My guess is
that the heroin just got here. Gupta has to keep it somewhere till
he can ship it out. He wouldn't keep it at the house. But Jamal did
give me a list of other properties Banerjee owns here under different company names. That's where we have to look."

"He owns a produce warehouse here in Margao," Sapeco said.

"Good," Sansi said. "A market center close to the port. Plenty of activity to screen the movement of drugs and plenty of export cargo in which to hide them."

"You want to watch the warehouse?"

"No," Sansi said. "I have to get inside the warehouse. I have to know if the drugs are there. I have to get the name of a ship and a sample of heroin to establish the point of origin."

Sapeco started to look queasy. "If the heroin is there it will be well protected," he said.

"No doubt," Sansi said. "But Gupta can't be everywhere and his goons are not as clever as he is. I am going to take a look at the warehouse."

Sapeco seemed about to argue but changed his mind and lapsed into a nervous silence.

"We have to do something, Doctor," Sansi said. "We can't just watch and wait and hope they make a mistake. There isn't enough time for that. We have an opportunity here—and we have to take it."

Sapeco nodded, but Sansi could see that the real problem remained. Sapeco was afraid and there was nothing that Sansi or anyone else could do to make him unafraid.

Sansi looked at the pictures on the line and pointed to the hippie couple on the motorbike.

"What about these two?" he asked. "Where do they fit in our puzzle?"

Sapeco hesitated a moment then stepped forward so he could see the picture properly. "I know the man," he said. "I can't tell you his name, but I know he is American and he has been around Goa for some time. He likes to present himself as a guru to the other hippies. He sells drugs, too. Undoubtedly he works for Gupta."

"He wasn't very welcome at the house. They wouldn't let him in the door."

"He is a small-time pusher," Sapeco said. "He probably has an exaggerated idea of his importance. Americans are like that."

"So he's a long way down the ladder in Gupta's organization."

"One pusher among many." Sapeco shrugged. "Gupta has hundreds working for him."

"And the girl?"

"I don't know her. She is very pretty. I would remember if I had seen her before. She is probably one of his followers. Some of the hippie women are beautiful, but they have no brains."

Sansi unpinned the prints and was about to drop them onto a pile of discards to be destroyed before he left for the night when he hesitated. Then he put the prints to one side. He wasn't exactly sure why, he already had his lead, but he would hang on to them for a while. Just in case.

CHAPTER 13

nnie stepped out onto the verandah in her bikini and picked her *lungi* off the back of a chair where it had been drying in the sun. She examined it carefully and decided she had succeeded in scrubbing most of the newness out of it. It ought to be acceptable for a cool place like Anjuna.

She wrapped it around her waist and went back inside to look at herself in the bedroom mirror. It was better, she thought. More natural and definitely more bohemian. She pushed it down over her hips and stopped just above the pubic line, the way she'd seen others wear it. It was quite an effect, she had to admit. But not for public consumption. She was a sensualist, not an exhibitionist. She hitched the *lungi* back up to her waist and fastened it securely. Then she put on her hippest T-shirt, a deep magenta that went with the rich colors of the *lungi*.

She did a last-minute check of her makeup then picked up the phone and called the front desk to order a taxi. She hung up, plucked her hat off the corner of the mirror, and started for the door. Then she stopped and looked at the hat, at the scarf wound around the crown, and she wondered if she was trying too hard.

But she decided she liked it anyway and left it where it was. She was prepared to make some concessions to the ambience of Anjuna, but she wasn't willing to cancel herself out entirely. She detoured through the living room to pick up her purse and sunglasses, then let herself out just as the black-and-yellow taxi was pulling up outside.

"Anjuna," she said as she slid into the backseat.

The driver cruised back down the hill toward the resort, turned right at the main gates, and took the road that led toward Panjim. After about a mile he took a left fork and turned onto the single-lane blacktop that led north to Anjuna. Within minutes the environment changed dramatically—just as it had on the beach. It was as if she had crossed an invisible line between resort world and postcolonial India. The narrow blacktop with its wide, dusty shoulders took her past coconut groves and rice paddies, and through a series of villages where water buffalo, cattle, chickens, dogs, and mobs of children roamed the streets and routinely stopped all traffic. The character of the buildings changed from resort-style uniformity to a chaotic mélange of mud-brick homes, Portuguese bungalows, funky guest houses, art galleries, craft shops, open-air tavernas, and ramshackle restaurants. The tourists were replaced by a ragtag assortment of half-naked young people and aging hippies with receding hairlines and tie-dyed T-shirts, the likes of which Annie hadn't seen in twenty years. Every few minutes a motorbike howled past, piloted invariably by a bare-chested man with a flimsily dressed woman clinging to him like a backpack, their long hair knitted together into a banner-length piece of macramé. All shared the same fixed expression, a look of constipated smugness that said riding around in the sun half-naked on a motorbike was more fun than sex, but they were far too cool to let it show.

Annie knew they were getting close to Anjuna when they had to pass a police checkpoint. The driver slowed down while a couple of policemen peered into the backseat. Annie assumed she had passed inspection because they waved the driver through. On the other side of the checkpoint she saw that some of the bike riders had been pulled over and the police were going through their things. She understood why. They all looked like outlaws. They all looked as if they could be carrying. They were all guilty by appearance. Most of the men who had been stopped had tattoos and sun-streaked dreadlocks that reached to the waist. The women looked like gypsies with nose rings and multiple chains. Annie saw a girl of no more than twenty whose head was shaved except for a long ponytail. She had ugly black tattoos that covered the outsides of both legs.

These weren't people who were taking a walk on the wild side during a year's leave of absence from a computer job in Cincinnati. These were people who had crossed the line and were never coming back. Next to them, in her newly laundered *lungi*, her magenta T-shirt, and her stylish straw hat, Annie felt like Mary Poppins.

A hundred yards farther, the driver turned onto a narrow road that led into a densely planted coconut grove. Then he stopped and said he could go no farther. The narrowing road had become jammed with people on bikes and scooters, and there were hundreds more on foot walking to and from the market. Annie paid the driver and got out of the cab. She joined the rest of the crowd and followed the road, barely a trail now, as it snaked toward the beach. On both sides were pastel bungalows and palm-thatch restaurants with lush gardens where it would be easy to lose an afternoon, or maybe a month or two, over a cold drink.

At last she saw the market ahead of her, a bright pastiche of banners and canopies stretched between the palm trees, providing shade for a maze of stalls, benches, and mats spread out across a broad stretch of sand at the head of the beach. As she came closer she saw that some of the banners were clothes for sale, draped over lengths of rope tied between the trees. Beneath them were dozens of metal camp beds laid end to end and piled high with T-shirts, blouses, skirts, pants, and *lungis* in every color and combination.

Annie wandered slowly down the first row of stalls but saw nothing that interested her. Most of the clothes were cheap and trashy. So were the leather and plastic sandals and the poorly woven tote bags. She drifted around to the next row and then the next. She came to a row that was no more than a line of coconut mats spread on the ground and covered with jewelry. Silver and copper bracelets, chains, necklaces, earrings, medallions, jewelry boxes, wallets and purses. Most of it was gaudy and charmless, but some of the silver bracelets looked like antiques and were elegantly engraved. She hunkered down to examine them more closely and was quickly drawn into a haggling duel with the vendor, a young man of no more than nineteen or twenty. She was interested in a bracelet with a tag that said six hundred and fifty rupees, but when he would go no lower than two hundred and fifty rupees, she got up and walked away. It was all part of the game. If he ran after her, they would make a deal at her price, which was two hundred rupees. If he let her go she would save herself a few dollars. She smiled to herself as she walked on. He was letting her go. She might have to go back and eat crow later on, she thought. She liked the bracelet and ten bucks wasn't a lot of money.

She walked past a stall that sold solid ivory chess sets and wondered at the evil of killing an elephant to make such trash. She passed a tattooist where a hippie man was having a serpent tattooed on his right shoulder blade. Blood streamed down his back from the punctures in his skin, but he refused to have it wiped off, preferring to parade his machismo for a while. She passed a stall where a darkly tanned blond woman in her fifties sold health food—whole-grain breads, rolls, carrot cakes, date loaves, coconut slices, and brownies. She passed a young man sprawled in the sand beside a beach towel on which he had laid out a camera, a watch, a Walkman, and a couple of T-shirts. He wore baggy shorts and a T-shirt with an Australian flag. His curly dark hair was cut the way an accountant might wear it. She paused and he looked up at her with a melancholy mixture of need and humiliation. A sudden chill passed through her and she forced herself to walk on. He was selling his possessions to get money to buy drugs, she realized, to bleed out a few more highs in paradise. Next he would sell his return air ticket and then maybe his passport. In another week or two he would go crawling to the consulate, destitute, addicted, infected with hepatitis or worse, and he would beg them to send him home.

She walked past a row of pretty, lacquered jewelry boxes without really seeing them. She had almost grown accustomed to seeing Indians as victims, prostrated by disease and poverty in the streets of the big cities. But the sight of this healthy young man prostrated by the need for drugs in this pleasant, beachfront idyll was disturbing in a particular way. She knew she ought to feel pity for him. But all she could think about was the opportunities he must have spurned to get himself to this level of degradation—opportunities that the poor of India would never know. Compared with him, there was a dignity in their suffering.

The insistent bass thud of loud rock music was a welcome intrusion on her dark thoughts. She traced the sound to a sprawling bamboo shack at the top of the beach where a banner identified the Sea Breeze Bar and Restaurant. She knew the song. It was the Hendrix version of "Wild Thing." Primitive, sexual, compelling. Party music for those who wanted to party to the grave.

She ducked through the narrow doorway and paused to let her eyes adjust to the gloom. The only lighting came from outside—through the open sides of the building or filtered through the palm-thatch roof. It created a soft sepia tone that gave the restaurant an eerie, dreamlike quality. The bar and the dining room were both crowded and there was a steady drone of conversation beneath the music. Most of the customers were young, men and women with long hair and little clothing lounging around a junky assortment of tables and chairs, drinking, smoking, talking, some of them just staring. Despite the alfresco ambience the air was dense with cigarette smoke . . . and something else—the sweet pungence of marijuana. Annie hadn't smelled so much dope in one place since she had left college.

She lingered a moment too long in the doorway and found herself elbowed to one side by a hippie man who came in with his girlfriend. She was too surprised to complain. She had always heard that hippies were tolerant and gentle. She decided to get herself a drink and took a step toward the crowd at the bar.

"Hey, Valley girl. . . ."

Annie recognized the voice. She peered through the haze at the faces in the restaurant section and spotted Cora, smiling and beckoning to her. She was at a table with a striking dark-haired woman and a little blond girl about nine or ten years old. Annie navigated her way between the crowded tables and sat down gratefully next to Cora.

"There's only one thing I want to know," Annie said.

Cora waited.

"After I've breathed the air in here for a while, how the hell am I supposed to get back on my feet?"

"Don't worry about it." Cora smiled. "We've been here since breakfast."

Annie laughed, though she suspected Cora wasn't kidding. She put her purse on the table, took off her hat, and put it on top of her purse. Then she shook her hair loose and grabbed a handful at the back so she could hold it up and let the air cool her neck while she looked around. After a moment she realized that both Cora's friend and the little girl were staring at her.

"Hi," she said, and nodded to both in a friendly manner.

They stared back at her but said nothing.

"Honey, this is Annie," Cora told the little girl. "She's the nice lady I met the other day."

The little girl continued to stare suspiciously.

"This is Sara, my daughter," Cora added. "She's pissed at me because I won't let her have a banana smoothie. Correction . . . her second banana smoothie."

"I have heard that too many smoothies are bad for the figure," Annie said, trying to stay neutral.

Sara flashed her a hostile look and turned away.

"Then again . . ." Annie added with a wry smile.

"You have a very powerful aura," the dark-haired woman said suddenly.

Annie looked at her. She was somewhere in her early twenties with tangled black hair and the kind of figure that made enemies of other women. She wore a semitransparent cheesecloth smock that showed she was wearing pants but no bra, and she spoke English with a heavy German accent.

"Do you know there is a great deal of indigo in your aura?" the woman added.

Annie sighed. She could tolerate hippies. Especially when they were as down-to-earth as Cora seemed to be. But she couldn't tolerate flakes. And she had no pain threshold at all for any kind of half-baked, mumbo-jumbo, new age mysticism.

"This is Monika," Cora said. "She reads auras."

"Uh-huh," Annie said. "I think I better have a cigarette." She hesitated, then said to Monika, "Would that obscure my aura?"

Monika smiled. "Would you mind waiting just one minute before you light your cigarette?"

Annie sighed and took her hand back out of her purse.

"Let me tell you something about yourself and then see if you are still the skeptic," Monika said.

"You sure you can see my aura clearly enough in this light?" Annie asked. From the corner of her eye she could see Cora smiling. It made her feel better.

"The brow chakra is not usually so strong in people your age," Monika said.

"Is that good or bad?" Annie asked.

"It depends. . . ."

"No kidding."

"The brow chakra is the seat of intuition," Monika persisted. "In most people it is weakened by fear and insecurity. The fact that yours is so strong tells me you are a very instinctive person and you have learned to trust your instincts."

"Okay," Annie said. "What exactly is a chakra?"

"You have many chakras in your body," Monika explained patiently. "They are places where your life energy comes into contact with your physical being to create a vibration that is visible outside your body as light waves."

"Ahh." Annie nodded. "I see."

Monika leaned forward across the table and stared at Annie in a way she found unsettling.

"Would you do something for me?" she asked.

"What?"

"Stand up for a moment, in the light."

"Oh, come on. . . ." Annie protested.

"Please," Monika persisted. "I ask you to do it only for one moment . . . and then I will prove something to you."

Annie looked at Cora, but this time Cora's expression was unreadable and she just shrugged. Annie sighed. She was on her own.

"Okay," she said. "Just to prove that I am not afraid to make a fool of myself, I will . . . stand up."

She got out of her chair, stepped over to the light and waited, and felt like a fool. There were people at other tables nearby who had stopped what they were doing and were watching her. Annie noticed that the expressions on their faces were not the kind of amusement she would have expected but open curiosity and the expectation that this woman, this Monika, was about to do something extraordinary. Perhaps, she thought, they could see her aura, too. To Annie it felt like one of the longest moments of her life. At last she threw her hands in the air and sat down.

"Too fast?" she said. "Want to see it again?"

Monika made a face. "Longer would be better. . . ."

"Sorry . . ." Annie murmured, then took her Kents out of her purse and lit one up.

"You have a lot of dark red in your root chakra," Monika said. "That tells me you are a dominant personality and you have a powerful temper."

"Bravo," Annie said. "I'm Italian. But you could never have known that by looking at me. Maybe I shouldn't have plucked my eyebrows last night."

"The naval chakra has a definite orange glow, which means you are a very confident person. . . ."

"Well, we're just clipping along, aren't we?" Annie said, and pulled on her cigarette.

"Your solar-plexus chakra has a good underlying yellow emanation," Monika went on, undaunted. "Though it is not as strong as it should be. Which means you are a career-minded person, but you have suffered from some health problems lately."

"Not bad," Annie conceded with a smile. "That one is . . . very not bad."

"The indigo in your brow chakra is so strong it says very clearly that you are a seeker of truth."

"You sure it's not the reflection off my shirt?"

"I think you must have chosen a career where the pursuit of truth is very important to you," Monika continued. "You are a very honest type of person. Sometimes you are quite brutal about it. You demand total honesty in yourself and from those around you, and you can be very hard on them when they do not live up to your standards. You can also be very unforgiving."

Annie was still smiling, but she also felt a slight prickle of unease. She pushed it away. It was coincidence. A lucky guess, that was all. There was no way this woman could know what had happened between her and Sansi lately. Nobody knew.

"I think you might be reaching just a teeny little bit," she said.

Monika smiled again. She had found the chink in Annie's armor.

"You have made the pursuit of truth your life's work," she added. "You are so committed to the pursuit of truth you have risked your life to find it and you will do so again in the future."

Annie felt her self-assurance crumble another fraction.

"But you are also a cynic," Monika proclaimed confidently. "Cynicism is your greatest weakness and causes you to doubt your judgment in others when there is no need for doubt. The blue in your throat chakra tells me you have made your life and your career in the business of communication. You are not a teacher because your ego is too strong for that . . . and so is your temper. You are not in advertising because advertising is full of lies. I think you are successful in the media. Television or radio. I think maybe, when you are in America, you are a television re-porter."

She could see by the look on Annie's face that she had come close. And she was clever enough to know when to stop. She leaned back in her chair and smiled triumphantly.

"Your aura lays your soul bare, Annie," she said. "It is the one truth you cannot hide."

"You must have told her something," Annie said to Cora.

"I just met her here, now, today. . . ."

"Sure . . . but you two do know each other?" Annie insisted.

"Yeah." Cora laughed. "But this is the first time I've seen her since I saw you. I didn't tell her anything. Honest, we weren't talking about you before you got here."

"I'm not buying it." Annie shook her head. "Something smells."

"I am right, aren't I?" Monika said. "You are a reporter on television in your country."

"Close," she said. "Except this is my country for now and I work for a newspaper, not television."

"But you are thinking about a career in television?" Monika persisted.

"Oh, yeah . . . sure," Annie hedged. "But everybody in journalism thinks about a career in television at some time."

"But you will do it," Monika said. "It is in your character; you have made up your mind. . . ."

"Jesus." Annie smiled feebly. "I think I need a drink."

The people at the other tables looked appropriately impressed. A man, bearded and hollow-gutted in a pair of faded green board shorts, got up from the table and gave Monika a reassuring squeeze on the shoulder.

"Far fucking out," he said.

Then he glanced at Annie, pitying her in her cynicism, and returned to his table to join the buzz of conversation.

"You charge for this kind of thing?" Annie said to Monika.

Monika shook her head. "I could," she said. "But I don't. And now you know . . . it is not as you first thought. It is not bullshit."

"I'm impressed," Annie admitted, though part of her clung to the notion of inspired guesswork. "I am definitely impressed. Consider me a chastened skeptic."

At that moment a waiter passed nearby and Annie signaled him to come over.

"I want a Limca please . . . and a banana smoothie."

Sara's head whipped around at the mention of her favorite treat. Annie looked apologetically at Cora.

"I might need some help with it, if that's okay?"

"It's okay." Cora smiled her approval. Then she looked pointedly at her daughter. "As long as this little girl promises to eat some real food sometime today. You can't live off banana smoothies all the time."

"I promise," Sara said solemnly. Then she turned to Annie with a whole new appreciation in her eyes. "Thank you, Annie."

Annie smiled and was about to answer when Monika started to gather her things together.

"I hope I'm not driving you away?" Annie said, only partly sincere.

"No," Monika responded lightly. "I want to get some things from Aggie before her best stuff is all gone." She paused and then added, "I am giving a dinner party at my house on Saturday. You should come."

For a moment Annie was surprised by Monika's generosity, especially in the face of such open sarcasm.

"Thank you," she said. "I . . . I'll try."

Saturday was several days away and she suspected she might run into some opposition from Sansi.

"You might find it interesting," Monika said. Then, with a backward glance, she added, "But you should come with an open mind."

Annie watched her go. Then she looked at Cora. "An open mind?" she repeated with heavy irony.

Cora smiled. "It's always the innocents who are the most dangerous," she said. "They're the ones who get you when you're least expecting it."

The waiter returned and set the banana smoothie and a bottle of Limca with a plastic straw in front of Annie. She slid the smoothie across the table to Sara then picked up the Limca and took a long drink of lime soda. It had a chemical tartness that resembled lime, but it was cold. She put the bottle down and watched while Sara went through her banana milkshake in two minutes.

"Slow down," Cora warned her daughter. "You'll get cramps if you drink it too fast."

Sara said okay and finished it anyway.

Cora arched her eyebrows at Annie and Annie felt a twinge of guilt.

"Can I go play now?" Sara asked, squeezing out from her chair.

"Sure," Cora said. "But stay close, okay? I don't want you

wandering off on your own. We'll be going home in a little bit and I want to know where you are."

Sara promised, then darted out of the restaurant and disappeared quickly into the market crowd. Cora watched her go, a look of uncertainty on her face, then sighed and leaned back in her chair.

"You can't watch them every second of the day," she said. "You have to let them live a little—or what's the point, you know?"

Annie nodded. She understood. It was one of the reasons she had decided never to have children. In her work she had seen too many mothers who had lost sons and daughters to all manner of horrors. It was selfish and cowardly, she knew. But she also knew that the pain of such a loss was unendurable.

"You don't have to wait till Saturday, you know," Cora said.

"I'm sorry?"

"If you're bored with the hotel . . . you don't have to wait for an invitation to come back. Just come when you want. I'm around most of the time."

"Oh," Annie said, touched by Cora's easy offer of friendship. "Thank you."

She offered her pack of cigarettes and Cora took one. The two of them smoked, enjoyed the music, and watched the stoned theater of the restaurant crowd for a while.

"You think Monika invited me to her dinner party just so she can humiliate me some more in public?" Annie asked.

"No," Cora said. "She's a lot of things, but she's not a phony. What you see is what you get. She's really a very generous person."

Annie sensed that Cora was holding something back.

"But . . . ?"

Cora shrugged. "I'd probably be a lot more comfortable with her if she wasn't fucking my old man."

Annie smiled a small, embarrassed smile. It wasn't the answer she was expecting, and she wasn't sure how to react.

"Does she . . . know that you . . . ?"

"Oh yeah," Cora said. "It's not exactly a secret around here—and I really can't blame her."

"But you do blame your husband?"

Cora responded with a curiously ambivalent smile. "I wish he wouldn't," she said. "But I would never try to stop him. We've never laid that kind of trip on each other. We've always believed people should stay together because they want to, not because they have to, because they feel obligated or trapped or something. There's no such thing as a little bit of freedom, you know? Either you're free or you're not."

"What about you?" Annie asked. "Are you . . . free?"

"I can go with other people if I want," Cora said.

"But you don't?"

"After the kids came along I never really wanted to."

"You have a son?"

"Yeah," Cora answered. "He's twelve years old now. He and Sara were born in India. He's out there somewhere." She waved at the market crowd. "Probably playing cards with the other kids, trying to get their money."

"You mind if I ask you how long you've been married?"

Cora had to stop and think about it. "Sixteen, seventeen years, I guess. We don't keep track. We don't believe in that kind of anniversary thing."

Annie repeated the words in her head. *Anniversary thing.* They had been said with such undisguised scorn.

"We were married in L.A.," Cora added. "We came out here in seventy-nine."

"You came right here, to Goa?" Annie asked.

"No. We lived at an ashram at Pune for the first year. Then we went up to Manali."

Annie nodded. She had heard of Manali, another infamous hippie redoubt in the Himalayas.

"We came here first in eighty-one, I think," Cora said. "We didn't come to live until eighty-three, when they started the ashram."

"And you've never been back to the States in all that time?"

"We've been to Europe a couple of times," Cora said. "Drew travels more than I do. He does a little business in Manali. He gets our passports and visas updated every few years. He usually goes to Italy. It takes him a couple of weeks. I haven't been outside of India for six or seven years."

"Drew?" Annie said. "Is that your husband's name?"

"Yeah," Cora answered. "His name is Andrew but everybody calls him Drew."

"Well"—Annie shrugged—"it sounds like a lot of fun for Drew."

She didn't tell Cora what she really thought, that for a free spirit she appeared to be leading a startlingly conventional life. She stayed at home, kept house, and raised the kids while her husband lived the life of a traveling salesman—playing the field and doing pretty much whatever he felt like. It was a classic fifties kind of marriage where only the props were different. Instead of roses around the front door, it was bougainvillea. Instead of an apron, Cora wore a *lungi*. Instead of martinis before supper, she and her husband smoked ganja. And instead of going faithfully to the church social, they went faithfully to the ashram.

Cora shook her head as if amused by Annie's incomprehension. "I trust my husband," she said. "I trust him completely."

This time Annie's reaction was spontaneous and open. She was stunned.

"Excuse me?"

Cora smiled. "The thing about Drew," she said, "is that he has never lied to me."

Annie felt an incipient dismay.

"Think about it," Cora added. "What is one thing that every woman knows about men?"

Annie shrugged. "They all lie . . . I guess."

"Exactly," Cora said. "But before they lie, they screw around. I mean, all men screw around and then they lie about it, right?"

Annie thought about Sansi. It was only a matter of days since she'd caught him lying to her. But that had been in relation to something else. She was certain he wasn't seeing other women. As certain as she could be. She shifted uneasily in her chair.

"They're not all bastards," she hedged. "They don't all screw around."

"Oh." Cora chuckled. "I'm sorry . . . yours doesn't. But mine does. And so do ninety-nine-point-nine percent of all men between the ages of fifteen and fifty-five. The difference is that my old man is honest about it. He tells me what he's doing and he tells me why. And that's all I need to know—I don't want to hear about the rest. But at least he doesn't creep around behind my back doing it and then insult me by lying about it later. And you want to know something else?"

Annie waited.

"He loves me and I know that he loves me . . . and I still love him."

Annie stubbed her cigarette out in the ashtray and expelled a long plume of smoke. "I couldn't be that cool about it," she said. Then she added, "I walked out on my marriage because of it."

"What?" Cora said. "Because your old man went with somebody?"

"There was a little more to it than that," Annie said with a hint of self-mockery.

Cora leaned back in her chair, her eyebrows raised in anticipation.

"His name was"—Annie hesitated—"is Michael. He was the night editor at the *L.A. Times*. That's where I worked before I came here. I was twenty-two years old and he was this streetwise crusader type, you know? The tough guy with a brain who wasn't afraid of anybody. Fight city hall, fight big business, fight the governor, that kind of deal. When I was with him I felt like I could look the whole world in the face and never be afraid of it again. And you know what else?"

"What else?" Cora asked eagerly.

"He always wore his shirtsleeves rolled up and his tie loose at the collar, so you could see some of his chest hairs sticking out at the top of his shirt. He was just like the reporters in old forties movies. But he was the real thing. He wasn't phony. It wasn't an act. It was all real with him."

Cora nodded. "So when did he break your heart?"

"When I found out he was fucking an eighteen-year-old girl. She was some kind of trainee."

"And you thought that was unforgivable?"

"Yes," Annie said. "I did. And not just because he was unfaithful. There was a lot of other stuff that went with it."

"Of course," Cora said. "He lied about it."

"If he'd told the truth, I would still have left him," Annie said levelly.

Cora waited.

"Michael was a rising star," Annie said, "destined for big things. They couldn't afford to lose him. But they also couldn't afford to have somebody hanging around as a reminder of this unfortunate flaw in his character. So they got rid of the girl. And he went along with it like it was exactly how it should be. It made me sick to my stomach. He was a coward and a liar and a phony. He was everything I thought he wasn't."

"And that's why you left the paper?"

"Pretty much," Annie said. "It's a big newspaper—but not that big. I just didn't want to be anywhere near him."

She reached for her pack of Kents and took out another cigarette. At that moment the waiter passed close by, and Cora asked if Annie felt like some tea. She did, and the waiter poured for them both.

When the waiter had gone, Cora said, "Drew has had three affairs in the last ten years. I knew about every one of them. Two of the women were friends of mine."

Annie took a breath and then slowly shook her head. "And you forgave them all."

"It isn't a matter of forgiving," Cora said. "It's a matter of living with what's real."

CHAPTER 14

"He uses many aliases," Jamal's voice echoed tinnily down the telephone line from Bombay. "But his real name appears to be Chandra Khan."

"*Acha.*" Sansi wrote the name down on a sheet of hotel notepaper.

"He is Afghan by nationality though he is based in Lahore," Jamal added. "He is one of Banerjee's oldest suppliers. He brings the drugs across the Thar Desert by camel train and down through Rajasthan. You know how impossible it is to patrol that section of the border with Pakistan."

"*Acha.*" Sansi and Sapeco had both been proven right. The man in the turban at the pink house was Afghani and he was a drug runner.

"He never accompanies the camel trains himself," Jamal went on. "He usually crosses at another time and place and meets up with them later when it is safe. Then he takes care of delivery and payment personally. If he is in Panjim, then he is certainly delivering to Gupta."

"With Banerjee's knowledge?"

"Perhaps . . . perhaps not. But I can't wait until those two have a falling-out. I need something now, Sansi. What have you been doing down there?"

It sounded so much like old times that Sansi had to remind himself he was no longer in the commissioner's service. The call had started badly with Sansi breaking the news about Rao's flight from Panjim. The silence on the other end of the line told Sansi how shaken the commissioner was by news of yet another desertion. Sansi had taken the opportunity to remind Jamal that Rao may have leaked information about Sansi's investigation to Gupta or Gupta's lackeys in the police department. It was Sansi who was most in danger now. There was another silence on the line but this time only for a moment. As usual, the commissioner was worried more about his own skin than anyone else's.

"I may have something else for you in forty-eight hours," Sansi said. "Now we are sure Gupta has a new consignment in town, I think I know where to look. But it takes time, Commissioner. I am only one man. I cannot be in twelve places at once."

"What about Sapeco? He is reliable—he's helping you, isn't he?"

Sansi smiled at the idea of the doctor doing anything more than offering advice and support. "He's doing all he can," he answered truthfully. "But if he were capable of getting the kind of evidence you need, I wouldn't be here, would I, Commissioner?"

Once again Jamal fell uncharacteristically silent. *"Acha,"* he said, and Sansi heard an unfamiliar resignation in his voice. "I will expect your call in forty-eight hours."

Sansi broke the connection, then dialed the hotel operator and placed a call to his chambers in Bombay. While he waited Annie emerged from the bathroom wearing a robe and a towel around her hair. She sat on the end of the bed and watched him at the bureau as he toyed with his pen and pondered his notes, waiting for the phone to ring.

"Busy?" she asked.

Sansi turned, saw how lovely she looked, and smiled. "Yes," he said. He looked at his watch. Twenty-three minutes to eleven. He had to be at the market in Margao by midday to meet Sapeco. "Not enough time," he mumbled to himself.

"Was that Jamal?"

Sansi nodded.

"He ought to know how it feels to sweat for a change," she said.

Sansi smiled. He had been thinking the same thing himself.

"There's something I've wanted to talk to you about for a couple of days now," Annie said.

Sansi stopped playing with the pen.

"I met a woman in the hotel the other day, an American woman. She's from Los Angeles, not far from where I grew up."

"That's nice."

"She seems very nice. I met her again on Wednesday for tea—at the market in Anjuna. She's a hippie."

"You know her name?" Sansi asked.

"It's Cora . . . Cora Betts."

He wrote it down on his notepad.

"I think she's okay," Annie said. "She's married, two children, a beautiful daughter. I didn't get to meet her son. I don't know what her husband does. The whole family has lived here for eleven, twelve years."

"They are certain to be involved in the drug culture," Sansi said.

"Sure . . . to some extent, but I don't think they're into hard drugs. They look too healthy. She's a very nice-looking woman, she looks like she takes care of herself . . . and her daughter is beautiful."

"They could be trouble."

"I don't think so," Annie said. "I think they're just . . . hippies. That's all."

"It would be safer if you stayed close to the hotel."

She shook her head. "There's no way I'm going to be confined to the hotel," she said. "I have to be able to get out. I was thinking of going up there this afternoon, just for a couple of hours."

"To Anjuna?"

"Yes. And there's a dinner party I've been invited to tomorrow night. I think I'm going to go. I wanted you to know."

"I don't think you should," Sansi said. "Even if you are right and these people are harmless, you don't know who their friends are. You have no idea what dangers you could be exposed to."

"The invasion of the body snatchers?"

"It is not a joke, Annie."

"No," she said. "It's a racket run by the police that preys on the gullible and unsuspecting tourist—you said so yourself. But I don't think these people are any friends of the police, and they seem to have survived here just fine for a long time."

"Did your new friend tell you about the hippie child who was murdered at Anjuna last month?"

Annie fell silent.

"A little girl, nine years old," he went on. "Strangled or drowned—it doesn't make much difference, she was still murdered. It is difficult to see how your friend could not know about it."

Annie looked uncomfortable. "I don't know," she said. "There was no reason, I guess. She strikes me as a very honest type of person . . . painfully honest if—"

The phone rang and cut her off before she could finish. Sansi signaled her to wait and put the handset to his ear. A moment later Mukherjee's voice sounded down the line. Music could be heard in the background.

"Hello, hello . . ." Mukherjee was saying. "Mr. Sansi's chambers."

"Yes," Sansi said. "This is Sansi here."

"Yes, this is Mr. Sansi's chambers. How am I helping you?"

"Mukherjee?"

"This is Mukherjee speaking now, who is this speaking to me?"

Sansi sighed. "Mukherjee, switch off the radio."

"What?"

"Switch . . . off . . . the . . . radio," Sansi shouted.

There was a sound of scuffling at the other end of the line, and then the radio went dead. A moment later Mukherjee returned.

"Hello?" he said, his voice timorous and uncertain.

Sansi struggled to be patient. "This is Sansi speaking," he started again. "I am calling from Goa. I want you to do something for me."

"Oh, Sansi sahib." Mukherjee sounded relieved. "How charming you are to call. Are you enjoying your holiday, sahib? And your hotel, is it charming also? And how is—"

"Mukherjee?"

"Yes, sahib."

"Shut up."

"Yes, sahib."

"Did a large brown envelope addressed to me arrive at my chambers yet?"

"Oh yes, sahib, most unnecessary. The person could have given it to you in Goa because that is where you are. I am sending it to you there now, sahib."

"Mukherjee?"

"Yes, sahib?"

"I sent it. I don't want it back here. I want it there."

There was a silence at the other end and then a puzzled-sounding "Oh."

"I addressed it to myself at my chambers because I want it there when I return. Do you understand?"

"Oh yes, sahib," Mukherjee answered, sounding bewildered.

"What I want you to do is to keep it safe for me," Sansi pressed on. "It contains some very important photographs and

I don't want anything to happen to them. They could be evidence in a case and I want you to put them somewhere where they will come to no harm until I get back."

"Absolutely, sahib," Mukherjee responded. "You can be depending on me. My uncle Bakul has a safe. I will put them there until you get back."

Sansi could tell that finally it all clicked into place for Mukherjee. He had realized that Sansi was up to something shifty, behavior which Mukherjee simply hadn't expected from his employer. Now that it had happened he was on familiar ground again, and his tone of voice indicated new respect for Sansi.

"Good," Sansi said. He had no idea whether he would ever need the pictures again, but experience had taught him that evidence had a way of disappearing from police files. It never hurt to keep a set of duplicates hidden away somewhere.

"All right, Mukherjee. I will call you again if I need you."

"Sahib?" Mukherjee said before Sansi could hang up.

"Yes?"

"Uncle Bakul gave me a very good price on the paint."

"Excellent," Sansi said. "I hope you are doing a good job."

"Oh yes, sahib," Mukherjee reassured him. "It is as beautiful as the gulmorh flower."

"The gulmorh?"

"Yes, sahib. It is most charming."

"Mukherjee, the gulmorh is yellow."

"Yellow?"

"Yes."

"Oh . . ."

"I said ivory. Not yellow. Ivory."

There was a long pause. Sansi could picture Mukherjee looking around the empty chambers, surveying his handiwork, an expression of dismay on his face.

"It is an ivory kind of a yellow," Mukherjee said finally.

"No," Sansi said. "I want it ivory. You are a graduate of the

University of Bombay, Mr. Mukherjee. You should know what
ivory is. If you do not paint my chambers ivory, I will make you
do them all over again when I get back, at your own expense. Do
you understand?"

There was another pause, then a disconsolate "Yes, sahib."

"Are Bapre." Sansi hung up, knowing Mukherjee would soon
be on his way back to his uncle Bakul and this time the two of
them would have to get the paint mix right. He looked at his
watch again. It was almost eleven and he still had to drive to
Margao. He got up to go. But before he left, there was one last
thing he had to do. He crouched down in front of Annie, took her
hands in his, and looked in her eyes.

"I don't want you to go," he said. "There is nothing innocent
about this place, Annie. You can trust nobody here. Nobody. So I
am begging you—don't go back to Anjuna."

She paused. "You could come with me."

"You know I can't," he said.

"Well, I'm going," Annie said. "Maybe I don't know this
woman very well, but I don't think she could hurt me. From the
little I know about her, I don't think she could hurt anybody.
I'm certainly not prepared to write her off on somebody else's
orders."

■　■

Sansi navigated his way through the busy town center of Margao
and parked the Maruti a couple of blocks north of the market.
Then he walked to the ancient and mildewed arcade whose stalls
spilled into the surrounding streets in a clamorous labyrinth
shaded from the sun by a patchwork of palm thatch and rusting corrugated iron sheets. It was a perfect place and it was
an impossible place to conduct a clandestine meeting. The
jostling crowds offered ideal cover because it was impossible to
know who was with whom. But it would be just as easy to miss
someone, or to lose him in the crowd, especially a man like

Sapeco, who barely came up to Sansi's shoulder and who had insisted that neither he nor Sansi could acknowledge each other's existence.

Sansi hovered around the southeast corner of the market and tried to look like a shopper. It was a pleasant enough way to pass the time. Sansi loved markets. He loved the look, the color, and the texture of all the different produce. He loved to taste things he had never seen before. He saw real beauty in the piles of limes, mangoes, papayas, yams, jackfruit, and glistening, sinuous chilis, in burlap bags filled to overflowing with different kinds of rice, grains, beans, brown lentils, yellow lentils, red lentils, split peas, green peas, and chickpeas—all as hard and as shiny as gemstones. He loved the festive colors of the spice stalls with their earthenware pots filled to the brim with salt, garlic, coconut, crimson cayenne, yellow turmeric, ruby marsala, fenugreek, cardamom, jaggery, coarse-grained cumin, dried mint, green and brown coriander, green and dried ginger, ground and dried chilis. Most of all he loved the smells. He loved to savor the promiscuous, commingling aromas of the marketplace. The market was a microcosm of India, a full frontal assault on all the senses that left one pleasantly reeling.

He bought a bag of plump red chilis for no other reason than that he liked the look of them. He stopped at a nut stall and bought a bag of unshelled cashews so he could nibble while he waited.

A hand gripped his arm as though someone were trying to squeeze past. Sansi had become so accustomed to the constant pushing and shoving he almost didn't notice. Sapeco gave him an extra squeeze to make sure he understood then continued through the crowd. Sansi turned, saw the doctor, and started after him, trying to keep no more than a half-dozen steps behind.

Sapeco stayed in the main aisle on the south side of the arcade, though, like Sansi, he stopped occasionally and bought things so he would look as if he was doing some shopping. A couple of times Sansi lost sight of the doctor and was afraid he would lose him in the crowd, but Sapeco knew enough to dally until Sansi caught up with him again. The doctor led the way out of the market and continued up a dusty side street where a few of the more modest vendors had spread out garden produce and fly-blown fish on plastic sheets on the ground. On the opposite side of the street was a graying two-story cement warehouse caked with grime and mildew. A few old signs hung from its walls advertising agricultural machinery, spark plugs, batteries, and pumps. There were no windows and a cement ledge ran the length of the building a couple of feet above ground level. Sansi counted eight loading bays. Only two had their doors open. One was vacant, except for a few *kulis*, some of whom gnawed on strips of dried chilis while they waited for the next load. In the other a ramshackle truck had either just delivered a load or was waiting to take something away. The ground was littered with scraps of fruit and squashed, rotting vegetables. Flies swarmed thickly and the air was rotten with the smell of putrefaction. Mean, bony dogs patrolled the length of the street and fought viciously over the choicest tidbits. At night, Sansi knew, the street would belong to the rats.

Sansi assumed that this was Gupta's warehouse, but in case there was any doubt, Sapeco led him around to the front of the building. There, the doctor leaned against the warehouse wall and pretended to examine something on his shoe before continuing up the street and leaving Sansi to conduct the rest of his reconnaissance alone.

Sansi unshelled a couple of cashews and ate them while he studied the facade of the warehouse. There was a set of wooden doors painted green and two sets of windows, one at ground level, the other at the second-floor level. Sansi assumed that this was where the offices were situated. The name of the building's original, Portuguese owner was barely visible in an ornate, banner-style script over the door. A smaller wooden sign had since been screwed into the cement and said simply GOA PRODUCE COMPANY in English and Sanskrit.

Sansi continued his slow circumnavigation of the building. He estimated the warehouse was seventy-five meters long by thirty meters wide. He thought there would only be two floors at the front of the building so that the main body of the warehouse could be filled to the roof. There were another eight loading bays on the opposite side of the warehouse and all were closed, with their steel roller doors padlocked shut. Sansi knew he could open any one of them in less than a minute. The rear of the warehouse was a cement wall with a couple of peeling signs and a window near the roof that looked as if it hadn't been opened in years. There was no evidence of burglar alarms or wires and certainly no electronics. The building was a rudimentary fortress that relied on nothing more than muscle as its main line of defense. In India it was cheaper and more efficient to hire a dozen goons than it was to install and maintain an alarm system that would alarm no one—least of all the police. Sansi thought he could get in. The only allies he would need were a pair of bolt cutters, a flashlight . . . and an effective diversion.

He walked back up the street where the two loading bays were open, stopped to buy a bag of tomatoes from an old woman, and then continued in a meandering way that took him close to the open bay. He ignored the curious stares of the idle *kulis* and peered into the gloomy interior of the warehouse.

The warehouse looked half-full, mostly with sacks of rice, though there were a few large crates stamped MACHINE PARTS. He had guessed right about the interior layout. There was only one floor except for the front of the building, where an iron staircase led up to a row of offices. There were lights on in the offices and a kind of gantry from which an observer could see the whole interior of the warehouse. Sansi heard voices and saw other *kulis* inside with handcarts. In a corner near the ground-floor office there were a couple of ice chests and a cold-drink machine. Still there seemed to be no security guards. Suddenly Sansi became acutely aware of the interest the *kulis* were taking in him. He had lingered a little too long for innocent curiosity, he realized.

"Where's the boss?" he asked abruptly. "Isn't anybody in charge around here?"

He spoke Konkani and made sure his voice was loud and authoritative, as if he had business there.

The *kulis* looked blankly back at him. Then one of them pointed toward the second-floor office. Another told him he would have to use the front door. Sansi thanked them brusquely and continued up the street. Just before he turned the corner to the front of the building, he snatched a quick glance back and was pleased to see that no one was watching him. He kept going, past the front doors and down the street. It was the opposite direction from where he had parked his car, but he still needed to check out the area around the warehouse.

Most of the surrounding streets were taken up by warehouses, though there were a couple of garages, machine shops, a few houses, and the odd taverna. But what interested him most was the works depot that occupied a large corner lot, two blocks from Gupta's warehouse. There, behind a high, chain-link fence, were a half-dozen pieces of heavy construction equipment—earthmovers, backhoes, and generator trucks—though there was room for much more. The sign at the front gate said ASHOKA CONSTRUCTION.

Sansi tried to keep a smile from appearing on his face. The Ashoka Construction Company was one of the shady contractors Sapeco had told him were involved in the building of the Konkani Railway. This was all Sansi needed. He was going to break into Gupta's warehouse tonight, and he knew exactly how he was going to do it.

■   ■

At the same moment that Sansi was working his way through the maze of warehouses back to where he had left his car, the gates of the pink house at Miramar were opening to admit the man on the red-and-white Yamaha motorbike.

This time the silver-haired hippie was alone. He parked the

bike in the shade of the portico and walked over to the side door. Unlike his previous visit, he did not have to knock and wait. The door was opened by the same man who had escorted him outside last time. The goon patted him down in the hallway, though it was obvious there weren't many places where Drew might hide a weapon under a pair of jeans and a T-shirt. When he was satisfied, the goon waved Drew inside with a smirk. Drew felt relaxed. He had prepared himself before coming. Gupta and his goons weren't going to rattle him today with any of their crude little power games.

Once inside, Drew had to walk across an elaborate circular mosaic of Surya the sun god and his seven-horse chariot that took up most of the entrance-hall floor. Its irony was not lost on Drew. Surya was one of six paths worshipers could take to find God. Drew stepped down to the sunken living room where Prem Gupta, latest avatar of Rajiv Banerjee in Goa, sat in a creamy leather armchair alternately scribbling into a large-lined notepad and tapping figures on a calculator. Gupta wore an expensive cream silk shirt and matching pants. His feet were bare and his long brown toes worked restlessly in the pile of the carpet. His longish hair was parted in the middle and swept back. His neck was long and slender, like his toes, and surprisingly delicate for a man with a reputation for brutality. In front of him was a marble coffee table with a cream-and-caramel grain that made it look like a giant piece of candy. On top of it were a couple of plastic binders and several loose sheets of paper with figures written on them.

The room was at the front of the house, so that its windows overlooked the lawn and let in huge shafts of sunlight. With its airy interior, clean design, and muted color scheme it could have been the home of a senior executive. Gupta himself looked every inch the young executive as he caught up on his work at home. The only dissonant touches were the goons sprawled on a leather sofa drinking Kingfisher and watching a German porn video on a big-screen TV.

Nobody acknowledged Drew's arrival. He selected an empty chair, sat down, and watched the porn movie for a while.

"You want something to drink?" Gupta asked without looking up. He spoke with a heavy accent, though it was not the same comic accent that afflicted most Indians who spoke English. It was a monotone—flat, dead, emotionless.

"Sure," Drew said.

"Beer?"

"Yeah."

Gupta waved a finger at one of the goons and the man got up without a word and went to the kitchen. He returned a moment later with a quart bottle of Kingfisher and thrust it at Drew. There was no offer of a glass. Drew noticed that Gupta had his usual bottle of mineral water and an empty glass on the table in front of him.

Everything went back to the way it had been. Drew sipped his beer and watched the movie. Occasionally the goons sniggered and spoke to each other in Marathi, which Drew didn't follow. Gupta said nothing. He concentrated on the sheets of paper on his lap, checking them against the figures he tapped onto his calculator. He made no effort to hide what he was doing. The entries were almost certainly something to do with Gupta's enormous cash flow and would have made fascinating reading. But Drew understood none of it. He did understand that this was Gupta's way of insulting him, of telling him he was so unimportant he offered no threat to anyone.

"How are things at Anjuna?" Gupta asked after a while.

Drew looked away from the feverish threesome on the TV screen and shrugged. "Slow," he said. "We're getting close to the end of the season. Business is winding down. We're not moving as much stuff. We might have to drop our prices soon."

Gupta nodded but said nothing. He kept punching in figures and making new entries on his notepad.

Almost as an afterthought Drew added, "Dias isn't helping. He's making everybody paranoid. He had his guys at the market again on Wednesday, hassling everybody, so nobody wanted to make any buys. Sometimes I wonder whose side that guy is on."

Gupta merely nodded again. It was precisely the nonreaction Drew had expected. But he'd done what he wanted to do. He had planted the seed. Gupta might not show it, but he would think about Dias now. The drug-squad chief was a constant source of trouble. He might take money from Gupta, but he remained a law unto himself. He controlled the biggest armed gang in the state. Someday Gupta would have to take care of Dias the way he had taken care of Sharma. In the meantime Drew was happy to make life as hard as he could for both of them. Anything that sowed doubt and suspicion among his enemies would only work to Drew's benefit.

Gupta understood that perfectly. But it didn't mean that Drew's comments about Dias weren't true.

He finished what he was doing, threw the calculator and the notepad back onto the marble table, and looked at Drew for the first time since he had arrived. Drew looked back at him and tried not to blink. It was impossible. Gupta never blinked. He had the unnerving stare of a reptile that said he could kill you on a whim and only sleep better for it.

"What about the girl?" he asked.

Drew hesitated, then decided there was no point in playing stupid. "She doesn't know anything," he said. "She's a babe. I'm screwing her, that's all."

"You could have got her killed," Gupta said.

"She doesn't know who you are. She doesn't know anything about this house. I wasn't going to bring her in. Even if I had, it wouldn't have mattered. She doesn't know what's going on. She doesn't look at the world the same way as you and me. She reads auras, for fuck's sake."

"Auras?" Gupta said.

"Yeah, fucking auras." Drew gave a small, lopsided smile. "We're all supposed to be surrounded by colors, right? Cosmic vibrations? She can see them and then . . ." He slipped into parody. "She can tell you what kind of a person you are."

Gupta smiled faintly. "What kind of person are you?" he asked.

"I am . . . a teacher."

"Of what?"

"Of serenity through truth," Drew said.

"Acha," Gupta said. "Which country is she from?"

"Germany."

"Could she be of some use to us?"

"Maybe."

"All right," Gupta added. "You keep your eye on her. Let me know if there are any problems. I'll tell you if we need her."

Drew nodded.

Gupta sat silently for a while, thinking. He didn't like Drew. There was nothing unusual in that. He disdained all white people. They thought they were superior to people like him. Indians . . . anybody with black or brown skin. He believed he was superior to all of them. He thought they were weak and spoiled and arrogant. He despised them. Failures in their own countries— rich, soft countries filled with easy opportunities—they came to India to mooch off its poverty. He'd heard of Indians who had gone to America and become rich in one or two years. From what he'd heard, anybody with half a brain could make money in America. India was harder. Life was harder. People were harder. Certainly he knew of no white man who could survive the life he'd had—orphaned at birth in the slums of Dharavi, passed from family to family, fed from scraps and missionary kitchens until he was old enough to join the gangs. He begged, stole, and fought to make a living. He had committed his first murder when he was eleven years old—a fifteen-year-old who tried to rape him while he slept on the street. Gupta had stabbed the boy frenziedly as if to repay the world for all it had done to him. By the time he was fifteen, he ran a gang thirty to forty strong and was challenging other gangs for a share of the rackets. He learned figures by dealing with money. He learned languages by dealing with people. He learned psychology by dealing in fear. Everything he needed to know about the world he learned the hard way. It was Banerjee who had come to him, not the other way around. Gupta knew there wasn't a white man alive who could come from the same cruel beginnings and get to where he was by the age of twenty-seven.

"There is something I want to show you," he said.

At last, Drew realized, he was going to hear why Gupta had sent for him.

"Something different," Gupta continued. "Something special. I want you to tell me if it is something the foreigners would like."

"What?" Drew asked. "Some new kind of dope?"

"Something like that."

"A synthetic?"

"No." Gupta shook his head. "This one is natural . . . untouched by human hands."

The goons smirked.

"Okay," Drew said. "Let's take a look."

"Not now," Gupta said. "Tonight. We have to go somewhere."

Drew frowned. There was a dinner party at Monika's tonight. He had planned on being there. He wanted to meet his wife's new friend, the newspaperwoman from L.A. She sounded interesting. She could turn out to be useful, too. But to him. Not Gupta. He would just have to be late, he decided. Now that he was here, there was no way Gupta would let him leave until they'd completed their business.

"Well," he said with a resigned shrug, "there's always a market for something new."

"I never said it was new. Hindus have been using it for five thousand years."

"And you think I don't know about it?"

"There are many things about India that have never been revealed to outsiders," Gupta said. "The British were here for two

hundred years and they never discovered all our secrets. Our secrets are our power. They are ours to share, ours to sell."

"Whatever it is"—Drew was growing tired of Gupta's nee-
dling—"I can probably handle it."

"That is what I like about Americans," Gupta murmured.
"You are such . . . adventurous people. Always looking for the
next big thrill. The ultimate experience."

"And you think this is it?"

"It is stronger than heroin, more powerful than LSD, and
more dangerous than either of them. It is the ultimate experience
because it gives you the experience of death. It takes you on a
journey into the depths of your own soul. You see all your karma
at once—all your past lives, all your future lives. If you are strong,
you survive. If not . . ." He concluded with a shrug.

"Any side effects?" Drew asked, deadpan.

Gupta smiled. "It takes . . . a certain kind of person," he said.
"It is for those who have tried everything and are still not satisfied. Amongst Hindus it is believed that this is only for the lowest
in our society, for those who are completely depraved. But if you
do it once, you have to go back. That is the beauty of it. There is
no other experience like it."

"That's the funny thing about this business, isn't it?" Drew
said. "Depravity just doesn't go as far as it used to."

CHAPTER 15

"**Y**ou want some?" Cora held out a newly lit joint and waited. Annie took it, held it awkwardly between her fingers, and studied it for a moment. She hadn't touched marijuana in years. Not since she was at USC, when she had smoked it just about every weekend. But everybody had done that then. After she graduated, her exposure to it declined, and when she married Michael, it stopped altogether. It was he, of all people, who said they had to live clean. A record for possession was a good way to scuttle a career in the media, especially when that career depended on an ability to shake skeletons out of other people's closets without rattling any of your own. And that was how she had viewed it ever since.

She had avoided dope in India for the same reason, though it was cheaper than liquor and proffered on every street corner. But she had nearly succumbed the previous afternoon when she had spent the afternoon with Cora and a few of her hippie friends. Cora had taken her to a place she called the garden, a sandy hollow in the dunes with a spectacular view of the beach. There had been about half a dozen women and Annie had sunbathed while the others meditated, some of them topless, some completely nude. Afterward she had swum a little then joined in a game of volleyball. Some of the women had played topless and it had emphasized the fact that there was a certain distance between them and her. Annie liked going nude, when it felt right, but there was an element of exhibitionism in playing volleyball topless on a public beach that didn't appeal to her. She wasn't surprised when a few Indian men drifted down to watch, though it didn't seem to bother the other women. Later they had gone back to the garden and a couple of joints had been lit, but Annie had left before she had to make a choice, saying her boyfriend would be worried about her. Now she was being tempted again.

She put the joint to her lips and took a couple of tentative pulls. It burned and she started to cough. She had forgotten about the burn. She hacked out a series of pungent blue cloudlets and passed the joint back to Cora while she caught her breath.

"Bit out of practice," she croaked.

"You lose your tolerance for it," Cora said. "I lay off for a couple of days and the first time I go back, it knocks me right on my ass."

She took two short pulls then expertly nipped the end into a tight bud, tapped the embers into the ashtray, and set the roach to one side for later. It was good dope and there was too much left to justify throwing it away. Annie sank back into the pile of cushions on the floor, glad she could fall no further. She had absorbed no more than a trace of smoke and already she felt a little woozy. It wasn't unpleasant. A slight dreaminess and a touch of déjà vu reminded her what it had been like all those years ago. She would have to be careful when she was offered more later. It was strong. She could easily get out of her depth. She felt a flutter of alarm. Maybe she shouldn't have come. Maybe Sansi was right and she was wrong. She pushed it away, dismissed it as a paranoia rush. She was out of practice, that was all.

It was a little before nightfall and they were in the small and untidy living room of Cora's house, two houses back from the

beach, within earshot of the surf. The house was a five-room
mud-brick bungalow painted pastel yellow. There was a garden
at the back enclosed by a brushwork fence and a verandah out
front shrouded in fine-mesh fishing net that served both as an
adornment and as protection from mosquitoes. They had decided to meet there so Annie could go with Cora and the kids to
Monika's dinner party. It was the first time Annie had seen the
inside of Cora's home, and it had been like stepping into a time
capsule.

The furniture was a random assortment of wicker, bamboo,
and cheap, painted hardwoods. There was a wood-frame sofa
painted pale blue, its thin upholstery hidden beneath elaborately
patterned covers and cushions of all shapes, sizes, and fabrics.
The floor was covered with coir matting, and there was a low
bamboo table in the middle of the room buried beneath weeks,
perhaps months, of household detritus. Bottles, glasses, cups,
ashtrays, books, magazines, music cassettes, a glass bong, a tobacco pouch, cigarette papers, incense sticks, a couple of flashlight batteries, a bottle of Mercurochrome with a few used Q-Tips,
and a bowl of moldering cashews with a tortoise-shell barrette
among them, a few blond strands of hair still attached. Whatever
else Cora might be, Annie realized, she wasn't house-proud.

Two electric lightbulbs hung from the ceiling, one shaded by
a beaded skirt, the other by a bowl of darkly lacquered rattan.
There were a couple of table lamps, too, one of which had a shade
of yellowing rice paper stretched across a crooked wire frame,
the other with a length of red gauze draped over it so it would
cast a rosy red glow when lit. There were fat, garishly marbled
candles, trinket boxes, and ornaments made of wood, silver, and
stained glass. Wind chimes made from seashells hung outside the
back door, while other chimes of copper and stained glass hung
in the windows and splintered the sunlight into giddy, vivid he-
liograms. The walls had been covered with pictures so that barely
an inch of plaster was visible—snapshots of friends and family,
pictures of old rock stars, gurus, and Hindu gods, and most

prominent of all, posters from the sixties—fading originals, dog-eared and timeworn but nevertheless intact. That was what had grabbed Annie's attention when she first arrived—these authentic remnants of the sixties, portholes to the psychedelia of the past. Jim Morrison at the Whiskey. Janis at the Coliseum. The portrait of Juicy Lucy from the Hendrix album *Electric Ladyland*. The foldout cover from *Sergeant Pepper*. The movie poster of *Woodstock*. The Blind Faith poster of the nymphette with the plane. A Bill Graham concert at the Filmore featuring the Grateful Dead, Quicksilver Messenger Service, Iron Butterfly, and Jefferson Airplane. Collector's items, most of them, Annie thought.

"You want a lime juice?" Cora asked.

Annie nodded. "Straight. Ice if you have it."

Cora got up and padded into the kitchen on her bare feet. She wore white cotton harem pants and a man's white undershirt with no bra. Her hair was braided into a thick rope that swung like a pendulum when she walked. She looked very cool and very hip, Annie thought. And she gave the impression that she looked that way without even thinking about it. By comparison, Annie felt as if she had tried too hard to look casual, and all she was wearing were blue jeans and a black T-shirt. Maybe it was the jeans. Maybe they looked too dressy here.

Cora took a pitcher of lime juice out of an ancient electric refrigerator and filled two glasses. Her daughter, Sara, was at the kitchen table playing a game with her Indian dolls—the Indian equivalent of Barbie dolls, Annie assumed. She had yet to meet Paul. He was out surfing, though it was getting dark and Cora had told him to be home by sunset. If he wasn't back soon, she said, she would go down to the beach and get him.

The wooziness had passed, so Annie got to her feet and went back to browsing the snapshots on the wall. She had already found pictures of Cora and the children taken at different places and different stages of their lives, as well as pictures of friends and parties and good times long gone. The other recurring figure was a handsome, bearded man with narrow Celtic features and long black hair that had silvered with great elegance over the years.

"Is this Drew?" Annie asked, nodding to a picture on the wall as Cora returned with the drinks.

"Yeah, that's him," Cora said, and took a sip of her drink.

"Nice-looking man," Annie said. Even as she said it she knew it sounded like an understatement.

"Tell me about it," Cora said. She put down her glass, picked a tape up off the table, and slotted it into the cassette player. There was a ripple of electronic beeps and then the haunting lament of a sinuous tenor sax.

Annie paused.

"I know this."

Cora waited.

A minute passed and then Annie shook her head.

"Gato Barbieri," Cora said. *Los Desperadoes.*"

Annie nodded and went back to cruising the wall, the melancholy saxophone playing in the background. "You've got a lot of good memories tied up in this place."

"We should have left while we still had them."

Annie turned and looked at her. "Mixed feelings?"

"Oh yeah," Cora said. "But it's like I said the other day. We know our time is finished here. This time next year, maybe the year after, there'll be a big, luxury hotel here. The swim-up bar will be about where we are now."

"Property's moving here, too?"

"All the time," Cora said. "Our lease expires in three months. We expect this place will be sold out from under us before then. The bulldozers will move in the day we vacate."

"Where will you go?"

"Back to the States."

This was surprising. "You'd go back home?"

"Not to California," Cora said. "The desert probably. Me and Drew have talked about it. Arizona, New Mexico, west Texas maybe. Somewhere nobody else wants to live so the land is real cheap. We'll buy a few acres and build a place." She smiled and looked around. "We don't need much."

"You'd be a long way from the beach," Annie said.

"They don't make 'em like they used to."

"What would you do?"

"Go back to teaching, probably. Find an alternative school somewhere, or maybe start my own."

"You're a teacher?"

"Well, I'm qualified. But I've never actually done it, apart from my own kids, friends' kids."

"You'd really leave India after all these years?"

"We have to," Cora said. "Times have changed, the place has changed. People here have grown so greedy. We have to face it, you know? Everywhere's pretty well fucked now. Sooner or later the assholes always find a way to your door. All you can do is try and buy yourself a little time."

Annie nodded. They weren't her words, but she knew the tune. It went with the mood, a pall of cynicism that had settled over the whole world, the feeling that the last of the good times had slipped away when nobody was looking. She turned her attention back to the tanned, happy faces on the wall, suspended in eternal unawareness.

"Who's this?" she said, pointing to a snapshot of Cora with another woman in front of what looked like a ruined temple.

Cora came over and looked at the photograph.

"Her name is Cass. That's what everybody called her. I guess you can see why. Her real name is Karen . . . Karen Henke. This picture was taken at Old Goa. It's the place where all the deserted churches and cathedrals are, where the missionaries first came. She was my best friend."

"Was?"

"She left last month. She and her old man, Rick, went back to Ann Arbor. They used to have the house next door, the place that's empty now."

There was a tension in Cora's voice that hadn't been there a moment ago, and Annie realized she was pushing into a delicate area. But she was impelled to go on, to know more about the life Cora had led in Goa—and to know just how much she should trust Cora.

"Why did they leave?" she asked, her voice carefully neutral.

For a moment Cora stood so still she seemed not to breathe. Then she exhaled slowly. She moved slightly to one side and pointed to a snapshot midway up the wall, a picture of two little girls, both blondes, both about seven years old. They were so alike they could have been sisters. One of them, Annie recognized instantly as Sara. The other little girl she didn't know. But looking at her gave Annie an unsettling feeling.

"That's Cassie's daughter," Cora said, pointing to the second girl. "Her name is Tina. She and Sara were best friends, too."

She stopped for a moment, struggling to suppress a tremor in her voice. "She died last month, right here at Anjuna, on the beach. I was one of the first to find her."

"Jesus," Annie breathed. Her feeling had been right. It was the child Sansi had told her about.

Cora turned away from the gallery of memories. "Come out the back," she said, and gestured toward the kitchen where Sara was still playing.

Annie picked up her cigarettes and lighter. Then she followed Cora through the kitchen and down a narrow hallway that led past the bathroom and the bedrooms and out onto the back verandah with its fishnet screen. There were a few dilapidated pieces of wickerwork, a couple of chairs, stools shoved up against the wall to provide back rest, and a table latticed with cigarette burns. A couple of beach towels hung over the back of one chair and an empty bottle of feni was glued to the cement floor. Cora took a chair where she could face Annie and still keep an eye on the houses facing the beach and the sandy path where her son, Paul, should soon appear. Annie took one of the stools and leaned back against the wall, still warm from the heat of the day.

"How is Sara coping?" she asked.

"Not very well," Cora admitted. "But none of us are. We're just better at hiding it than a nine-year-old kid, I guess. She has nightmares. She asks questions. Sometimes I think she understands that Tina's gone and then she asks me something like will she be able to write to Tina." She paused for a moment. "Yesterday was a bad day. She found some things she'd forgotten about. A few plastic bracelets, some beads and necklaces, a couple of rings. It was their secret treasure. She and Tina had hidden it in the yard when they were playing together. They'd put one of my rings in there, too. Some other time I probably would have been pissed at the both of them."

Annie picked up her cigarettes and offered one to Cora, but Cora shook her head.

"I'll finish that joint after Paul gets back," she said. "I need to mellow myself out before we go to Monika's."

Annie lit a cigarette and took a long, hard pull. She welcomed the smoke as it scorched deep into her lungs. Her throat felt sore and constricted and she was afraid it was about to close.

"How did she die?" she asked.

"The cops said she drowned," Cora answered. "But nobody believes that."

"Why not?"

"She was murdered," Cora said. "Everybody knows she was murdered."

"How can you be so sure?"

"She was with us the night she was killed," Cora said. "You know the place in the dunes, the place we call the garden?"

Annie nodded.

"There was a full-moon party that night, and that's where we were because that's where we always go when there's a full-moon party."

"Full-moon party?"

"It's kind of a tradition here," Cora explained. "Every full moon there's a big beach party somewhere on the coast. Thousands of people come. There's music and dope and dancing.

There was supposed to be one this month, but it was canceled. It's finished now, for the season, maybe forever. Last month it was here. There were maybe two thousand people on the beach. It was a mob scene. That's why we were up at the garden."

"Who was there?"

"Me and Drew and the kids," Cora said. "Cass and Rick and Tina, Aggie and her old man. A whole bunch of people. Fifteen or sixteen of us at least."

Annie nodded.

"We had the kids with us so we'd know where they were," Cora went on. "We were all pretty stoned. There'd been a lot of dope and booze and everybody crashed out. Tina was with her mom, for Christ's sake, asleep right next to her. They must have been touching. Paul and Sara were with me.

"Somebody must have been watching us. When we were asleep they crept into the garden and got hold of Tina and took her down to the water. Whether they killed her on the way or she was unconscious when they put her in the water, it doesn't matter. She didn't drown. She was murdered. And I know it could have been any of the kids—but they chose Tina."

"And part of you feels guilty?"

"Yeah," Cora said. "Because I was so goddamned relieved it wasn't one of my kids."

"What about your friend Cass?"

Cora shook her head. "She was catatonic. For days. We were all scared. We thought we were going to lose her, too. Drew couldn't leave Rick alone for a minute because all he wanted to do was OD."

"What, he blamed himself, too?"

"Rick has a few problems," Cora said. "Dope, booze . . . he was wasted the night it happened. He was so out of it, it was two days before he could understand that his daughter was dead."

"And there's no chance she could have drowned?"

"No way," Cora said emphatically. "I mean, what nine-year-old kid gets up in the middle of the night and walks a hundred yards down the beach to go for a swim?" She paused. "Besides, I saw her body, remember? There were marks on her neck. Bruises. Somebody choked her."

"Then why would the police lie about it?"

Cora looked at her. "Because it was the cops who killed her."

"The police?"

"Yeah," Cora said. "The fucking cops killed her."

"Why would they want to kill a child?" Annie asked. "What possible threat could a nine-year-old girl present to the police department that would result in her being murdered?"

"It wasn't Tina who was the threat," Cora said quietly. "It was all of us. Tina just got singled out, that's all, as the best way to deliver the message. That's why it could just as easily have been one of my kids if either one of them had been sleeping a little closer to the edge."

"You mean it's all because of real estate? They want you off the land so they can buy it up faster?"

"What else?" Cora said. "The cops and the government are in it with all the other land sharks. The cops are just hired muscle for the developers. That's why we've had this harassment campaign for the past six months. It's been getting heavier and heavier all the time. More and more busts, roadblocks, hassles everywhere you go. They hate us. Not just because we're in the way but because a lot of people here are opposed to the railroad and they're helping out with the environmental campaign. The sharks are scared somebody in Delhi will notice, so they want to put an end to it now. This is their way of telling us our time is up. They've finished screwing around. They want us out—tomorrow. So what do they do? They kill somebody. But not just anybody. Not some tourist passing through or some hippie that nobody cares about. They kill a kid who lives here with her family, so everybody notices. Now everybody is scared."

"And that's the real reason you're getting out?"

"You don't think it's enough?"

"What I don't understand is why you're still here," Annie said.

"I can see you've got a lot of time and sentiment tied up in this place, but I have to tell you, if it was me and my kids, I'd have been on a plane weeks ago."

Cora remained silent for a long time. Then she looked pointedly at Annie.

"Can I trust you?" she said. "I mean, if I tell you something, I really need to know I can trust you."

Annie felt a sudden surge of guilt. "Yes," she said. "You can."

Cora hesitated a moment longer, then nodded. "Okay," she said. "You've seen how it is with dope around here?"

Annie nodded.

"Well," Cora went on, "there aren't a lot of ways to make money in this place. Drew gets a share of the donations to the ashram, but it's not enough to live on. So he does a little dealing on the side. Nothing heavy. Only grass, hash, acid, a little opium. He doesn't do heroin. And he only sells to people he knows."

"Uh-huh."

"He has a couple of connections," Cora went on. "One of them is a guy called Gupta. A big-time hood from Bombay. He lives in a big pink house out at Miramar. Drew went to see him, just to put the word out, try to make things right for a while. He wanted to tell them we got the message, we're going, and Drew would use his influence to make sure there were no more problems with the environmental thing, no more fighting the railroad, no more pipe bombs at the work sites, no more protests. All we wanted was a couple of months to get it together, you know?"

"Is there a chance this guy, Gupta, could be behind Tina's murder?"

"We don't know who gave the order. All we know is that it was the cops who did it. They could have been acting on their own."

"And you think you bought some time?"

"All Drew knows is that Gupta said he'd see what he could do. That's where Drew is tonight, trying to make sure everything is okay."

"Jesus . . ." Annie lapsed into silence. It was just as Sansi had said. On the surface Goa looked like paradise. Underneath, it was a murderous cesspool of vice, drugs, and greed, where nobody could trust anybody and nothing was the way it seemed. Sansi had been right. But Annie's instinct about Cora had been borne out, too. Cora had been completely truthful. She had confirmed everything Sansi had said . . . and more.

A small dark shape appeared suddenly in the footpath between the houses. A moment later a handsome young man with a surfboard under his arm bobbed toward them through the dusk. He leaned the surfboard against the verandah rail, ducked under the fishnet, and grabbed a towel from the back of a chair to dry himself. His long blond hair trailed down his back in a serpentine slick and water ran in small rivulets from his fashionable, knee-length shorts. Cora got up with a relieved smile on her face, gave him a brief hug, and kissed him on top of his head. When Cora stepped away from him, there were big wet sandy patches on her shirt and pants.

"Annie," she said. "This is my son, Paul."

"I'm very pleased to meet you, Paul," Annie said formally.

Paul looked frankly back at her, weighed her carefully for a moment, and said, "Yeah." Then he threw the towel back onto the chair and went into the house.

"There's fresh juice in the refrigerator," Cora called after him. "And you better put on something dry. We're going to Monika's in a few minutes. She's doing supper tonight."

"I'm sure everybody says the same thing," Annie said. "But he is almost an exact replica of his father."

"I know," Cora said. "I sometimes wonder if I'm his real mother."

Annie smiled. Cora remained standing and Annie knew she was about to go back inside to see to the needs of her children and finish that joint that was waiting. But there was something more Annie wanted to know before they were finished.

She said, "You seem pretty sure it's the police who are responsible for Tina's death."

Cora nodded. She used a bare toe to trace a pattern on the floor in the puddle of seawater her son had left behind. "Have you heard of a cop called Tony Dias in Panjim?"

Annie shook her head.

"He's the chief of the drug squad," Cora said. "And he's really, really dirty. He was here the night of the full-moon party, the night Tina was killed. He and a few of his thugs, hassling people, looking for busts. But that was just a cover."

"That doesn't mean he's the murderer," Annie said.

"It was Dias or one of his thugs," Cora said with an air of finality.

"You said yourself there were two thousand people on the beach that night. That means two thousand suspects."

Cora looked up from the pattern on the floor. "You know how the cops pick up a little extra cash in Goa?" she asked.

Annie thought she knew what was coming. She tried to keep her eyes and her face blank.

"They hang on to the bodies of dead foreigners until their next of kin pay a bribe. Cass and Rick were told they couldn't have Tina's body back until they paid the cops two thousand dollars. They didn't have that kind of money and there was no way they could get their hands on it. Like I said before, they were zombies. They just wanted to go home. So Drew paid the bribe for them. Drew took care of everything for them. And that's why we have to stay on here a little longer. We're a little low on cash right now. We need the time to get some money together so we can save our own goddamn lives."

Annie could scarcely believe the feelings that were swirling around inside her. For the first time in her life she knew what it was like to feel sympathy, maybe even admiration, for a drug dealer. What was insane was that, in the inverted logic of India, it made a certain kind of sense.

"There's something else I didn't mention," Cora said.

Annie waited.

"You know how some people believe that when a person is murdered, the image of the murderer is trapped in their eyes and you'd know who it was if you could only find a way to get it out?"

Annie believed there were others who believed such things, but she had never bought into that kind of superstition.

"Yeah," Cora said, reading her expression. "I know how it sounds—but I believe it now. Because I saw Tina's face. And I swear the image of her killer was still in that child's eyes. She knew who it was and she was trying to tell us . . . if we could only read her eyes."

■   ■

It was almost two o'clock in the morning and Sansi waited in the darkness of the deserted market, across the side street from the warehouse owned by the Goa Produce Company, and wondered if Dr. Sapeco would find the nerve to go through with it. So far the situation was pretty much the way he had expected it to be. The street was dimly lit and thick with concealing shadows, but it was never empty. Dogs prowled and squabbled and chased after rats. People slept at the side of the road on mattresses made from hemp stretched across bamboo frames. Some slept in the dirt amid the rotting produce. A few huddled together beneath an occasional streetlight, smoking, drinking chai, chewing *paan*, and passing the night away.

Sansi had driven past the front of the building once already and seen that the front door was open. Three security guards had set up stools in the doorway where they could enjoy the slight breeze instead of sweltering inside the warehouse. From where he hid, Sansi could see that every few minutes one of the guards would go to the corner and glance down the street to make sure everything was all right. Once, in the hour he had been waiting, he had seen two of the guards do a slow patrol around the entire building. Once again Sansi felt a pang of uncertainty. No matter how confident Gupta might be, it didn't seem like anywhere near enough security if several million dollars' worth of heroin was hidden away inside. Unless there were guards inside, too, which he would discover soon enough.

He looked at the luminous hands of his watch again. It was two o'clock. Everything depended on Sapeco now. There was nothing Sansi could do but hide in the shadows, ignore the scuffing and scuttling of rats all around him, and wait. He opened and closed his fingers on the steel handles of the bolt cutters in his right hand and then did the same with the flashlight in his left hand. His fingers had grown stiff and his hands were slippery with sweat.

Three blocks away, Dr. Francesco Sapeco, general practitioner, senior surgeon at Margao Hospicio, former police surgeon and forensic examiner for the government of Goa, tootled through the streets on his mission of terror. He had already made one pass by the Ashoka Construction Company's works depot, but there had been too many people in the area and he had kept going. This time the corner was deserted, but Sapeco felt even more afraid. He had no excuse now for not going ahead with it. He rolled past the front gates and the big company sign on the chain-link fence with the heavy machinery parked in rows behind it. He slowed down a fraction, but his nerve faltered and he tweaked the accelerator and sped away. Then he applied the brakes again. Firmly this time. Enough to make sure he was committed. The scooter shimmied and the gasoline-filled bottles in the luggage compartment clinked menacingly. He jumped down before the scooter had come to a complete stop and stood it against the curb. He opened the lid of the luggage compartment and grimaced as the stench of gasoline fumes rushed up at him. He pulled out two tightly capped bottles, looked at them briefly, then turned and lobbed them over the chain-link fence at the nearest piece of machinery, a bulldozer on a flatbed truck.

Sansi had made up the bottles for him and told him what to do. It was simple enough. Of the six bottles, five were sealed and

only one had a fuse. Sansi had assured him that only one was
needed to ignite the gasoline.

The bottles arced over the fence and smashed against the
bulldozer. Sapeco watched as the gasoline spread a wet, shiny
stain down the side of the bulldozer, dripped onto the truck, and
formed sinister little puddles on the ground. He heard a growling
sound on the other side of the fence, then a rush of noise and violence as a large German shepherd hurled itself furiously at the
chain mesh. The voices of security guards sounded from the
other side of the depot. Hurriedly he grabbed two more bottles
and lobbed them over the fence, too. He directed them all at
the same target. Sansi told him it was better to put them all in the
same place rather than try to start a lot of little fires. This way he
could be reasonably certain of getting one good blaze started.

Sapeco hurled the last of the capped bottles over the fence
then picked up the bottle with the fuse. His hands shook as he
held the bottle upright and fumbled for the lighter in his pants
pocket. He had tried not to get any gasoline on his clothes, but
the bottles had been smeared with it and his hands and clothes
stank of it now. The voices drew closer. The sound of running
feet. Something moved on the sidewalk, only a few feet away.
Sapeco started in alarm. It was a beggar, another pile of rags
asleep on the street, now a dazed witness to Sapeco's act of
terrorism.

Sapeco flicked the cheap plastic lighter. It flared and he gave
a small, involuntary gasp of fear, convinced he was about to turn
himself into a human torch. He held it to the twisted rag stuffed
in the neck of the bottle and it caught immediately, a lurid blos-
som of flame. Panicked, he threw it over the fence, but he threw
low and it hit the top of the fence. For one dreadful moment
Sapeco thought it would explode all over him. It didn't. The
bottle burst and its contents splashed over the ground, leaving the rag caught in the mesh at the top of the fence, burning
harmlessly.

A figure in uniform came into view on the other side of the fence, running toward him between the dark ranks of machinery. Then another and another. Their voices grew louder, warning him to stop. The dog launched itself at the fence in a frenzy. Sapeco looked at the lighter, useless in his hands. He flicked it into life again and flung it over the fence toward the dripping pile of machinery, but it snapped shut and the flame died before it landed. Sapeco knew it was too late. He had failed.

He hurried back to his scooter, opened the accelerator wide, and sped off up the street, gasping to himself with fear. He was fifty to sixty yards away when the burning rag on the fence disintegrated into a dozen tiny pieces and a few fiery fragments fluttered into the compound like drunken fireflies and landed on the fuel-soaked dirt. The effect was spectacular. The ground erupted in a vivid, fiery mosaic. A few spidery tendrils leaped wickedly at the flatbed truck and the bulldozer. The puddles beneath the truck ignited all at once and a monstrous wall of flame erupted around the big machines with a terrifying roar.

The guard dog scrabbled away yelping, its fur singed and smoldering. The security guards threw themselves backward, away from the instant inferno. One of them turned and ran for the security hut to call the fire department. The others picked themselves up and scrambled to move the machines nearest the blaze before the bulldozer and the truck could explode.

Six blocks away, Dr. Francesco Sapeco, urban terrorist, heard the whoosh of the explosion and saw the buildings on both sides of the street illuminated briefly by a brilliant yellow light. But he didn't slow down or stop to survey his handiwork. He didn't glance back over his shoulder to see what damage he had done. He kept going, away from the town center, away from Margao, as quickly as his scooter would carry him.

From his hiding place in the shadows of the market arcade, Sansi watched the effects of Sapeco's terrorist act with illicit satisfaction. First there was the thump of the explosion, then the radiant glow of the fire behind the rooftops—and then instant uproar. All the sleeping bodies stirred at once and struggled to their feet as the alarm spread. Those who were already awake ran to the main street to see what had happened. Within moments the side street was almost empty and the street in front of the warehouse was filled with shouting, running people.

He stepped out of the darkness and crossed the street at a fast walk. When he got to the first loading bay, he climbed onto the ledge and knelt down beside the roller door. He worked the blades of the bolt cutters around the steel arm of the padlock and squeezed hard. It split apart with a single loud crack. He lifted the door no more than a foot and a half, quickly rolled underneath, and pulled it shut behind him. Then he lay still and listened. It was better than he had hoped for. The uproar outside would have masked everything. No one could have heard him come in.

The rear of the warehouse was dark, where Sansi was, and there were shadows between the high stacked rows of produce, but there were lights in the offices at the front of the building that spilled through the dirty windows and gave the front half of the warehouse a dusky amber glow. Sansi found himself in an aisle wide enough to accommodate a forklift between sacks of rice piled to the top of the walls. He eased forward a few feet and peered down the next aisle toward the front of the building. The warehouse contained thousands of sacks of rice. He couldn't search every one. What he had to look for was something that was different in some small way from everything else in the warehouse, and he didn't have long to find it. He gave himself half an hour, no more. By then the shock of the firebomb attack should have worn off—and there was always the possibility that the guards might come back sooner.

Sansi crept along the aisle, patting the bags of rice as he went, looking, feeling, sniffing, searching for that one small thing that didn't look quite right. There was nothing. He came to the end of the first aisle and turned into the second—more bags of rice, all stamped with the name of the company and the words APPROVED

FOR EXPORT—INDIA CUSTOMS, though they had never passed under
the eye of an honest customs officer and probably never would.
In the next aisle the bags of rice gave way to a series of wooden
crates marked GENERATOR SPARES and PUMPING UNIT PARTS. A couple of crates stood alone from the others and looked as if they had
been opened recently and resealed.

Sansi took out his penknife and started working the screws
loose on the corner of the first crate. It was several minutes before he was able to slide a single wooden bar to one side. He
shone the flashlight inside and saw wads of packing foam. He
reached in and probed through the squeaky chunks of foam until
his fingers closed on something cold and heavy and metallic. He
lifted it out and examined it in his flashlight beam. It was a small
carburetor wrapped in clear plastic, exactly the kind of spare part
that would be needed for a portable generator. It could have been
cast with a hollow center to hold a kilo of heroin, but it felt too
heavy, too solid. He put the piece back and rummaged around
until his fingers closed on something else—another carburetor.
He put it back, replaced the wooden bar, screwed it quickly in
place, and moved on to the next crate. This time he found filters,
filter caps, and O-rings, all genuine spares for pumping machinery. He glanced at his watch. He had been in the warehouse for
almost twenty minutes. He decided he would waste no more time
on the packing crates. He set off down the next aisle, probing and
patting the stacked bags of rice. Still he found nothing unusual.
At the rear of the warehouse he looped around into the next aisle
and started working his way forward again.

When he came to the end of the aisle, he looked around the
open area at the front of the warehouse. There were perhaps
twenty feet between the last bags of rice and the ground-floor office. The office door had a frosted-glass panel set into the top half
that showed the light was on, though there was no sign of movement on the other side. There was also a metal staircase that led
to the second floor. Beside the staircase was a soft-drink machine
and a couple of ice chests that Sansi had glimpsed on his first

brief reconnaissance. Next to one of the ice chests was a large, steel washbasin. Next to the basin, fitted snugly into the corner, was an L-shaped workbench. Beneath the workbench were a number of paper bags and what looked like several rolls of clear plastic.

Sansi crept through the amber twilight and ran his flashlight beam over the workbench. The bench was covered with a thin sheet of metal, scratched and dented by years of use. Half its surface was covered by a clutter of tools, industrial cutters, staple guns, bits and pieces of plastic, balls of twine, and rolls of tape—nothing that didn't belong in a working warehouse. The other half of the workbench was strangely bare, as if it had been wiped clean to remove all trace of whatever work had been done there. Sansi leaned down and examined the surface more closely. He came so close that his cheek touched the metal. It felt cold, and when he moved away he left a smudge of condensation. He ran his fingers over one long scratch in the metal surface and held them up. He could see white powder, the grains so fine he could barely feel them. He put his fingers to his nose and sniffed. The powder had a slight chemical odor that he didn't recognize. Heroin had no odor. But it could be a chemical used in the manufacture of heroin. It was possible that Gupta was running his own laboratory in Goa.

Sansi rubbed his fingers clean. Then he knelt down and trained his flashlight on the bags underneath the bench. There were at least a dozen of them made from heavy-duty packing paper stitched shut with plastic twine. Some were unmarked, though others had words stenciled on the side. Sansi leaned closer.

"*Bakwas,*" he muttered, the Hindi word for "bullshit."

According to the stenciled descriptions, the bags contained plaster of paris.

He took out his penknife again and nicked the bottom corner of the nearest bag so it would look as if it had been gnawed by a rat. A column of fine white powder spilled out through the hole and formed a neat cone on the floor. Sansi took a small plastic bag from his shirt pocket and used his penknife to spoon in the equivalent of two tablespoons of powder. Then he tied a knot in the neck of the bag and tucked it back in his pocket.

When he was finished he dipped his fingers into the ruined cone and sniffed them again. The powder smelled the same as the sample he had gotten from the top of the workbench. He wiped his hand on his pants, stood up, and looked around. He was starting to feel desperate, thinking he might have made a mistake. Sweat dripped off his forehead and left shiny blotches on the metal surface of the workbench. The only other containers that might hold something illicit were a couple of metal drums under the washbasin. One was a large blue drum labeled detergent; the other was smaller and a dull, grayish green and identified only by a black skull and bones, the poison symbol. He prized the lid off the blue drum first. It was half-full with a viscous yellow liquid and gave off a powerful detergent smell. Even so, he took another plastic bag from his pocket and helped himself to a sample. Then he put the lid back and turned to the second, smaller drum. It opened easily, and when he shone his flashlight inside, he saw that it was three-quarters full of white powder. This powder had a sharp, acrid smell. There was something familiar about it, though he couldn't remember where he had smelled it last—and he was almost certain it wasn't heroin. He took out another of his bags and helped himself to two spoonfuls anyway.

He put the lid back, got to his feet, and checked his watch again. His thirty minutes were up. He wiped the sweat from his face and looked around. Still there was no one. The uproar outside continued unabated. Far away he thought he heard the bells of a fire engine.

Sansi hesitated. He had no samples of anything that seemed to be heroin. Without the drug—and the name of a ship or destination for it—all their risk and effort would be wasted.

He ran his flashlight along the bench again. There was something on the wall over the bench. An untidy thicket of papers held together by heavy clips. This might be what he needed—export documents, consignment notes—anything to connect the Goa Produce Company to a ship.

He leafed quickly through the papers, but they turned out to be lists of machinery parts, the contents of the wooden crates. He turned his attention to the offices at the front of the warehouse. They were the center of the warehousing operation. If incriminating paperwork was to be found anywhere, it was almost certainly in one of those offices. Sansi moved quickly to the ground-floor office. He turned the handle and pushed, but the door was locked. He couldn't risk breaking into the office, because then they would know there had been an intruder. He hesitated. There wasn't time to do anything else. He turned to go, his eyes resting briefly on the ice chests. He hadn't thought to check them.

Sansi walked to the nearest ice chest and cautiously lifted the lid. A cold fog hissed out at him and coated his face with a clammy sheen. The fog cleared and he peered inside. The chest held about a dozen bags of ice and a couple of clear plastic bags packed with what looked like frozen meat. He reached inside and moved the meat bags so he could see underneath, but there was nothing except more ice. He lowered the lid and went to the other ice chest. When he opened it the same cold fog wheezed out at him, misting his face and eyes. With it came a harsh, chemical odor that was completely unexpected—the acrid stench of formaldehyde, the same smell that enveloped him in the autopsy room at crime branch in Bombay and clung to his clothes for days afterward. Then the fog cleared and he found himself looking at the open-jawed face of a corpse.

Sansi recoiled, and the lid slipped from his grasp and slammed shut. His heart thudded painfully in his chest. He looked around, listening for voices or the sound of running feet, but there was nothing. He lifted the lid carefully and looked back into the ice chest. The body was that of a young white man inside an open plastic body bag on top of the ice. His legs had been

drawn up at the knees to fit him into the freezer. His skin was
bluish gray. His hair was medium length and thickly encrusted
with ice particles, so it was impossible to be sure what color it
was. He was clean shaven and his eyes were closed though the
jaw was wide apart, locked in rigor mortis. The tongue was a
twisted rag that protruded slightly from the side of the mouth.
Frost particles glistened on the teeth and inside the nostrils. Unpleasant as the face was, what disturbed Sansi most was the condition of the torso.

The chest had been cleaved apart cleanly and expertly from
the throat to the pubic bone and opened as if prepared for an autopsy. But instead of the internal organs, exposed for examination, there was nothing. The corpse had been gutted like an
animal in a slaughterhouse. This was the husk of what had once
been a human being—reduced to nothing more than a meat-and-
bones carcass.

Sansi heard something—a door slamming, then footsteps. He
lowered the ice chest lid quickly and carefully and hurried back
into the shadows. Another door opened and the voices of two
men rang loudly through the warehouse. Sansi ran as fast as he
dared back to the unlocked roller door. He eased the door up a
fraction, dropped to the ground and rolled outside. The lights
came on just as he closed the door behind him. He took a sec-
ondhand padlock from his pocket and snapped it shut on the
door. Then he picked up the broken lock, the flashlight, and bolt
cutters and scurried across the street, back to the enveloping
darkness of the market arcade. A few people saw him pass, but no
one paid him much attention. The streets were full of excited,
running people.

Sansi walked briskly past the darkened storefronts where
many *kulis* remained stubbornly asleep on the bare boards of the
stalls despite all the noise. He threw the broken padlock high
over the buildings to his right, and a few yards farther on, he
dropped the bolt cutters into an oil drum filled with rotting produce. Carrying only the flashlight, he continued to the end of the

arcade before turning to look behind him. Nobody was following. Nobody had noticed. Nobody cared. He stopped for a moment to catch his breath, but the stink of putrefaction was everywhere and it flooded into his lungs like a thick and noxious vapor. The image of the gutted corpse in the ice chest came back to him— and with it the awful realization of what had been in the other ice chest—the frozen lumps of meat. He tried to suppress the nausea that boiled up inside him, but it was no use. He grabbed wildly for something to hang on to, to try to steady himself. Then, noisily and violently, he emptied the contents of his stomach onto the pavement.

CHAPTER 16

Prem Gupta's smoke-blue Contessa nudged its way through the heavy traffic on Heliodoro Salgado Road until Gupta grew impatient with their slow progress and told his driver to pull over. He and Drew got out of the car and continued on foot, with Gupta's two goons following a few paces behind.

It was a little after eleven and the streets of Panjim were raucous with vice and commerce. The stores were all open, their brightly lit windows full of cheap jewelry, electronic junk, and trashy souvenirs. The tavernas and restaurants were crowded, spilling laughter, loud music, and clouds of marijuana smoke into the fumey night air. All along the street hustlers, beggars, and pimps harried the passing parade of tourists the way wild dogs would harry a herd of cattle.

Gupta led the way to the end of the block then turned down a gloomy backstreet. In Bombay it would have been jammed with slum shanties, but because Panjim was small and prosperous, it was almost empty except for a few scavenging dogs and the odd group of men engaged in something illicit. There were houses on both sides of the street, most of them converted into offices and small businesses with apartments over the top, where the occupants could be seen through open windows eating, drinking, laughing, arguing—acting out the intimacies of their lives in public. Occasionally the back door of a taverna would open and a kitchen wallah would step outside to smoke a *bidi* or decant a bucket of swill into an overflowing garbage bin.

The houses were all two or three stories high, old town villas painted brown and blue or rusty red and linked together in a haphazard way, so that their rooftops lurched and swooped into each other at all different heights and angles. With their painted exteriors and brilliantly lit interiors, they looked like a chain of paper lanterns. It could have been the waterfront in Lisbon rather than India.

Drew tried to project an aura of calm, but inwardly he was afraid. If Gupta wanted to kill him, it would happen something like this—lured to some squalid backstreet under the guise of business as usual, then a sudden and unpleasant death. His fingers wandered nervously over the heavy brass buckle on his belt, which could be twisted and jerked loose to reveal a short knife blade. Its complete inadequacy under the circumstances only added to his fear. He shouldn't have come. He had miscalculated badly. His early-warning system, usually reliable, had let him down this time. His relationship with Gupta had always been fractious, and now Gupta had grown tired of him and elected to teach him a lesson. Drew thought about making a run for it. It would be better to risk making a fool of himself than to tough it out and wind up dead.

A raw-ribbed dog darted in front of them and lunged at something in the shadows. There was a scuttling sound, a high-pitched squeal, then the dog reappeared with a rat twitching in its jaws. Gupta gave Drew an amused glance. Drew looked straight ahead, his muscles tense, ready to run.

At last they came to a small print shop with a solid-looking door at the side. The shop was closed, but Gupta banged on the door hard. There was a moment's delay, then the door opened a crack and a man's face appeared—thin, dissipated, and wearing a ragged turban. He knew Gupta and opened the door wide, pressing his hands together and murmuring the words *"Namaste sahib"* over and over. Gupta told the two goons to wait outside and stepped into the shop. Drew hesitated, peered through the open doorway, and saw an empty hall lit by a single lightbulb. Then he looked at the goons. He was relieved that Gupta was leaving them outside. Maybe his instincts had been right after all. Maybe there was no danger. Maybe Gupta was only playing with him, the way he always did. Drew's instincts had always served him well in the past. He summoned up all his nerve and followed Gupta into the building.

The hall was dingy and bare and smelled of machine oil. There was a door to the right that seemed to lead into the print shop and a narrow staircase directly in front of them. The door-man shut the door behind them and pointed to the stairs. Gupta went first, with Drew a short distance behind. When they were out of sight, the doorman squatted back down on the bottom step, took a *bidi* out of his shirt pocket, and lit it.

At the top of the stairs was a high-ceilinged, poorly lit corridor that ran toward the front of the building with two or three doors on each side, all of them closed. Drew assumed they were in a private apartment over the print shop, but the shop only occupied the back half of the building. There was no indication of what was at the front. Gupta kept going toward a door at the end of the corridor. He turned the handle and the door opened onto a room that was in total darkness. He turned and beckoned impatiently for Drew to follow. Again Drew hesitated, his fingers clasped around the belt buckle.

"What's going on here, man? What is this place?" He tried to sound calm, but he could hear the fear in his voice.

"Shut up," Gupta whispered. "I want you to see something."

Drew moved slowly forward. His legs felt weak and wooden. Sweat poured down his back, soaking his T-shirt and the waistband of his jeans. He was within a few feet of the open door when he realized that the room was not completely dark. There was a pale yellow glow at floor level, a window of some kind with a light behind it. Drew looked quickly around the room and saw the outline of some furniture—junk piled in a corner, a sofa, and a few straight-backed metal chairs arranged in front of the window to form a kind of viewing gallery. The only figure visible seemed to be Gupta.

"Come in and close the door," Gupta said. "And don't make any noise."

It took every last bit of nerve that he possessed, but Drew did as he was told. With the door closed, the room became dark and threatening, and Drew felt vulnerable again.

"Sit down and watch," Gupta said. "And whatever happens, you don't say or do anything."

Gupta moved to a chair at the far side of the window and sat down with his back to Drew, telling him there was nothing to fear. The fear crested in Drew's throat, then subsided again. He felt his way numbly through the darkness and took the seat next to Gupta. Then he looked down at the window at his feet.

It wasn't a window at all, he realized, but a glass-paneled louver, one of many that would allow cool air to circulate from the downstairs of the house to the upstairs. The building had once been a commodious town house owned by some Portuguese grandee, though it had long since been bastardized and partitioned into numerous shops and apartments.

Drew tensed as Gupta leaned toward him in the darkness.

"If I wanted to have you killed," Gupta said, "I wouldn't go to this much trouble."

Despite his fear, Drew smiled. His instincts were right. Gupta had only been playing with him. But his nerve had held and Gupta still didn't know how close Drew had come to running.

He turned his attention to the window at his feet and found himself looking into a bare-walled room with a single door, no windows, and no furniture except a single mattress on the floor. The distant hum of the city told him the room was situated in the middle of the house, which made it virtually soundproof. There was a man in the room, sitting cross-legged on a thin black cushion with his back to the wall facing the door. Drew could not see his face because it was obscured by a large, grayish turban with a puggaree that hung down his back. He was dressed in a white *kurta dhoti*, the shirt and loincloth favored by traditional Hindus. His bony hands were folded comfortably in his lap, the fingernails a bright pink against skin the color of jute. At his side was a stick with a cushioned handle at one end. It looked like a crutch, though it was only a couple of feet long. In front of him, on the floor, was a crumpled burlap bag.

Drew stared at the bag. Something inside it stirred.

"Goddamn . . ." Drew said. "What is it?"

Gupta reached over to him and squeezed his arm hard. Then he jabbed a finger at the window, and suddenly Drew understood. The louvers were open slightly. Anything that was said in this darkened room could be heard downstairs. And everything that was said downstairs could be heard above.

If the man in the room below had heard, it didn't show. He remained quite still, like a guru or a swami, meditating. Drew settled down to wait. He would show them. He could wait, too. However long it took.

After a while the door downstairs opened and a man dressed like a house servant appeared. He padded across the tiled floor on bare feet, whispered something to the swami, then turned and went back out of the room. The swami gave no indication that he had seen or heard anything. A few more minutes passed and then the servant reappeared with two men in their twenties who looked like *kulis*. Their clothes were dirty and their hair was long and matted. Whatever money they made wasn't spent on their appearance. The servant spoke softly to them and they slipped off their sandals, pressed their hands together, and bobbed respectfully to the swami. He did not acknowledge them in any way.

"Who are they?" Drew whispered.

"Laborers," Gupta answered. "They have come down from Bombay to work on the railway."

Drew leaned forward so he could see better, his fear supplanted by the morbid fascination of the voyeur.

The servant set two more cushions on the floor in front of the swami, one in front of the other, then stood back against the door. One of the *kulis* took off his shirt, folded it, and put it on the mattress like a pillow. Then, bare-chested, he stepped across to the first cushion and sat down, cross-legged, so that he faced the swami, the burlap bag between them. The other *kuli* followed and squatted on the cushion behind his friend.

For a long time no one moved and no one made a sound. All three men remained perfectly still with their heads slightly bowed. Then the murmur of a chant began to emanate from the swami, a high-pitched nasal mantra that Drew had not heard before, either in the ashram at Pune or the temple at Madurai. He strained to hear the words, but the swami ran them together so rapidly they blurred into an unintelligible drone. Drew thought he heard the name Ananta. He listened closely and this time he was certain. The swami said the name Ananta several times, but repeated it so quickly it was almost indistinguishable through the monotone.

Drew recognized the name. Ananta was the many-headed cobra in Hindu mythology, the force of eternal life.

The swami moved for the first time, precisely and fluidly. He gripped the bottom two corners of the burlap bag, shook it gently, and lifted it into the air. A tightly coiled cobra slid out onto the floor in front of him. The swami put the bag down at his side and picked up the stick with the padded handle. He held it by the shaft with the handle pointed away from him. The snake remained motionless. The swami reached forward with his free hand and prodded the cobra out of its defensive coil. The snake reacted sluggishly, reluctantly, and did not attempt to strike. Instead it rippled the length of its shiny black body and started to

move across the floor, away from the swami, looking for a means
of escape. The swami wielded the stick quickly and deftly. He
aimed the handle at a point just behind the reptile's head and
pinned it to the floor. This time the snake reacted angrily. Its
thick body whipped and thrashed as it tried to get away. From his
position overhead Drew heard the harsh scrape of the cobra's
scales against the floor. Still, no one else had moved. Drew
watched, transfixed. He knew what was about to happen and still
he couldn't quite bring himself to believe it.

The swami kept the cobra's head pinned to the floor beneath
the padded handle of the stick then reached forward with his
other hand. He spanned the snake with his thumb and forefinger
and ran his hand up the warm dry body until he came to the flat
bulge of the head. He stopped for a moment. Slowly, carefully, he
worked his hand the last few inches, feeling the tough, rubbery
cartilage under the scales, until his fingers were right behind the
jaw. Again he stopped. This was the most dangerous moment.
The moment when everything had to be coordinated just right.
He pinched his thumb and forefinger together fractionally until
he could feel the hinge of the cobra's jaw. If he pinched too
tightly, he would choke the snake and kill it. If he pinched
too loosely, it would break free and bite him.

The cobra writhed violently, coiling and uncoiling around his
arm. The swami dropped the stick and lifted the enraged snake
into the air. Its hood flared, its fangs glistened, and a loud, threatening hiss filled the room as it fought to escape its tormentor. The
swami got up onto his knees and used both hands to try to hold
the cobra still. The *kuli* on the first cushion leaned back to avoid
the serpent's thrashing tail. His friend held him by the shoulders
and patted him on the back. In the room above, Drew felt his
flesh grow cold and clammy.

"Shit . . ."

At last the swami brought the snake under his control and
settled back on his haunches. Then he turned to face the man in
front of him. Slowly, he held out the serpent's head, offering it.

The *kuli* paused, preparing himself. His chest rose and fell quickly. Sweat glistened on his thin body. Then he too leaned forward. Slowly and deliberately, he closed the gap between himself and the cobra's darting tongue. With only inches separating them, he extended his own tongue toward the snake. As if to taunt it. To taste it. To savor the moment of contact, the catalyst that would plunge him into the primal energy stream and carry him to that dark and dangerous place that lingered somewhere between life and death.

His companion edged up behind him, holding him, bracing him. The man leaned closer. The cobra's tongue flickered and brushed the extended human tongue. The man flinched and gave a slight gasp, but he didn't pull back. Instead, he leaned closer. The swami leaned closer, too, and closed the gap between them. The cobra extended its fangs, lunged, and bit deep into the offered flesh. The man uttered a choking cry of pain and tried to pull away. But his friend held him firm and the swami followed with his hand so that the cobra continued to pump its venom into the sensitive tissue. Once, twice, three times. Then the swami jerked the snake's head upward and back in a single swift motion so that the fangs came out quickly and cleanly, without tearing the tongue.

The *kuli* fell backward into his friend's lap and gave a series of short, breathless cries. His eyes stared wildly, his face was an agonized grimace, and his arms and legs spasmed uncontrollably. His companion held him and whispered to him, but he seemed unable to hear. Inside his body, behind the staring eyes, the neurotoxins in the cobra venom burned through his bloodstream like napalm, searing the nervous system, shutting down the respiratory system, assailing the muscles of the heart, and igniting an hallucinatory firestorm in the synapses of the brain.

He slipped deeper and deeper into coma. His breathing became shallower and he mumbled in Marathi. Then his voice weakened and faded to nothing. The fibrillations in his heart stopped and his pulse started to fall. His chest stopped moving and his limbs stopped twitching as paralysis became complete. Finally, his head lolled to one side, his eyes half-closed, his mouth open and slack. Blood from his punctured tongue trickled thickly down his chin and dripped onto his chest. Then that, too, stopped.

For a moment nobody moved or spoke. Then the swami picked up the burlap bag and dropped the writhing cobra inside. Returned to its dark nest, relieved of its venom and its fury, the cobra became still and docile again. The swami pushed the sack against the wall and settled back to wait. The servant beside the door stepped forward and helped the other *kuli* lift his companion onto the mattress. They wiped the blood from his face and chest and arranged him so that he was on his side, his head cradled on one arm. The man's companion sat down to wait. The servant opened the door and disappeared. The swami sat on his cushion, silent and indifferent.

Drew felt something brush against his arm and he gasped and pulled away. Gupta took him by the elbow and prodded him toward the door. It was only when they were outside again in the jaundiced light of the corridor that Drew realized how fiercely his heart was pounding. How afraid he was—and how excited. He pushed his hair back from his face. It was soaked with sweat. His body was slick with it. He wiped the palms of his hands nervously against his pants. Gupta watched him with an amused half smile.

"That guy's not dead, is he?" Drew asked. "He can't be dead?"

"No," Gupta answered. "There wasn't enough venom for that. He will be in a coma for about twenty-four hours. When he comes out of it, he will feel as if he has been born again."

"Okay," Drew said, though he still did not understand. "What happens to him now, for the next twenty-four hours?"

"He has already experienced many fantastic things," Gupta said. "In his mind he has been killed. He has experienced terror and tranquillity. Now he knows nothing. That is how it will be for the rest of the night. Tomorrow he will see more things in his mind. He will fly through the universe like Garuda and he will speak with the gods. He will look down on his own life as if he were a god and it will give him strength. When he comes back he will feel a great hunger for life."

Gupta paused and then added, "When his senses are reawakened, they will be very great. Food and drink will taste better than they did before. Everything will feel better . . . and his appetites will be great. For a while he will be able to go with a woman many times. Maybe more than one woman, maybe many women."

Drew paced agitatedly along the corridor, innumerable questions swirling through his mind. "How do you know he won't die?" he asked. "People die of snakebite in this country all the time. It's not like you use a measuring cup or anything?"

"Sometimes they do die." Gupta shrugged. "Sometimes the handler makes a mistake. He milks the cobra in the morning, but he doesn't take out enough venom. Or maybe he gets the cobra confused with another that has not been milked."

"There are more?"

"Of course," Gupta replied. "Or there would be no money in it. The handler has twenty or thirty cobras. He will have many customers tonight. Tomorrow we make more money from the whores they need. That is the beauty of it. One need feeds upon another . . . and so it goes."

Drew looked at the closed doors along the corridor. That was what the rooms were for, he realized. They were for the johns to use while they tripped out on the cobra venom and then tested their prowess with Gupta's whores.

"And now you tell me something," Gupta added quietly. "You think this is something foreigners would like? This is something we can sell to the tourists?"

"Jesus . . ." Drew's mind swarmed with the possibilities. It was the most bizarre ritual he had ever seen—and it had the potential to earn him a fortune. "To do it or to watch it?" he asked.

This time it was Gupta who looked surprised. "You think people would pay to watch that?"

"That's where you'd make most of your money," Drew said. "You'd need the right kind of place, but they'd pay. That's why they come to places like India. This is exactly the kind of shit they want to see."

Gupta nodded, his expression thoughtful. Clearly, it had never occurred to him that foreigners would pay to watch others take a snakebite.

"Americans . . ." he said. "There is nothing you won't sell." Then he turned and walked back along the corridor, down the stairs, and out onto the street. Drew hurried to catch up to him, his head still full of unanswered questions. Gupta's bodyguards were waiting outside and they obediently fell into step a few yards behind Gupta and Drew.

"Why do they do it like that?" Drew asked. "How come they can't drink it or shoot it? Why do they have to let the fucking thing bite them on the tongue?"

"You know about drugs," Gupta said. "The tongue is very sensitive. Plenty of blood. When you inject directly into the tongue, the effect is immediate."

"Sure." Drew nodded. "But do they have to let the snake do it?"

"It has always been done this way," Gupta said. "The venom is pure. No refrigeration, no syringe, no AIDS. It works as well today as it did five thousand years ago."

They came to a streetlight and Gupta stopped and looked at Drew.

"I don't expect you to understand," he said. "All you care about is the thrill, the pleasure. But this is the Indian way. You taste the pain before you taste the pleasure. And the pleasure is like the pleasure you had the first time you had a woman, a feeling no man can have twice in one lifetime—unless he is prepared to die and be reborn."

Drew looked at him. "How come you know so much about it?"

Gupta paused. "Every Indian should do it once," he said.

"You've done it?"

Slowly Gupta extended his tongue. Halfway along, at the fleshiest part of the pad, were two tiny pink buds. Scar tissue. And the moment Drew saw them he knew he would have to do it, too. Just once.

CHAPTER 17

It was a little before dawn when Sansi got back to the bungalow at Aguada. He let himself in carefully so he wouldn't wake Annie and felt his way up the hallway in the dark. When he reached the living room, he switched on a table lamp and went to the bar. He opened the refrigerator, took out the ice-cube tray, and shook a half-dozen cubes into the sink. He molded the plastic bags and their contents into the empty squares then covered them with water and put the tray back in the fridge. Then he went to the bathroom, removed his contact lenses, threw his clothes in a corner, and took a quick shower.

After he had dried himself, he turned off the lights, padded naked to the bedroom, and quietly opened the door. The room was in total darkness and he had to feel his way to the bed. He pulled back the top sheet and climbed in carefully, listening for some sign that he might have disturbed her. There was nothing. Sansi was glad. She must have been in a deep sleep. He settled down and reached across to give her a reassuring pat, the way he usually did, only to find that her side of the bed was empty. He sat up and turned on the light. The bed hadn't been touched since it had last been made up.

He got out of bed, put on a robe, and went hurriedly from room to room. The house was empty. It looked as if she hadn't been there all night.

"Maderchod," Sansi swore, afraid for her, angry at himself.

She had been going to Anjuna to visit her new hippie friend. Something must have happened to keep her from coming back. He put on a clean change of clothes, snatched up his car keys, and headed for the door. He had a name—Cora Betts. It wasn't much, but it was enough to get him started. He would find Annie if he had to search every hippie hovel in Goa.

The moment he switched on the hall light he saw the envelope lying on the floor just inside the door. A hotel envelope. He hadn't seen it earlier because he hadn't turned on the lights. He picked it up and tore it open. The message inside said, *Staying over with Cora and family. Don't worry. Everything fine. See you in the morning. Love, Annie.* At the top of the page was a note that the message had been received at 11:07 the previous night.

Sansi sighed. He walked slowly back to the living room and put the note down on the coffee table. He looked at his watch. Almost 5:30. It could be another six hours before she got back and he wasn't supposed to worry?

A wave of exhaustion washed over him. He had been going for twenty-four hours and he had to rest. He sat down on the sofa, dazed and fretful. He would rest for a little while, he decided. He would try to nap for an hour or so, until the sun was up, then go looking for her.

He pushed off his shoes, lay down on the sofa, and closed his eyes. For a while it was impossible to sleep. Vivid and dreadful images scrolled erratically across his brain, jolting him back to wakefulness each time he dozed. Eventually the anesthetic of exhaustion took over and he slipped into a shallow and restless sleep.

He woke up with the sun in his eyes and a stale taste in his mouth. His neck ached and he had pins and needles in both feet where they had hung over the arm of the sofa. He looked at his watch. It was a little after ten. He had slept for about four hours. He looked around. The bungalow was quiet and had an empty feeling to it. Annie hadn't come back yet. He swung his legs off the sofa, limped to the bathroom, and looked in the mirror. The face that looked back was the face of a sixty-year-old man. He was shocked by how much silver there was in a day-old growth of beard. He knew he ought to shave but couldn't spare the time. He brushed his teeth and doused himself with cold water in an effort to revive himself. It only made him feel worse. He pushed his dripping hair back from his forehead and was about to leave when he saw the case for the contact lenses. He had almost forgotten them, his only disguise. His eyes felt sore and teared furiously when he put them back in. It was a moment or two before the blur faded and he could see clearly again. Then he went back to the sitting room and wrote a note to Annie on the back of her message in case he missed her.

Stay here until I get back, was all it said.

Outside, the sky was clear and blue and blameless. The sun was not yet hot enough to burn, and the ocean looked serene and inviting. Sansi enjoyed none of it as he walked back down the hill to the hotel. He had left the Maruti in the main parking lot—a minor precaution, though it was unrecognizable now beneath its sunbaked coating of dirt. It would look better after a good wash, he hoped. Though soap and water wouldn't wash away the scrapes and gouges all along the right side. His precautions were probably all for nought, he decided. The car-rental company would have him arrested when he took the car back.

As he walked past the main entrance of the hotel, he smelled coffee and fresh pastries and remembered that he hadn't eaten since lunchtime the previous day. His stomach felt queasy, but he thought some coffee might help lift the fog from his brain. He detoured through the lobby to the restaurant and helped himself from the urn at the buffet table. Two cups of black coffee with extra sugar. He drank them quickly, almost scalding himself. As he left he picked up a couple of pastries to eat in the car, hoping they might mop up some of the acid in his stomach.

He was on his way back through the lobby when he noticed an older white woman with shortish gray hair ambushing guests with leaflets she was handing out. He had seen her before and assumed she was with some tour group. He cut across the lobby in the hope of avoiding her, but she saw him and crossed over to him, a sheet of paper in her outstretched hand.

"I'm sorry to bother you," she said in a dry, scratchy voice that said she wasn't sorry at all. "But if you'd just take a look at this and, please, let us know if you've seen the girl in the photograph. Our names are at the bottom and we can be contacted here at the hotel anytime."

Her accent was American. He guessed she was in her late fifties or early sixties. It was hard to tell with Americans. She had pleasant features turned fleshy with age, though there was a hardness in her eyes and in her voice. Sansi nodded politely, took the leaflet, and kept walking. He glanced at it as he continued outside and down the steps to the parking lot. There was a picture of a young woman and a plea for information. The word *reward* appeared prominently in English and Hindi—a hundred and fifty thousand rupees for any information that resulted in her being found.

Another missing daughter, another stricken family, another mother and father in search of a truth that would only break their hearts. He looked at the picture of the girl. She was about twenty years old with the same features as the gray-haired woman in the lobby, though her hair was long and reddish brown and her smile brimmed with the confidence of youth. Sansi felt a pang of guilt. Part of him wanted to help, but he suspected it was already too late for this girl, whoever she was. By the time the parents came looking, it was almost always too late.

Then he saw the name beneath the photograph.

Cora Betts, it said, aka Cora Gilman of Los Angeles, California. Now forty-two years old. Married to Andrew Betts, also of Los Angeles. Two children, a boy aged twelve and a girl aged nine. All believed resident of Goa.

Sansi stopped at the bottom of the steps. It was Annie's friend at Anjuna. The name Cora was written in the message that now lay on the coffee table up at the bungalow. Sansi stood silently for a moment, forcing his tired brain to think. He looked at the paragraph at the bottom of the flier. It said anyone with information should contact Mr. and Mrs. D. and J. Gilman through the Fort Aguada Hotel or any U.S. consular office. Sansi made up his mind. He turned and walked back up the steps and into the hotel lobby. She was still there, handing out her leaflets.

"Forgive me," he said as he approached her. "I assume you are . . . related to this young woman?" He already knew the answer but he needed to hear it from her.

"Yes," the woman answered. "I'm her mother. Why, have you seen her? Do you know where she is?"

Sansi shook his head. "I'm sorry . . ."

He wouldn't tell her anything till he knew a little more himself.

"It's an unusual name," he said. "I think I may have heard it somewhere."

Sansi saw the hope in her eyes replaced by suspicion and wariness. He knew how he must look to her with his haggard appearance and day-old growth of beard. He took a business card out of his wallet and handed it to her.

"My name is Sansi," he said. "George Sansi. I am an attorney-at-law. If I can be of any assistance . . ."

The woman took the card, looked at it, then back at him. Her eyes told him she was unimpressed. Then he realized what she was thinking. The American word for it was *shyster*.

"Well, thank you, Mr. Sansi," she said, the hardness in her voice more apparent. "I appreciate your offer, but if you don't have anything definite . . ."

She left the sentence hanging but her meaning was clear. If

she had been in India any length of time, she must have met a dozen lawyers who would have promised to move the Himalayas to find her daughter, if it meant they could get their hands on thousands of American dollars in legal fees.

"Do you have any idea where your daughter might be, Mrs. Gilman?" he asked.

"We have it on good authority that she is here," she answered shortly, and went back to handing out fliers.

"Yes," Sansi persisted, "but do you know where exactly?"

Joy Gilman sighed. He was beginning to be a nuisance.

"Look, Mr. Sansi," she said, "I appreciate your interest, but unless you have something genuine to offer, I'd appreciate it if you'd just leave me to get on with my business."

"There may be something I can do—" He stopped himself when he realized how phony it sounded, even to him.

"Maybe I can help." It was a male voice, an American, firm and authoritative. Sansi turned. He hadn't seen the man approach. Blond, balding, in his midthirties, tanned beet red by the sun, his jaw was set and his manner decidedly unsympathetic. He was too young to be Mrs. Gilman's husband, Sansi thought. Perhaps a bodyguard?

"Thank you, Terry," Mrs. Gilman said. "This is Mr. Sansi. He says he wants to help us."

The way she said it made it clear what she really thought of Sansi. The blond man nodded.

"You have information about Mrs. Gilman's daughter?"

"Do you mind telling me who you are?" Sansi responded bluntly. He could help these people if he had a mind to, and more than they realized. But they seemed determined to drive him away before they had any idea what he had to offer.

The blond man reached into his shirt pocket and produced a badge.

"I'm Terence Coombe," he said. "I'm with the U.S. State Department, attached to the American consul in Bombay, and I'm here to assist Mrs. Gilman. Now, if you have anything to offer,

we'd be delighted to hear it. Otherwise, you're just wasting our
time and yours because we have access to all the local expertise
we need." He paused and, with unnecessary emphasis, added,
"Do you understand me?"

"Yes, Mr. Coombe," Sansi responded soberly. "I understand
you . . . perfectly well."

The blond man nodded. If he detected any irony in Sansi's response, it didn't show on his face. He put his badge back in his
pocket and took up a confrontational stance that challenged
Sansi to press his case.

"I am sorry to have bothered you, Mrs. Gilman." Sansi nodded formally to her, then turned and walked back through the
lobby.

Back in the Maruti, he rolled down the windows, and waited a
few moments to let the interior cool down. He assumed Mrs.
Gilman's husband was somewhere else distributing more fliers.
He knew nothing about the relationship the Gilmans had with
their daughter, but it couldn't have been too good if this was how
they had to go about finding her. He also knew that if their daughter didn't want to be found, her parents couldn't have come up
with a better way of driving her underground than by papering
Goa with wanted posters. But Sansi was beginning to understand
something more about Americans. They didn't like anybody
telling them what to do. Even in a foreign country. And Sansi was
not about to force his help onto people who didn't want it.

■   ■

The drive up the coast from Aguada to Anjuna would have been
enjoyable on any other day. The road meandered through shady
coconut groves and pretty villages filled with bustle and color,
and there were occasional glimpses of the ocean between the
palm trees. But Sansi was not in the mood for sight-seeing. He
was tired and scared—not for himself, but for Annie. No matter
how she tried to reassure him, he was convinced she had no idea
how much danger she was really in. Somehow he had to keep her

safe for another three or four days. That was all it would take to finish his end of the investigation. And if that wasn't good enough for Jamal, the commissioner would have to find some other way to save his skin.

The drive was uneventful until Sansi entered the small town of Calangute, about halfway between Aguada and Anjuna. There he found himself tacked onto a slow-moving line of traffic until, at last, he came to a complete stop. Something was wrong. Traffic was backed up through the town in an angry, heated mass of cars, buses, trucks, taxis, motorbikes, and scooters. There was no sign of traffic from the opposite direction. Sansi assumed there had been an accident. It could be a while before the traffic started moving again. He rested his forehead against the hot plastic of the steering wheel and muttered a string of curses under his breath. He considered turning around and finding another way to Anjuna, but he didn't know the roads and could easily get lost. He switched off the engine, opened the door, and stood up on tiptoe to try to see what kind of accident it was, to get some idea of how long he might be delayed.

The traffic stretched ahead in an unbroken line for a hundred yards or so and ended at a large and excited crowd in front of a square government building. There was some kind of a commotion going on in front of the building and more and more people were hurrying up the road to join the crowd of spectators. Sansi asked a couple of passersby what was going on, but they didn't seem to know. He would have to go and see for himself. He took the keys out of the ignition, closed the car door, and joined the stream of curious people hurrying up the road.

As he drew closer he saw that the building was a police station and the crowd was noticeably divided about whatever it was that was taking place in front of it. Some were angry and agitated, while others were amused and seemed to be enjoying themselves. Some people argued and taunted each other and there was much pushing and shoving and the occasional violent scuffle. The noise had melded into a single roar that rose and fell with the temper of the crowd. Sansi had seen many riots in Bombay and he thought the mood of the crowd was escalating rapidly to the same pitch.

Something happened in front of the building and the noise reached a crescendo. It was accompanied by a terrible, inhuman shriek that cut through the roar of the crowd like the scream of a factory whistle, then another and another. The screams were followed by a series of high-pitched howls, then the sound of glass breaking. All of it came from inside the police station.

Somebody must have gone berserk, Sansi realized—a prisoner or somebody under the influence of drugs. He strained to see over the heads of the crowd, but it was hopeless. There were at least a thousand people in the road now, a volatile, seething mass, and all he could see was the flat, dun-colored roof of the police station. Some people had climbed onto the roofs of cars and buses to see what was going on, and he realized that he would have to do the same. He looked around and started to work his way through the crowd toward a restaurant where there was a mud-brick wall crammed with cheering hippies. Finally he made it inside and found himself on a long, narrow terrace where there were still a few empty chairs and tables. He pushed a chair against the wall and climbed up so he could see between the shoulders of the hippies. At last he was able to get a clear view of what was going on in front of the Calangute police station.

Several uniformed policemen were rolling in the dirt punching and kicking at each other while a couple of sergeants struggled hopelessly to pull them apart. At the same time an enraged inspector wearing a red-banded cap and brandishing a *lathi* was standing in the doorway urging a cowering group of officers back into the building. But the policemen hung back, too afraid to go inside and face whatever it was. At the same time the sounds of destruction seemed only to grow in intensity. Loud bangs and crashes echoed through the building, and the dirt apron in front of the police station was strewn with broken glass, splintered pieces of furniture, and torn police files. In the midst of this havoc two police clerks scurried back and forth, picking up sheets of paper and snatching them away from the grasping hands of the crowd.

The uproar swelled to a new crescendo when a man appeared at the entrance to the police station, a policeman, dazed and bloody, his uniform shredded, his arms and torso freshly scarred with welts. He was clutching his left arm, and Sansi saw that the arm was scarlet with blood and a strip of flesh hung loosely from the elbow. Two of the policeman's comrades hurried up the steps and helped him to safety. There was a renewed chorus of screams from inside the building and another avalanche of police files spewed from a broken window. Sansi watched as the files burst open and sheets of paper fluttered over the crowd like huge white butterflies. Dozens of hands grabbed at the papers and tucked them away. There was a sudden blur of movement at the same window and a lull from the crowd as a dark and demonic shape appeared. Then, in a snarling rush, the shape hurtled from the building and into the surrounding trees, scattering a trail of papers behind it as it flew, chattering, through the treetops.

"Monkeys . . ." Sansi said disbelievingly.

The police station at Calangute had been attacked by monkeys.

He looked around till he found somebody who looked like a waiter. Speaking Konkani he asked what had happened. The man told him that a tribe of monkeys had lived in the area for years, though they had never harmed anybody before. Then, about an hour earlier, the entire tribe had swarmed out of the trees and attacked the police station.

"*Bhagwan*," Sansi murmured. "Is it rabies?"

The waiter shrugged and Sansi turned back to the bizarre spectacle on the other side of the road. It was the logical explanation. Rabies was common in India and monkeys were often carriers. In which case the entire tribe must have been infected and would have to be destroyed.

Suddenly it all made sense, a fantastic, surreal, Indian kind of sense. The police service in Goa was divided almost equally between Hindus and Christians. To Hindus the monkey was the physical incarnation of Hanuman the monkey god, symbol of duty, devotion, and love. To harm a monkey would be an act of sacrilege that would deny the perpetrator the attainment of nirvana. Unless there was a clear and obvious threat to human life, the Hindus in the Goan police service would simply stand aside and do nothing, no matter what damage the monkeys did to police property. It was embarrassing, perhaps, and expensive. But the monkeys might not be rabid. There might be some higher, cosmic rationale for their behavior and it would be wrong to interfere. Therefore, the monkeys would be allowed to finish their rampage and return to the trees they had come from. Later the Hindus would consult their priests for an interpretation of the portents.

The Christians, however, suffered no such constraints. They must have tried to drive the monkeys out. In which case the Hindus present would not be able to stand idly by while the physical incarnation of Hanuman was attacked. Which was why so many policemen were now rolling in the dirt, settling their religious differences with their fists.

It was funny, Sansi knew. Funny and farcical and tragic. Several policemen had been hurt and at least one badly mauled. At any moment the situation could erupt into a full-scale riot. If this were Bombay and the crowd were divided between Hindus and Muslims, a riot would already have started with the potential to kill dozens of innocent people. In India, farce and tragedy went hand in glove.

He decided he'd seen enough. He would go back to the car and find another way to Anjuna. He climbed down from the chair and made his way back out to the road. The crowd was bigger and more boisterous than before, and he found it harder to push his way through. Only those who had scooters and motorbikes found it easier to bulldoze a path. That was when he noticed the silver-haired hippie he had observed at the pink house a few days earlier, the American Sapeco identified as a small-time pusher who liked to masquerade as a guru to impressionable women. He passed only a few feet away, nosing determinedly through the crowd on his red-and-white Yamaha. This time he had a different woman with him. This time the woman on the passenger seat was Annie.

CHAPTER 18

At the moment the tree monkeys of Calangute began their assault on the police station, Prem Gupta was standing at the
living-room window at the pink house, waiting to receive some
visitors.

He watched, expressionless, as a cream-colored Ambassador
pulled through the gate and drove slowly up the gravel drive. He
waited until the car disappeared around the side of the house and
under the portico, then signaled his bodyguard to go and greet
his visitors.

The first man out of the car was Detective Sergeant Costa, a
heavyset man with thinning hair who looked older than his
twenty-nine years. The second was Detective Perez. He was a
couple of years younger than his colleague and about the same
height, but he was thinner and his movements were quick and
nervous. Despite the heat they both wore ill-fitting jackets to con-
ceal the weapons they carried. Those who knew them knew that
Perez was the more dangerous because he was skittish and inclined to overreact when he felt threatened. The last man out of
the car was Inspector Dias, chief of the Panjim drug squad and

258

the most highly decorated officer in the Goan police force. Dias
was a slender man, of medium height, with a neat mustache and
hair that glistened with oil. He wore a pale blue safari suit with
short sleeves and a paisley shirt with its collar outside the collar
of the jacket. Like his goons, he carried a pistol under his jacket.
As an added precaution, a police truck with sixteen armed constables waited outside the gate.

The door opened and Costa led the way inside, followed by
Dias and then Perez. The three of them stepped into the entrance
hall and onto the gorgeous mosaic of Surya the sun god, where
Gupta's bodyguard waited to pat them down. Costa and Perez
stiffened and looked to Dias for their cue. Dias looked irritated.
The same thing happened every time he came to the pink house
and every time with the same result.

"Touch one of us and it's assault of a police officer," Dias
said.

Gupta's bodyguard hesitated, looked over his shoulder to
where Gupta waited. Gupta shrugged and signaled the bodyguard to let his visitors pass. The three visitors walked noisily
across the marble floor and stepped down into the sunken living
room. Gupta waited, hands in his pockets, back to the window.
He greeted Dias cordially but spoke Marathi, not Konkani. Another of the games he liked to play to remind Dias who wielded
the real power in Goa.

Dias didn't mind. Like many Indians he was proud of his ability to speak several languages. It was evidence of his higher intel-
lect. He took a seat on the sofa nearest the corner and directed
Costa and Perez to chairs well apart from each other, where they
could see all the approaches to the room. Gupta noticed and was
amused, though his expression didn't change. Dias was stupid. If
Gupta wanted him dead, it wouldn't happen here and now. It
would happen when he least expected it. In a traffic jam in Panjim or at some drug den in Anjuna, Baga, or Calangute.

"You want a drink?" Gupta offered, observing the minimal
obligations of a host.

Costa and Perez asked for Thums Up with ice, Dias for sweet lime. Nobody wanted alcohol. Nothing to blur the senses until business was concluded. Gupta gestured to his bodyguard, who went off to the kitchen, leaving Gupta alone with Dias and his two goons. Gupta turned and gazed out the window, showing his visitors his back, showing them how little he had to fear from them.

For a long time nobody spoke. Dias felt himself getting angry. He was old enough to be Gupta's father. He had twenty-six years in the police service. He had his own power base, his own businesses, and he cut his own deals. The way he saw it, he was his own man. These people paid him for his goodwill so they could do business in Goa and he could do them the occasional favor. And it was Gupta who had asked for this meeting, not Dias. Now this upstart from the slums of Bombay dared to turn his back on Dias, making him wait, treating him like a *kuli*.

Gupta saw it differently. Dias was on the payroll. Another corrupt cop. High ranking and dangerous, perhaps, but in the hierarchy of the underworld, about one step up from an informer. He had come because Gupta had told him to come, not because he wanted to. Gupta would get down to business when it suited him. He knew how to handle a man like Dias, how to get him off balance, how to get him angry. It was another way of loosening Dias's tongue, to get him to say what was really on his mind.

The silence lengthened and expanded until it filled the room like something brittle and crystalline. Gupta's bodyguard seemed to be taking a long time to get the drinks. Despite the air-conditioning, Costa sweated so much the collar of his shirt looked damp. Perez shifted in his chair, his eyes flitting everywhere, his hand returning constantly to his jacket, feeling the comforting hardness of the gun underneath. Dias rested his foot on one knee and absently tapped a finger against the heel of his shoe. Still Gupta stood with his hands in his pockets, gazing out the window, as if he had forgotten they were there.

At last Dias lost patience. "You asked for this meeting," he said.

Gupta turned and looked at Dias as if the policeman had interrupted him in the midst of other, more important thoughts.

"Did I?" he said distractedly.

"*Bakwas . . .*" Dias grunted.

Gupta smiled. He didn't want to push Dias too far. He stepped away from the window, sat down in his big leather armchair, and smoothed the creases from his trousers.

"You've been busy these past few weeks," he said. It was a statement more than a question.

"I am a busy man."

"Your arrest quota is up."

"It's about the same."

"That's not what I hear."

"What do you hear?"

"The tourist season is winding down, but you're busier than you were two months ago. More arrests, more confiscations. Maybe you decided you weren't making enough money? Maybe you changed our arrangement without telling me?"

"The arrest rate will be the same this month as it was last month and the month before."

"And the drugs you've seized?"

"You want to change the arrangement?" Dias said bluntly. "Is that what this is about?"

"If you are making more arrests, if you are taking a bigger share of the product, people are going to notice. They're going to get scared. And you'll only hurt the market. The customers have to know they can come here and consume their drugs in peace. We can't have Goa getting a bad reputation."

"It would be easier if the hippies didn't make trouble all the time."

"They're a nuisance," Gupta agreed. "But they have a place. We need them to keep the young people coming. They spread the word that Goa is kind to junkies."

"Do you know about the firebomb attack in Margao last night?" Dias asked abruptly.

Gupta hesitated. He'd heard that somebody had set fire to some machinery at the Ashoka Construction depot a couple of blocks from his warehouse. It was an obvious target for the anti-railroad protesters. His men had assured him there was no problem at the warehouse and he had thought little more about it.

"The terrorists get much of their support from the hippies," Dias said. "If the hippies want to support terrorism, they are going to get big trouble from Panjim. It has nothing to do with the drug squad. It is a security problem. If Panjim can't show Delhi they are on top of the situation, the next thing that will happen is the army will be here looking over our shoulders and everything will be more complicated. If the hippies want to stay in Goa, they should stay out of politics . . . sit on the beach and smoke ganja like they've always done."

Gupta nodded. He had already discussed this with Drew. The American had promised to use his influence to persuade his countrymen to pursue other, nonviolent forms of protest rather than giving bomb-making lessons. If some Americans ignored the warnings and continued to stick their noses into a fight that was none of their concern, they would get everything they deserved.

"The business with the railroad will pass," Gupta said. "The demand for drugs will always exist. When the free port comes, Goa will be a playground for the world. Millions of people will fly in here every year. The demand for drugs will be greater than ever. The money will come like waves from the sea. It would be a pity to risk a share of that by getting greedy now."

This time it was Dias who was amused. Gupta was a hoodlum with twenty or thirty armed men at his command. Dias had the resources of the entire police force at his disposal—three thousand armed men. He was confident he could launch an operation against the gangster from Bombay and persuade the commissioner and the chief minister later that it was necessary. There

would be no trial, no unwelcome publicity, no protests. Gupta
and his thugs would be slaughtered during a raid by a police assault force, and afterward Dias would be in a position where he
could dictate terms to all the gangs.

"If you're being cheated you should look elsewhere," Dias
said. "I am a man of honor. When I make a deal, I keep to it. If I
want more—I will tell you."

Gupta remained silent. Either Dias was a better liar than he
expected . . . or it was Drew who was lying. But if the American
was lying, what purpose would it serve to set Gupta and Dias at
each other's throats? To take the heat off Drew while he skimmed
Gupta's dope and blamed it on the market? If that was the case,
the American was risking his life for a distinctly short-term
gain. Even for a hippie, it was dumb. Was Drew really that stupid, Gupta wondered, or was he smarter than anyone thought?

The door from the kitchen opened and Perez put his hand
inside his jacket. Gupta's bodyguard reappeared with a middle-
aged *bai* carrying a tray of cold drinks. Perez slowly withdrew his
hand and wiped it on his pants. The *bai* put the tray down on the
candy-colored table, bobbed respectfully to Gupta, and left.
There were two bottles of Thums Up, a sweet lime, three glasses
filled with ice, and a bottle of mineral water for Gupta. He waved
to his guests to help themselves and waited while everyone took
a drink, letting some of the tension leach out of the air. He knew
all he needed to know from Dias. What he had to do now was to
nudge the policeman back into a more productive frame of mind.

"Have you found someone to take over the police surgeon's
job?"

"Yes," Dias said. "There is someone in Panjim."

"Is he qualified?"

"He has a medical certificate on the wall," Dias said. "He is an
abortion specialist and he drinks too much, but he will do what
he is told."

"Can he do postmortems?"

"I have seen so many, I could do them," Dias answered.

"Will the board accept him?"

"The board will not present a problem," Dias said. "Some people from the hospicio might not like it, but they know to keep their mouths shut."

Gupta nodded. "What about that last man, what is his name . . . ?"

"Sapeco?"

"Will he keep his mouth shut?"

"He is out of the way now," Dias said. "His friends found him a job at the hospicio. He is just another complainer."

"Just another complainer?" Gupta said quietly. He liked that. "Too many of these complainers could give Goa a bad name. I don't want Goa to have a bad name. The future of Goa depends on the tourist trade."

It was then that Dias understood. This was the real reason he had been asked to come to the pink house today. Everything else had been a diversion, a game so Gupta could show how tough and how smart he was. But what he was really worried about was Sapeco. He was worried that the former police surgeon would talk too much about the things he had seen in the autopsy room at police headquarters.

Dias gave a small grunt of acknowledgment. It was easily solved. He had already thought of doing something about it himself. He looked over at Costa and Perez and saw that they understood, too. Gupta saw the look as it passed between them and was reassured. Dias was a fool. A fool with a bad temper, bad manners, and bad taste in clothes. But he had his uses. The best servants were never too bright.

■   ■

"He gave me a ride back to the hotel. I don't see that there's anything wrong with that."

"Do you know who he is?"

"Yes, I know who he is."

Sansi stood in the bedroom doorway. Annie was seated at the

dressing table in a hotel bathrobe. The curtains were drawn against the sun, so that the room was filled with a melancholy twilight. She had only just gotten out of the shower and was brushing her still-wet hair when Sansi got back. Now she sat sideways to the mirror and played with the hairbrush in her lap while Sansi waited for an answer.

"He's Cora's husband," she said. "I spent the night at their place. I sent you a message—I know you got it. He gave me a ride back this morning to save me the hassle of getting a taxi."

"Why did you spend the night with those people?" Sansi asked. "After everything I told you?"

She picked absently at the gold-embossed letters on the handle of the hairbrush.

"Did you take drugs?" he added. "Is that why you didn't come back?"

Annie looked at him. She hadn't lied to him yet and she saw no reason to start now.

"I smoked some grass," she said.

"*Are Bapre . . .*" Sansi leaned one arm against the doorjamb.

"It was only grass," she added. "I've smoked it before. I just got a little ripped, that's all. I didn't plan on staying over."

"You just got a little . . . ripped?"

"Ripped . . . stoned."

"You got high, so high you didn't know what you were doing."

"I wasn't completely out of it. I knew what I was doing."

"Where were you?"

"I told you, at Cora's place."

"Is that where you smoked the ganja?"

"I shared a joint with Cora before we went to the dinner party. There was dope at the party, too, grass mostly. A few people brought some hash . . . and some of the food had hash in it. There's a woman there who makes hash brownies. I didn't have any."

"But you smoked more ganja?"

"There was dope going around the whole time I was there. I

guess I don't have the same tolerance for it that these people have."

"They're junkies."

"I didn't see anybody do anything hard," she said. "I didn't see any needles or shit like that. If I had I would have been out of there."

"Did you pass out?"

"I got back to Cora's place okay. I figured I was safe there. We'd done a lot of talking. I trust her. Sometimes you just feel like you know somebody."

Sansi didn't answer right away. He stepped away from the door and sat on the edge of the bed so he could see her better. She looked back at him through eyes that were skeined with fatigue. He reached over to her and stroked her leg.

"How do you feel?"

"Tired."

"The ganja takes a lot out of you."

"So does a mattress on the floor."

"You look terrible."

"So do you."

"This isn't my idea of a holiday," he said. "Are you sure it's what you want?"

She smiled and shook her head.

"You should have come back," he added.

"I know," she said. "But it was late and I was stoned and I didn't feel like wandering around Anjuna in the dark looking for a cab. I think that would have been more dangerous."

"Was your friend's husband there?"

"Drew?"

Sansi nodded.

"I only met him this morning," she said. "He wasn't at the party last night. Cora said he was out somewhere, doing some business. I guess he didn't get back till late."

"When you were alone and passed out from the ganja?"

"Nothing . . . happened," she said, giving each word separate and equal emphasis. "When I woke up, the guy was in bed with his wife. Asleep. I got up with the kids, I had some coffee. Cora got up and I talked to her for a while. I was going to get a cab when Drew got up and said he'd give me a ride. I thought he was being nice. They're not all freaks up there, you know."

"You know what he does for a living?"

"Yes." She put the hairbrush on the dresser and reached for her Kents. "He teaches meditation . . . and he's a dealer."

"So you know he deals in drugs," Sansi said. "But he's a nice kind of a dealer and his wife is nice and his children are nice . . . and so everything is all right?"

"No." She paused to light a cigarette. "There's a lot about this place that I don't think is all right. But it isn't really important what I think. It's the way these people are, the way they want to lead their lives. I'm just passing through, I'm not going to spend the rest of my life here."

"Oh." Sansi nodded. "And none of it will touch you because you are on holiday? You're just passing through and your neutrality will protect you like an invisible shield—like all those other people who thought they were just passing through?"

Annie looked away, too tired to argue. It had been a long time since she had smoked so much dope and she had forgotten about its aftereffects—the light-headedness, the bloodshot eyes, and the peculiarly jittery lassitude that craved the comfort of another joint. All she wanted to do now was to sleep it off and wake up with a clear head.

"You know, Drew is involved with the man I am investigating here in Goa," Sansi said.

Annie looked at him, startled. "With Banerjee?"

"One of his lieutenants, a young hoodlum called Gupta. He runs Banerjee's drug operation here. Drew knows him quite well."

"Cora says he only sells soft drugs. He doesn't deal heroin. I'm sure she would know."

"I am sure she does."

"You don't know that he deals heroin."

Sansi heard how unwilling she was to believe the worst of her new friends—that they might have deceived her completely.

"Annie, I know these people," he said. "I've been watching Gupta's place since I got here. If Drew is involved with them, he is selling heroin. It is the cornerstone of their business."

"Does this guy Gupta live in a big house at Miramar?"

"Yes, he does," Sansi answered hesitantly, wondering how she knew.

"Cora told me," Annie said. "She told me about him, she told me why Drew has been talking to him. She told me a lot of things."

Sansi was skeptical.

"You know the little girl who was killed? You made a big production about the fact that Cora hadn't said anything to me about it. Like she was hiding it or something?"

Sansi nodded.

"She wasn't hiding it," Annie said. "She knew that little girl. Her name was Tina and she was nine years old. Cora's daughter, Sara, used to play with her all the time. They were best friends. I saw the way Cora looked when she talked about that kid. Not wanting to talk about something like that is not the same as hiding it."

"She knows the family?"

"They lived next door to each other for two, three years."

"Did she say how the child was murdered?"

"She was strangled and her body was dumped in the ocean. Some half-assed attempt to make it look like a drowning."

So far this matched the account Sansi had gotten from Sapeco.

"Did she offer any theories on who might be responsible?"

"She said it was the cops."

"Why does she think it was the police?"

"That's what everybody up there thinks. There was no investigation, you know. Nobody in authority gives a shit, and the cops aren't about to investigate themselves."

"Does she have any proof it was the police?"

"Not really," Annie conceded. "But she was there the night it happened."

"She was there the night of the murder?"

"She and two thousand other people. There was a big beach party. The hippies throw them every full moon during the holiday season. Cora and Drew were there with their kids, and this little girl was there with her parents."

"Do you know their names?"

Annie had to stop and think. "The mother's name is Cass. No, her real name is Karen. It's Karen Henke. The father's name is Rick and they're from Ann Arbor, Michigan."

Sansi nodded.

"Well," she gave a tired sigh, "it was this big party and everybody was having a good time. But the cops were there, too, looking to make trouble. Some guy called Dias from the drug squad and a bunch of his goons."

"And Cora thinks this Dias was responsible?"

"Him or somebody like him—definitely a cop."

"That's prejudice, not proof."

"It's more than that."

"What then?"

"You know what. . . ." Her exasperation began to show in her voice. "They're hippies, they're in the way, they're stopping all these rich bastards from getting richer. And the cops are on the take from all of them. It was you who told me the cops are dirty. There's a pattern of harassment here that goes back months— arrests, rape, torture. Killing a hippie kid was the next step, a way to increase the pressure."

"Is that what Cora told you?"

"Yes, and it's working. They're getting out."

"They're leaving?"

"Sure. They don't want to stay here, the way things are. They have kids of their own. They're going back to the States."

"When?"

"As soon as they can get the money together." She stopped and looked pointedly at him. "You wouldn't think it would be so hard for a big-time dealer like Drew to scrape together the cash to buy a few plane tickets, would you?"

Sansi recalled the first time he had seen Drew at the pink house and the way he had been treated. He had thought then that Drew was only a small player in Gupta's operation. Sapeco had confirmed as much. And much of what Cora had told Annie was true. In which case it was possible that everything else was true as well—that Cora was an innocent participant in a drama that was not of her making, that her husband was a not-so-innocent hustler who had ensnared himself in something far bigger and far deadlier than either of them had imagined.

"You want to know why Drew can't fly his family back to the States right now?" Annie intruded on his thoughts. "You want to know why he went to see Gupta?"

Sansi waited.

"When that kid was murdered, her parents went to pieces. It was Drew who got them through it. It was Drew who took care of all the official stuff, the documents and the bribes and all the other shit. It was Drew who gave them the money to fly back to the States with their daughter's body." She paused a moment, then added, "That's why you saw him at Gupta's place—not because he's one of Gupta's dealers. He was trying to buy some time. He was begging Gupta to get the cops to lay off the hippie community for a while so those who want to leave can leave. So nobody else has to get hurt."

Sansi considered what she had told him. It was plausible enough, all of it. But there were a few things that jarred. The woman Sansi had seen with Drew at the pink house was not his wife. Sapeco had mentioned that Drew was something of a guru to the other hippies and a compulsive womanizer. Certainly everything about Drew suggested an ego out of all proportion to his position in life. It seemed unlikely to Sansi that such a man would take his girlfriend with him when he planned on begging for the lives of his family.

Sansi looked at Annie and said, "You're quite sure it was Drew who took care of the arrangements to transship the child's body back to the United States?"

"Yes," Annie answered. "Without him it wouldn't have happened. The Henkes didn't have any money, and from what I understand, Rick Henke wasn't much use at the best of times."

Sansi looked at her. "This Drew must be a very caring—what is the word?—nurturing kind of person," he said.

Annie smiled, despite her tiredness.

"Well." Sansi got up to go. "Your friends won't have to worry about going begging to someone like Gupta for much longer."

Annie watched him while he took the flier out of his pocket and handed it to her. "I would say their tickets out of Goa just got here," he said.

CHAPTER 19

Sansi followed Sapeco down a narrow aisle with shelves filled with specimen jars on one side and a row of refrigerators on the other. They came to a cramped corner office with a name on the door that said DR. R. FALEIRO. EPIDEMIOLOGY. The door was open, and inside, a woman in a lab coat worked at an L-shaped desk with a microscope, specimen slides, and a stack of analysis charts.

"I am sorry to trouble you, Dr. Faleiro," Sapeco said from the doorway.

"This is not a good time for me, Doctor," she answered without looking up. "Leave the samples with Sitaram. We won't be able to get to them today. Perhaps tomorrow."

Sapeco looked at Sansi and Sansi shook his head. Sapeco sighed, stepped into the office, and lowered his voice to a whisper.

"Rohini," he said. "This is important . . . a favor." Her shoulders tensed, and for a moment she seemed unwilling to look at him. Then she lifted her head and noticed Sansi for the first time. She smiled, politely but warily, then looked back at Sapeco. She was an attractive woman in her early thirties with a severe, hospital haircut and tired eyes. There was no *thikka* on her forehead, which suggested that she was unmarried or Catholic like Sapeco.

"I am sorry, Dr. Sapeco," she added wearily. "But unless it is an emergency . . ."

"I would not trouble you if it was not an emergency, Doctor," he said.

Dr. Faleiro beckoned them inside and Sapeco closed the door. It was not a big room, and with the three of them inside it was crowded.

"Rohini is the best friend of my eldest daughter," Sapeco said, looking at Sansi. "They went to school together. Anna wanted to get married and have babies. Rohini wanted a career in medicine. She is too good to waste her life here, but . . ." He shrugged. "Like many others in Goa, she wants to help her own people."

Rohini Faleiro smiled at Sansi, this time with more warmth, and he saw that she was not merely attractive but beautiful, despite the dark circles under her eyes. A woman who could have done better for herself but had opted for a life of scientific drudgery in a provincial hospital dedicated to helping the poor. There were others like her, he knew, people whose goodness somehow transcended the mire of cynicism and corruption. Without them, India wouldn't function at all.

Sapeco explained what was needed. Sansi took out three clear, plastic bags and put them on Faleiro's desk. The first two contained white powder, one of them coarse and granular, the other fine-grained. The third contained a viscous yellow gel that puddled into a squat oval shape on the desktop.

Faleiro took the bag of fine-grained powder first and swiveled her chair to the side where she kept her microscope and a rack of specimen slides.

"They're obviously not corrosive," she said as she opened the bag. "Are any of them toxic?"

"You should treat all of them as if they are toxic until we can identify them," Sansi said. "One of them is supposed to be plaster

of paris, though I have reason not to trust the label on the bag.
The other came from a metal drum that said it was poison. I have
smelled something like it before and I have an idea what it might
be. The liquid came out of a drum of detergent and that is how it
smells to me. I want to know if either of the powders is heroin or
if any one of them is a chemical that could be used in the manufacture of heroin."

"You think they might be using plaster of paris to cut the
heroin?" Sapeco asked.

"It's possible," Sansi answered. "Usually it is white sugar or
flour, but as you know, if they are not too fussy about repeat customers, they will use bleach, laundry powder—or plaster of
paris."

"But you think the gel is liquid soap?"

"It could be anything," Sansi responded. "It could be a masking agent to deceive customs inspectors at the other end. It could
be a suspension fluid for hashish oil. These people come up with
new tricks all the time."

Sapeco looked unhappy. To him it seemed they had risked
much and gained precious little except more of Sansi's theories.
He was about to say something when Dr. Faleiro opened the first
bag and sniffed tentatively at the contents. Both men fell silent
and watched her closely.

"It smells like gypsum," she said after a moment.

She plucked a clean wooden spatula from a cup, took a por-
tion of the powder out of the bag, and spread it carefully on a
glass slide. She put the slide under the microscope and peered
through the lens.

"It isn't heroin," she said. "The composition of the crystals is
nothing like heroin."

She took the slide out again, added a few drops of water from
her flask, and stirred it with the spatula till it formed a smooth
white paste. Then she sniffed it again.

"Calcium sulfate," she said. "You were right the first time, Mr.
Sansi. It is plaster of paris."

Sansi nodded but said nothing.

Sapeco leaned forward, dabbed a finger in the paste, smeared it between his fingertips, smelled it, and nodded.

Faleiro turned next to the bag with the coarse-grained powder that Sansi had warned her might be poisonous. She was about to open it when she stopped and looked around.

"That's strange," she said.

Sansi and Sapeco looked at her.

"I can smell petrol," she said. "Do you smell petrol?"

Abruptly Sapeco leaned away from her.

Sansi put his hands in his pockets and smiled. "I stopped at a petrol station on the way here," he said. "I got some on my hands."

"Ah." Dr. Faleiro nodded and went back to the bag of white powder.

Sansi looked at Sapeco, trying to reassure him with his eyes, but the expression on Sapeco's face said he was beyond any reassurance that Sansi could offer.

Dr. Faleiro opened the bag, sniffed it, grimaced, and pulled sharply away. "I think I know what this is," she said, looking curiously at him. "If I am right, I would like to know where you got it."

"I think it would be better, Doctor, if you did not know," he answered. His tone was friendly but firm, and Faleiro did not argue.

She selected a clean new spatula, dug a sample of powder out of the bag, and tapped it onto a clean slide. This time it took her a little longer to deliver her verdict.

"There are some simple chemical tests I could do," she said as she sat upright. "But I'm quite sure it's paraformol."

"Paraformol?" Sansi repeated.

"Yes."

Sapeco looked puzzled. "What would they want with paraformol?" he murmured.

But Sansi was too preoccupied to answer. Dr. Faleiro had the bag of gel open in front of her and was sniffing at it carefully. She sniffed again, deeper, more confident, then a third time.

"Borax concentrate," she said. "I'll test it for additives, but I'm quite sure it's borax. We use it here all the time."

"Liquid detergent?" Sansi asked.

"Yes."

She tied a knot in the neck of the bag and put it with the other samples. "The paraformol is a restricted substance. The other two are easily obtained, especially the borax. We buy it in bulk with the medical school at Bambolim."

She looked briefly at Sapeco then back at Sansi. "You do know why the paraformol is restricted, don't you?"

"Yes," Sansi said. "It is used for the preservation of human tissue . . . dead human tissue."

Dr. Faleiro nodded. Then she leaned back in her chair and waited. The room became very quiet, the atmosphere thick with unanswered questions. Sapeco was the first to speak, his voice an echo of his growing frustration.

"These chemicals don't have anything to do with the manufacture of heroin," he said. "These are things we use in hospitals and medical schools—"

"And mortuaries," Sansi said.

Sapeco hesitated, then said, "Yes, we kept them at the mortuary in Panjim."

"That is almost certaintly where these came from," Sansi said.

Sapeco stared at him. "Why would anybody take them from the mortuary?" he asked. "Why would anybody outside a medical establishment have any need for them?"

"Because they are an important means of getting the heroin out of Goa," Sansi said.

"But how?" Sapeco demanded, his impatience becoming more apparent. "As masking agents?"

"No," Sansi answered quietly. He looked around for something to sit on. He wasn't used to such physical rigors as he had undergone in the past few days, and his back and his legs felt tired and achy. But Dr. Faleiro's office seemed designed to discourage loitering. Sansi suspected it was deliberate. He contented himself by leaning against one of her massive metal filing cabinets.

"When I was with crime branch I attended more postmortems than I care to remember," he said. "I became quite familiar with the smell of formaldehyde." He paused and looked at Sapeco. "If I remember correctly it is made by adding water to paraformol?"

Sapeco sighed. "Yes."

"Approximately one-third water to each measure of paraformol," Dr. Faleiro said.

"But it is only when formaldehyde is mixed with methanol that it produces formalin," Sansi continued. "Which is the main chemical used by coroners to preserve organ samples, I believe."

"Yes," Sapeco said.

"But the formula for embalming fluid is quite different?"

"Of course," Sapeco answered. "When the primary concern is the preservation of organs for forensic examination, there is no need to worry about odor or appearance. Embalming serves an entirely different purpose. It is all about cosmetics—the elimination of odor and the good appearance of the corpse."

"There is no methanol in embalming fluid, is there?" Sansi asked. "The main ingredients are formaldehyde and borax?"

"Generally yes," Sapeco answered. "Some embalmers use other things, too, like glycerine and carbolic acid and wax, especially when a corpse has been disfigured and some restoration work is necessary."

"But we live in a country where three-quarters of the population is Hindu and believes in cremation," Sansi said. "Muslims do not practice embalming and neither do Sikhs or Parsis. The demand for it must be very limited."

"Goa is the only place in India where embalming is performed on a regular basis," Sapeco confirmed.

"Because Goa is the only place where most of the population is Christian," Sansi concluded. "And the Christian tradition is to present the corpse for public viewing, for the paying of respects prior to burial."

"In many cases."

"So there are a number of practitioners in Goa, and a number of places where embalming can take place?"

"There are a few licensed practitioners," Sapeco said.

"I would assume that embalming in Goa is practiced according to Western standards and traditions?"

"It was brought here by the Jesuits," Sapeco said. "They did it to preserve the bodies of saints and nobles of the church. The most obvious example is the body of Saint Francis Xavier, the patron saint of Goa. He has been on public display here for four hundred years."

"And what about you, Doctor?" Sansi asked. "Did you perform embalmings at the mortuary?"

Sapeco hesitated before answering, and when he spoke it was with a certain reluctance. "Our situation was different," he said. "Almost without exception it was restricted to foreigners . . . I think you know why."

"Because the corpse of a foreigner has to meet certain safety standards before it can leave the country?"

"There are international laws governing the transshipment of corpses. The airlines won't carry a corpse unless it has been cleared by the appropriate health authorities and the consul."

"And when a corpse arrives in the home country, what happens then, Doctor?"

"As far as I am aware, it is examined by the health authority at the port of entry, and if everything looks all right and the documentation is in order, it is turned over to the family for burial."

"Would there be any need to open the corpse up?" Sansi asked. "Any need to go inside?"

"Not unless the local health authority had . . . a reason. . . ."

His voice ebbed away as the momentum of Sansi's questioning bore down on him like a dreadful crushing weight. A look of
panic came into his eyes. He tried again, and again the words
shriveled in his mouth.

"Not unless they had a reason to . . ."

"A reason to be suspicious," Sansi finished for him.

Sapeco leaned against the wall to steady himself. He nodded
blankly.

"Are you all right, Doctor?" Faleiro asked.

It was a moment before he could answer. When he finally
said "Yes," it sounded flat and unconvincing.

"Would you like some water?"

Sapeco nodded and Faleiro poured him a glass of water from
a metal flask. He drank it in a series of rapid swallows and put the
empty glass back on her desk.

"I still don't understand about the plaster of paris," Sansi
said, determined to finish what he had started. "I assume it serves
some purpose in the embalming process?"

It was directed at Sapeco, but the doctor, distracted by his
own inner turmoil, seemed not to hear.

"It is used to harden and preserve the internal organs,"
Dr. Faleiro answered for him.

Sansi nodded. "I take it the postmortem procedure in Goa is
the same as it is in Bombay?"

"I believe it is a standard procedure," she said.

"You take out everything—heart, lungs, viscera . . . everything?"

"Yes," Sapeco interjected. His voice sounded strained and he
stopped for a moment to clear his throat. "We follow . . . we always followed procedure."

"You take samples of the various organs for examination?"

"Yes."

"And what happens to everything that is left?"

"We soak it in formaldehyde, sprinkle it with plaster of paris,
and put it back."

"All of it? Everything goes back into the torso?"

"Yes."

"Excuse me," Dr. Faleiro interrupted softly.

Both men looked at her.

"You forgot about the brain."

"The brain?" Sansi echoed.

"Yes." Sapeco nodded. "The brain."

"What happens to the brain?"

"We always remove the brain," Sapeco answered. "We take samples to look for lesions and abnormalities, and what is left we soak in formaldehyde and sprinkle again with plaster of paris. Then we put it in a plastic bag and put it inside the torso with the other internal organs."

"*Acha*," Sansi said. "But the skull is put back together and the facial tissue replaced?"

"It is a straightforward procedure," Sapeco said. "The facial tissue peels off like a mask and goes back the same way."

"So the family at the other end can have an open casket if they wish?"

"We always proceeded on the assumption that they would," Sapeco said.

"And no one would know that the skull was empty?"

"No one except the health authorities . . . and whatever other authorities were part of the interment process."

"And the brain goes back inside the torso—in a plastic bag?"

"As long as it is returned with the rest of the remains, we have fulfilled our obligation under the law."

"I would assume that if the authorities at the other end were to reopen the body, they would find everything in order?"

"Yes."

"Because you are a good coroner," Sansi said. "And they would know that by looking at your work."

"Yes." Sapeco's voice faltered again.

"And if they were to conduct an autopsy of their own?"

Sapeco glanced nervously at Faleiro before answering. "In the case of every foreigner we sent back, they would find traces of massive heroin overdose," he said.

"Despite the presence of all these other chemicals?"

"There would be a very strong residual and that would be preserved, too."

"Which would only corroborate the cause of death on the death certificate."

"Yes."

"Presumably they would only need a few minor tissue samples."

"Of course."

"There would be no need to take apart the hardened mass of internal organs?"

"No."

"No need to go into the skull again?"

"There would be no reason," Sapeco answered dully. "No reason at all."

An oppressive silence descended upon the three of them, making Dr. Faleiro's office feel even more claustrophobic.

"You were right to leave when you did," Sansi said.

"I had no idea," Sapeco said. "I would never be part of such desecration."

"I know," Sansi said. "It was your respectability they wanted. The quality of your work was your signature. It is just as you said; these people are arrogant and stupid and evil. The only way they find strength is through their willingness to do evil. They won't replace you easily, Doctor. They will make mistakes and they will get caught. We are only accelerating the process."

Sapeco didn't say anything. His face seemed to be crumpling in slow motion, like the mask of a doll in a fire.

"I think you should give serious consideration to getting yourself and your family out of Goa for a while," Sansi added. "I will help you all I can."

Sapeco did not answer right away, and when he did he made

no mention of Sansi's offer. "How much do you estimate they're moving out?" he asked.

Sansi paused. "Three, perhaps four kilograms to each corpse," he said. "Four or five times a month. That's thirty to forty million dollars a month in the West."

The doctor glanced at Faleiro. "One month would pay for a new hospital," he said. "A year would pay for a comprehensive immunization program for the entire country."

Dr. Faleiro looked back at him but said nothing. She had heard enough to confirm that the less she knew the safer she would be.

Sansi said, "I think Dr. Faleiro wants to get on with her work."

He retrieved his samples and put them back in his laundry bag. "Thank you, Doctor," he said.

"Thank you, Rohini," Sapeco said. He glanced briefly at her as he turned to leave, too humiliated to look her in the face.

"I'm glad I could help," she said.

She said it hurriedly, as if anxious to reassure him. But Sapeco was beyond the solace of words. Clearly he was desperate to get back to his own office, where he could lock the door and be left alone for a while. Sansi thanked Dr. Faleiro again and turned to follow Sapeco.

"Wait a minute," Faleiro said.

Sansi stopped and waited as Faleiro got out of her chair and reached into a cardboard box on a shelf behind her desk. She took out a small oblong package wrapped in yellow wax paper and handed it to him.

"Here," she said. "It's a special solvent soap I use . . . it will help get rid of that petrol smell on your hands."

■   ■

It was dusk when Sansi got back to the bungalow. Annie was on the verandah with a cup of coffee and a cigarette and *The Na-*

maste Book of Short Stories facedown on the table beside her.
When she heard him in the hallway, she got up and went inside.
She looked fresher and better rested than the last time they had
seen each other, though there was still a trace of redness in her
eyes. Sansi looked awful and knew it. His hair was lank and
greasy, he still hadn't shaved, and his shoulders were stooped
with fatigue.

"You look whacked," she said.

"Whacked?"

"Tired . . . beat."

"In that case," he said, "I am most whacked."

"Why don't you have a shower and go to bed?"

"I can't. I have to call Jamal, then I have to go out again."

"Where?"

"Not far. Here in the hotel."

"Have you eaten?"

Sansi tried to remember. "I had something this morning."

"You want some coffee?"

"Please."

He slumped down on the sofa and picked up the phone.
Annie poured him a cup of coffee while he booked his call with
the switchboard. When he had hung up, he leaned back and tried
to rub some life back into his face. His lengthening chin stubble
rasped against his fingertips and his eyes ached behind the
silicone shield of his contact lenses. He was desperate to take
them out, but he didn't dare until he'd seen Mrs. Gilman again.
He tried to ignore the discomfort, took a sip of coffee, and
hoped the caffeine would keep him awake for another hour or
two.

"You want me to order you something from room service?"
Annie offered.

Sansi had to think about it. He ought to eat something, but he
was so tired he felt bilious. "You might see if they have some mulligatawny soup," he said.

Annie picked up the phone, punched in the number, and waited. "What is a mulligatawny anyway?" she asked.

"Chicken soup with a pinch of curry," he said.

"Ah." She nodded. "Jewish penicillin by any other name."

Sansi looked puzzled. "Mulligatawny soup isn't Jewish," he said.

At last someone answered from the kitchen and Annie ordered the soup and a fresh pot of coffee. Then she hung up and looked back at Sansi.

"You'd probably feel better if you had a shower," she said. "It's going to be a while before your call comes through."

Sansi nodded. He knew he would have to clean himself up before he went to see Mr. and Mrs. Gilman.

"I'll finish my coffee," he said. He reached for his cup and noticed that the flier he'd given her earlier that day was faceup on the table. "You looked at it?" he asked.

"Yes," she said, following his gaze. "I looked at it."

"What do you think?"

"It reads like a goddamn wanted poster."

"Yes," Sansi said. "I thought it was a little like that myself. It reads as if they do not expect to find her easily, as if they are looking for her with the understanding that she does not want to be found."

"Maybe she doesn't," Annie said. "Not by her mother at any rate."

Sansi looked questioningly at her.

"She can't stand her mother," Annie said. "They haven't spoken to each other in a long time."

Sansi considered the matter for a moment. "That isn't the only thing that seemed odd to me," he said.

Annie waited.

"They're doing everything they can to make this search harder than it ought to be," he went on. "All it takes is a few discreet questions. They could find out where their daughter lives in a wet afternoon. But something like this . . ." He gestured dismissively at the flyer. "It is like sending out a warning. It is calculated to drive her away."

"It's not subtle," Annie said. "But it's Joy Gilman's way."

"You know Mrs. Gilman?"

"I don't know her," Annie answered. "I know of her. She was big in local politics in L.A., a big self-promoter. Her family always came second except when she needed them to fluff up the image at election time. Cora confirmed a lot of my suspicions about Joy Gilman and all those other politicians like her."

"Well, she is making a mistake," Sansi said. "Or she is listening to someone who is giving her very bad advice."

"Listening to other people was never one of her strong points," Annie said. "It's one of the reasons her daughter stopped talking to her."

"She is listening to someone now."

"Like who?"

"Mr. Coombe—he's from the consul. He was with Mrs. Gilman when I met her in the lobby this morning. A man with a most unfortunate manner, considering his prospects for success here depend upon his ability to get along with the natives."

He gave the word *natives* a particularly British tone of condescension and it made Annie smile. Only Sansi, with the dual personality of the Anglo-Indian, could carry off something like that.

"What strikes me as most curious about this," he added, "is why Mr. and Mrs. Gilman should come here now."

"What surprises me is why they would come at all," Annie said. "They must know how their daughter feels about them."

"Yes," Sansi said. "Something must have happened. They must want to see her very badly. They must be very afraid for her."

"Afraid?"

"There is much to be afraid of here," he said, looking point-edly at her.

"They're getting old," she speculated. "Intimations of mortality and all that. Maybe they want to patch things up before they die."

"Perhaps," Sansi said. "But in my experience, such sponta-neous outpourings of forgiveness are rare in long-standing fam-ily disputes. Even rarer in the disposition of people such as Mrs. Gilman. No, something must have happened to make them choose this particular time."

"Yes, but what?"

"Mrs. Henke, perhaps."

"Karen Henke? She was Cora's best friend. She would know how much Cora despises her mother."

"She is also aware how dangerous a place Goa can be—espe-cially to children."

Annie paused. "So what are you going to do?"

"I am going to try and talk to the Gilmans," he said. "I am go-ing to find out why they are here."

"What good will that do?"

"I'm not sure," he said. "It depends largely on what they have to tell me, or whether they will tell me anything."

"Are you going to tell them where to find Cora?"

"I haven't decided what I will tell them."

"Are you?" Annie persisted.

"What makes you think she needs to be protected from them?" Sansi asked. "It might be the best thing for her and her children if her parents were to find out where she is."

"You don't know that," Annie said. "You're interfering in someone's life. You have no right to do that."

"But you do? Because you mean well and I don't?"

Annie paused to take a breath and to calm herself. "I could at least speak to Cora first to see if she wants her parents to know where she is."

Sansi hesitated, wondering how much he should tell her. He

didn't know yet whether his suspicions were anything more than unsupportable misgivings.

"You told me something this morning about Drew," he said. "Something I think could be important."

Annie gave a short, disbelieving laugh. "You won't let it go, will you? You just won't let it go."

"You said he took care of the arrangements for the transshipment of the Henkes' daughter. You said he gave them money so they could accompany their daughter's body back to the United States."

"Yes," she said. "That's why they're stuck here now."

Sansi nodded. "I know you told me, but where is it the Henkes' live in the United States again?"

"Ann Arbor, Michigan."

"And that is where their daughter is buried?"

Annie nodded.

"And Drew and Cora hope to be leaving soon?"

"As soon as they can."

"Do you know where they are going in the United States?"

"New Mexico, I think. At least that's what Cora says."

"New Mexico?"

"Yes."

"Why New Mexico?"

Annie shrugged. "Because it's warm and it's cheap and it's got a kind of spiritual side to it and a lot of history. A lot of hippies and new age types go there because they can do their thing and people will leave them alone."

Sansi nodded. "Do you know if they will be stopping over in Michigan on the way to New Mexico—to see their friends the Henkes?"

"I don't know," Annie said. "I guess it's possible. Cora never said anything to me."

"It would be surprising if they didn't, given the close connection between the families," Sansi mused out loud. "The extent to which they relied on Drew and the . . . nurturing type of person he is."

"You've never met him and you sound like you hate him," Annie said. "That's a kind of prejudice I never expected to hear from you."

Sansi looked at her. "Yes," he said. "I am prejudiced. I am prejudiced against parasites. And Drew is a parasite. He lives off the weaknesses of others. He draws gullible people to him, preaches to them about peace and harmony, then sells them the drugs they need to kill themselves. He may look like a low-level hustler, Annie, but I am not so sure. He may be a lot more dangerous than you realize."

Annie looked at him closely. "You know something," she said. "You know something, don't you?"

"I don't know what I know," he said. "I need a few more days—then we will both know."

She wanted to press him further, but his eyelids began to droop and she realized that if he didn't do something to revive himself, he was about to pass out on the sofa.

"Come on," she said. "Let's see if a shower helps."

He put down his coffee cup, levered himself out of the sofa, and with Annie by his side, walked woozily to the bathroom. She waited while he undressed, then took away his soiled clothes and brought him a complete change. He climbed under the shower, soaped and shampooed himself methodically, and turned the water up as hot and as hard as he could bear it in a vain attempt to sluice his exhaustion down the drain. Shaving was a little harder. The razor felt clumsy in his hand and he steered it around his face as if in a dream, as if it were someone else's face he was shaving. By the time he had dressed and combed his hair, Annie came back to tell him his mulligatawny soup had arrived. As a final act of desperation he doused his face with aftershave and hoped the pain from the razor nicks would keep him awake for an hour or so.

His soup was waiting for him on the dining-room table, but

when he sat down he found he had no appetite. He managed a mouthful of bread and a half-dozen spoonfuls of the soup, then he stopped and pushed the bowl away from him.

"Bad mulligatawny?" Annie asked from across the table.

"Good mulligatawny," he said. "It's me. I'm too tired."

"More coffee?"

He nodded and she poured him a fresh cup. He had just put it to his lips when the phone rang. Annie got up and brought it over to him. He smiled appreciatively.

"Don't get used to it," she said.

Sansi picked up the phone and waited while the switchboard completed the connection with Bombay. There was a series of clicks, a grating burst of static, then finally Jamal's voice, a sonorous echo of Sansi's own weariness.

"Jamal."

"It's Sansi, Commissioner."

"You have something?"

Sansi heard the same urgency he had heard when Jamal had visited him in his apartment. Obviously, the situation in Bombay was no better.

"I may be getting somewhere," he said cautiously.

"What have you got?"

"I think I know how they are getting the heroin out to Goa," Sansi said. "But there are a few things you have to do at your end."

"What things?"

"You have to contact all the consuls for Western Europe," Sansi told him. "You must go directly to the consuls them-selves—the junior staff are not trustworthy—and you must get the names of all foreign citizens who were shipped home after dying of a drug overdose in Goa during the past two years."

"*Bakwas,*" Jamal swore. "Do you have any idea how long that will take?"

"That is up to you, Commissioner," Sansi said. "You know how much time you have got."

There was a long silence at the other end. Both men knew that Sansi would never have spoken to him that way if he had still been working at crime branch. And both men knew how much had changed since Sansi had left.

"What is the purpose of this?" Jamal asked.

"Every one of them will have to be exhumed," Sansi replied. "Every one of them will have to be examined."

"They will be turning over half the cemeteries in Europe," Jamal protested. "What are we looking for?"

"Evidence of interference after interment," Sansi said. "Traces of heroin inside the corpse separate from any residue in the tissue."

There was a loud clacking sound and Sansi looked up to see that Annie had put her cup down so hard it had cracked at the base and a puddle of coffee was spreading over the shiny surface of the table. Instead of hurrying to the kitchen to get a cloth to clean it up, she stayed where she was, staring at him while the puddle spread wider and wider.

"That is how they've been getting it out?" Jamal asked, his voice rising.

"Yes," Sansi answered. "They have been hiding it inside the bodies of overdose victims."

"You are absolutely sure of this, Sansi?"

"I have all the evidence we need at this end," Sansi said. "All we need now is one corpse with traces of heroin in it at the other end. I don't know when the last body went out, but if you move quickly you might find one with all the heroin still inside."

"*Are Bapre* . . ." Jamal sighed, his voice a long exclamation of relief.

"I have one more request," Sansi added. "The name of a probable American victim."

He looked at Annie and saw that her eyes were wide with disbelief. The silence on the phone seemed to seep out into the room, so that everything was silent except for the rhythmic drip of the coffee as it spilled from the table to the floor.

"Her name is Tina Henke. A child, nine years old. The parents' names are Rick and Karen Henke and they live in Ann Arbor, Michigan. The cause of death is listed as accidental drowning. I believe the real cause to be death by strangulation. The body was interred sometime within the past eight weeks. I suspect the heroin may still be in there."

CHAPTER 20

Sansi knocked on the door of the Gilmans' room. There was a long pause and he was about to knock again when he heard someone moving behind the door. The lock turned, the door opened, and a man in his early sixties appeared wearing a checked, short-sleeved shirt and khaki pants. He was gaunt and round-shouldered, so that his clothes hung loosely on him, and he had a high forehead with thinning gray hair and the jaundiced, desiccated look that many Americans seemed to acquire in old age. His eyes, pale brown and watery, had a tentative look.

"Yes?"

"Mr. Gilman?"

"Yes."

"My name is George Sansi. I am a lawyer from Bombay. I wonder if I might speak with you for a moment."

Gilman hesitated and Sansi heard someone speaking furtively from inside the room: Gilman's wife telling her husband to send Sansi away.

"I met Mrs. Gilman this morning," Sansi added. "We did not

have the opportunity to speak properly. I wonder if I might have a word with you both now?"

"I'm sorry, Mr. Sansi," Gilman said in the unhappy manner of a man who would rather avoid confrontation. "Unless you have some information about our daughter . . . I . . . I don't think there is anything for us to discuss."

"It is your daughter I want to discuss," Sansi said.

"Yes, I know," Gilman answered. "But I think my wife spoke for both of us this morning . . . this is a very difficult business for us . . . please."

He went to close the door. Reflexively, Sansi put up his hand and held it open. Gilman looked alarmed, unsure what to do next.

"Please . . . take your hand away from the door."

Sansi heard a click and the sound of Mrs. Gilman tapping the telephone keys.

"Tell him I'm calling hotel security," she said in her dry, scratchy voice.

"Your daughter has a friend who used to live in Goa," Sansi said quickly. "Her name is Karen Henke and she lives in Ann Arbor in the state of Michigan. She had a daughter named Tina who died here. I think Mrs. Henke is the reason you are here?"

Gilman dithered, his expression shifting from alarm to recognition to hopelessness.

"Please, Mr. Gilman," Sansi said. "Ask your wife to wait a moment. My interest here is entirely reasonable. I may have some information that will assist you, and I assure you, I am not interested in a reward."

It might have been the note of entreaty in Sansi's voice or his use of the word *reasonable* that tipped the scale. Or it might have been the suggestion that if Gilman were to impose just a little restraint on his wife, they might learn something to their advantage. Whatever it was, it was enough to prompt Gilman into a decision.

"Hold on a minute, Joy," he called back into the room. "Maybe we ought to hear what Mister . . . ?"

"Sansi."

". . . what Mr. Sansi has to say."

There was a slight pause, then the sound of the handset settling into its cradle. A moment later the door opened wider and Mrs. Gilman appeared.

"He knows about Karen Henke," Mr. Gilman said.

Joy Gilman looked suspiciously at Sansi. "I'll go get Terry," she said. "If we're going to talk, I think he should be here."

Sansi recognized the name of the man from the consulate who had discouraged him from speaking further with Mrs. Gilman that morning.

"I think it would be better if we spoke privately," he said.

"I bet you do," Joy Gilman said, and moved to go around him.

"Please, Mrs. Gilman," Sansi said. "I just told your husband— I have no financial interest here. But I do have information relating to your daughter and I believe it would be in your best interests to listen to me, if only for a moment."

Joy Gilman hesitated, looked at her husband then back at Sansi. It finally seemed to occur to her that she might be in danger of driving away a man who had something to offer.

"Okay," she conceded. She made it sound as if she was doing Sansi a favor. "We'll hear you out."

Sansi nodded politely, though he had already decided that much of what he had heard about Joy Gilman was right. She was abrasive, impetuous, and mistrustful, a woman who had decided early in life that the best way to get what she wanted was to walk over everybody. To that end she had surrounded herself with weaker mortals, like her husband, to make sure she got her way.

Sansi stepped inside while Mr. Gilman closed the door behind him. The room was small and poky compared with the spacious and elegant bungalows up the hill, a standard double with a sitting area and balcony overlooking the beach. Joy Gilman took a chair near the balcony door while her husband gestured for Sansi to take the tiny two-seat sofa. Mr. Gilman remained standing for a moment, looking awkward. Then he stuck out his hand and introduced himself.

"My name is Don Gilman."

He and Sansi shook hands and Mr. Gilman sat down in the remaining armchair. Joy Gilman waited, her face set, eyes wary. Neither of them offered Sansi a drink.

"You must understand, Mr. Sansi, we've met a lot of people in this country who want to take advantage of us," Don Gilman said. "We know nothing about India. This is our first time here—"

"And the last," Joy Gilman said.

"We have to be careful," Don Gilman added. "We never know who we're dealing with. The consul has been very helpful to us in that regard."

"Yes," Sansi responded. "I met Mr. Coombe this morning."

His tone was acute enough to convey his low opinion of Coombe. It seemed to rankle Mrs. Gilman. Obviously, she depended on Terry Coombe. He was their guide and adviser, their lifeline in an alien culture.

"You told us you have some information," she said.

"I have a good idea where your daughter is, Mrs. Gilman," he said, growing tired of her bad manners. "And I suspect Mr. Coombe knows where she is, too."

The hardness in her eyes wavered for a moment, though she recovered quickly. "Where is she?"

"She lives at the hippie colony at Anjuna, about five miles up the coast from here. I don't know which house exactly, but you could have taken a taxi up there at any time and found her in about an hour. Except now, of course. It's too late now."

"Too late . . . ?" Don Gilman repeated. "Why is it too late?"

"She knows you're here," Sansi told them. "And I suspect she'll try to avoid you. But you already know that, don't you?"

The Gilmans looked uneasily at each other.

"I assume it was Mr. Coombe's idea to print and distribute the reward posters?" Sansi said.

"Is there anything wrong with that?" Joy Gilman retorted. "From what I understand, money is the only way to get anything done in this country."

Sansi allowed himself a small smile. "From what I understand, Mrs. Gilman, money speaks rather loudly in your country, too."

She looked away, peeved.

"You could not have gone about your search in a less effective manner if you had tried," Sansi went on. "You have told all Goa what you are doing here. Naturally that will bring out the criminal element. And if you are not careful, most of your time will be taken up dealing with them. If you had used some discretion, if you had looked around quietly on your own, you would have found your daughter at the coffee shop in the resort next door to us. She comes in two or three times a week for coffee. Or she did until you started passing out your reward posters."

For a moment there was only pained silence. Don Gilman leaned forward, elbows on his knees, and rubbed his face roughly with both hands. Joy Gilman pressed her lips together tightly, wavering between uncertainty and hostility.

"We'll go to the police if we have to," she said. "They've promised us full cooperation in finding Cora."

"The police?"

"Yes. We'd prefer Cora to contact us voluntarily, but the police will find her and hold her for us, if it comes to that."

"They could bring her to you now if they felt like it," Sansi said. "They know where she is. They know where all your daughter's family are. Your son-in-law teaches meditation in the ashram at Vagator—among other things. He is very well known in Goa."

"Terry Coombe wouldn't lie to us," Joy Gilman protested. "He's worked his butt off on our behalf."

"I'm sure he has been by your side ever since you got here," Sansi observed. "I doubt you can go anywhere without him."

The expressions on both their faces told him he was right.

"What are you saying?" Don Gilman asked. "That we've been taken for a ride by our own consul?"

Sansi hesitated, choosing his words carefully. Then he looked directly at Joy Gilman.

"When I saw what you were doing this morning, Mrs. Gilman, when I met Mr. Coombe—I thought it was more a matter of ignorance. A lot of consular people live in India for some time and think they know the country. They think they know how to deal with the people. I thought that perhaps Mr. Coombe meant well and his only mistake was overzealousness. But the more I thought about it, the more I came to believe you were being manipulated. Something very wrong is happening in Goa and I think Mr. Coombe is part of it. I don't believe he is here to help you at all. I believe he is working very hard to create the illusion that he is helping you when all the time he wants to make sure you never get in touch with your daughter. It would explain his behavior when I tried to speak with you this morning, Mrs. Gilman. It was more than ignorance. He did not want to take the chance that you might learn something from me. It is only by keeping people away from you and filtering all local contact through him that he can make sure your search goes nowhere."

Sansi watched as his words hit home, saw the cracks widen in Mrs. Gilman's veneer. Her husband looked dazedly at Sansi.

"You're telling us that Terry Coombe is a crook?"

"I think there is a real possibility that Mr. Coombe is involved in ongoing criminal activity," Sansi answered.

"What reason . . . what kind of criminal activity?"

"Drugs," Sansi said.

Don Gilman moaned softly and seemed to shrivel further inside his sack of tired yellow skin, as if his worst fears had all been confirmed.

"We don't know that any of this is true," Mrs. Gilman said. "Any of it . . . it could all be bullshit."

"Mrs. Gilman, your son-in-law is a drug dealer," Sansi said quietly. "He is involved with some of the biggest heroin traffickers in India. I have reason to believe he may be smuggling heroin into the United States, and if that is the case, someone inside the consulate is helping him. I think there is a good chance that person is Mr. Coombe. I have set certain inquiries in motion which ought to confirm that in the next day or two. If I am right, it would explain why Mr. Coombe is working so hard to prevent your getting near your daughter and her family. He isn't working for you or the consul, Mrs. Gilman. He is working for your son-in-law, and your son-in-law doesn't want you anywhere near his family. You would know better than I do why that is so, Mrs. Gilman."

Joy Gilman looked stung, as Sansi had intended.

"Mr. Sansi, you seem to know an awful lot about what goes on here," she said. "You're not exactly a disinterested party, are you?"

Sansi hesitated. It was time for some accommodation, an effort to take some hostility out of the air. The Gilmans had confirmed some of his suspicions, but he still hadn't obtained everything he needed from them.

"I am a lawyer," he said. "But I was also a police officer for twenty years, at crime branch in Bombay. It is the equivalent of your FBI. I have been in Goa for some time, conducting a private investigation. But you are right, Mrs. Gilman, it is not a coincidence that we have crossed paths. The reason you are here is the same reason I am here. It is all tied up with the consequences of the drug industry. You are right to be suspicious. It is impossible to know whom you can trust in Goa. Certainly you cannot trust either the police or the government."

"But we can trust you? We can take your word over the word of a man who works for our own government?"

"You and your husband are alone in India, Mrs. Gilman," Sansi said. "You must rely on your own judgment."

"For God's sake, Joy," her husband interjected. "It's not like we didn't know what to expect."

Sansi looked at Don Gilman.

"The son of a bitch was dealing drugs when our daughter got tied up with him twenty years ago," Gilman said. "Of course he's going to be doing the same thing here—and a hell of a lot worse, I don't doubt."

Sansi listened, trying to look sympathetic.

"Karen Henke told us they were all at this Anjuna place together," Gilman added. "It sounded like some kind of commune or something. It was Terry Coombe who said it was too risky for us to go up there, that we should let him handle it."

This time Mrs. Gilman did not contradict her husband. She stared blankly at the floor, resigned to the probability that Sansi was right, that Terry Coombe had been manipulating them ever since they had arrived because he was part of the drug trade, too.

"You've spoken to Karen Henke?" Sansi asked.

"Yes," Gilman answered. "You're right, Mr. Sansi. She contacted us a few weeks back. She told us what happened to her daughter. She said she was worried about Cora . . . about the kids. . . ."

Gilman's voice faltered. He stopped and struggled to compose himself.

Joy Gilman finished her husband's sentence for him. "That was when we found out we had grandchildren," she said.

"You didn't know?"

Mrs. Gilman shook her head. "We aren't on good terms with our daughter. We haven't spoken to her since she got married, seventeen years ago. The last we heard was when she and that bastard decided to move to India. Until three weeks ago we had no idea we had a grandson and a granddaughter. Our grandson is almost a teenager . . . and we've never seen him."

"And you have no illusions about your son-in-law?" Sansi said.

"None," Mrs. Gilman added. "The son of a bitch destroyed our family."

"Because he was a drug dealer?"

Joy Gilman paused for a moment. A multitude of emotions seemed to pass behind her eyes. A half smile formed briefly on her lips, then vanished.

"I'm retired now," she said. "Before I retired I spent my whole life in local politics. Twenty-two years ago I was the first woman to be elected mayor of Glenvale. It was quite an achievement at the time, and one of the reasons I won was because I stood for something. I had a solid family values platform. I also had a family. Don was in the design department at Lockheed. Cora was at teachers' college. Our son, Robert, was in the twelfth grade, an honors student. I know what an important part image plays in politics, Mr. Sansi. I'm sure it's not a whole lot different here."

Sansi nodded his agreement.

"So," she continued, "I guess you can appreciate that we had a few problems when our daughter told us she was dropping out of college so she could move in with a convicted drug dealer."

The more Sansi heard, the more he realized that in a bleak, predictable way, there was much about Joy Gilman that made sense.

"But you know what?" Mrs. Gilman added.

Sansi waited.

"I was reelected five times in a row. That's a record that's going to stand for a long time, Mr. Sansi. The voters stuck by me. I took that as the greatest compliment of all. And, by God, I was there for them every day. I never let them down."

Sansi smiled ambiguously. He had no doubt that Drew was some kind of a monster. But so was Joy Gilman. And Cora Gilman had been caught between the two of them.

"Which of you spoke to Karen Henke?" he asked.

"We both did," Joy Gilman said.

"Did she tell either of you how her daughter died?"

Both Don and Joy Gilman hesitated. It was Mrs. Gilman who answered first.

"She said it was murder. She said there was some kind of land boom under way. She claimed it was some kind of big government scam and the hippies had been targeted because they were in the way and the developers wanted to be rid of them."

"Did she say who she thought was responsible?"

Mrs. Gilman thought for a moment, then shook her head.

"She told me she thought it was the police—or people working for the police," Mr. Gilman said. "She wasn't too clear about a lot of it, like she was still in shock from what had happened. But she was definite about getting Cora and the kids out. She said they were in a lot of danger and we had to get them home."

"Did she mention Drew at all?"

"She said he gave them money, helped them get back home," Mrs. Gilman answered. "Which doesn't sound like him, I have to tell you. Not the way I remember him."

"You don't think it is the kind of thing he would do naturally, out of concern for his friends?"

Mrs. Gilman emitted a mirthless laugh. "He never did anything for anybody unless there was something in it for him. I don't know what he looks like today, but he used to be pretty cute—cute as any movie star. And a real glib tongue on him. The girls went for him in a big way. Cora wasn't the only one. But he saw what a meal ticket she was. And once he had a hold on her, he spent all her money and used her to get more money out of us. He only cares about himself, Mr. Sansi. Being a drug dealer is the perfect profession for him. He doesn't care how many people he kills as long as there's money in it."

"Do you have a telephone number where Karen Henke can be reached?" Sansi asked.

"Sure," Don Gilman answered. "You want to speak to her?"

"It might be helpful," Sansi said. "Perhaps you could call her

first. Tell her I will be calling . . . that I am a lawyer and I am trying to help."

"We'll call her tonight if you want," Don Gilman said.

He pulled an address book off the telephone table, copied
Karen Henke's number onto a piece of hotel notepaper, and
handed it to Sansi. Sansi nodded. Now he had everything he
needed. He started to get up but Mrs. Gilman wasn't quite ready
to let him go.

"What about Terry Coombe, Mr. Sansi?" she asked. "What
are we supposed to do about him?"

"Don't do anything about Mr. Coombe," Sansi replied. "Go
along with him as if everything was normal, and don't say or do
anything to make him suspicious. In the next day or two I suspect
Mr. Coombe will receive an urgent summons to return to Bombay. Then he will cease to be a problem."

"Then what happens to us?" Don Gilman asked. "We can't
find Cora on our own."

Sansi felt a pang of disquiet.

"You want me to do it?"

There was an awkward silence between the three of them and
then, speaking in her business voice, Mrs. Gilman said, "We'd
like to give Cora the opportunity to come back with us, Mr. Sansi.
But if she doesn't want to, that's her decision. It's the children we
want."

Sansi looked from one to the other, his disquiet deepening.
"What makes you think they will come without their mother?"

"It isn't Cora's decision anymore," Mrs. Gilman said. "She is
an unfit mother. She decided to throw her life away—nobody
else. But she has no right to throw away the lives of those two
children. They're Americans. They are entitled to all the rights
and privileges of American citizenship. They don't belong in this
third-world shithole with a pothead for a mother and a pusher
for a father. We came here with a federal court order granting us
guardianship of our grandchildren, and it's our understanding
that the Indian government will not stand in our way. We're go-

ing to find our grandchildren, Mr. Sansi, and we're going to take them home and give them the lives they deserve. And what Cora wants or doesn't want really doesn't have a hell of a lot to do with it anymore."

A wave of giddiness engulfed Sansi. There were suddenly too many conflicting demands, and he felt incapable of sorting them out. Neither Don nor Joy Gilman seemed to notice.

"So," Mrs. Gilman said, "you're obviously a man who cares about what's right, Mr. Sansi. Will you help us rescue our grand-children?"

CHAPTER 21

Sansi looked at the bland surroundings of the bedroom, almost as familiar now as his bedroom in Bombay. The bedside clock told him it was a few minutes after ten. He had slept for almost twelve hours. He ought to feel better. Instead he felt weak and drained, as if he needed twelve more. As if he needed a holiday. He smiled faintly. Annie gave his hand a squeeze.

"You had a bad night," she said. "You woke me up a couple of times tossing and grumbling. You couldn't have got much rest."

"No," Sansi said. "Perhaps when we get back to Bombay?"

She smiled and got to her feet. "You think you can handle some juice . . . or coffee?"

"Coffee."

He was just as bad as Annie with her cigarettes and the hippies with their dope, he thought. All he needed was a fix to get him through—caffeine, sugar, whiskey, whatever. Temporary solutions to last a lifetime, as long as it was a short life.

Annie returned after a few minutes and he disentangled himself from the sheets and propped himself up against the pillows so he could drink his coffee without spilling it. Annie sat on the edge of the bed, anxious to know how his meeting with the Gilmans had gone. She had waited up for him the previous night, but he had been too exhausted to talk and she hadn't pushed him. Now she could wait no longer.

"So," she prodded him. "What are they like?"

"Who, the Gilmans?"

"No, the Kennedys."

Sansi hesitated, wondering how much he should tell her when there was still so much he was unsure of himself. "As you said, Mrs. Gilman is a . . . strong personality, the kind of person who always thinks she's right, no matter how much damage she does. Her husband seems a decent enough chap, but he is weak. He goes along with her to keep the peace, even though there is no peace."

"Did they say what they're doing here now?"

"Karen Henke called them."

"So"—Annie nodded—"you were right."

"After so many years, it was the only explanation."

"And what do they expect to accomplish now that they're here?"

"They want to see their daughter."

"Isn't it clear to them that their daughter doesn't want to see them?"

"Oh, it's clear to them," Sansi said. "But they are not overly concerned with what Cora wants—and they certainly don't care about Drew."

"Well, what then?"

"They want their grandchildren," he said. "They have come to save their grandchildren from the drug culture. They want to take them back to America."

"Oh Jesus . . ." Annie breathed.

"And they asked me if I would help them."

Annie stared at him. "What did you say?"

"I told them . . . I would think about it."

Annie felt a stab of disbelief. When she spoke it took considerable effort to keep her voice under control.

"Are you saying that you'd actually consider it? That you'd help them take Cora's kids away from her?"

Sansi put his cup down on the bedside table. "I am trying to deal with the situation that exists," he said. "At the worst, it might not be a bad thing if Cora was to talk to her parents."

"You have no right to make that decision," Annie said, her voice rising. "What goes on between Cora and her parents is none of your business."

"They want to go back to the United States," Sansi added.

"Yeah, but maybe not on Joy Gilman's terms."

"It is something they could discuss," he said. "The Gilmans would prefer to make peace with their daughter."

"And Drew?"

Sansi shrugged.

"There's no place for him in their plans, is there?"

Sansi remained silent.

"Jesus Christ."

"Annie, he is hardly the ideal role model—"

"You're not the goddamn child welfare authority," she snapped.

"You think it is all right for children to grow up with a drug dealer for a father?"

"That's not the point."

"It is as far as the Gilmans are concerned. Drew has convictions for dealing drugs in America. He won't stop when he gets back. The Gilmans have a right to be concerned about their grandchildren."

Annie shook her head. "Cora is a good mother. It would destroy her if you took her kids away."

"Cora had a choice. Her children should know they have a choice, too."

"You're talking about breaking up a family."

"Perhaps this is one family that deserves to be broken up."

Annie gasped. "I don't believe you said that."

"You only have to see what kind of man Drew is to appreciate the caliber of Cora's judgment."

Annie sat quite still on the edge of the bed and stared blankly at the bedroom floor.

"As awful as Mrs. Gilman is, I think she represents far less of a threat to the children than their father," Sansi said. "I think the Gilmans deserve a chance to see their grandchildren."

Annie nodded and lifted her eyes to meet his. "You think it's okay to make deals with that shithead Jamal," she said quietly. "I was willing to go along with that because you and I are grownups and we can live with the consequences." She got up and took a couple of steps toward the bedroom door before turning to look back at him. "But I am not going to let you make deals with the lives of those children."

"Annie . . ."

He leaned forward and reached for her hand, but she backed away. An invisible chasm opened between them, its dimensions defined only by the terrible silence that rushed in to fill it. Then she turned and left the room. A moment later he heard the front door close behind her.

"Bhagwan," Sansi said.

■   ■

It was late morning when the call he had placed got through. He hurried in from the verandah and picked up the phone and the operator told him to stand by. There were several minutes' delay, a sustained screech of static, then at last, a clear ringing tone. It rang for a long time before a woman answered, a woman on the other side of the world in Ann Arbor, Michigan.

"Mrs. Henke?"

"Yeah."

"My name is George Sansi. I am an attorney-at-law. I believe you are expecting my call?"

"Yeah, hours ago," Cass said. "So, what's going on over there?"

She was standing in the kitchen of a rented duplex on West Herkimer Street. On the other side of the kitchen windows, the long northern winter had not yet loosened its grip and the street was coated with a rind of dirty snow. Rick was sprawled on a sofa in the living room, smoking a joint and channel-surfing the late-night TV. Cass had lost weight since she had left India, but it hadn't done much for her appearance. Her skin was sallow, her hair greasy, and her eyes permanent hollows. No combination of grass and Prozac seemed potent enough to give her even one good night's sleep.

"Mrs. Henke, I am involved in an ongoing investigation into certain corrupt activities in Goa, and I have come into possession of material concerning the death of your daughter."

"What . . . kind of material?"

Fifteen thousand miles away he heard the catch in her voice.

"Material that might give us the identity of the person responsible for the death of your daughter," he said.

"Yeah, and what's that going to cost me?"

Sansi paused, wondering what exactly Don Gilman had told her about him. "There will be no cost to you, Mrs. Henke," he said. "What I am seeking is your cooperation . . . to establish beyond doubt who is responsible for this crime."

"And what good is that supposed to do?"

Sansi understood her reticence. As far as she was concerned, it was already beyond doubt. The police had killed her daughter, and corruption was so much a part of official life in Goa it was unlikely they would ever be brought to justice. If Sansi was some crooked lawyer looking for a way into the case so he could squeeze her for a buck, he wasn't about to get very far.

"The situation in Goa is very complicated, Mrs. Henke."

"Tell me about it."

"It may not be exactly as you think."

"Are you saying it wasn't the cops who killed my daughter?"

Sansi heard the anger in her voice and realized he was in danger of losing her. "The material I have acquired suggests the investigation should be expanded to include individuals outside the police force."

"What individuals?"

"I cannot say with certainty, Mrs. Henke. I have suspicions, but it could be one of several people."

"Who are you working for?" she asked abruptly.

"I am part of an out-of-state investigative unit," Sansi said. "It is the only way the issue of corruption in Goa can be approached with confidence."

"You're not with the government?"

"Not the government of Goa," he answered.

There was a silence, then she said, "What do you want from me?"

Sansi gave a sigh of relief. "Mrs. Henke, I need to know if there has been any official examination of your daughter's body since it arrived in the United States?"

There was a long pause at the other end.

"Mrs. Henke . . . ?"

"You mean an autopsy?"

"Yes."

"Why do you want to know something like that?"

"Please, Mrs. Henke, it is relevant to the investigation."

"That was all handled by the consul," she answered. "We told them what really went down and they acted like they sympathized, but they didn't do anything. They got a copy of the official report from the coroner's office in Panjim, but that was all bullshit. They said there was nothing they could do except refer it to Washington for some kind of advice or follow-up or something, but we knew there was nothing ever going to come of it."

"So, Tina was buried as soon as you got her back from India?"

"Yeah, two days . . . two days after we got back."

"Do you remember who it was on the consular staff you dealt with?"

"I'm not sure," she said. "A friend of ours took care of all of that for us. Drew Betts. He was our neighbor at Anjuna. If he hadn't helped us, we wouldn't have got through it. The cops tried to screw us right to the end. It was Drew who called the consul. We just signed the papers."

"Do you remember the name of the man from the consul?"

"I'm not sure," she answered. "Cook or something, I don't really remember. I wasn't really functioning at my best at the time."

"Could it have been Coombe . . . Terry Coombe?"

"Yeah, it was," she said. "A blond guy . . . losing his hair."

"Thank you, Mrs. Henke." Sansi took a breath and added, "There is something else I have to ask you now, something very important."

There was an uncomfortable silence at the other end.

"Your daughter's body must be examined by an American coroner," Sansi said. "I have requested an exhumation order through the American consul in Bombay, but I am afraid it may not get very far. It would expedite matters greatly if you were to contact the authorities in Ann Arbor directly and tell them you want an autopsy performed immediately. You know your daughter was murdered, Mrs. Henke. You have to convince the coroner in Ann Arbor that the death certificate from Goa is a fraud."

"Is that where it came from?"

"You didn't know that?"

"No, I thought the consul had something to do with it. I didn't know, I wasn't thinking clearly."

"No. And the people who did this were counting on that. That is why you must question it now. Please, will you make the application?"

"You want us to dig up her body so we can find out what we already know?"

"Mrs. Henke, I know that your grief over your daughter's murder must overshadow everything you feel and do," Sansi said. "And I know you must have asked yourself why? Why did it happen to her? There was a reason. She wasn't selected at random. Your daughter's death was part of an elaborate, evil scheme. I think I know why she was killed, Mrs. Henke, and I want to put an end to it. But I need your help. I can't finish this without your help. . . ."

His words faded into a tinny echo and for a moment there was only the answering hiss of static. Then Karen Henke's voice came back, dull and oddly detached.

"Why was she killed, Mr. Sansi?"

"The evidence I have acquired suggests your daughter was murdered so that her body could be used to transport illegal drugs into the United States."

There was another achingly long silence at the other end then the same flat voice. "You think somebody used Tina's body to smuggle drugs into the country?"

"Yes," Sansi replied. "I don't know that this will make any difference to you, but your daughter was not the only one. There were others, perhaps twenty or more, from a number of different countries. We're still trying to find out how many."

There was a sharp rasping sound, then nothing, and Sansi thought she had fainted.

"Mrs. Henke?" he called. "Are you there? Are you still there?"

In the kitchen of her home the telephone had grown unbearably heavy in her hand, and Cass had let it slip down by her side. Somehow she found the strength to put it back to her mouth.

"I'm still here."

"I won't insult you by telling you I know how you must feel," Sansi said. "I don't . . . and I hope I never do."

"No," she said. "That's why you can call me up like this and tell me I have to go through it again, do it over and over . . ."

Her voice faltered and broke and Sansi waited, knowing there was nothing more he could say.

"You expect me to do this when you know there's no good that will come of it?" she added. "When there's nobody in that stinking goddam country of yours who will lift a finger against the people who did this?"

Sansi took a long and shaky breath.

"I can't promise you justice," he said. "But once I know who did this, one thing I can promise you—they won't do it again."

Cass let the phone hang by her side once more while she tried to collect her thoughts. The truth was she did not know what she felt anymore. Sometimes she no longer felt anything. Not even grief. Just a barren, crushing emptiness. She looked at Rick on the sofa, glassy eyed, slack jawed, clicking from station to station. It had never been much of a marriage. A couple of losers who gravitated toward each other out of a desperate need for undemanding companionship. Tina had been the bonus, the blessing. Somebody who loved Cass unreservedly, whose eyes lit up whenever she saw her because Cass was the center of her life. Tina was the source of her hope, her happiness, and her future. Now she was gone and Cass was utterly alone. She picked up the phone.

"I'll go to the coroner's office in the morning," she said.

"Thank you, Mrs. Henke."

"Yeah."

"You'll have them call me with the results?"

"Yeah."

He gave her the number for his office in Bombay, then hung up the phone. Despite the warmth in the room he felt cold and bleak, as if a chill had seeped through the telephone line from the other side of the world.

■　■

Annie paid off the cabdriver and hurried along the dirt footpath that threaded through the coconut palms toward Cora's house. Along the way she passed a few familiar faces, friends of Cora's who seemed pleased to see her. They were beginning to accept her, she realized, just as her world was conspiring to destroy them. She felt like a traitor in their midst.

She reached the bungalow, knocked on the flimsy wooden door, and waited impatiently. There was no response. Drew's red-and-white Yamaha was propped against the wall, but the house was quiet and looked empty. She tried the latch and the door opened to reveal an empty living room in its usual state of untidiness—cushions on the floor, plates, bottles, dope debris, a plastic bag with a couple of ounces of ganja for everyone to see. But no sign of Cora, Drew, or the kids. Then she heard something. The melodic lilt of sitar music from the back of the house.

"Hello . . . ?" she called, and took a step forward. "Anybody home?"

Nobody answered.

She crossed the living room tentatively, feeling like an intruder, and looked down the hallway past the empty kitchen and the bedrooms. The door to the verandah was open, so that sunlight streamed through the fishnet screen and painted a grid on the hallway floor. The other doors in the hallway were open, too; the only room that was dark was the main bedroom. That was where the music was coming from. A tape on the cassette player.

"Hello?" she tried again, a little louder. "It's me, Annie. Is anybody home?"

Again there was no response. She decided she ought to go. If Cora and Drew were home, they could be enjoying the kind of recreation husbands and wives liked to enjoy when somebody else was watching the kids. As if to confirm her suspicion, there was a grunt and a soft moaning sound, then a voice drowsy and discouraging.

"Who is it?"

It was Drew and she had woken him up. She hung back, then decided the damage was done.

"It's Annie. I'm looking for Cora."

There was a pause and then he said, "I think she's down at the garden."

"Thanks." She turned to go. "I'm sorry I disturbed you."

"That's okay," he answered. "What time is it?"

She looked at her watch. "Just after eleven."

"Shit."

"What's the matter?"

"I'm supposed to do the midday session at the ashram," he mumbled.

She smiled. Life in the fast lane. "You'd better hustle," she said.

"Hey," he called after her, "I'm glad you're here. I want to ask you about something."

She stopped, then retraced her footsteps cautiously till she was just outside the bedroom door. "What about?"

She didn't share Sansi's dark suspicions about Drew, but she didn't mistake him for a guileless love child either. She thought it would be a mistake to go into his bedroom when there was no one else around.

"It's okay," he said, sensing her hesitation. "You can come in."

"I don't think so," she answered.

There was another pause and then, "Any problems with your old man about the other night?"

"No."

"He wasn't jealous?"

"He has no reason to be."

"That's good. Jealousy is like cancer, except it eats away at the soul."

She smiled. Ashram patter—the banal presented as the profound. The hippies probably loved it.

"I'm going to see Cora," she said.

Before she could go, he appeared in the doorway, naked, his eyes half-open and his long silver hair tousled from sleep. He rubbed his beard and then, without a hint of self-consciousness, dropped his hand to his crotch and scratched himself there, too.

"Jesus . . . Drew . . ." She walked back down the hallway.

"What . . . ?"

He seemed genuinely not to understand. She felt a pang of doubt. Maybe she was overreacting. She stopped in the living room but kept her back to him.

"You want to talk to me, put something on."

"Oh," he said, as if he only just understood. "What's the problem? Can't you talk to me without staring at my cock?"

"Can't you talk to a woman without showing her your cock?"

She heard him laugh softly. "Okay," he said. "Just a minute."

A moment later he reappeared, fastening a *lungi* around his waist as he walked barefoot into the kitchen. He stopped by the refrigerator, took out a bottle of mango juice, and took a series of long swallows. Then he put it back, padded into the living room, and sat down on the sofa. Annie stayed where she was, in the middle of the room.

"Grab a seat," he said. "I want to talk to you for a minute."

She stayed where she was. "What about?"

"About the States."

"What about the States?"

"It's a while since we were there. I want to know how much things have changed."

"I don't know anything about the southwest."

"Who said anything about the southwest?"

"Isn't that where you're going? Cora said she—"

"It's one of the places we're considering," he said. "We haven't made up our minds yet."

He used the word *we*, but from the way he spoke, Annie knew he meant *I*. Despite the appearance of a liberated marriage, it was Drew who made all the major decisions.

"I'm thinking of starting an ashram," he said. "And I figure maybe L.A. would be better than New Mexico. What do you think?"

"I don't know," Annie shrugged. "I really don't."

"You just came from L.A.," he said, gentle but insistent.

"More than a year ago now."

"You still know it better than we do."

Annie sighed and decided it would be easiest to tell him what little she knew. "Well, you wouldn't be the first to try it," she said. "The question is could they fit another one in?"

"Mine wouldn't be like the others," he said. "I've been in India a long time, you know? I know stuff nobody else knows. I can introduce people to experiences more intense than anything they ever dreamed about. Not just meditation and transcendentalism, anybody can do that shit. I can show people how to confront their fears. I can show people the reality of reincarnation. I can take them on a journey to the other side of death."

"They can get that on the freeway."

He smiled, leaned toward the coffee table, and started to roll a joint. "Which part of L. A. do you think would be best?" he asked. "Venice . . . or maybe more upscale? The canyons have better vibes. What are the canyons like these days? What does it cost to buy into Topanga or Santa Ynez?"

It sounded real enough, but she couldn't avoid the impression that he was working her. She was used to getting information out of people and she knew when it was being done to her.

"Look, Drew, I'm leaving soon and I want to see Cora before I go. I just came to say good-bye."

"You're leaving?" He looked surprised.

"Yes, going back to Bombay."

He sealed the joint with a lewd stroke of his tongue, put it between his lips, and lit it. "You only just got here."

"I have a job to go back to," she said.

He inhaled, held it for a moment, then blew a long column of smoke at the ceiling. Then he offered the joint to her.

"I have to go," she said. "Good luck with the ashram."

"What do you want to tell Cora?"

She hesitated, reluctant to tell him though she wasn't sure why. "There are some people here looking for you," she said.

He nodded and took another pull on the joint.

"They've been handing out fliers around the hotel. They're offering a reward to anybody who can tell them where you are. I thought you should know."

She stopped because she didn't want him wondering how she

came to know so much. She wanted to discharge her obligations to Cora as a friend, that was all. After that, it was up to them what they did.

"Ma and Pa Kettle," he said.

"You know about them?"

"Yeah," he said. "I've seen the fliers. It's Cora's folks. They won't let it rest as long as she's with me. It's nice of you to tell us, though. It's nice of you to be concerned."

"What will you do?"

"Stay out of their way."

"What if they come here?"

"We'll know," he said. "We have more friends here than they do."

"You're not that hard to find."

"They'd still be wasting their time," he said. "We covered that territory a long time ago."

Yes, Annie thought, but that was before the Gilmans knew they had grandchildren. "Does Cora know?" she asked.

"Sure."

"How does she feel?"

"She doesn't like it," he said. "That's why she's not here right now. She and the kids are going to be at . . . different places for the next little while."

"Okay." Annie decided she had been more than polite. "I'd better go see her."

She opened the door and stepped outside. Drew got up, slipped on his sandals, and strolled out after her. He flicked what was left of his joint into the sand, then grabbed hold of his motorbike and wheeled it over to the footpath.

"Maybe we'll stop by and see you on the way through Bombay," he said.

"That'd be nice," she lied. She liked Cora, and felt for her, even though she didn't entirely approve of the way she lived her life. But she didn't really expect to see any of these people again—

and part of her was relieved. She had already stuck her neck way out on their behalf, and she still had no idea yet how she was going to square things with Sansi.

Drew hitched up the *lungi*, threw his leg over the bike, and let it roll forward a few feet. "There's something else I wanted to ask you."

She sighed, no longer trying to hide her impatience.

"Are you a religious person?"

She stared uncomprehendingly at him.

"Not especially."

"But your folks are religious, right?"

"They're Catholic, if that's what you mean."

"Yeah," he said, apparently pleased by her answer. "That's what I thought."

He kicked the starter pedal, and the 250cc engine hummed into life, then he eased open the throttle and rode off through the trees, his tinselly hair glistening in the bright sunlight. She watched him go, just out of bed, unwashed, half-naked, and high, riding his bike to the ashram to lead his first meditation of the day, and she marveled at such raw and unbridled ego. He didn't once look back, but raised his hand in a sardonic wave, knowing she was still watching him. From that single, arrogant gesture she knew she was right. He had been playing some kind of game.

She felt a pang of unease, then turned and followed the footpath down to the beach. She walked quickly, as if by hurrying she could leave her unease behind her in the shadows of the coconut palms. She was right to warn Cora, she reminded herself for the thousandth time since she had left Aguada, and she would not be diverted from doing it.

The sneering drone of the Yamaha faded behind her to be replaced by the soothing murmur of the surf. Minutes later she came to the sandy hollow amid the dunes that the hippies called the garden. The only people there were Aggie and Sara, sitting in the shade of a thatch shelter, though there were bags and mats and towels scattered around that suggested others were not too far away.

"Hello," Aggie said in her thick Danish accent. "You can't stay away from this place, hey?"

Annie tried to smile, but her face felt rigid, as if it had been locked in a frown.

Aggie's eyes narrowed. "Are you all right?"

"Oh sure," Annie said quickly. "Had trouble sleeping last night, that's all."

"What . . . mosquitoes?"

"No," Annie said. "Overactive imagination."

"Ah." Aggie nodded sagely. "The curse of the restless mind. You should try a cup of lukewarm cardamom tea before you go to bed. It is good for the nerves."

"Yeah . . . I probably should," Annie answered vaguely, and looked around. If Sara was here, then Cora couldn't be too far away. There were a few people on the beach playing baseball and a few in the water, but they were too far away to see clearly. There were also a half-dozen board riders trying hard to wring some excitement out of the swells, all of them Indian except for one long-haired blond boy. Paul was easy to find.

"Is Cora around?" Annie asked.

"She's having a swim," Aggie said. "She'll be back in a minute."

"I'll go down and see her," Annie said. "I have to talk to her."

Aggie seemed about to say something more, but she decided against it and went back to the piece of jute cloth she was working on with Sara, turning it into something decorative. Annie knelt down, watched Sara work for a minute, then lightly stroked her hair.

"How you doin', sweetheart?"

"Okay," Sara said.

"Just okay?"

"Yeah."

"I came to tell you good-bye," Annie said. "I might not see you again, so you have a great time in America, okay?"

Sara looked up from what she was doing. "Will we see you in America?"

"I can't promise," Annie said. "But I hope so . . . and if we do, we'll have a banana smoothie together. A big banana smoothie, okay?"

"Okay." Sara smiled.

Annie patted her one last time, then got back to her feet.

"Everybody is leaving," Aggie said. "Pretty soon Gus and me will be the only ones left."

Gus was Aggie's boyfriend, a Chilean in his sixties and a woefully inept artist.

"Maybe you and Gus ought to think about leaving, too," Annie said.

"No," Aggie said. "We have been here since 1967. We were the first, and now, I suppose, we'll be the last."

"You're not scared?"

"No," she said. "Mad . . . bloody damn mad for what they're doing here. But not scared. We're too old to be scared."

Annie gave her a wan smile. She didn't want to think about what would happen to the people who stayed.

"Bye, Aggie," she said. "Bye, Sara."

"Bye, Annie," Sara responded.

"Next time you're in Goa, you come see us," Aggie added. "We'll still be here."

Annie trudged down through the grassy dunes and across the hot sand. At the water's edge she slipped off her sandals and soothed her burning feet in the foam. A group of four women with Velcro bats hit a ball back and forth nearby, all of them topless, while a half-dozen Indian men in shirts and long pants stood around and watched. Some of the men watched Annie, waiting for her to take her clothes off, too. She turned away and strolled through the shallows, sandals in one hand, searching for Cora among the bobbing heads in the water. Her eye was drawn to a swimmer with one arm in the air, and she realized it was Cora waving to her. She waved back and waited while Cora finished her swim. A moment later Cora emerged through the waves, pausing only to wring the water from the long braided rope of her hair. She was wearing black bikini pants and looked so young and pretty she could have passed for twenty-two instead of forty-two.

"Hi," Cora said breathlessly as she walked up onto the sand. "You're not going in?"

"Not today," Annie said. "I just came by to see you."

Cora nodded and walked over to where she had left her clothes. She picked up her towel, dried herself quickly, wrapped her *lungi* around her waist, and pulled her T-shirt over her head just as the first two voyeurs wandered up.

"Bug off," she snapped, and gave them a dirty look. But they held their ground, hoping perhaps that she would decide to get undressed again just for them.

"Let's go back," she said to Annie, and started across the sand.

"I really wanted to talk to you alone," Annie said.

"Oh." Cora looked surprised. "All right, let's walk a ways."

The two of them turned back down to the water's edge where the sand was wet and firm and began a slow stroll southward along the beach. Their audience followed briefly, like lampreys, then decided there was more entertainment back at the ball game and did an about-face.

"Some things I won't miss," Cora said, observing their departure. "When we first came here, we had none of that."

"It'll only get worse before it gets better," Annie said. "Maybe in twenty or thirty years they'll wonder why people stopped coming."

"Yeah," Cora said. "If I have to go, I guess I'd rather go now and remember it the way it was."

"You know when you're going yet?"

"Soon," Cora said. "There's a little extra pressure on us now."

"Your folks?"

She gave Annie a quick sideways look. "I guess everybody in Goa knows by now, huh?"

"They weren't trying to keep it a secret."

Cora shook her head. "So stupid," she said. "So typical of my mother."

"Their timing is a little off," Annie said.

"It's Cass," Cora answered. "She probably thought she was helping. She's so fucked up at the moment."

"Cass couldn't have talked them into coming. They must have wanted to come."

"It makes sense only if you know my mother."

"Sansi saw them at the hotel."

"What . . . your boyfriend?"

"Yes."

"He talked to them?"

Annie hesitated, then said, "It's kind of hard to avoid them."

"My mother had to do this," Cora said. "Cass would have called her and told her we were in trouble. That meant my mother couldn't live with herself unless she proved to herself and the whole world that she'd done everything in her power to save us from ourselves. That's my mother's role in life, saving people from themselves. You wouldn't believe the shit we went through."

"You know, if you go back to L.A., they'll just find you there," Annie said.

"We're not going to L.A.," Cora responded. She looked surprised that Annie should even suggest it.

"Drew said he's thinking of starting an ashram there," Annie said. "He was pumping me for information on L.A."

Cora gave an emphatic shake of her head. "He wants to open an ashram—but in Taos, not L.A. New Mexico is more our kind of place. We couldn't go back to L.A."

Annie lapsed into silence, wondering whether Drew was lying to her, his wife, or both of them at the same time.

"He seemed pretty definite about it to me," she said. Then she saw that Cora had a small, embarrassed smile on her face and she understood. "Ah . . . he doesn't trust me."

"He doesn't trust anybody," Cora said. "It's a defense mechanism. He tells everybody something different so nobody knows what he's going to do. It's the way he is, the world has made him that way."

Annie nodded. It was a wife's rationalization and she didn't buy it. But she didn't have to. And it was easier to pretend to agree. "But you trust me?" she said.

Cora stopped and looked directly at her. "We're going to New Mexico," she said. "And when you get back to the States, I hope you'll come and see us. We won't be that hard to find."

Annie smiled, feeling reassured. They started walking again.

"Tell me something," she said. "Are you guys planning to stop off in Ann Arbor and see Cass?"

Annie felt guilty about asking, as if some of Sansi's suspicions had rubbed off on her. But it kept coming back, a small nagging voice at the back of her mind: what if she was wrong about these people and Sansi was right?

"I want to," Cora answered. "I'm kind of mad at her for calling my folks, but . . . I can understand. I know she's in bad shape. A lot depends on money. One of us will try to stop by and see her on the way through, me or Drew. Just to see if there's anything we can do."

Annie nodded. It made sense. All of it made sense.

"You want me to call somebody for you in the States?" Cora asked.

"No." Annie shook her head. "But thanks."

They walked on in silence, Cora seemingly happy to walk all day if that was what Annie wanted.

"I didn't just come to say good-bye," Annie said at last. "I wanted to tell you something . . . about your parents."

"You're not going to tell me you think my mother and me should try and patch things up, are you?" Cora said.

"No, I'm not." Annie smiled wanly. "I'm going to make things worse . . . a hell of a lot worse."

Cora looked at her.

"They didn't come here just because of you," Annie added.

"They came here because of the kids. They want to take the kids away from you and take them back to the States."

Cora exhaled sharply. Every muscle in her face seemed to contract into tight sinewy knots beneath her skin.

"The fucking bitch," she said breathlessly. "The evil fucking bitch."

"I'd rather not be doing this," Annie said. "But I had to warn you. They asked Sansi to help them. They'll probably ask somebody else."

"They asked your boyfriend to help them take my kids away from me?"

"I wasn't prepared to let him do it."

"He wanted to?"

"He doesn't know you the way I do."

"How much did they offer?"

"I don't know . . . he never mentioned money."

"Oh." Cora nodded. "It's a moral crusade. He thinks my folks are good, honest people and me and Drew are a couple of hippie deadbeats."

"He thinks . . . what he thinks," Annie said. "I happen to disagree, or I wouldn't be here."

Cora's voice was agitated now. "I told you everything," she said. "I told you where we're going . . . everything. You can't let him tell my parents. You have to promise me you won't let him tell my parents."

"It's okay, I promise," Annie said. "I wouldn't do anything that would harm you or the kids."

Cora took a series of deep breaths to try to restore herself to some level of calmness. Then she looked at Annie and smiled thinly.

"Thanks for telling me," she said.

"You know. You can protect yourselves," Annie said.

"Yeah." Cora nodded. She smiled again, a more relaxed smile. "And thanks for being a friend."

"It's okay," Annie said. "I feel bad I have to do this. You just keep yourself and the kids safe somewhere and get the hell out of here as soon as you can."

"Don't worry," Cora said.

Annie hesitated, not knowing quite what to say next.

"I'm sorry," Annie said. "I wish it wasn't like this."

Cora nodded. Then she stepped forward and embraced Annie tightly. Annie stiffened, taken by surprise, then relaxed and hugged Cora back.

"I feel like I just made a great new friend and now it's ending before it started," Cora said as she stepped back. "Before we get a chance to know each other."

■   ■

Sansi pushed the Maruti along the river road toward Panjim as fast as he dared.

He and Sapeco had arranged to meet outside the Basilica of Bom Jesus in Old Goa so Sapeco could return the surveillance photos of the pink house. The basilica was the mausoleum of St. Francis Xavier and one of the biggest tourist attractions in the state. Sansi thought the location ironic, though Sapeco had suggested it merely because it was convenient for both of them and always busy.

Sapeco had sounded flustered on the phone and Sansi was worried about him. The doctor seemed to be coming apart under the weight of all that ridiculous Catholic guilt. More urgently, when things blew up, Sapeco would be in considerable danger from Dias and Gupta. Sansi wanted the doctor to forget about his job at the hospicio and get himself and his family out of Goa for a while. He knew several places that were secure and distant and he was determined to get Sapeco into one of them.

The line of cars at the river crossing inched forward with maddening slowness. Sansi waited impatiently as the two overworked ferries shuttled sluggishly back and forth across the Mandovi and the line crawled forward. At last it was his time to board. He made the crossing without getting out of the car. Once on the other side, he drove up the ramp, turned left onto Dayanand Bandodkar Road, and followed the river upstream toward Old Goa. Traffic turned out to be inexplicably heavy and the drive took him longer than he expected, though he honked his horn and cursed like a *kuli* every foot of the way.

By the time he reached the squalid stalls and shanties that clustered beneath the Viceroy's Arch at the entrance to the old city, the traffic was almost at a standstill and he decided he could make better progress on foot. He pulled over to the side of the road, parked atop a scrubby embankment where there was no shade, and set off at a fast walk in the direction of the bloodred towers and domes of the abandoned city that had once been known as the Rome of the Orient.

Despite the mid-afternoon heat, the approaches to the old city seethed with visitors and the parking lot in front of the Viceroy's Arch was a simmering logjam of taxis and tour buses. Sansi knew why. The former capital of Goa stretched along the riverbank for a mile and a half and offered acres of walled gardens and cool, shaded cloisters where tourists could escape the worst of the day's heat while they browsed among the ruins of the Jesuits.

Sansi threaded his way through the slow-moving crowds, past the broken ramparts of St. Augustine's Church, whose walls, like the walls of every other building in the old city, had been stained red by oxides weeping from the stone, so that they all seemed afflicted by the same stigmata. Back in the sixties, Sansi knew, after the Portuguese had been forced out by the Indian army, the local villagers had come to plunder these buildings for stones to build their homes and had found hundreds of tiny skeletons hidden in the narrow spaces between the walls, the remains of long-dead infants. The product of illicit liaisons between monks and nuns, who would rather commit murder than look for forgiveness from their Jesuit overlords.

Once inside, the crowds thinned dramatically as they dispersed among the giant, decaying monuments. Sansi picked up his pace and cut across the vast square in front of the Church of St. Cajetan, a full-scale replica of St. Peter's in Rome and a sight to test the faith of every Catholic who saw its hollow grandeur. When he left the square he followed a long and almost deserted cloister that skirted the Convent of St. Francis of Assisi until he came to the massive Se Cathedral, one of the biggest and most opulent Christian churches in Asia, whose bell had tolled throughout the Inquisition to drown out the screams of burning heretics.

Sansi checked his watch. It was a few minutes before two. He was nearly an hour late.

The Basilica of Bom Jesus was just across the square from the cathedral, and as usual, it had attracted the largest number of visitors. Inside, in a silver casket, were the remains of St. Francis, patron saint of Goa and a four-hundred-year-old testament to the art of the embalmer. Somewhere amid the crowd that covered the steps in front of the basilica, the doctor ought to be waiting.

Sansi tried to look like just another tourist as he strolled across the open square toward the broad stone steps of the basilica. It was only when he reached the bottom of the steps that he realized something was wrong. The crowd seemed unnaturally subdued. The mood was not the same holiday mood he had seen elsewhere in the city. And the people at the entrance to the basilica weren't moving. Instead, they had arranged themselves in a mute semicircle at the top of the steps as if engaged in some kind of ceremony. Sansi felt a tingle of apprehension. It wasn't the silence of ceremony at all. It was the morbid silence of a crime scene.

Sansi hurried up the steps, pushing his way roughly through the crowd. Some people pushed back and others were quick to curse him, but when they saw the look on his face, they knew he was connected somehow to what had happened at the top of the stairs and they stepped aside so he could pass. Abruptly, he found himself in an open space beneath the walls of the basilica. In front of him, lying on the dusty flagstones, was the body of a small, slightly built man wearing expensive gray pants and a white shirt. It would have been apparent to anyone that this was not the kind of man who would like to be seen lying on the ground, robbed of his dignity.

He lay on his left side, his face partially obscured by his right arm, as though he had fallen asleep that way. One of his shoes was missing, the sock underneath was torn, and there was a graze on the foot. A thick pool of blood surrounded his head. The blood was a startling red color, so red it seemed fake. It was already drying in the sun, trapping many of the flies that had been drawn to it. On the other side of the body was a group of policemen, some in uniform, some in civilian clothes. One of them was twirling a chipped blue crash helmet carelessly in his hand. There was no sign of a folder or an envelope that might have held photographs.

Sansi stepped forward and knelt down by the body. He put his hand on Sapeco's shoulder as if to wake him. Then he smelled something sweet and fragrant. Aftershave, he realized. But there was something else, too, something acrid, faint but insistent. Then Sansi realized what it was. It was the smell of gasoline. Dr. Faleiro's solvent soap hadn't been able to get rid of it after all.

"Don't touch the body," someone said.

Sansi looked up and saw a man with bad skin and a thin mustache. He was wearing a short-sleeved safari suit. Sansi knew he was looking at Inspector Dias, chief of the Panjim drug squad.

"You should cover him up," Sansi said. "There must be something you can use to cover him up."

"Do you know him?" Dias asked.

Sansi lowered his head, afraid he would give himself away. "How did he die?"

"He fell," Dias said. "These old buildings are very unsafe. We warn people not to go up the stairs."

Then he repeated his question. "Do you know him?"

Sansi got slowly to his feet and looked at Dias. "He's a friend. I was supposed to meet him here. He was going to show me around the basilica."

Dias stared at Sansi and Sansi knew the policeman didn't believe him for a moment.

"What is your name?" he asked.

"Sansi. George Sansi. I'm an attorney from Bombay."

"An attorney?" Dias said.

"Yes."

"And what is the reason for your presence in Goa, Mr. Sansi?"

"Holiday," Sansi said. "I am here on holiday."

Dias studied him silently. "Where are you staying?"

"Fort Aguada," Sansi said. "The Hermitage."

Dias nodded. "You must be a very successful attorney, Mr. Sansi."

Sansi didn't answer.

"Are you staying in Goa long?"

"This is my last week. I think my holiday is over."

Dias looked unconvinced. "I am Inspector Dias, Mr. Sansi. I will want to talk to you again. You are not to leave Goa until I say you can."

Sansi didn't have to pretend to look shocked. "You can't do that. . . ." he began.

"I can keep you here as long as I like," Dias said matter-of-factly. "Dr. Sapeco's death will be investigated to see if there was foul play. You can stay at the hotel or be my guest at police headquarters, Mr. Sansi. Which do you prefer?"

"I can't tell you anything. . . ."

"You are confined to Goa for the duration of the investigation, Mr. Sansi."

He turned to go, then stopped and looked Sansi directly in the eye. "Don't think you can sneak out of Goa without me knowing about it," he said. "By the end of this afternoon every police officer in Goa will have your description—and I don't think you are that difficult to recognize, are you, Mr. Sansi?"

It was only then that Sansi realized he had left the hotel that morning without remembering to put in his anonymous brown contact lenses.

CHAPTER 22

"I should have heard from Jamal by now. It's been three days."

"Call him."

Sansi shook his head.

"If he knew something, he would call me. Something has gone wrong. Something must have gone wrong."

"Maybe somebody got suspicious," Annie said. "Maybe they dumped him already."

Sansi stared gloomily at his glass of iced tea on the verandah table. It was possible. Everything else had gone wrong, why not that?

"You should call Mukherjee," she said.

"He knows he is to call me the moment he hears from America," Sansi said. "I think I made myself clear."

"He could tell you if something's happened to Jamal."

"You're the one who wanted to stay, no matter what I said," Sansi said. "Now you can't wait to get us out of here."

"When the cops tell us to stay, that's when I know it's time to leave."

"You don't have to stay," he said. "You could leave now."

"I'm not going without you."

Sansi sighed in defeat. "American women."

"You could always find yourself a nice tame Indian girl, like Pramila."

"If I haven't heard anything by the end of today, I'll call Jamal," Sansi said. "And unless there's a compelling reason to stay, we'll leave. We'll leave tomorrow."

"Considering how far you stuck your neck out for him, I'd like to hear what suggestions he has for getting the cops off your back so we can get out of here without any hassle."

Sansi looked at her, sitting across from him on the verandah, her coppery hair stirring in the inshore breeze. It had been a long three days since Sapeco's murder, and they had spent most of it under self-imposed house arrest. Annie had used the time to work on her tan, and her oiled skin had turned betel brown, which had the effect of making her look even more Italian.

The melodic chimes of the front doorbell sounded inside the house and Sansi and Annie looked at each other.

"I didn't order anything," she said.

Sansi nodded. He got up and walked through the bungalow, preparing himself for whoever was outside. He stopped at the door and asked who it was, first in Konkani, then, when there was no answer, in Hindi.

A man's voice sounded tentatively on the other side of the door: "Mr. Sansi, is that you?"

It was the voice of Don Gilman.

Sansi opened the door and looked into the harried face of the American.

"I'm sorry to bother you," Gilman said. "I got your number from the front desk. Something's happened and I have to talk to you."

Sansi nodded and stepped aside, then he shut the door and led the way back to the living room. Gilman followed, taking in the spacious surroundings, so much more elegant than the accommodations he and his wife shared.

"Annie," Sansi called out. "This is Mr. Gilman from California. I believe I mentioned that he and his wife were staying at the hotel."

Annie stepped in from the verandah, trying not to look too uncomfortable.

"This is my friend Annie Ginnaro," Sansi said, completing the introductions.

"Hi," Annie said, and put out her hand. "It's . . . nice to meet you."

"You're American?" Gilman asked.

"Yes."

They shook hands, but when they let go Gilman continued to stare at her. Sansi didn't know which of them was more surprised, Annie at having Don Gilman in the room or Gilman at finding Sansi in the company of an American woman.

"You work together?" Gilman asked.

"No," Annie said.

Gilman nodded, but he looked confused and Annie wasn't about to volunteer anything that might make him less confused.

"Can I offer you something?" Sansi said. "A soft drink, beer, whiskey, or tea perhaps?"

Gilman realized he had been staring and became acutely self-conscious. "Ah, no thank you," he said.

Sansi gestured to the sofa and Gilman sat down stiffly. His gaze drifted back to Annie.

"Which part of the States are you from?" he asked. "If you don't mind me asking."

"California," Annie said.

"California?"

"Yes."

"Which part of California?"

"Los Angeles."

"My gosh—Los Angeles," Gilman said. "Which part of Los Angeles?"

"Brentwood," Annie said. It was where she had lived when she was married, not where she had grown up.

"Ah." Gilman nodded. "We live in Chatsworth."

"I live in Bombay now," Annie said, trying to put an end to the questioning.

"There is something wrong, Mr. Gilman?" Sansi said.

"What . . . ?" Gilman looked more confused.

"You said something has happened."

"Yes." Gilman seemed to remember suddenly why he had come. He looked nervously at the two of them.

"I don't want to appear rude," he said. "But I wonder, would it be possible to speak privately with you, Mr. Sansi?"

Sansi looked at Annie. Gilman must have known that the two of them would discuss everything that would be said, but he seemed to feel the need to maintain the pretense of some confidentiality, if only for his own comfort. The look in Annie's eyes said she would be happy to go along if it would hasten Gilman's departure.

"I'll be on the verandah," she said. She nodded politely to Gilman and turned to go.

"Thank you, Miss Ginnaro," Gilman called after her.

"No problem," she said as she stepped outside and closed the French doors behind her, leaving them fractionally ajar.

Sansi sat down opposite Gilman, who sat with his elbows on his knees, his hands clasped in front of him, sliding his wedding band back and forth.

"Terry Coombe has gone," he said. "Not so much as a by-your-leave. Just . . . gone."

"He didn't say anything to you?"

"We didn't know he'd gone till we saw the maid making up his room this morning," Gilman said. "The front desk said he checked out soon after midnight."

Sansi was surprised. Not so much by Coombe's sudden departure, which he had expected, but because it suggested some kind of upheaval at the American consul in Bombay—the kind of upheaval that might follow a high-level request from crime branch for the exhumation of an American child who had died in Goa and whose body was believed to have been used to smuggle heroin into the United States. And still Sansi hadn't heard from Jamal.

"Things seem to have worked out pretty much the way you said they would," Gilman added. "Now we don't know where we go from here. We can't just turn around and go home. We need your help, Mr. Sansi."

Sansi paused before answering. "I am sorry, Mr. Gilman, but I don't know what I can do."

"You can help us find our daughter, get her to talk to us."

"I don't think she would talk to me."

"So now what do we do?" Gilman asked, a note of hopelessness entering his voice.

"You should talk to the American consul in Bombay," Sansi said.

"What good will that do us if Terry is back there?" Gilman protested. "You said he was up to his neck in this drug business."

"I doubt very much that Terry Coombe is back in Bombay," Sansi said. "The moment he heard there was a flap about a drug-smuggling operation involving the consulate, he knew his time was up. At this moment, I suspect, Mr. Coombe is on an airplane out of the country. Probably en route to Dubai, which has a more flexible banking policy than Zurich and flight connections to a great many places."

Gilman exhaled sharply. "If Terry was a crook, how do we know we can trust anybody there?"

Under other circumstances Sansi would have found it amusing that the Gilmans were now willing to trust him more than their own consular staff.

"With Mr. Coombe gone, I think you'll find they're quite anxious to help you find your daughter, Mr. Gilman."

"So they can nail that bastard she's married to?"

Sansi nodded.

"I'd love to help them do that, Mr. Sansi," Gilman added. "But that means another trip to Bombay and a lot more wasted time. We're here and you're here and you know your way around this place better than anybody from the consul. We'll pay you. Just find our daughter and set up a meeting. That's all we want you to do. And we'll take it from there."

Sansi saw a movement from the corner of his eye and realized that Annie was leaning close to the French windows. "I think you should try and work with your consul, Mr. Gilman," he said.

Gilman stared at him in mute incomprehension.

Sansi held his gaze unwaveringly, but inside he felt wretched, as if he were in the process of betraying the Gilmans and their grandchildren. If he was right about Coombe, he was right about everything else—including Drew. Whether Cora knew it or not, her husband, the father of her children, was a man willing to defile the body of a friend's child in an endeavor to make himself rich.

"Let me think about it, Mr. Gilman," he said. "I will see what I can do."

"You'll help us?" Gilman said.

From the corner of his eye Sansi saw Annie stiffen. "I don't know yet. Let me make some inquiries. There might be something."

Gilman nodded. His eyes were watery and his hands trembled. It wasn't everything he had wanted, but it was something.

"Now, if you will excuse me," Sansi said, "I have some things to do."

"Of course." Gilman got up to go.

Sansi walked him back down the hallway and held the door for him. At the last moment Gilman stopped in the doorway and looked at him.

"We would be willing to pay you a great deal of money if you could help us get our grandchildren out of here safely, Mr. Sansi," he said. "A great deal of money."

Sansi nodded. "Let me work on it, Mr. Gilman," he said. "We will talk later about the money."

Sansi closed the door and walked back down the hallway. Annie was waiting in the middle of the living room, staring balefully at him.

"I won't let you do it," she said.

Sansi looked back at her. "Annie, my dearest darling," he said. "I think it is time you shut up and learned something."

■   ■

It was after five when Sansi finally got through to Jamal. When the commissioner came on the line, he sounded rushed and peremptory, more like the old Jamal than the pitiable, beleaguered creature Sansi had known lately.

"I was going to call you, Sansi," he said. "But things have been moving so quickly there has been no time. I cannot talk with you for long. I have a meeting with the chief minister in forty minutes."

"The autopsies," Sansi said. "They've come up with something?"

"There hasn't been time for an autopsy," Jamal said. "It only happened a few hours ago."

Sansi was confused. "You said things have been moving quickly, Commissioner?"

"Yes, there is a tremendous flap going on. Those scoundrels in cabinet don't know which way to turn. That is why the chief minister wants to see me so soon. He is desperate to save his skin and he needs my help."

"I'm sorry," Sansi said. "I have no idea what you're talking about. What flap . . . what is going on up there?"

"You don't know?"

"I haven't had any news from Bombay in several days, Commissioner."

"Rajiv Banerjee was assassinated this morning," Jamal said. "He was shot to death outside the Shiv Sena office in Bhandup."

For a moment Sansi was too stunned to speak. Then all he could manage was, "Banerjee's dead?"

A few feet away from him, Annie got up from her chair, a look of astonishment on her face.

"Yes," Jamal said. "They did a good job—an AK47 at close range. The whole magazine. There is no shortage of witnesses. He was waiting in the street for his car and the killers were inside the car."

"*Bhagwan,*" Sansi breathed.

"His bodyguards have all disappeared," Jamal continued. "Either they did it or they were in on it. Everybody is talking as-sassination, but it has nothing to do with politics. It was a gang killing, somebody on the inside."

"Gupta?"

"He is one possibility."

"He has plenty to gain," Sansi said. "With Banerjee gone he can do what he wants in Goa."

"The biggest problem with this investigation," Jamal said, "is that I might have to put my own name on the list of suspects."

"*Acha,*" Sansi said. "It will be a long list."

"My only regret is that I was denied the pleasure of watching him suffer," Jamal said. "Now there will be a state funeral and I will have to listen to everyone saying what a splendid fellow he was."

"What is your position with cabinet now?" Sansi asked.

"The chief minister called me three hours after Banerjee was killed. He wants to be reassured that the investigation will be handled discreetly. He can think of no one he trusts more than me to be in charge. I may use the opportunity of this meeting to strangle him."

"Then it is over," Sansi said. "They can't touch you."

"There will be no more talk of transfers for Jamal," the com-missioner answered with a hint of the old hubris. "They need me to get their money back and I am the only one who knows where it went. I would say that secures my position for a long time to come, wouldn't you?"

"You have no further need of me here, then?"

"There is no more need for you and your lady friend to hang around down there dipping your toes in the water at my expense," Jamal said. "I appreciate all you have done for me, Sansi. Make sure you give me a call when you get back to Bombay. Just allow some time for the dust to settle. Things will be a little busy here for a while."

"Commissioner?" Sansi spoke quickly before Jamal could hang up.

"Yes, Sansi?" A note of impatience crept into his voice.

"You did approach the consuls with a request for names and exhumation orders of the drug overdose victims?"

"Yes, I did," Jamal said. "Though I have to tell you, I thought it a little extreme, and so did some of the consuls. There has to be a better way of dealing with this, Sansi. We will discuss it when you get back."

"What about the Americans?" Sansi asked. "Have you heard back from the Americans?"

"No, not yet."

"We cannot allow these people to keep trading in human corpses, Commissioner. We can't forget about it just because Banerjee no longer poses a threat to you."

"Don't be impertinent, Sansi," Jamal retorted. "Of course we won't forget about it. But at this point I have a more immediate crisis to deal with. I will decide on the appropriate course of action for this other business when I have the time."

"One last thing, Commissioner?"

There was an exasperated silence at the other end.

"Your friend Dr. Sapeco?"

"Sansi, you know better than anyone, I have always valued loyalty. I will call him as soon as I can."

"Dr. Sapeco was killed three days ago," Sansi said. "By the same people who are using corpses to smuggle heroin. But he can rest peacefully now, knowing how much you value his loyalty."

Sansi put down the phone and stared blankly in front of him. He sensed rather than heard Annie move closer to him, then the touch of her hand on his shoulder.

"Well . . ." He drew in a deep breath. "It looks like your friends at the *Times* will be busy updating their obituary pieces about Banerjee, and saying all the things they couldn't say about him when he was alive."

"And Jamal is off the hook, so all is well with the world."

"You see." Sansi smiled feebly. "You do understand Indian politics."

Annie paused a moment, then said, "I can't say I'm surprised."

"No," Sansi acknowledged. "There has never been any secret about Jamal's priorities."

"Despite all your efforts on his behalf, I doubt you endeared yourself to him with that last remark."

"In that case," Sansi said, "next time he finds himself in difficulty, perhaps he will think twice about coming to me for help."

"So." She sat on the chair beside him. "Where do we go from here?"

"We go home," Sansi said.

"What about the Gilmans?"

"I can't tell them anything," Sansi said. "They will have to take their chances with the consul."

Annie nodded. "That's fair," she said. "As long as we stay—"

The telephone rang.

Sansi stared at it.

"Jamal?" Annie said.

"No," Sansi said. "He wouldn't call back."

He picked up the phone and listened.

"*Sansi sahib?*" It was Mukherjee.

"*Acha.*" Sansi sighed. "You are a little late, Mr. Mukherjee."

"I have been trying to call you all afternoon, sahib."

"We know about Banerjee," Sansi said, hoping to forestall one of his assistant's long-winded expositions.

"*Acha, sahib.* The stock market is up three points."

"I thought you were supposed to be painting my chambers and attending to the phone."

"The painting is all completed, sahib, and it is most beautiful, if I am saying so myself. And the Americans called around two o'clock, but the telephone lines have been very busy because of the assassination of Rajiv."

"The Americans?" Sansi got up out of his slouch. "What Americans—Mrs. Henke . . . the coroner's office . . . ?"

"It was a gentleman from the embassy in New Delhi, sahib."

"The embassy?"

"A Mr. Darius Pope, sahib. I wrote his name down. Very peculiar."

"What did he say, Mukherjee?"

"He said he was with the American Drug Enforcement Agency, sahib. He said he is most interested in arranging a meeting with you and is preparing to come to Bombay at your earliest convenience."

"Did he say anything about the autopsy?"

"Oh yes, sahib. That is why he is wanting to meet with you. He told me to tell you the autopsy took place on Tuesday and your information was quite correct."

"They found heroin?"

"They were finding three kilograms of heroin inside the body of the child, sahib."

"Three kilograms?"

Sansi looked at Annie and saw a growing expression of horror on her face.

"Yes, sahib," Mukherjee went on. "Mr. Pope is also wanting you to know that the coroner is confirming that death was due to strangulation and not to drowning, which was the cause of death stated on the death certificate."

"*Acha*," Sansi said. "Mukherjee, I want you to call Mr. Pope back and tell him on my behalf that I will be delighted to meet with him as soon as I am back in Bombay."

"Yes, sahib."

"Mukherjee?"

"Yes, sahib?"

"The envelope I sent you is still safe?"

"Oh yes, sahib, I told Uncle Bakul this envelope is containing most secret documents and he is keeping it in the same place he is keeping his money and that is a most secret place, sahib."

"Make sure nothing happens to him," Sansi said. "You have done well, Mukherjee. I will see you in a few days."

"Thank you, sahib. And I hope you and Miss Annie are enjoying the last few days of your holiday."

Sansi hung up the phone, jumped to his feet, and paced across the living room. "We don't need Jamal," he said in a burst of unrestrained triumph. "The Drug Enforcement Agency is sending someone to see me. They want to stop it, Annie. They want to stop this."

Annie looked at him, devastated.

"They found heroin in Tina's body?"

Sansi stopped when he heard the pain in her voice. "Yes," he said.

"It's true then, isn't it?" she said. "Drew is involved."

Sansi hesitated a moment, then nodded. "I wasn't looking for him. I never saw him as a major player in this operation. Like you and Sapeco, I thought he was just another silly, self-important hippie. But he wouldn't go away. Everywhere I looked he was there, always hustling, always up to something. All that was missing was the cellular phone. It was only when you told me he lived next door to the murdered child that I started to take him seriously. Because he was the only person who stood to profit from Tina Henke's death. Gupta and Banerjee never sent drugs to America. They had Europe, they didn't need America. But Drew does. He is going back there and he knows it takes a lot more money to live in America than it does in India. He saw his chance and he took it. He knew how Gupta was getting the drugs out. He saw how well it worked. He handled all the arrangements to get Tina's body out of the country. He paid for the fake death certificate, he paid off the police, he paid off Terry Coombe, and he kept paying him to keep Mr. and Mrs. Gilman busy when it looked like they might complicate matters."

"And he paid to have Tina murdered?"

Sansi shrugged. "It is all part of the service. If Dias and his goons are willing to kill for Gupta, why wouldn't they kill for Drew?"

Annie seemed to shrivel in front of him. "This will destroy Cora," she said.

"If she doesn't already know," Sansi said.

The hurt in Annie's eyes was eclipsed by a flare of anger. "She doesn't know anything about this. There is no way on God's earth she could know about this."

Sansi nodded. "In that case," he said, "you have a decision to make."

Annie looked at him.

"Either you can tell her now, or you can let her find out for herself when Drew goes to pick up the heroin and the DEA is waiting for him."

CHAPTER 23

"**S**ansi, there's somebody in the garden."

He was coming out of the bedroom when he heard Annie's warning. He stopped in the darkened hallway and peered through the curtain of light on the verandah. She was right. In the gloom beyond the verandah there was a man watching the house and making no attempt to hide himself. Sansi couldn't make out his features, only his size and posture, which was muscular and threatening.

At that moment the front doorbell rang and there was a loud and insistent knocking.

"This is the police," a voice said. "Open the door."

"Shit." Annie looked at Sansi. "What do we do?"

"Open the door," he said. "Just try and keep them there for a minute."

Before she could answer, he disappeared into the bathroom, shut the door behind him, and switched on the light. Quickly and carefully he took out his contact lenses, slipped them into their case, tucked the case inside a roll of toilet paper, and set it on top of the cistern. Then he stepped back into the hallway in time to see Annie retreating from the front door as Inspector Dias and another man bulldozed their way inside.

"You're a little late, Inspector," Sansi said amicably.

Dias hesitated, surprised by Sansi's tone.

"You have a lot of explaining to do, Mr. Sansi," he said.

"Well," Sansi responded cheerily. "What's been keeping you?"

Then he turned and walked into the living room, stopping briefly by the French windows to call to the sinister figure in the garden, "I presume you are all together."

Without waiting for an answer, he went to the sofa, sat down, and tried to make himself look a great deal more comfortable than he felt. Dias and his goon filed into the living room, followed by Annie. The second goon came in from the garden.

"You have already met Miss Ginnaro," Sansi said. "And these gentlemen are . . . ?"

Dias tilted his head to one side and looked searchingly at Sansi for any sign of mockery. "This is Sergeant Costa," he said, gesturing first toward the heavyset man from the garden and then to the thin man at his side. "And this is Detective Perez."

"Good," Sansi said. "Well, we were just about to have some chai. I am sure you would like some chai, wouldn't you? Annie, would you mind getting out a few extra cups for Inspector Dias and his friends?"

Dias looked suspiciously at Annie then back at Sansi, while Costa and Perez walked around the room, looking at everything. Annie had left her purse open on the bureau and Costa started poking his finger through its contents.

Annie snatched it away from him. "Do you mind?" she said angrily, pulling the drawstrings tight.

Costa looked at Dias and waited.

The atmosphere in the room was precarious, as Dias seemed to be trying to decide which way he wanted to go.

"Do sit down, Inspector," Sansi interjected. "I have people

waiting for me in Bombay, so I would like to get this business out of the way as quickly as possible."

Dias hesitated a moment, then stepped across to an armchair on the opposite side of the room from Sansi and sat down.

"What are you . . . *kshatriya*?"

"*Vaishya*," Sansi lied, glad to build on the inspector's secular ignorance. "My family is from Gujarat."

"What about her?"

"Miss Ginnaro can speak for herself," Sansi said.

Annie looked at Sansi, read his eyes, and said, "I'm a journalist . . . with the *Times of India*."

"A journalist?" The inspector seemed unimpressed, though Sansi thought there was a trace of uncertainty in his voice. It was what he wanted. He had to keep Dias off balance. The moment the inspector knew how helpless and alone they really were, they were dead. He also noticed that Dias's two goons had positioned themselves so they blocked both exits from the room.

"You work in Bombay?"

Annie nodded.

"What are you doing here?"

Annie looked at him for a moment then looked away as if the answer were so obvious the effort of a reply was beneath her. Sansi could have kissed her.

"I think we'll have that chai now," he said.

Annie went into the kitchen, put down her purse, and tried to go calmly about the business of making tea for three murderers. Dias watched her go, then turned his irritability on Sansi.

"You told me you were here on holiday," he said.

Sansi smiled amiably.

"You're not, are you?"

Sansi shrugged.

"Mr. Sansi, I am not a patient man."

"I have business in Goa."

"What kind of business?"

"Legal business."

"It would be a mistake to provoke me, Mr. Sansi." This time the inspector's voice was little more than a growl, and Sansi thought he might have gone too far.

"I am looking for someone," he said.

"Who?"

"Children," he said reluctantly. "I am looking for two children."

The anger in the policeman's eyes receded and was replaced by calculation and mistrust. "What children?"

Sansi paused, as if it pained him to answer. "Two American children."

"What do you want with American children?"

"I have been retained by my clients to find them."

"And who are these clients?"

"Inspector . . ." Sansi tried to protest.

"Who are these clients, Mr. Sansi?" Dias repeated.

Sansi sighed. "Their names are Gilman. Donald and Joy Gilman from Los Angeles, California. They want to find their grandchildren. They are staying here at the hotel."

Dias looked surprised, as if disconcerted by the sudden appearance of the truth. Parents came to Goa in search of their children all the time, why not grandparents? Certainly it was easy enough to check. He looked at his two cohorts then back at Sansi.

"What does this have to do with Dr. Sapeco?" he said.

Sansi sucked in a breath. "You are not naive, Inspector. You know that information comes from many sources."

"What kind of information did Dr. Sapeco have?"

Sansi decided it was just about time to introduce the prospect of a little remuneration for Dias. "Inspector," he said. "We are both professional men. I trust we can reach some accommodation on this."

"What kind of information did Sapeco have?" Dias repeated.

Sansi sighed, as if intimidated by a more resolute mind. "He said he knew the children's parents."

"What was he doing at the old city?"

"You know—he was supposed to meet me there."

"Yes, so the two of you could go sight-seeing."

Costa smirked.

"He said he had something for me."

"What?"

"Photographs."

"What kind of photographs?"

Sansi looked uncomfortable. "Photographs of the parents, the children's parents, so we would know what they look like."

Sansi hadn't dreamed how glad he would be that he hadn't thrown out the pictures of Drew and the hippie girl at the pink house.

"We recovered a package from Dr. Sapeco's body," Dias said.

"Photographs?"

"There were pictures of many people."

Sansi shrugged. "I am only interested in pictures of the children and their parents."

"How much were you paying him?"

"Inspector, I—"

"How much?"

Sansi hesitated. "Five hundred American dollars."

Dias nodded. "That is a lot of money."

"It goes on the bill," Sansi said. "My clients don't mind, as long as they get what they want."

"How did you find Sapeco?"

"His name was given to me by someone in Bombay."

"Who?"

"Commissioner Jamal of crime branch."

Sansi had been waiting to drop Jamal's name into the conversation and he was not disappointed by the reaction it got. Dias looked as if he had been slapped.

"You know Jamal?"

"I used to work in crime branch," Sansi said.

Dias no longer seemed quite so sure of his ground. Whoever else Sansi was, he had some powerful friends.

"But now you're a lawyer?"

"Yes," Sansi said. He was about to say more when Annie returned with the tea. She put the tray down on the table and dutifully filled four cups from the pot.

"There's cream and sugar there if you want it," she said. Then she walked around to the sofa and sat down next to Sansi. She had made the tea for them, but she was damned if she was going to serve it as well.

Dias and his two goons looked at the tea as if it might be poisoned. Then Costa walked over, selected a cup, added three spoonfuls of sugar and a generous splash of cream, and took it with him so he could lean against the wall and drink it. A moment later Dias took a cup, though he added neither cream nor sugar. Only Perez seemed to have no taste for tea. Sansi leaned forward to take his cup, sipped it, and pretended to enjoy it.

"You know the law, Inspector," he said, returning to their conversation. "There is more money in manipulating it than enforcing it."

Dias offered no reaction. He sipped his tea, put down the cup, and looked at Annie.

"You should boil the milk," he said.

"Sorry," Annie said.

"She is learning the Indian way," Sansi added.

"Why would Sapeco know where to find these children?" Dias asked, looking back at Sansi.

Sansi shrugged. "They're hippie children. Sapeco was supposed to know all about the hippie colony."

"They live at Anjuna?"

"That is what I have been told."

"What are their names?"

Sansi steeled himself for the final bluff. "The family name is Betts. The parents are Andrew and Cora Betts. The children are Paul and Sara. The boy is twelve years old, the girl is nine."

"That's the posters we saw," Costa interjected.

"You are working with the grandparents to find these people?" Dias asked.

Sansi nodded.

Dias took another drink of tea. "What do you think you are going to do when you find them?"

"The grandparents have never seen their grandchildren. There were problems in the family. They want to make peace."

Dias nodded.

An awkward silence stretched out between them, seeming to last an eternity. Sansi waited, willing Dias to make the final connection for himself.

"You haven't come to Goa to set up a kidnapping, have you, Mr. Sansi?" Dias said.

"No, no, not a kidnapping," Sansi answered quickly. "A reunion . . . a repatriation." He stopped and looked at Annie. "That is why Miss Ginnaro is here."

Dias looked at her. "You are covering this for your newspaper?"

"It's a great human-interest story," she said.

For the first time since he had arrived, Dias did something that resembled a smile, a thin reptilian smile. "Kidnapping is against the law, Mr. Sansi."

"Mr. and Mrs. Gilman have legal authorization to assume the guardianship of their grandchildren," Sansi said. "That authorization has been recognized by the government of India."

Dias looked thoughtful.

"Mr. and Mrs. Gilman have offered a substantial reward to anyone who can deliver their grandchildren safely to them," Sansi added.

"How much?"

"One hundred and fifty thousand rupees," Sansi said.

It was around six thousand American dollars.

"That is for telling them where the hippie lives?" Costa asked.

"No," Sansi said. "We know where he lives. We want to talk to him. We want to see the grandchildren." He paused and then continued, "They might be willing to go higher—but only if it guarantees the safe delivery of the children."

The inspector's thin face remained expressionless, but Sansi could see the calculation in his eyes.

"Police assistance could prove very useful at this point," Sansi added.

"That depends, Mr. Sansi."

"On what, Inspector?"

"On a great many things. But mostly it depends on whether you are telling the truth."

Sansi tried to look confused.

Dias got to his feet and signaled to his two goons that it was time to leave. "You'd better not be lying to me again, Mr. Sansi," he said, and started for the front door.

"I will be hearing from you soon then, Inspector?" Sansi asked, getting to his feet.

"Oh yes, Mr. Sansi," Dias answered. "You'll be hearing from me very soon."

Sansi watched the door close behind his uninvited guests. A moment later he heard a car engine and listened until it faded down the hill. He walked around the house and checked all the doors and windows, but there seemed to be no one outside watching. When he walked back to the living room, Annie was waiting anxiously. She slipped her arms around his waist and pressed herself hard against him.

"We served them tea," she said. "I can't believe we served them tea."

"We bought ourselves some time," Sansi said.

"How much?"

"A day, perhaps two."

"Then what?"

Sansi felt the heat of her against his chest, smelled the perfume of her hair. "Then it all starts to come apart," he said.

■   ■

Annie waited for Cora at a clearing in the coconut grove at Anjuna, not far from the main road so Sansi could wait by the

Maruti and see that she was safe. It was midmorning, the sky was clear, and shafts of sunlight slanted through the trees as clean and as sharp as knife blades.

She hadn't gone to the house this time. She couldn't bear the thought that she might run into Drew again. And if Cora was in hiding, as Drew had said, neither she nor the kids would be there anyway. So Annie had gone to Otto and asked him if he would mind taking Cora a message.

At last she saw Cora coming toward her through the trees. She wore a long white skirt with a matching T-shirt that made her look as dark as an Indian, and she was smiling, surprised perhaps, but obviously pleased to see Annie again. Annie shifted from one foot to the other. She felt as if she was caught between the lines, in no-man's-land.

"Hi," Cora greeted her easily. "I thought you'd be back in the big city by now."

"Yeah, hi," Annie said. "Ah no, we had to stick around a little longer."

She was tired and tense. She had been up all night thinking about this meeting—preparing what she was going to say and how she was going to say it, going over and over it in her mind, trying to anticipate every nuance, every inflection, every exchange of words, and knowing, in the end, that nothing would work.

A shadow passed across Cora's eyes. "What's wrong?" she asked.

Annie said, "Something has happened. I have to tell you—and I don't know how to do it."

A look of alarm appeared on Cora's face. "You haven't been talking to my folks, have you?"

"No," Annie said. "I met your dad. I didn't tell him anything."

"You met my dad?" Cora said, her voice rising.

"Yeah, I . . . he came to the room . . . that's not what I'm here to tell you." Already she realized it was spinning out of control.

Cora looked around, nervous, fearing a trap. She saw Sansi waiting by the car at the side of the road.

"Who's that?"

"That's Sansi," Annie said.

"What's he doing here?"

"He wanted to be with me . . . to make sure I'm okay."

"Did he bring my folks with him?"

"No."

"But he's going to tell them where I am?"

"No, it's nothing like that," Annie protested.

Cora's hand went to her hip. She looked away and took a breath that seemed to transform everything about her—the way she stood, the way she looked.

"I trusted you," she said. "That's the fucker who wants to take my kids away."

"He isn't going to take your kids away," Annie said.

The two women stared at each other. The only sounds were the swish of the palm leaves overhead, the chatter of parrots, and the distant rending screech of a monkey, ripping the peaceful calm of the morning.

"Drew was right," Cora murmured, more to herself than to Annie. "You can't trust anybody. He warned me. He told me you'd try to fuck us just like all the others."

"I came here to help you," Annie said.

"All right." Cora nodded. "The damage is done. Tell me what you want. Then go."

Annie flinched. Whatever hope she had had of keeping the meeting civil was gone. All she wanted to do now was get it over with. "We got some information about Tina," she said.

"Tina?" Cora looked puzzled. "What about Tina?"

"She was murdered."

"We know that."

"She was strangled, not drowned."

"We know all this," Cora said. "I told you, remember?"

"Somebody used her body to smuggle heroin into the States."

"What . . . ?"

"Karen Henke arranged for an autopsy," Annie said. "They found three kilograms of heroin in Tina's body."

Cora looked stunned.

"That's how Gupta has been getting the heroin out of Goa," Annie said. "Inside bodies."

"They found heroin in Tina's body?"

"Yes," Annie said. "Somebody used Tina's body to smuggle heroin from here back to the States. That's why she was killed."

Cora looked around blankly. "Gupta did this?"

"No," Annie answered. "Gupta's market is Europe, it's always been Europe. Somebody else sent these drugs to the States."

"How do you know this?" Cora demanded. "You never said anything about this before."

"Sansi's been working here," Annie answered. "He's been looking into the wheeling and dealing behind the free port for a client in Bombay. He wasn't looking for this. He found this out by accident."

"That's bullshit," Cora said, as if amazed that Annie would attempt such a blatant lie. Then a look of comprehension flooded across her face.

"How come all this just happened now?" she said. "Cass just happened to ask for an autopsy now? My parents just happened to come here looking for us now?"

"It's not like that. . . ." Annie tried to explain, but Cora refused to listen.

"It's my parents, isn't it?" she said. "They're using Cass to get what they want. They're trying to make out that we're smuggling heroin into the States so they can get the kids away from us."

"It's not your parents. . . ." Annie's voice rose to a shout as she struggled to make herself heard. "It's not me, it's not Sansi, it's not Gupta, it's not the rest of the goddamn world ganging up on you. It's Drew. Why can't you face it, Cora, it's your husband and nobody else?"

"Drew?" Cora looked outraged. "You're saying Drew killed Tina?"

"I don't know if he killed her, but he's part of it. He works for Gupta and so do the cops who've been doing the killings. He's in on it, Cora. He's been in on it since the beginning. But he's the only one with a reason to send heroin to Ann Arbor, and he's the one going there to pick it up."

"You sold me out," Cora hissed. "I trusted you and you sold me out."

"I'm trying to help you," Annie insisted, her voice faltering under the strain. "If you go back to the States with Drew, the DEA is going to be waiting for him and then you will lose the kids. If you'd just stop and think for a minute, you'd see that I'm trying to help you."

"You sold me out. . . ." Cora screamed heedlessly. Then what little control was left snapped, and she launched herself at Annie in an explosion of fury and frustration. Annie stumbled backward and tried to protect herself as Cora's fists flailed about her head and shoulders, slapping, stinging, punching. Sansi shouted at Cora to stop and ran through the trees toward them. Cora saw him coming and backed away.

"You and your boyfriend better get away from here," she panted. "Because if you come back, I'll kill you myself."

■   ■

It was early afternoon when the taxi pulled up at the gates to the pink house, and a man wearing a tan suit with a pale blue shirt and black-and-red-striped tie got out.

"Here." Sansi handed the driver a five-hundred-rupee note. "Wait for me."

He paused and looked around for a moment before he approached the gates. The house looked quiet, as it usually did. There was no movement, no sign of life. His eyes traveled past the house and the clay brick wall at the back with its coronet of broken glass, up the hill to the screen of dense green jungle from which he and Sapeco had observed the parade of scoundrels coming to pay homage to Gupta. Now it was Sansi's turn to come and kiss Gupta's feet, to bargain with him, to try to outwit him, to do what so many others had tried to do and failed. For a moment he pictured himself up there in the jungle, watching himself through binoculars, and he wondered whether he looked as transparent as all the others. He shrugged the thought from his mind, smoothed the creases from his jacket, and approached the stainless-steel gates.

"Hey," he called in the direction of the gatehouse. "My name is George Sansi. I am an attorney from Bombay. Tell Prem Gupta I want to see him."

There were two guards visible behind the darkened glass of the gatehouse windows. One of them got up and came outside.

"You have business?"

"Yes, I have business."

"What business?"

"Tell Gupta I want to talk to him about his investment portfolio."

The guard disappeared back into the gatehouse and huddled briefly with his companion. Sansi saw him pick up a phone and speak to someone. He waited awhile then bobbed his head, put the phone down, and stepped back outside.

"Mr. Gupta is not here," he said.

Sansi nodded.

"Tell him I have a message for him from Rajiv Banerjee."

The guard looked at Sansi dumbly.

"Just tell him," Sansi said.

The guard hesitated, then stepped back into the gatehouse and picked up the phone again. A moment later he reappeared, waited for the guard in the gatehouse to buzz the gates open, and beckoned Sansi inside.

"You can go," he said, and waved in the direction of the house.

Sansi stepped inside and heard the gates close behind him

with a soft metallic click. The guard looked at him with the same detached curiosity he might have had for a condemned man. Sansi started up the long curving driveway toward the house, the crunch of gravel beneath his feet announcing each footstep. When he reached the portico he was sweating. Two of Gupta's goons were waiting for him, one at the side door, one at the bottom of the steps. Sansi recognized both of them from his surveillance. The goon at the door had a pistol in his hand, though he seemed quite relaxed and held it loosely by his side. Both of them had the same look in their eyes as the guard at the gate.

"I have a message for Prem Gupta," Sansi said. He spoke Marathi, telling them he knew who they were and where they were from. Neither of them said anything in return.

The goon at the bottom of the steps stepped forward and gestured to him to put his hands in the air. It was a thorough search. The goon even ran his fingers around Sansi's shirt collar and the seams of his jacket and pants cuffs, feeling for wires. He found nothing because there was nothing to find. No weapons, no wires, no personal effects, nothing. Every pocket was empty.

He stepped away and grunted to the man at the door. The goon opened the door and casually waved Sansi inside. A wave of cool air rushed out and enveloped Sansi with an air-conditioned sigh, chilling the sweat on his skin, making him feel clammy. He walked up the steps and into the house, one goon in front of him, one behind.

He found himself in a large entrance hall whose floor was occupied by a lurid mosaic of Surya the sun god. He hadn't been sure what to expect. Most gangsters had the taste you would expect of hoodlums who had suddenly accumulated great wealth and whose idea of luxury was gold, glitz, and big-breasted whores. But this house had once belonged to Rajiv Banerjee and he had paid others to give him the taste he needed to be respectable. Now it was occupied by a young psychopath who had butchered the previous occupant with a sword.

Ahead and to the left Sansi saw a large, sunken living room

furnished with leather, silk, and marble in varying shades of cream and caramel and a wall of high windows that overlooked the front lawn. One of the goons put his hand on Sansi's chest, telling him he could go no farther. Then the three of them waited in the hallway, Sansi standing on Surya's golden chariot, the two goons idling nearby.

After a few minutes Sansi heard the swish of approaching footsteps on the marble floor. He was reminded that marble floors were favored by many wealthy Indians, not only because they were cool and durable but because they were easy to clean. Bloodstains in particular could be wiped off without leaving a trace.

Gupta appeared. He wore cream silk slacks and shirt and a pair of jeweled, felt-soled slippers. His hair looked damp, as if he had just come out of the shower. As he came closer Sansi was struck by how young and innocuous he looked. He was slender and fine-boned, with features that were delicate to the point of effeminacy, and his gaze was unnervingly blank, as if there was no one on the other side. Sansi knew he would be unable to read Gupta's emotions from his facial expression. Whatever he said, whatever expressions mobilized those fine features, would bear no relation to whatever he felt on the inside. And that, Sansi knew, was what made him so dangerous.

When he had come within a few feet, he stopped, hands in his pockets, and looked Sansi over the way he might look over a new car.

"You've got blue eyes," he said. His voice was young and gentle, like his appearance. "Your mother or your father?"

"My father was British," Sansi said.

"You're the same Sansi who worked with Jamal at crime branch?"

"I left the police service last year. I'm a lawyer now."

Gupta studied Sansi a moment longer. Sansi noticed that he hardly ever blinked.

"You have a message for me from Banerjee?" Gupta said.

"Yes," Sansi said, meeting Gupta's blank-eyed stare.

Gupta was a head shorter than Sansi, fifty pounds lighter, and fifteen years his junior. He had grown up in the worst slums in Asia and hadn't had a day's schooling in his life. It took every scrap of composure Sansi had not to feel intimidated by him.

"It is a little late now, isn't it?" Gupta said.

"Sometimes the message outlives the sender."

"You knew Banerjee?"

"I never met him," Sansi answered. "But, like many people, I feel I knew him quite well."

"And he gave you a message for me?"

"In a manner of speaking."

Gupta looked at Sansi with something approaching amusement. He enjoyed a good game as much as anybody. Sometimes more.

"What was it he wanted you to tell me, Mr. Sansi?"

"It is what he didn't want me to tell you that matters," Sansi responded.

Gupta took his hands out of his pockets, folded them loosely across his chest, and waited.

"Banerjee had many friends in government," Sansi explained. "But Jamal was not one of them. Similar temperaments and similar aspirations, I think. Each of them saw the other as a rival for the affections of cabinet. But Jamal knew that Banerjee's business dealings were not always aboveboard and he saw that as a way to undermine Banerjee's support in cabinet."

Gupta listened, his eyes and face expressionless.

"Jamal had compiled quite a comprehensive dossier on Banerjee over the years," Sansi continued. "He could show that it was Banerjee's practice to acquire legitimate businesses, which he would then subvert and use as a cover to conduct various illegal activities."

"Illegal activities?" Gupta repeated, arching an eyebrow.

"Extortion, land fraud, tax fraud, phony title transfers,

bid rigging, stock swindles, development scams—that kind of thing."

"Jamal could prove this?"

"And more," Sansi said.

"What was he waiting for?"

"Banerjee had become too powerful," Sansi answered. "Jamal had to find a way to deprive him of the protection of cabinet. He saw his opportunity when Banerjee embarked on a series of investments in Goa in advance of the free port."

"Why would Jamal care what happens in Goa?"

"He doesn't," Sansi said. "What interested him was that Banerjee persuaded several members of cabinet to join him in those investments. Banerjee thought it gave him respectability and an extra level of protection, which it did. But it left the government vulnerable because money from several ministers was mixed in with Banerjee's money, which came from a number of questionable sources and was destined for a number of questionable investments. Jamal knew he could turn that vulnerability to his advantage, but he needed somebody down here to tell him what was going on. He needed a little more information about Banerjee's wheelings and dealings in Goa so he could go to cabinet and tell them that if they wanted any kind of a future in politics, they would have to distance themselves from Banerjee before Jamal laid corruption charges."

A slight smile formed on Gupta's lips. "Blackmail," he said.

"Influence."

"And that is why you are in Goa, Mr. Sansi, to look at Banerjee's investment portfolio?"

"I think I have been successful in contributing certain pertinent material to Jamal's evidence file on Banerjee's interests here."

"Certain pertinent material?"

"Yes."

"And where is this material now?"

"With Jamal in Bombay."

"It won't do him any good now that Banerjee is dead."

"It still gives him a considerable degree of influence in cabinet."

Gupta hesitated. "This is all very interesting, Mr. Sansi," he said. "But what does it have to do with me?"

"You were one of Banerjee's business partners in Goa," Sansi answered. "There were others, not all of them quite so meticulous as you."

Sansi wanted there to be no misunderstanding about his meaning, though he had to be careful not to say anything that would bring Gupta's anger down on him.

"You look tired," Gupta said. "Why don't you sit down and have a cold drink?"

"Thank you," Sansi said. "A salt lime would be most welcome."

Gupta told one of his goons to bring some drinks, then turned and led the way into the living room. Sansi followed and took a seat on the sofa while Gupta went to a large leather armchair that commanded the room like a throne.

"I have always admired Jamal," Gupta said. "He knows how to use power. He trades influence the way others trade gold."

"To him it is the same thing," Sansi said.

"What about you, Mr. Sansi? Do you admire Jamal? Do you want to trade influence for gold?"

It was said with such deceptive mildness that Sansi could not help but feel a pang of apprehension, a queasy presentiment that to take a wrong step now would mean catastrophe.

"I am not here to blackmail you," he said. "I am here to offer you information. What you do with that information is up to you."

"What information is that, Mr. Sansi?"

Sansi nodded. "For quite a few years there have been rumors that Banerjee was connected to the heroin trade," he said. "Nobody was ever able to prove anything, but the rumors stuck."

Gupta shrugged. "They never slowed him down."

"Jamal thought Banerjee might be moving heroin out of Goa through one of his newly acquired business partnerships," Sansi continued, afraid that if he stopped, his throat would close up. "A legitimate business partner would have reasonable cause to be concerned that Banerjee might use one of his companies to ship heroin out of Goa."

"A reasonable concern," Gupta agreed.

"Two months ago a child was drowned at Anjuna. An American child. Her body was flown back to the United States with her parents. They did not know it at the time but there were three kilograms of heroin inside her body."

Gupta's expression never shifted beyond mild curiosity. "That's interesting," he said. "How did they find something like that?"

"The body was exhumed at the mother's request," Sansi said. "She had reason to suspect that someone had interfered with the body before it left Goa."

"Somebody must have told her," Gupta said.

"Somebody did. The police surgeon at the time was Dr. Sapeco. He knew what was going on, though he didn't like it. It seems he was forced to participate against his will, then suffered an attack of conscience and told several people before he died. The police seem to think it might be suicide. Either way, it is all a bit of a mess. Especially now that the DEA is involved."

"The DEA?"

"Yes," Sansi said. "The Drug Enforcement Agency in the United States. They are very interested in the source of this heroin. They have ordered their agents at the embassy in New Delhi to follow it up. It is quite ironic really because, as you say, with Banerjee dead there really isn't much they can do now. Though I would imagine anyone who was remotely connected to Banerjee in a business sense would be trying very hard to distance themselves from him now. The last thing anyone wants is a lot of American drug agents sniffing around."

Gupta seemed quite unperturbed by it all, though behind that blank-eyed stare, Sansi knew, wheels were turning. He waited, feeling the sweat snake coldly down his back. If he was wrong, Gupta knew about the operation involving the girl and had approved it. If he was right, Gupta knew nothing about it— and had just learned that Dias and Drew had not only cheated him but had brought the DEA down on their heads in the process.

"Does Jamal know about this, too?"

"Yes," Sansi said. "But it is as I said. He does not care what happens in Goa. He is content to leave it to the DEA and the federal government."

"Does anybody else know—apart from yourself?"

"No one knows how many people Sapeco talked to before he died," Sansi answered. "I also took the precaution of having copies made of all my evidence and sent to a location in Bombay the address of which is unknown to me. If anything happens to me, that evidence will be turned over to the DEA."

Gupta smiled faintly.

A door opened and the goon reappeared with a salt lime for Sansi and a mineral water for Gupta. Sansi sipped the salt lime and tried to remain calm.

"If you don't want money, Mr. Sansi, what do you want?" Gupta asked amiably.

It was then that Sansi knew it had worked. He was right. They had been cheating Gupta. He looked at the floor for a moment, took a breath, then looked up and spoke the absolute truth.

"I want to be left alone," he said. "I want to go back to my job in Bombay and I want to be left alone."

Gupta nodded. "That's funny," he said. "That's all I ever wanted, too."

Sansi looked at the dead eyes in the young and gentle face

and found it impossible to tell whether Gupta was playing with him or not.

■   ■

Drew sat lotus fashion on a thin black cushion in the cobra house. His bare feet were tucked into his thighs, his arms extended, balanced on his knees so that his hands hung loosely in the air, the third finger of each hand lightly touching the thumb. His head was tilted backward and his eyes were closed. His hair hung halfway down his back and shone dully in the amber light. Softly, he recited his mantra, over and over in a fluid monotone.

> *"Brahman Satyam, Jagan Mitya.*
> *Jeevo Brahmaiva Naparah."*

> Brahman alone is Truth, the world is unreal.
> The individual soul is the only Brahman.

There were three other people in the room with him, the swami and two servants. One stood at the door, the other squatted on the cushion immediately behind Drew. It was this man who tapped Drew on the shoulder to tell him the swami was ready.

Drew ended his chant, looked at the swami and then at the crumpled burlap sack by his side. The swami's face was narrow and blunt-featured, his skin almost black against his white puggaree and *kurta dhoti.* He met Drew's gaze with a look of serene indifference. Drew was disappointed. If he was the first white man to take the bite of the cobra, the swami was not impressed.

Drew took a series of short breaths and braced himself. He had made a promise to himself. He would show them how strong he was. He wouldn't cry out like the others.

The swami began his chant, invoking the spirit of Ananta, the many-headed cobra. Drew listened to every word, every inflection, his senses honed to a preternatural keenness. It was only seconds away now. The ultimate trip. A journey through the terrors of death to the ecstasy of rebirth.

The swami chanted a little longer, soothing the cobra. Then he picked up the sack, opened it, and slid the snake out onto the floor. Drew flinched, an involuntary reflex, the instinct for self-preservation.

The first time he had been to the cobra house he had seen the snake at a distance, from maybe twenty feet away. It had looked smaller then, more manageable, something a man might subdue quickly if he had nerve enough. This close, it looked terrifying—four, maybe five feet long, its black scaly body the thickness of a man's forearm. Slowly it eased itself out of its coil, lifted its head, and surveyed its surroundings.

The swami waited till the cobra had lifted itself a few inches off the floor, then lunged forward with the cushion stick and pinned the snake's head to the floor. The cobra writhed furiously and tried to get away. The soft rasp of its scales against the floor tiles became a harsh scraping sound. Drew felt a surge of fear and anticipation. A tide of endorphins flooded his veins. He was already high.

Until now he had thought cobras were a grayish-black gunmetal color. Now he saw every scale in exquisite sharp focus, and he realized they were not dull and monochromatic at all but varying shades of purple and mauve, rich and subtle and polished like steel, so that all the colors in the room were reflected in each platelet. The same terrible, mesmeric beauty that made the serpent the symbol of all that was evil in the West was the same quality that made it the symbol of strength, potency, and eternal life in the East.

The swami spanned the cobra's body between his thumb and forefinger and ran his hand upward until it was just behind the hinge of the jaw. He waited till he was sure of his grip and then he let the cushion stick fall to the floor with a deafening clatter. He hoisted the snake into the air and tried to wrestle it under his control. His first grab missed and the snake wound itself around his arm as far as the shoulder, flexing and thrashing. The swami grabbed a second time and this time he held it fast, one hand at the jaw, the other two-thirds down the body. Then he turned and held it so it could confront its prey for the first time.

Drew's heart hammered painfully in his chest. His breathing became shallow and rapid. Fear clawed at his insides, draining, enervating, robbing him of his resolve. He forced himself to lean forward and, as if in a dream, extended his tongue toward the snake.

The swami leaned closer and the cobra's hood flared, sending out its first warning. Its tongue flickered and teased the narrow space between them, scenting his sweat, tasting his fear. It hissed, a malevolent, threatening sound. Drew forced himself to look into the cobra's eyes. Two soulless black beads. The only life in them was his own, the ghostly image of his face, curved, refracted, and miniaturized, as if he had already been absorbed into the karma of the snake.

The swami's hand moved closer. The snake's tongue flickered again. This time it brushed lightly across his face, danced across his tongue. It felt hard and dry like a thorn. Then the black, scaly lips peeled back to reveal a pair of glistening fangs. At the tip of each fang a globe of venom trembled, innocent as a teardrop.

The voice of reason screamed at Drew to run. He was close to breaking. But he wanted the scars. He had to be able to show the scars. If he didn't do it now . . . he leaned closer. The swami relaxed his grip and the snake struck, its fangs biting deep into the exposed pink pad.

The pain was more than Drew had ever known, jolting and burning at the same time. He reared backward, trying to get away, flailing with his arms, but the swami's servant pinned him and held him tight. The cobra's head bobbed, once, twice, three times, and each time Drew felt the venom pulse into his body. It poured into his bloodstream like a torrent of molten metal. Alien and lethal, it seared his throat, boiled through his arteries and

veins, scorching everything in its path, snatching the breath of
life from his body and squeezing his heart to stillness.

He wanted to scream, but it was too late. His body was no
longer his. His limbs felt loose, trembly, and uncoordinated. The
swami jerked the cobra's head up and back, extracting the fangs
in a single clean motion. Drew barely felt it. All sensation had
been scourged from his body. The burning was replaced by a
creeping, numbing coldness. He coughed, and the servant lifted
his head and turned him to the side so he would not choke on his
own blood. A trickle of red from his puncture wounds trailed
from the corner of his mouth and spooled thickly onto the floor.
His eyes bulged as he fought to draw a breath, but his lungs were
unable to respond. He was suffocating, dying. Panic flared briefly
in a retreating circle of consciousness. There had been a mistake,
there was too much venom, it was too strong.

He felt himself falling, gathering speed, faster and faster
through the rushing darkness. There was no fear anymore. All
the struggle and sorrows of the world had been left behind. All he
felt now was a cold, rushing wind against his face, whipping his
long hair as he plunged through the earth's chill depths. Then,
through the darkness, he saw a pinpoint of light, a fluid nucleo-
lus of bright, changing color that pulsed and expanded rapidly as
he fell toward it. He felt an inexplicable surge of ecstasy as it
leaped up to meet him. Then it burst around him in shards of
burning iridescence . . . and he was gone.

His head lolled forward and his eyes stared blindly at the
floor. The swami's assistant reached down, closed his eyes, and
wiped the blood from his chin. Then he looked at the louvered
window high up in the wall and signaled that everything was exactly as it should be.

Upstairs in the gloom, Cora dared to breathe again. This was
what he had promised her. This was what he wanted her to see.
This was what he wanted to take back to America.

She watched as they lifted him onto the mattress and waited
while his heart and breathing stabilized. One of them checked his

pulse and listened to his heartbeat, then nodded to the other. Cora got up from her chair and wiped the palms of her hands against her skirt. Their room was waiting. In a few minutes they would bring him upstairs and she would watch over him through the night, protecting him, sharing his experience the way she shared everything else with him. And in the morning they would make love with an intensity that would be better than anything they had ever known.

CHAPTER 24

It had been a routine night so far—trucks carrying produce north, buses bringing tourists south, cars and taxis carrying passengers back and forth between the small towns and tourist shrines of the north shore, and hippies on motorbikes heading from one party to another.

Sergeant Patnaik squatted beside a small fire at the side of the road, a cup of chai between his hands. Two constables shared the campfire with him, sipping their tea, their ancient 303 rifles beside them on the ground. Three more constables took their turn on the road, flagging down the northbound traffic, checking drivers and passengers, occasionally poking around in the back of a truck in case something or somebody was hidden there.

Patnaik looked at his watch. It was a little before five. Another hour and the sun would come up. An hour after that and his relief would come to take over the checkpoint. He could go home and sleep for a few hours and perhaps take his son fishing in the afternoon, as he had promised. He yawned and rubbed a hand roughly around his face, trying to wake himself up.

An overloaded bus from Bombay, swaying from side to side, slowed down when the driver saw the police with their 303s in the road, but they waved him on. They weren't interested in people coming into Goa tonight, only those going out. The bus accelerated and disappeared into the night, and for a moment the only sounds around the fire were the chirp of cicadas, crickets, and frogs in the surrounding rice fields and ditches.

A pair of headlights swept from the south, and Sergeant Patnaik heard the roar of a truck engine through a broken muffler, then the grinding of gears as the driver slowed down when he saw police uniforms in the firelight. The truck pulled up at the checkpoint. It carried a gigantic load of cashews held in place by a net of frayed rope.

Sergeant Patnaik heard his men ask the driver for his papers. He put down his cup, got up from the campfire, and took a slow stroll around the truck. There were two men in the cab and the driver looked nervous. A constable told Patnaik the driver had identity papers from Bombay but no driver's license. The driver protested that he had left it in another truck. Both looked to Patnaik for some sort of solution. Patnaik decided they would forget about the license, but the driver would have to pay five hundred rupees for overloading his vehicle. The driver said he thought two hundred was fair. Patnaik started to walk away and the driver went up to three hundred. At that moment another pair of headlights came into view behind the truck. Patnaik shut out the entreaties of the truck driver and watched as a battered, mud-encrusted Maruti limped to a halt behind the truck.

The sergeant walked over to the car and looked inside. There were a man and a woman. The man wore *kurta* pajamas, a vest, and an old pillbox hat. The woman was dressed all in black and wore a veil. Muslims.

"Papers," Patnaik said.

"No papers," the man answered. He spoke Konkani, though he had a strong accent. Urdu, the sergeant guessed. He cleared his throat and spat into the road. He was Christian not Hindu, so he had no problem with Muslims.

"Where do you live?" he asked.

"Panaji," the man answered. It was the Hindi name for Panjim.

"Where are you going?"

"Bicholim."

"What is the purpose of your journey?"

The man looked offended. "We are going to the mosque," he said. "Morning prayers."

Patnaik nodded and stepped away from the car. There was only one mosque on the north side of the Mandovi and it was at Bicholim. More of the faithful would be coming soon. He waved them on and walked back up to the truck to see if the driver had come up with three hundred rupees yet. The Maruti pulled around the truck and drove off into the darkness in the direction of Bicholim.

A half hour later the Maruti drove into Bicholim, passed the mosque, and kept on going until a few miles farther on it crossed the boundary with Maharashtra. Two miles the other side of the state line it turned north near Maneri and headed in the direction of Bombay.

"I don't know how those poor women stand it," Annie said as she unfastened the veil and took her first clear breath of night air since she and Sansi had left Aguada. "Can we stop soon? I need to take the rest of this stuff off before I suffocate."

Sansi looked at her through the opaque shields of his contact lenses and smiled.

"I think we're safe now," he said.

The description Dias had circulated was of a high-caste Hindu lawyer with blue eyes traveling to Bombay in the company of a white American woman. No one was looking for an anonymous brown-eyed Muslim and his wife going to early-morning prayers at Bicholim.

■   ■

"You want something to drink?"

Dias thought about it for a moment then nodded. "Pepsi," he said.

Costa had parked their unmarked police car under the cover of a mango tree about thirty yards in from the road to Anjuna. Dias sat in the back while Costa and Perez sat in the front. Costa was at the wheel and he was thirsty. He looked at Perez, but Perez shook his head. Costa grunted, opened the door, and climbed out.

There was a stall selling cold drinks a few yards down from the checkpoint where uniformed policemen were conducting their usual random search of hippies going to the flea market at Anjuna. It was still early and already there had been a few busts. The police truck had a half-dozen hippies in the back and it looked like another two were about ready to join them. A constable had found a packet of something on a bare-chested man with rainbow-colored dreadlocks. His girlfriend had a shaven head, nose rings, and tattoos, and she was refusing to get off the back of her boyfriend's motorbike.

They never learned, Costa thought. Every week the checkpoint was here and every week they tried to drive past it with their drugs, betting they wouldn't be pulled over. All they had to do was leave their drugs somewhere else for the day. But they had to take the chance, knowing that if they lost, they would be a long time in Panjim jail before they came up for trial and eventual deportation. Another few minutes and the truck would leave for the police station at Calangute and then come back for the next load. Stupid hippies.

Costa strolled down to a drinks stall, bought a Pepsi for Dias, and a Thums Up for himself. Everybody seemed to prefer Pepsi now that it had been allowed back into the country, but Costa was used to the taste of Thums Up. Even though the sugar in it was bad for him, he was going to stick with it. He paid for the drinks and took them back to the car. He noted, as he walked back, that the car was barely visible in the dense shade of the mango tree. That was why they always parked in the same place. Dias could see everything from the comfort of his backseat, but nobody could see him.

Costa opened the door and handed the Pepsi to his boss. Dias took it without taking his eyes away from the scene at the checkpoint. He liked watching the busts. He always had. He liked watching the women in particular, watching how they behaved, speculating on how they would behave later when they came to understand just how much power he had over them.

"I have to stretch my legs," Perez said.

Dias nodded. Now that Costa was back, it was okay. He insisted that one of them be close by at all times. But Perez was always restless. He could never sit still for too long. Sometimes it got on Dias's nerves.

Perez climbed out of the car and strolled to the edge of the shaded area beneath the tree. He took a packet of *bidis* out of his pocket and lit one with a plastic lighter. He looked back at the car. Dias was invisible in the backseat. Costa stood a few feet away drinking his Thums Up. Another day at the market. He turned his back on the noise and clamor of the road, the shouts and protests of the hippies as they were led away to the police truck, and looked in the direction of the beach, which was hidden behind a screen of scrubby trees and high dunes. There were a few old villas and houses scattered around, most of them destined for demolition in the next year or two if Dias was right. One day this whole coast would be gilded with luxury hotels, resorts, and condominiums. World-class. Better than anything in America. And one of them would be his.

"Deciding where to put your house?" Costa asked.

Perez looked around. He hadn't heard him. Costa could move quietly for a big man.

"Over there." Perez nodded in the direction of the highest dune. "That way I could see everything for miles."

Dias looked away from the checkpoint to see where his body-guards were. He saw them through a slivered tangle of light and shade on the far rim of the umbrella, looking toward the high dunes. He turned his attention back to the checkpoint. One of the constables had dragged the woman with the shaven head off the motorbike, and she had gone crazy, screaming, spitting, and scratching. It had taken three men to subdue her. They had her on the ground now and were putting handcuffs on her. If she didn't shut up, he would order them to gag her. He couldn't understand women who deliberately made themselves ugly by shaving off their hair and covering themselves with tattoos.

The doors on each side of him opened at the same time and Dias looked around expecting to see Costa or Perez. Instead he saw two men he didn't know. Instinctively he lifted his hands to protect himself and opened his mouth to shout. One of them grabbed an arm and clamped a hand over his throat, choking off his cry for help. The other grabbed Dias's free arm and pinned it to the seat. Then he brought his other hand around in a tight arc.

The man jammed the hypodermic needle deep into Dias's left eye and thumbed down the syringe button, injecting forty milliliters of pure heroin into the policeman's brain. A drenching wave of pain flooded through the policeman's body. He bucked and kicked, but his killers held him fast till the syringe was empty. Then the man with the syringe jerked it loose and watched a thin jet of blood spurt from the punctured eyeball. He used Dias's jacket to wipe off the needle, then put it in his pocket and leaned back out of the car. The other man let go of Dias's throat and the two of them walked unhurriedly away.

Dias screamed. Behind the agony, in the dying recesses of his mind, it was a scream to pierce the heavens. Beyond the confines of the car it was an agonized sob. A surge of soothing warmth swept over him, swallowing the pain and the fear. He lifted his hands, tried to hold on to the seat in front of him and pull himself out of the car. He felt as if he were swimming in blood, warm and thick, pulling at him, weighing him down. Then the warmth was gone and in its place there was a sickening, drowning cold. He was dying, the way he had watched others die. He felt himself falling into a well of darkness as he toppled slowly through the open door of the car. His legs caught between the seats and he stopped, suspended halfway out of the car, his head upside down a few inches from the ground, a glistening scarlet thread spooling from his eye, inscribing a grotesque calligraphy of death in the dirt.

A short distance away Perez reluctantly withdrew from his dream of the future and looked back at the car.

"Mother of God," he muttered. He threw the smoking *bidi* to the ground and started toward the dying Dias. Then he felt Costa's powerful hands on his shoulders, holding him, stopping him from going any farther.

"He's gone," Costa said calmly. "Let him go."

CHAPTER 25

A black-and-yellow auto-rickshaw nagged its way through the bedlam in Dalal Street and stopped at the curb outside Lentin Chambers. Annie climbed out and handed the driver twenty rupees. She wore a white blouse with long khaki pants and looked like a wealthy American tourist. The driver looked at the money as if she had spit in his hand. The fare was eighty rupees, he protested, his face a grimace of betrayal, his voice a practiced whine.

No, it wasn't, Annie answered politely in English. The right fare was somewhere between twelve and fifteen rupees. She smiled, told him to have a nice day, and disappeared into Sansi's building, leaving the rickshaw driver muttering behind her. She had been much more relaxed about things like that in the month since she had returned from Goa. Things that had bothered her about Bombay before she went away no longer seemed quite so infuriating. Bombay was the same—the traffic, the chaos, the dirt, the greed, and the corruption—but she was different. Her perspective had altered and the city no longer drove her to distraction the way it had before. As a result, there had been fewer arguments with taxi drivers, fewer confrontations with street hustlers, and no more harsh exchanges in Hindi. Her friends and colleagues at the newspaper had all remarked on it. Her vacation had done her a power of good.

She paused briefly in the lobby to admire the new brass plate among the building's list of tenants, acknowledged the salute of the security guard with a smile, and continued to the elevator. Even the drafty old elevator cage that creaked down to meet her like a great mechanical spider amid a nest of greasy cables seemed more eccentric than sinister.

When she got to the top floor and opened the door to Sansi's chambers, she found them much tidier than the last time she had seen them, though there was a lingering smell of paint and the walls still looked more yellow to her than the ivory Sansi had wanted. The old, scaly linoleum in the outer office had been replaced by new, cream-colored linoleum, and Sansi and Mukherjee had arranged the old furniture into some kind of order and stacked the bookshelves with an impressive array of law books. Unfortunately, law books and high ideals did not constitute a thriving practice. The reception desk was empty and unattended, the only sounds were the wheeze and rattle of the air-conditioning, and Sansi and Mukherjee looked lost, each in his own office with the door open.

"Hello, Miss Annie," Mukherjee called brightly when he saw her, as if glad to see someone other than Sansi for the first time that day. "How charming you are to be coming again."

"Good to see you, Jeet." She smiled. "Dare I ask how business is going?"

Mukherjee shrugged. "I can go downstairs and get business but Sansi sahib will not let me," he said. "He says it is bad for the reputation."

"I know. He's very stuffy about his reputation."

Sansi appeared in the doorway to his office and looked around the corner at Mukherjee. "If we go on like this, Mr. Mukherjee will be back on the street sooner than he expects," he said.

"You still looking for a receptionist?" Annie nodded at the empty desk.

"Are you applying for the position?" Sansi asked.

"You really want me here?"

Sansi looked at her in a way that required no explanation.

"Well," Annie said. "I heard you had some time on your hands, so I came to buy you lunch."

"I will get my jacket," Sansi said.

"Appearances, appearances," Annie muttered, and started toward the door.

"It was Chakravarty who said you can tell everything about a man by his appearance," Sansi told her as he followed her.

"Funny," Annie said, "I thought it was Oscar Wilde."

"He stole it." Sansi paused in the doorway and called over his shoulder, "Mr. Mukherjee, you will keep the office open till I get back from lunch."

"Oh yes, sahib," Mukherjee answered. "You can be depending on me."

Annie and Sansi smiled at each other as they stepped outside. It seemed they had both heard something like that before.

They went to the New Café, across the road from the high court, and found a booth upstairs at the back.

"Have you heard from Jamal yet?" Annie asked as she looked over the menu.

"No." Sansi shook his head. "He won't call me unless he wants something. Otherwise he will wait for me to go to him."

"Are you going to call him?"

"No."

"Not even to be polite?"

"No."

"What about the politics of the situation?"

"These are the politics of the situation," he answered.

They ate lightly, a vegetable *biryani* with *chappatis* and bottled water. When they were finished, Sansi ordered a pot of chai for them both.

"How is the child-prostitution story going?" he asked, settling back in his seat.

"Great," she said.

"Great?" He seemed genuinely surprised.

"I decided at the beginning that it wasn't going to be the usual hand-wringing piece," she explained. "I decided I was going to make something happen."

Sansi's eyebrows arched.

"I found a twelve-year-old girl who survived the earthquake at Latur," Annie went on. "Her whole family was killed except for a brother who works as a *kuli* in Bombay, so she came here to find him. At the bus station she was picked up by pimps and sold to a brothel. She's been there ever since. The women's collective knows about her and they're doing a rescue tomorrow night. We're going to be there and we're going to reunite her with her brother."

"The paper is happy with that?"

"The paper loves it," Annie said. "We're doing something, we're exposing the whole child-prostitution racket, and it makes the paper look good while somebody else takes all the risks. The politicians will be falling over themselves to take some of the credit."

Sansi smiled. "You're beginning to sound cynical."

"I'm helping somebody who wants to be helped," Annie said. "It makes a difference."

"Not like Goa?"

Annie shook her head. "One thing I learned from Goa is that you can't save somebody who doesn't want to be saved."

"You don't have to apologize for trying," he said.

"I made a fool of myself."

"You are lucky that's all you did," Sansi added. "I could have gotten us both killed. And for what? To help Jamal."

"At least you knew the risks you were taking," Annie said. "I still can't believe that I couldn't . . . that I wouldn't see what was right in front of my nose."

"It is very hard to give up on someone you like."

"Yeah," Annie said, her voice little more than a sigh. "I still worry about the kids. I can't help wondering how they're going to turn out, you know?"

"I don't think Mrs. Gilman is the kind of woman who will give up on her grandchildren easily," Sansi said. "She will find someone to help her get them back."

Annie forced a smile. "It's very appealing," she said. "That whole way of life—hippies, flower children, freedom. You can see why so many people fall for it, why they never want to give up on it. And you want to give them the benefit of the doubt because all they want is their freedom. But it's freedom from everything—including consequences. I guess I'm just not that dumb."

The waiter brought their tea and they drank it in silence for a while.

"I haven't seen you in your *salwar khameez* since we got back," Sansi observed.

"Oh." She shrugged. "I'll still wear it—and my sari on special occasions. But I don't feel like I have to try so hard anymore. I'm an American living in India. No matter how long I live here, that is what I'll always be. There's no point in canceling myself out just to try and fit in."

Sansi gave her a slight smile but said nothing. They finished their tea and Annie called the waiter and paid the bill. Once outside, they walked back to Dalal Street and dallied together on the corner outside Lentin Chambers, neither one of them in any particular hurry to go back to work.

"Are you going to be all right?" Annie asked, glancing up at his top-floor office.

"I'll be all right," he said. "I may have to stoop to a few bar association dinners to squeeze my contacts, but if that is what it takes . . ."

Annie smiled.

Sansi turned to look for a cab to take her back to the *Times of India* building.

"Excuse me, Sansi sahib."

It was one of the Sikh security guards calling from the lobby of Sansi's building. "There is a lady in your office waiting to see the memsahib," he said. "An American lady. She asked for you, but she is looking for the memsahib."

"Did she give her name?" Sansi asked.

The guard looked abashed. "She said she was a friend of the memsahib's," he said.

They rode the elevator in silence. Sansi walked quickly to his office, followed closely by Annie. He opened the door, and there, sitting on the old railway bench in the reception area, was Cora.

She looked calmly at them as they stood together in the doorway, staring at her. "Hi," she said. "I'm sorry. I should have warned you I was coming."

For a moment neither of them was able to speak.

Mukherjee emerged from his office, a worried look on his face. "This lady said she was a friend of Miss Annie's—" he began.

"It's all right, Mukherjee," Sansi said, and waved him back into his office.

Mukherjee backed away, unable to take his eyes off the drama that had materialized so unexpectedly in front of him.

At last Annie found her voice, and when she spoke, it was more in bewilderment than in anger. "What do you want?"

"I wanted to see you," Cora said. She stood up and Annie saw that she was thinner than she had been when they had last confronted each other across the clearing at Anjuna. She was dressed differently, too. Instead of her hippie clothes she wore a plain, tan knee-length dress with sandals and a purse that matched. The clothes didn't look right on her and she held herself as if she knew it. Her hair was still long and worn in a braid, though she had tied it up in a tight loop so it didn't hang down her back like a length of rope.

"I wanted to see you before I went back to the States," she added.

"Cora, I don't think there is anything we have to say to each other," Annie said.

"You should go," Sansi told Cora, his voice firm to the point of harshness. "You have made a mistake in coming here, Mrs. Betts, and you should go now."

"My name isn't Betts anymore," Cora answered. "My husband is dead. I'm using my maiden name now . . . Gilman."

Annie shook her head, stunned.

"I wanted to apologize," Cora added. "I'm flying out tonight and I wanted to see you before I left. I promise, you won't see or hear from me again."

Annie looked at Sansi, and Sansi waited, willing to take his cue from her. Then she gave a slight nod of her head.

"All right," Sansi said. "You can use my office. I'll wait here."

Cora looked at him and smiled feebly. "You don't have to be afraid of me," she said. "Not anymore."

It was just as Annie had said. There was something about Cora that made him want to believe her.

"Leave the door open anyway," he said.

Annie led the way into Sansi's office, Cora just behind. There were three chairs, one behind the desk, two in front. Annie took the chair behind the desk. Cora sat in front, took a pack of Kents out of her purse, and offered one to Annie.

"One of the benefits of being back in Bombay," Cora said.

Annie shook her head. "I quit a month ago, when I got back from Goa," she said. "Something about what happened there seemed to put a lot of things in focus for me."

Cora nodded. She lit the Kent and inhaled deeply, as if she needed it to keep going.

"I went to your office," she said. "I didn't want to wait in case I missed you. They said I'd probably find you here."

Annie nodded but didn't offer a response.

"I am sorry about what happened, you know," Cora said. "I

mean it. I'm sorry about all of it. I know you were only trying to help. I know you cared about what was right for the kids, and I know how hard it must have been for you. I'm sorry I didn't believe you."

"It was your choice."

"Yeah, it was." Cora nodded. "It was always my choice."

"How are the kids?"

"They're okay," Cora said. "They're in L.A. with their grandparents."

Annie didn't want to show any emotion, but it was impossible not to be surprised. "You got together with your parents?" she asked.

Cora nodded.

"When?"

"A couple of weeks after you left."

Annie hesitated, trying to make sense of this news, wondering how much of it was true and how much of it was lies.

"Is it true?"

"About what?"

"About Drew?"

"Yeah, it's true."

"He's dead?"

"Yeah."

"Do the kids know?"

"Not yet."

"How did he die?"

"I killed him."

This time Annie could not keep the look of shock off her face.

"Not . . . by my own hand," Cora said. "But I arranged for it. . . . I arranged for it to happen."

Annie shook her head, unable to speak. For a long time there was only silence between them.

Then Cora said, "You remember when I saw you last at Anjuna?"

"You said you'd kill me."

"I meant it, too. I did everything else for him. I would have killed for him, too, if he'd asked me."

Cora paused a moment and looked out the window at the dirty skies of Bombay that were so unlike the clean blue skies of Goa.

"There was this thing he found," she said. "A ritual . . . a weird kind of drug ritual run by an old swami at a house in Panjim. This guy's a snake handler. You take a bite on the tongue from a live cobra and then you take a trip on the venom."

Annie felt an unpleasant chill. She recalled the conversation she'd had with Drew at his house when he had told her about something he'd discovered that would take people on a journey to the other side of death. Annie had scoffed at it at the time, believing he was just being melodramatic.

"Drew was fascinated by it," Cora continued. "He wanted to take it back to the States for his ashram. He figured there were plenty of people who would pay big money for something like that—to do it and to watch it."

"I'm sure he's right," Annie said.

"Yeah, well, he took me there. He wanted me to watch him do it. And I did. I watched him. And he wanted me to watch out for him like always. To watch his back. And he wanted the scars on his tongue to show people he'd done it. So he'd be the guru—the Man—like always."

She paused to take a puff on her cigarette before going on.

"What happens is the venom knocks you out for a long time. You hallucinate, you see things, hear things. Then, after nine or ten hours, you come out of it. But your senses are really keen, really sharp. Everything is heightened, everything tastes better. And everything feels better . . . especially sex."

Annie's feeling of foreboding became stronger.

"That was all part of it, too," Cora went on. "The sex—to make it seem like we were closer together. Except there was something he forgot. He forgot that when you hallucinate you see things you don't want to see and you talk about things you don't want to talk about. And he talked about the night at the beach, at the full-moon party, the night Tina was killed. What he said made me realize that it was him . . . it was Drew who killed her. Because he was talking to her and he was telling her to be quiet and not to wake up. And he carried her down to the water all over again in his mind . . . and he killed her. He choked her and he held her under the water until she was dead."

Her voice wavered and she had to stop. She lowered her head so that Annie could no longer see her face. Annie waited, expecting to see tears. But there were none; when Cora lifted her head up again her eyes were dry.

"I told you I saw Tina in the water the next morning," she said. "I saw her face and her eyes. And it was like she was trying to tell me who killed her."

"Jesus Christ," Annie whispered.

"He really got off on the cobra thing. He said it was the best, the best ride he'd ever had. Better than heroin, better than speedballs, better than anything. And he figured he could handle it the way he handled everything else. A couple of weeks later, when the scars had healed, he wanted to go back to the cobra house and do it again. But he didn't want me with him the second time. He wanted somebody younger, somebody better. So he took Monika."

Annie remembered the voluptuous German who had read her aura at the Sea Breeze.

"So I went to see Gupta and I told him," Cora said. "And he didn't say anything, he just listened. But I knew he would take care of it and he did. He told the swami what to do. When Drew went back, the swami gave him a bite from a snake that hadn't been milked. So Drew got the full shot. He got what he always wanted . . . he got to take the ultimate trip."

She stopped and looked into Annie's eyes for a moment. "There's something else you might like to know," she said.

Annie sat still and silent, her breath frozen in her throat.

"You remember the morning we walked along the beach and

you told me Drew had been asking you about setting up an ashram in L.A.?"

Annie nodded.

"He asked you about your family, too, right?"

"Yes."

"And about your faith and if your family was religious?"

"Yes," Annie said, "I thought it was strange at the time."

Cora nodded. "During the last year and a half, when they were killing tourists and smuggling the drugs out in their bodies, he was spotting for Gupta and Dias. He looked for tourists who would make the best mules, people with families who were sure to want the bodies back whatever the cost. Drew would make friends with them, then tell Dias who they were and where to find them."

Annie recalled her last image of Drew, as sharp and as clear as a snapshot in her mind. Half-stoned, half-dressed, convinced of his own invincibility, riding off on his motorbike to the ashram at Vagator to take the midday meditation. She remembered the sardonic wave of his hand and the strange intimation she'd had that he had been playing with her somehow.

Cora nodded. "He wasn't satisfied with just Tina. He needed backup in L.A. He was checking you out." She paused a moment, then added, "You were next."

ABOUT THE AUTHOR

PAUL MANN was born and educated in England. For the next twenty-five years he traveled the world and wrote for leading newspapers and magazines in London, New York, Montreal, and Sydney. For the past several years he has devoted himself to writing novels. He is the author of *Season of the Monsoon*, the first novel featuring George Sansi. He currently lives near Ottawa, Canada, with his wife and three daughters.